nowledge. 知識工場

Knowledge is everything！

Knowledge is everything！

知識工場
Knowledge is everything！

嚴選 透過完整句，全方位理解英文片語正宗使用法！！

隨書附贈MP3
完整對話光碟

一句話搞定萬用
狄克生片語

How to Master Dixon Idioms and English Phrases
with One Single Sentence

獨創狄克生片語短句學習法，日常考用兩相宜
片語、俚語、慣用語，一本全通透！！

run up 上漲

call it a day 結束一天

DIXON IDIOMS

up in the air 懸而未決

just now 剛才

精闢
解析

英文
會話

應考
無敵

張翔、薛詩怡 聯合編著　Brian Foden 審訂

透過完整句學習片語
才是王道！

時常有讀者跟我反應：從小到大學了這麼多年的英文，累積的字彙量不少，文法觀念也大多掌握得宜，然而還是有些明明看似皆為透過簡單的單字（或是都看得懂的單字）所組合而成的一個句子，反覆讀了好幾遍之後，卻還是不太能明白其意。就我的分析，我想這類的讀者所缺乏的，就是對於狄克生片語的掌握能力。

片語，是由兩個以上的單字所組合而成的詞組。詞組內的單字，因為與其他單字相互配合後，產生了化學變化，使得原本的字義被調整、扭轉、甚至化為另一個意思與獨立單字完全不同的片語。也由於片語如此神奇、使用上具備相對便利性，因此不僅在英文書寫中經常使用，在英語會話中的使用度也極高。

然而，坊間的片語學習書，多把片語拉出完整句外單獨教學，反而違背了片語應遁入句中、托出語句精義的實用價值；或將大量的片語塞入一則長篇對話中，反而混淆了學習的重點。因此，本書將英語學習回歸原實，透過完整句的形式，明確點出片語在句中的正確位置與用法，協助讀者理解如何正確使用片語，進而提升英語溝通力。

張翔

{作者序}

精通狄克生片語，
瞬間提升英語使用力！

英語的微妙之處在於，經過巧妙的文字組合，許多片語會意含不同於字面上堆砌的意思，而這些片語廣泛地被使用，充滿在日常英語使用的語境當中。但是這些片語往往也讓英語初學者十分頭大，也成為英語學習讓許多人卻步的最主要原因之一。

狄克生片語在近數十年間被廣泛認定為最有系統，也最容易入門的片語學習書，讀者可以由坊間書局架上動輒數十本不同的狄克生片語學習書可見。然而這些學習書籍無論多新，甚或是多暢銷，共通的缺點就是，其中提供的內容不外乎是片語整理以及例句示範。誠如筆者提過的，片語被廣泛地使用在日常生活中，也因此單單只有單一片段例句的學習方式，並無法滿足許多英語學習者希望進入英語生活語境的目的。

相信很多讀者都有過這種經驗，在對話的當下，聽到學過的片語時，腦海一片空白，只能用字面文字去理解，但卻因此造成很多尷尬的情況，等到事後，才懊悔地氣自己，怎麼沒有立即想起曾經背過的片語意思。

本書就是因此應運而生。經由生活情境對話，讓讀者可以真正有效地吸收學習這些片語用法，也可以更有效率地在英語學習上更上一層樓。

{ User's Guide }
使用説明

本書共計收錄**600**則片語，依難易度分為
初級、中級、中高級，依片語首字母排序。

① 首先，由**完整句**帶出**關鍵片語**。

②
緊接著完整句
的是每則片語
的**使用說明**。

③
透過MP3聆聽外
師原音對話，學
片語不忘精進英
聽能力。

④
每則片語補充
一篇**實用對
話**，協助讀者
不僅理解片語
語意，更能活
用片語。

---

001 **A lot of** people think wealth is the key to happiness.

很多人認為財富是通往幸福的關鍵。

a lot of為「很多」之意，可加在可數的複數普通名詞前，亦可加在不可數
之物質或抽象名詞前，為十分實用的不定數量形容詞。a lot of可以寫成lots
of加在名詞前，也可以寫成a lot加在動詞後，但不可寫成a lots of。

MP3
001

A: What do you think happiness is?
你覺得幸福是什麼？

B: A lot of people might think wealth is the key to
happiness, but I don't.
很多人可能認為財富是通往幸福的關鍵，但我不這麼想。

A: What do you mean?
你的意思是？

**B: I just want to lead a healthy life and spend time with
the ones I love.**
我只想過著健康的生活，並和我所愛的人共度時光。

相關用語 **many** 許多的   進階補充 **lead a...life** 過著…的人生

---

⑤
相關用語及**進階補充**，補充
與對話相關的單字或片語。

⑥
書後附上**A-Z片語索引**，
包含**片語、語意、難易度**
(初、中、中高)及**頁碼**，方
便查詢。

Index

contents

目錄

How to Master Dixon Idioms and English Phrases
with One Single Sentence

初級片語 Part 1

初級片語，係針對欲增強基礎英語能力、以及有心提升簡易日常英語理解力與使用能力者所設計。學完本章的初級片語，英語溝通力可達九年級程度，即有能力掌握基礎的英文聽、說、讀、寫，也能理解、並正確使用簡易的日常生活英文。

How to Master Dixon Idioms and English Phrases with One Single Sentence

{ *Part 1* }

初級片語

Basic Level

Dixon Idioms
and
English phrases

001 **A lot of** people think wealth is the key to happiness.

很多人認為財富是通往幸福的關鍵。

a lot of為「很多」之意，可加在可數的複數普通名詞前，亦可加在不可數之物質或抽象名詞前，為十分實用的不定數量形容詞。a lot of可以寫成lots of加在名詞前，也可以寫成a lot加在動詞後，但不可寫成a lots of。

A: What do you think happiness is?
你覺得幸福是什麼？

B: **A lot of** people might think wealth is the key to happiness, but I don't.
很多人可能認為財富是通往幸福的關鍵，但我不這麼想。

A: What do you mean?
你的意思是？

B: I just want to **lead a healthy life** and spend time with the ones I love.
我只想過著健康的生活，並和我所愛的人共度時光。

相關用語 → **many** 許多的   進階補充 → **lead a...life** 過著…的人生

002 I am looking for **a pair of** running shoes for my daughter. 我在幫女兒找一雙慢跑鞋。

a pair of為「一對、一雙」之意。pair的意思是由成對的兩部分所構成的一件物品，若把兩部分拆開來就不能使用，如剪刀、褲子、鞋子等。這類由成對的兩部分所構成的物品，才可用pair加以形容。由於用a pair of所形容的物品必須視為一個整體，因此需使用單數動詞，不可使用複數動詞。

A: May I help you?
需要幫忙嗎？

B: I am **looking for a pair of** running shoes for my daughter.
我在幫女兒找一雙慢跑鞋。

A: What is her shoe size?
她是什麼尺寸？

B: Five.
五號。

相關用語 → **a couple of** 一對、一雙   進階補充 → **look for** 尋找

003

There will be **a series of** discounts and sales.

將會有一系列的折扣和特賣。

a series of為「連續、一系列」之意。series單複數同形,是指類似或彼此相關的若干物,在時間或空間上形成連續;或物品們本身成組、成套之意。本片語後若接複數名詞,其後動詞亦以單數處理。注意series跟serious(嚴重的)看起來和讀起來非常相似,書寫和聽力上要多加留意。

A: Why are there so many people at that **department store**?

為何那家百貨公司那麼多人?

B: Oh, that department store is having an anniversary sale.

喔,那家百貨公司正在舉辦週年慶。

A: Is there anything interesting on sale?

有什麼有意思的特賣品嗎?

B: I'm sure there will be. I've heard there will be **a series of** other discounts and sales, too.

我相信有的。我聽說還會有一系列的其他折扣和特賣。

相關用語 ⊶ **set** 一套　　進階補充 ⊶ **department store** 百貨公司

004

Is John **absent from** class again?

約翰又缺課了嗎?

absent from為「缺席、不在」之意。absent可當動詞,也可當形容詞,但在用法上有差異。absent當動詞時:absent + O + from + (代)名詞,意指「缺席」;當形容詞時:be absent + from + 名詞,意指「缺席的」。

A: Where is John? Is he **absent from** class again?

約翰在哪裡?他又缺課了嗎?

B: He caught the flu and is very sick.

他感冒了,病得很重。

A: OK. Then can you **drop by** his house and give him his report back after school?

好的。那你放學後可以去看看他,順便把報告拿給他嗎?

B: Sure.

沒問題。

相關用語 ⊶ **away** 不在地　　進階補充 ⊶ **drop by** 順便拜訪

005

He makes the same mistakes again and again.

他一再重蹈覆轍。

again and again為「一再地」之意，通常放在句尾，為副詞片語，修飾前面的動詞。again為副詞，表示「再次」，again and again有加強語氣的作用。另有片語over and over again，用來表示「再三、反覆」的意思。

005

A: How is your team assignment going?
你的小組報告進行得怎麼樣？

B: Well, everyone is great, except for John.
嗯，大家都很棒，除了約翰以外。

A: Why? Is there something wrong between you two?
為什麼？你們之間有什麼問題嗎？

B: No. It's just he is very careless and makes the same mistakes again and again.
沒有，只是他很粗心，而且一再犯同樣的錯。

相關用語 → repeatedly 一再　　進階補充 → except for 除…之外

006

If you agree with the manager, then don't sign the contract. 若你和經理意見相投，就別簽合約。

agree to/with為「同意某事/某人」之意。agree是指「任何一方面皆和諧一致，且無矛盾或衝突」。agree to後接事情、提議、方案等，不接人；用法：S + agree to + 事情、提議、方案等。agree with則可接事物或人，但後接人較正式且正確。用法：S + agree with + 人。

006

A: If you agree with the manager, then don't sign the contract.
若你和經理意見相投，就別簽合約。

B: Why not?
為何別簽？

A: By signing the contract, it shows that you agree to disobey his orders.
簽署合約代表你同意違抗他的命令。

B: Oh, I see.
原來如此。

相關用語 → see eye to eye 同意　　進階補充 → sign a contract 簽約

007

Take three pills after each meal **along with** water.

餐後配水吞服三顆藥丸。

along with為「連同…一起」之意。單獨用along一字是「沿著」的意思，若加上with就有「隨同…一起」的意思。需特別注意的是，along與alone形音皆近，但後者alone為「單獨的」之意，需加以辨識。相似片語：all along「自始至終」；along the lines of + 物「與某物相似」；get along with + 人「與某人相處愉快」。

A: Take three pills after each meal along with water.
餐後配水吞服三顆藥丸。

B: Just water?
水就好了？

A: Yes, nothing but warm water.
是的，只要溫水就可以了。

B: OK.
好的。

[相關用語] → **together with** 連同   [進階補充] → **nothing but** 只有

008

I can't wait **any longer**.

我無法再多等了。

any longer為「再久一點、多些時間」之意，多用在疑問句與否定句。any在此為副詞，表「少許、若干」；longer則為形容詞，long的比較級；兩者相連則成為副詞片語。any用作代名詞時可接單數或複數型動詞，但用來表示「人」時，則多接複數動詞。

A: I can't wait any longer. When is the next train?
我無法再多等了。下班火車是什麼時候？

B: I am sorry for the delay. The next train should arrive within two minutes.
對於誤點我感到抱歉。下班車應於兩分鐘內抵達。

A: OK.
好。

B: Please have some tea while you're waiting.
等待期間，請喝點茶。

[相關用語] → **anymore** (不)再   [進階補充] → **sorry for** 為…感到抱歉

009

When will Grandma **arrive at** the airport tomorrow?

奶奶將於明日何時抵達機場？

arrive at表「抵達」，後接地點。come和arrive都有抵達某處或達到某一種地步的意思；come是強調到達某處或某地步的過程中，所涉及的進程或動作；arrive則是強調到達某處或目的地的概念。前者是以動作為主，後者則以概念為主。通常arrive at表示抵達小地方，arrive in則表示抵達較大的城市或國家；如不僅表示抵達且含有滯留之意時，則用in表示。

MP3
009

A: When will Grandma **arrive at** the airport tomorrow?
奶奶將於明日何時抵達機場？

B: Five thirty in the morning.
早上五點半。

A: I'm thinking about **picking her up** at the MRT station.
我想去捷運站接她。

B: That will be great. Grandma will be very happy.
那太棒了。奶奶會非常開心的。

相關用語 → depart 離開　　　進階補充 → pick + 人 + up 接某人

010

Why can't you study **as hard as** your sister does?

你為何無法像你姐姐一樣用功？

as...as...為「像…一樣…」之意，用於連接同等級形容詞的比較，表示「相同的程度」。用法：S + be V + as + adj + as + (代)名詞。like作為介系詞時也有「像」的意思，用法：S + be V + adj + like + (代)名詞。然而，as和like之間亦有不同之處，前者用於表示「關係上的等同」，而後者則指「形態或性質上相似，但並不等同」。

MP3
010

A: Why can't you study **as hard as** your sister does?
你為何無法像你姐姐一樣用功？

B: You mean be like a nerd?
你說像個書呆子一樣嗎？

A: Your sister is not a nerd.
你姐姐不是個書呆子。

B: To all my friends, she is.
對我的朋友們來說，她是。

相關用語 → as easy as abc 輕而易舉　　　進階補充 → such as 例如

011 Please come home **as soon as** you leave school.

請你一放學就回家。

as soon as為「一…就…」之意，指涉兩個動作的發生：動作一發生後，動作二緊接著動作一發生。用法：S + V1 + 受詞 + as soon as + S + V2 + 受詞。as soon as可置於句首，但在該子句最後須加上逗點，如：As soon as you arrive in New York, give me a call.「你一到紐約，就打電話給我」。若將本片語置於句中引導子句，則第一個as前不加逗點。

MP3
011

A: Please come home **as soon as** you leave school.
請你一放學就回家。

B: Why?
為什麼？

A: Today is your dad's birthday. We are going to **eat out** and celebrate.
今天是你爹生日，我們要上館子吃飯慶祝。

B: OK. I will come home as fast as I can.
好。我會盡快回家。

相關用語 → ASAP 盡快   進階補充 → eat out 上館子吃飯

012 Remember to hand in your assignment by tomorrow afternoon **as usual**. 記得照常在明天下午前繳交作業。

as usual其意為「照常、照例」，為副詞片語，可置於句首或句尾，修飾全句或句中動詞。usual為形容詞，通常做主詞補語或受詞補語。usual不可用usually代替；usually是副詞，放在一般動詞之前，be動詞之後。

MP3
012

A: Remember to **hand in** your assignment by tomorrow afternoon **as usual**.
記得照常在明天下午前繳交作業。

B: Miss Chen, can I have one more day?
陳老師，我可以遲交一天嗎？

A: Why?
為什麼？

B: My computer crashed.
我的電腦壞了。

相關用語 → as always 如常   進階補充 → hand in 繳交

013

Can I **ask for** a gift if I pass the test next week?

若我下週考試通過，可以要份禮物嗎？

ask for為「要求」之意。用法：S + ask for + 事情 = S + ask + 人 + for + 事情。相似片語：ask for it表示「自討苦吃」。其他和ask有關的片語有：ask for the moon「癡人說夢」；a big ask「不情之請」；Never ask pardon before you're accused.「別不打自招」。

A: Dad, do you **have a minute**?
爸，你有空嗎？

B: Sure. What is it?
當然有。什麼事？

A: Can I **ask for** a gift if I pass the test next week?
若我下週考試通過了，可以要份禮物嗎？

B: Well, I'll think about it.
嗯，我考慮一下。

相關用語 **request** 要求　　進階補充 **have a minute** 有空

014

You don't care about me **at all**.

你一點都不關心我。

at all為「絲毫、全然」之意，通常用於否定句，表示「一點都不」的意思來加強語氣。也可用在疑問句中，表示「究竟、到底」之意。"Not at all." 用來表示對別人謝意的客氣回答，其意思等同"You are welcome."「別客氣」、"Don't mention it."「不用提」和"No problem."「沒問題」。

A: You don't care about me **at all**.
你一點都不關心我。

B: Why do you say that?
你為何這麼說呢？

A: If you **cared about** me, you would remember my birthday.
如果你關心我，就會記得我的生日。

B: It's tomorrow, isn't it?
那不是明天嗎？

相關用語 **not at all** 一點也不　　進階補充 **care about** 關心

015

After taking the exam three times, I got the license **at last**. 考了三次試後，我終於拿到執照了。

at last是副詞片語，意思是「最後、最終」。此片語置於句首，可修飾全句；置於句尾，則修飾句中動詞。作「到底、究竟」的意思解時帶有責怪的意味，用於疑問句，特別是完成式的疑問句，並且要置於句尾。at last也可寫成at long last，但at long last 的語氣較強。

MP3
015

A: Have you got your driver's license yet?
你拿到駕照了嗎？

B: Yes. After taking the exam three times, I got it at last.
拿到了。在考了三次試以後，我終於拿到了。

A: I am glad you finally pulled it off.
我很高興你終於成功了。

B: Me, too.
我也是。

相關用語 → **in the end** 最後   進階補充 → **pull off** 成功

016

At least two kilograms of flour is needed.

至少需要兩公斤麵粉。

at least表「至少」，為副詞片語，也可寫成at the least或at the very least。此片語也可用作「無論如何」的意思解。和at least相反的片語是at most「至多」。相關片語有：least little thing「無關緊要、不可能的事」；line/path of least resistance「最省力的方法」。

MP3
016

A: Honey, can you bring me some flour from the grocery store?
親愛的，你可以幫我去雜貨店買些麵粉嗎？

B: Sure. How much do you need?
可以啊。你需要多少？

A: At least two kilograms.
至少兩公斤。

B: OK. Let me get my wallet.
好的。我拿個錢包。

相關用語 → **in the least** 絲毫   進階補充 → **grocery store** 雜貨店

017

I won't **be able to** have dinner with you.

我無法跟你吃晚餐。

be able to為「有能力的」之意。be able to + V = can + V，但兩者之間仍有區別，前者表示「有能力做到」，後者則為「可以做到」。be capable of也表示有能力勝任之意，但更為強調應付某種特殊工作的能力，且兩者後接的介系詞不同，須特別注意。

A: Are you OK? You look terrible.
你還好吧？你看起來很糟。

B: I won't be able to have dinner with you. I haven't finished my project yet.
我無法跟你吃晚餐了。我的企劃還沒完成。

A: Two heads are better than one. Let me help you.
三個臭皮匠勝過一個諸葛亮。我來幫你。

B: Thank you so much.
真是太感謝你了。

相關用語 **capable** 能⋯的　　進階補充 **be willing to** 願意⋯的

018

I **am afraid that** I might fail the class.

我擔心我可能會被當掉。

afraid常用來表示恐懼或情緒不安。用法：S + be V + afraid of + Ving/N，意為「害怕某事某物」。除了加of外也可加to，用法：S + be V + afraid + to + V，意思是「對某特定行動有所不能或不情願」。本片語後面還可加that + 子句，用法：S + be V + afraid + that + S + V，that可省略。

A: I am afraid that I might fail the class.
我擔心我可能會被當掉。

B: How come? You've been working very hard.
怎麼會？你一直很認真啊。

A: But Mr. Smith said he would like to talk to me about my grades.
但是史密斯老師說他想和我談談我的成績。

B: Don't worry. I believe you'll do fine.
別擔心。我相信你會沒事的。

相關用語 **in fear of** 害怕　　進階補充 **Don't worry.** 別擔心

019

Why **were** you so **angry with** Dave?

為何你這麼生戴夫的氣？

be angry at/with為「憤怒的、生氣的」之意。當angry的對象是指人的言行或事物時，介系詞要用at或是about。用法：S + be V + angry at/about + 人的言行或事物，其中about特別指對事；若要指對人產生怒氣，必須要用with。用法：S + be V + angry with + 受詞(人)。

A: Why were you so angry with Dave?
你為什麼這麼生戴夫的氣？

B: He broke my vase. It's the third one he has broken this month.
他把我的花瓶打破了。這已經是這個月他打破的第三個了。

A: Calm down. He is just a baby.
冷靜點。他只是個嬰兒。

B: A baby? He is already four!
嬰兒？他已經四歲了！

> 相關用語 • **be furious at** 狂怒的　　進階補充 • **calm down** 冷靜點

020

Whether you pass or fail will **be based on** your projects.
你能否通過，端看你的作業成績。

be based on為「根據、基於」之意。用法：S + be V + based on + (代)名詞。base有「以…為起點」之意義，形容詞為basic「基礎的」；名詞為basis「基礎」。在棒球運動上，base有「壘」的意思，相關棒球術語：base hit「安打」；base on balls「保送上壘」；baseman「內野手」。

A: Whether you pass or fail will be based on more than just your projects.
你能否通過，不只看你的作業成績。

B: What are the other criteria?
其他的評分標準是什麼？

A: Your attendance record and in-class performance.
你的缺席紀錄和上課表現。

B: OK.
好的。

> 相關用語 • **on the basis of** 基於　　進階補充 • **in-class** 課堂上的

021

I will **be** more **careful about** it next time.

我下次會更加小心。

be careful about為「注意、關心」之意。careful是指「對自己的工作或責任處處留心，以免發生錯誤或損害」的意思。用法：S + be V + careful about + 事情／人。其他相關片語：be careful with「對…小心」；be careful in「審慎做…」。

MP3
021

A: There are a lot of typos in your sales report.
你的銷售報告裡有很多錯字。

B: I am sorry. I will **be** more **careful about** it next time.
對不起。我下次會更加小心。

A: Please do. You waste both of our time with all these mistakes.
麻煩你了。由於這些錯誤，你浪費我們彼此的時間。

B: I know. I am very sorry.
我知道。真的很抱歉。

相關用語 ► be careful of 小心　　進階補充 ► cautious 謹慎的

022

I **am crazy about** Hello Kitty.

我愛死凱蒂貓了！

be crazy about為「狂熱的、醉心的」之意。用法：S + be V + crazy about + (代)名詞。crazy是形容詞，其動詞是craze、副詞是crazily、名詞是craziness。相關片語：be crazy as a betsy bug「精神錯亂的」；crazy bone「肘部尺骨端」。

MP3
022

A: Wow! It's a Hello Kitty bag! I love it! Thank you!
哇！是個凱蒂貓的袋子！我喜歡！謝謝你！

B: I am glad you like it.
我很高興你喜歡。

A: Like it? Are you kidding me? I **am crazy about** it! Thank you so much.
喜歡？你開玩笑嗎？我愛死它了！真的很謝謝你。

B: Do you want to try it on now?
你想要現在試揹嗎？

相關用語 ► enthusiastic 熱情的　　進階補充 ► zealous for 熱情的

023

We **are** quite **different from** each other.

我們和彼此很不同。

英文中在說到「與…不相同」的概念時，be different from是最普遍、簡單的一種說法，其中「from」也可以用「to」代替，但主要是英式用法。different是指人或物無相似之處，有時暗指對比或對立。

A: I never knew that you had a twin sister.
我從來不知道你有個攣生姐妹。

B: Yes, I do, but we **are** quite **different from** each other.
對啊，但我們和彼此很不同。

A: In what ways?
怎麼說？

B: Actually, we **have little in common**. We have different hobbies and interests.
事實上，我們沒什麼共通點。我們擁有不同的嗜好與興趣。

相關用語 **similar** 相似的　　進階補充 **have in common** 共有的

024

He must **be disappointed at** my performance.

他對我的表現一定很失望。

be disappointed at表「失望」。用法：S + be V + disappointed at + 事情。disappointed是動詞disappoint「使沮喪」的形容詞形式，表「受到挫敗的」，at後面接事情，最好不要接人；若要接人，則使用in。

A: I saw the way Mr. Watson was looking at me. He must **be disappointed at** my performance.
我看到華生先生看著我的樣子，他對我的表現一定很失望。

B: Come on. Don't be so negative. It's not your fault we lost the game.
拜託，別這麼悲觀。我們輸掉比賽並不是你的錯。

A: But it is! What if I didn't **drop the ball**? We might have won the game.
但是是我的錯！要是我沒犯錯，我們或許可以贏得比賽。

B: Don't say that! You did your best.
別這麼說！你盡力了。

相關用語 **frustrated** 失望的　　進階補充 **drop the ball** 犯錯

025

She is famous for great songs and her sense of fashion. 她以好歌和時尚感著名。

be famous for為「以…著名」之意。famous主要用於人、地、物、事等方面，表示廣為人知或常受談論，往往有稱頌之意。相較於famous而言，若是因負面傳聞而著名，一般使用notorious，意為「惡名昭彰的」。

MP3
025

A: Lady Gaga is going to give some concerts in Taiwan!
女神卡卡要在台灣開演唱會了！

B: Who is Lady Gaga?
誰是女神卡卡？

A: Come on! She **is famous for** great songs and her sense of fashion!
拜託！她以好歌和時尚感著名。

B: Oh, I remember now. Isn't she the one who wore a meat dress?
喔，我想起來了。她不就是那個穿生肉裝的人嗎？

相關用語 **well-known 出名的** 進階補充 **known for 著名於**

026

How about buying something he is fond of?

買他喜歡的東西如何？

be fond of為「喜愛、愛好」之意，為形容詞片語，後面接的動詞要變成Ving。fond在此為「喜歡的、愛好的」之意，另有「溺愛的、多情的、妄想的、難以實現的」等意義。

MP3
026

A: Little Joe's birthday is next Saturday. What should I buy for him?
小喬下週六生日，我該買什麼給他？

B: How about something he **is fond of?**
買他喜歡的東西怎麼樣？

A: For example?
像是？

B: Maybe you can get him a Transformers robot. He **wants one badly.**
或許你可以買個變型金剛機器人給他。他很想要一台。

相關用語 **prefer 更喜歡** 進階補充 **want sth. badly 非常想要**

027

You **are intent on** winning the championships, aren't you? 你專注於奪冠，對吧？

be intent on為「專注於、熱心於」之意。用法：S + be V + intent on + Ving/N。intent表「熱切的、專注的」，也可當名詞，意為「意圖、意向」；例如evil intent「意圖不軌」。在這裡是當形容詞，使用時要特別留意。

027

A: Why are you in such a rush?
你為何如此急匆匆？

B: I have to attend basketball practice.
我得去參加籃球練習。

A: Wow! You are intent on winning the championships, aren't you?
哇！你專注於奪冠，對吧？

B: The competition is around the corner. I want to win!
比賽馬上就要到了。我想要贏！

相關用語 • **be keen on** 熱衷於　　進階補充 • **in a rush** 倉促地

028

Is your brother **junior to** you?
你的兄弟比你年輕嗎？

junior是形容詞，表示「年紀較輕的」。應注意的是，junior to後面要加受格(me、him、her、you、us、them、it)，而younger than後面要加主格(I、we、you、he、she、it、they)，兩者不可混淆。

028

A: Is that your older brother over there?
那邊那位是你的哥哥嗎？

B: No, that's my younger brother, Tom.
不，那是我弟弟，湯姆。

A: He is junior to you? He looks at least two years older than you.
他比你小？他看起來至少比你大兩歲。

B: Ha-ha. He's a bit old for his age.
哈哈，他看起來比實際年齡稍長。

相關用語 • **younger** 較年輕的　　進階補充 • **be senior to** 比…年長

029

Jiang Xun is known to many art lovers for his **works.** 蔣勳的作品為許多藝術愛好者所熟知。

be known to表「為…所熟知」。known是形容詞，意思是指「被熟知」。相關片語之比較：be known for + 特性「以…特質聞名」；be known as + 身分、職業「以…身分聞名」；be known by「藉由…認識」。在known前加上well或widely等副詞，可強化知名的程度。

A: Who do you think we can invite for the speech next month?
你覺得我們下個月可以請誰來演講？

B: How about Jiang Xun? He is known to many art lovers for his works.
蔣勳怎麼樣？他的作品為許多藝術愛好者所熟知。

A: It's a good idea. How can we contact him?
好主意。我們要怎麼與他聯絡？

B: My sister is a friend of his. I can ask her for help.
我姐姐是他的朋友，我可以請她幫忙。

> 相關用語 → **familiar** 熟悉的 　　進階補充 → **a friend of** …的朋友

030

If you don't get up now, you'll **be late for** work.

若你現在不起床，上班會遲到。

be late for為「遲到」之意，late是指人或物抵達某地的時間較規定或約定的時間晚。用法：S + be V + late for + 名詞。late可以當名詞、副詞、形容詞，但不可以當動詞。相關諺語：Better late than never.「遲勝於無」；It's never too late to learn.「求知不嫌晚」。

A: If you don't get up now, you'll be late for work.
若你現在不起床，上班會遲到。

B: Alright. Let me go wash up.
好。讓我梳洗一下。

A: Your breakfast is downstairs waiting for you.
你的早餐在樓下等你。

B: Thanks, Mom.
謝囉，媽。

> 相關用語 → **early or late** 遲早　　進階補充 → **wash up** 梳洗

031

I believe your father will **be** so **proud of** you.

我相信你父親會非常以你為榮。

be proud of表「以…自豪」之意。proud為形容詞，這個字雖是「驕傲的、自豪的」之義，但它的含義可以廣泛到從個人持有適度的自尊心，到鄙視別人的高傲態度。用法：S + be V + proud of + 事情／人。proud後方也可以加to V「自豪地去做某事」或that + 子句「自豪某事」。

MP3
031

A: I believe your father will be so proud of you.
我相信你父親會非常以你為榮。

B: Why is that?
為何這麼說？

A: Haven't you checked the bulletin board yet? You won another first prize!
你還沒看到公佈欄嗎？你又得第一名了！

B: He will be over the moon at the news.
他聽到這消息一定樂翻了。

相關用語 ● **pride** 自豪　　進階補充 ● **over the moon** 欣喜若狂

032

He **is short of** experience and very arrogant.

他經驗不足，又非常自大。

be short of為「缺乏、不足」之意。short為形容詞，表示「短缺、短少」的意思，名詞形為shortage。用法：S + be V + short of + 東西／事情。相關片語：be short for「…的縮寫」；be short on「欠缺」；be short with「對…無禮」。

MP3
032

A: I don't want Jason on my team any more.
我不想要傑森在我的組裡了。

B: Why is that?
為什麼？

A: He is short of experience and very arrogant.
他經驗不足，又非常自大。

B: OK. I'll transfer him to Jessica's team if she agrees.
好的。若潔西卡同意，我會把他調到她組裡。

相關用語 ● **be lack of** 缺乏　　進階補充 ● **transfer to** 調任

033

Because of Jack, the whole class will have to cancel the trip. 因為傑克，全班必須取消旅行。

because of表「因為、由於」。because在作連接詞時，所接的子句通常出現在主要子句的後面。值得注意的是，because後面要接包含完整主詞和動詞的子句，但because of後面不能接子句，必須接名詞。

A: **Because of** Jack's carelessness, the whole class will have to cancel the trip.
由於傑克的疏忽，全班必須取消這次旅行。

B: That's too bad. Why?
太糟糕了。為什麼？

A: He lost all the train tickets.
他把所有的火車票弄丟了。

B: Oh, no!
噢，不！

相關用語 • **due to** 由於　　　進階補充 • **owing to** 由於

034

He will be a grown-up **before long** and leave us for college. 他將在不久後成年，離開我們去念大學。

before long表「不久以後」，為副詞片語，可放在句首、句中或句尾來修飾整個句子，若放在句中則需置於動詞之後。相關片語：as long as「只要」；in the long run「最後、終於」；so long「再見」；long time no see「好久不見」。

A: **Look at** our little Tommy. He is so adorable, isn't he?
看看我們的小湯米。他真可愛，不是嗎？

B: Indeed he is.
他的確是很可愛。

A: And he will be a grown-up **before long** and leave us for college.
他將在不久後成年，離開我們去念大學。

B: Come on. He is just a baby now. There are still many years left before we lose him.
拜託。他現在只是個嬰兒，還有很多年會和我們在一起。

相關用語 • **in a short time** 短時間內　　進階補充 • **look at** 看

035

Do you **believe in** ghosts?

你相信有鬼嗎？

believe in是指「對觀念、思想或宗教等的信心，或相信有鬼怪」的意思。
believe in跟believe的差別為：believe in是指對「人格、主義、行為抱有
信心」的意思；believe則是單純表示「相信某件事或某句話」，涵蓋的範
圍和程度不如前者廣與深。

MP3
035

A: Do you **believe in** ghosts?
你相信鬼嗎？

B: Not really. How about you?
不算是。那你呢？

A: I believe there might be a world **beyond our knowledge**.
我相信或許有我們不理解的世界。

B: So you are one of those people who watches ghost-hunting shows, aren't you?
所以你是會看捉鬼節目的人，對吧？

相關用語 → **trust** 信任　　進階補充 → **beyond knowledge** 無法理解

036

I don't think it **belongs to** any of us.

我想它不屬於我們任何一位。

belong to是指「屬於」的意思，若後面加人，意思是指「屬於某人」；加
上事物或組織，意思是指「屬於某個團體或組織」；相關片語：belong in
是指「放在、居於」的意思，其後要接地方。

MP3
036

A: Excuse me. Do you recognize the bag over there?
不好意思。你認得那個包包嗎？

B: No, I don't think it **belongs to** any of us.
不，我想它不屬於我們任何一個人。

A: Then we should give the unattended bag to the station staff.
那我們應該將無人所屬的包包交給車站職員。

B: We'd **better** do that.
我們最好要。

相關用語 → **belongings** 攜帶物品　　進階補充 → **had better** 最好

037 Which do you like better **between** this shirt **and** that one? 這件和那件襯衫，你比較喜歡哪件？

between A and B表「在A和B之間」。between和among都有「在…之間」的意思，而其中的差別為：between這個字多用於指稱兩者之間，而among則是指在三者以上之間。among另有變體amongst，為英式用法，在美國為較文言的用法。

A: Honey, which do you like better between this blue shirt and that striped one?
親愛的，這件藍襯衫和那件條紋衫，你比較喜歡哪件？

B: I'd go with the striped one.
我會選條紋衫。

A: Are you sure? But that one might make me look fat.
你確定嗎？但是那件讓我看起來肥胖。

B: Then just take the blue one.
那就挑藍色那件吧。

相關用語 **betwixt 在兩可之間**　進階補充 **in-between 中間的**

038 I **borrowed** the shirt **from** Kevin.
我跟凱文借來這件衣服。

borrow from為「從…借來」之意。用法：S + borrow from + (代)名詞。borrow後面一定要接介系詞from，不能接to。須注意此字與lend同為「借」之意，但borrow是「借入」，lend則是「借出」，不可混用。

A: I've never seen this shirt before. Did you buy this last week?
我沒看過這件襯衫，你上星期買的嗎？

B: No, I borrowed it from Kevin.
不是，我跟凱文借來的。

A: Kevin? Mr. Wally's son?
凱文？瓦利先生的兒子？

B: That's him. We sometimes swap clothes with each other.
就是他。我們有時會交換衣服。

相關用語 **lend 把…借給**　進階補充 **swap with 與…交換**

039 This bracelet **brought back** the old days.

這只手鐲使我憶起往日情懷。

bring back表「使憶起、再掀風潮」。當此片語的受詞為代名詞時，受詞要放在back的前面。bring的動詞時態屬於不規則變化，它的過去式和過去分詞均是brought。

A: Look at this! This is the bracelet you gave me ten years ago.

你看！這是你十年前送我的手鐲。

B: That's right! I thought it **rang a bell** when I saw it on your wrist.

沒錯！我一看到你戴在手腕上時就想起來了。

A: This bracelet **brought back** the old days when we first met.

這個手鐲讓我想起我們初識的那些日子。

B: I am glad you still love it.

我很高興你還喜歡它。

相關用語 → **recall** 使想起　進階補充 → **ring a bell** 模糊地記得

040 I was **brought up** by my grandparents.

我由祖父母撫養長大。

bring up在當「撫養」的意思解時，其同義字為breed。這個片語還有一些其他解釋，比如：「嘔吐、突然停止或停頓、准許發言、提出、將帳目或計算等轉載到次頁」等。

A: It's a nice picture. Are they your grandparents?

這張照片拍得真好。他們是你的祖父母嗎？

B: Yes, I was **brought up** by them after my parents died in a car accident.

是的，自從我雙親車禍身亡後，就賴他們撫養我長大。

A: Oh, I am sorry to hear that.

喔，我很遺憾聽到這些。

B: It's OK. They've been **taking** great **care of** me.

沒關係。他們一直很照顧我。

相關用語 → **raise** 養育　進階補充 → **take care of** 照顧

041

He is trying to build up his own business.

他正試圖自立門戶。

build up意指「建立、加強」。在當作「加強」的意思解釋時，多指加強一種力量，例如體能等等。此片語也可當「阻塞、創建、養成」的意思解。

MP3
041

A: I haven't seen Jack for a while. What has he been doing?
我好一陣子沒看到傑克了。他在忙什麼？

B: He is trying to **build up** his own business and thus is quite occupied these days.
他正試著創業，所以最近很忙。

A: Really? What is his business?
真的嗎？他做什麼生意？

B: He runs a pet grooming shop downtown.
他在市區經營一間寵物美容坊。

相關用語 ● strengthen 加強   進階補充 ● build on 以⋯為基礎

042

We met each other by accident.

我們偶然遇見彼此。

by accident是指「偶然地、意外地」之意；by accident of則是指「憑藉⋯機遇」的意思。accident可當「事故、災禍」解，也可當「機遇、偶然」解，在後者的狀況下與chance同義。

MP3
042

A: How do you know Dave?
你和戴夫怎麼認識的？

B: We met each other **by accident** at the World Car Exhibition.
我們在世界汽車大展上偶然遇見彼此。

A: What were you doing there? I didn't know you liked cars.
你在那裡做什麼？我不知道你喜歡汽車。

B: I don't, but the showgirls were excellent subjects for photos.
我沒有喜歡，但是展場女孩是攝影的好題材。

相關用語 ● by chance 偶然地   進階補充 ● fortuitous 偶然的

043 The contract was returned **by mistake**.

合約遭誤退。

by mistake為「錯誤地」之意，通常放在句尾，用來修飾整個句子的句義。mistake可當動詞也可當名詞，mistaken是形容詞，意為「錯誤的、被誤解的」；mistaken identity是「認錯人」的意思。

MP3
043

A: How come I haven't got the contract yet?
我為何還沒收到合約？

B: I am sorry. The contract was returned by mistake. I'll resend it today.
很抱歉。合約因疏失而被退回，我今天會重新寄出。

A: When can I receive the contract?
我何時會收到合約？

B: It should be tomorrow.
應該是明天。

相關用語 **by error** 錯誤地　　進階補充 **by fault** 錯誤地

044 I don't want to walk home **by myself**.

我不想獨自一人走回家。

by oneself是一種強調用法，強調某事由某人獨立完成，不假他人之手。當作副詞片語時，用來修飾句中動詞，oneself要視句中主詞而作改變。當作形容詞片語時，則表示「單獨的、獨自的」之意。

MP3
044

A: Do you mind walking me home? I don't want to walk home by myself.
你介意送我回家嗎？我不想一個人走回去。

B: Of course, and maybe we can have a drink before going home.
當然好，也許我們回家前可以喝點飲料。

A: That's a good idea. Where should we go?
好主意。我們應該去哪裡？

B: How about John's Bar?
約翰酒吧如何？

相關用語 **on one's own** 獨自　　進階補充 **how about** …如何

045

By the way, you left this paycheck in your pocket.

對了，你把薪水條忘在口袋裡。

by the way用作「順便一提」的意思解時，通常置於句首，或插入兩個沒有邏輯關係的句子之間。當作「在途中、在路旁、業餘性質地、隨意地」的意思解時，通常放在句尾。在書信當中常用縮寫"BTW"。

045

A: I've sent your suit to the dry-cleaner. **By the way**, you left this in your pocket.
我已經把你的套裝送去乾洗了。對了，你把這個忘在口袋裡。

B: Oh, it's my paycheck! Thank you so much!
喔，是我的薪水條！真是太感謝你了！

A: You have to be much more careful **next time**.
你下次得更加小心。

B: I certainly will!
我一定會的！

相關用語 → **mention** 提及　　進階補充 → **next time** 下次

046

I am tired of celebrating **by ways of** throwing parties.

我厭倦以舉辦派對的方式慶祝。

by way of 可以用through代替，表「經由」。用法：S + V + by way of + Ving/N。way在這裡可當成實體上的「道路、途徑」，也可作為抽象的「方法、手段」。相關片語：rub sb. the wrong way「激怒某人」；go a long way「成功」。

046

A: Dad's birthday is coming. How should we celebrate it?
老爸的生日快到了，我們該怎麼慶祝？

B: How about giving him a surprise party?
幫他辦個驚喜派對如何？

A: I am tired of celebrating **by ways of** throwing surprise parties.
我對於用舉辦驚喜派對來慶祝感到厭倦。

B: Then just meet up and have a nice friendly dinner together.
那就一起聚聚，吃頓溫馨的晚餐。

相關用語 → **via** 經由　　進階補充 → **be tired of** 對⋯感到厭倦

047

Jason has been **called up** for military service.

傑森已被徵召入伍。

call up主要用於美式英語，為「徵召入伍」、「打電話」之意。call up另有「傳喚、回想」的意思。作「回想」之意解時，受詞一律放在up之後；其餘用法，受詞若為代名詞時，一律放在up之前。用法：S + call up + 人 = S + ring up + 人 = S + give + 人 + a ring = S + give + 人 + a call。

MP3
047

A: Are you coming to Jason's party this Friday?
你這週五要來傑森的派對嗎？

B: A party? For what?
派對？什麼派對？

A: Jason has been **called up** for military service. He's leaving next Monday.
傑森要去當兵了，他下週一上路。

B: What a surprise!
真是出乎意料！

相關用語 → enlist 從軍　　進階補充 → phone call 電話

048

I am so glad that someone **cares about** me.

有人關心我，我很高興。

care about表「關心、感興趣」，用法：S + care about + (代)名詞。care是指「憂慮、疑懼、操心、責任」等足以成為心理負擔的事物，可當動詞也可當名詞。相似片語：take care of「照顧」；care for「喜歡」。

MP3
048

A: I hope you are better now.
我希望你好一點了。

B: Thank you. I am so glad that someone still **cares about** me.
謝謝你。我很高興還有人關心我。

A: What are you talking about? Jeff has been **worried about** you a lot.
你在說什麼？傑夫一直很擔心你。

B: Really? How come he never **pays me a visit**?
真的嗎？那他為何都沒有來看過我？

相關用語 → worry about 擔心　　進階補充 → pay sb. a visit 探望

049

I think he **caught a cold**.

我認為他感冒了。

cold一般是指因為少穿衣服或淋雨而得到的傷風或感冒,若是帶有過濾性病毒的流行性感冒,則用influenza。cold當名詞時是不可數名詞,但若加上動詞如get、have,則必須在cold前加上a。與感冒相關的詞語:sneeze「打噴嚏」;cough「咳嗽」;snivel「流鼻水」。

A: Peter isn't going to school today.
彼得今天不上學。

B: Why not?
為什麼不?

A: I think he **caught a cold**.
我想他感冒了。

B: Then we had better take him to Dr. Liang.
那我們最好帶他去看梁醫生。

相關用語 **runny nose** 流鼻涕　　進階補充 **sore throat** 喉嚨痛

050

You can always give me a call if you **change your mind**. 若你改變心意,可隨時電話連絡我。

change one's mind如果在後面加上介系詞about,再加上Ving,就代表「對於已決定的事有所變動或更改」的意思。相關片語有:make up one's mind「下決心」;speak one's mind「表明決心」;lose one's mind「失去理智」。

A: Are you sure you don't want to order our latest magazines?
你確定不想訂購我們最新的雜誌嗎?

B: No, thank you.
不用了,謝謝。

A: Then, you can always **give me a call** if you **change your mind**.
那麼,若你改變心意,可隨時打電話給我。

B: No problem.
沒問題。

相關用語 **come around** 讓步　　進階補充 **give sb. a call** 打電話

051

Cheer up! It's no big deal.

開心點！這也沒什麼。

cheer up是指人「從低落的情緒中振奮起來」的意思，可作及物或不及物動詞用。若當「鼓舞」之意解時，是及物動詞片語；當「振作起來」之意解時，則是不及物動詞片語。當及物動詞片語時，受詞若為代名詞，應置於up之前；若為名詞，則放前後皆可。另在美式口語當中，cheers可當「乾杯、萬歲、祝賀」等意思解。

MP3
051

A: You look awful. What's wrong?
你看起來糟透了。怎麼了？

B: I failed the driving test.
我沒通過駕照考試。

A: **Cheer up!** It's no big deal. Just take another test some time.
開心點！這沒什麼。就改天再考一次吧。

B: But it's the third test I have taken already.
但這是我第三次考了。

相關用語 ◦ **cheer on** 鼓勵　　進階補充 ◦ **cheer squad** 啦啦隊

052

Aren't you going to help **clean** this **up**?

你不打算幫忙清理嗎？

clear up在當「清理、澄清」的意思解時，其後要加名詞，不能加代名詞。clean和clear之間的差別在於，前者強調清潔乾淨，較接近neat和tidy；後者則著重清楚明白，較接近obvious。

MP3
052

A: Wait! Aren't you going to help **clean** this **up**?
等等！你不打算幫忙清理嗎？

B: Why me? Jason was also part of it.
為什麼是我？傑森也有份。

A: But Jason is only one person. Can't you be a dear and help, too?
但是傑森才一個人，你不能也出手幫忙嗎？

B: Fine. I'll do it.
好，我會的。

相關用語 ◦ **clean up** 打掃　　進階補充 ◦ **clean up on** 擊敗

053 You are **close to** David, aren't you?

你和大衛很熟，是吧？

close to為「親近、靠近」之意。close表示「中間幾乎沒有空隙地緊密接近」，可當形容詞和副詞。雖然close跟near的意思差不多，都是「在附近」，但close本身的「接近」，在程度上比near還要近。close既可當地理距離上的「靠近」，也可當心理距離上的「親近」。

A: Jeff, you are **close to** David, aren't you?
　　傑夫，你跟大衛很熟，對吧？

B: Yes. We are the closest roommates ever. Why do you ask?
　　沒錯。我們是最好的室友。為何這麼問？

A: I would like to ask you a favor and **introduce** me to him.
　　我想請你幫忙介紹我給他。

B: Sure. No problem.
　　當然，沒問題。

相關用語 ● familiar with 熟悉的　　進階補充 ● introduce to 介紹

054 Long skirts just **came back** this season.

長裙本季再度恢復流行。

come back意為「回來、再度恢復流行」，屬正式用法。口語上，則用be back，如：I will be back. = I will come back. 此片語另外還有「記起」的意思，但用法是某事 + come back to sb.，切記不可顛倒順序。

A: Look at my lace skirt. Isn't it beautiful?
　　看看我的蕾絲裙，很漂亮吧？

B: It's a bit too long. Short skirts are in fashion, aren't they?
　　有點太長了。短裙才時尚，不是嗎？

A: Come on! Long skirts just **came back** this season.
　　拜託！長裙本季再度恢復流行了。

B: Oh!
　　哦！

相關用語 ● get back 恢復　　進階補充 ● in fashion 合於時尚

055 Where do you **come from**?

你來自何處？

come from的原意是「來自何處」，但常用來說明或詢問某人的出生地或原籍，所以come from後面通常接地點。come from在作「起源於、源自、出生於」之意解時，為及物動詞，受詞放在from之後。此片語因時態的不同，意思也會跟著改變。用現在式時，常指「某人之出生地與原籍」；過去式是指「從哪裡來」。

MP3
055

A: Where do you **come from**?
你來自何處？

B: I come from Nantou.
我來自南投。

A: So it's true what they say about all beauties **coming from Nantou**.
所以「美女都是從南投來的」說法，一點也沒錯。

B: I am flattered.
過獎了。

相關用語 → **originate in** 來自　進階補充 → **derive from** 起源於

056 How are you **coming on** your new project?

你的新企劃進展如何？

come on為多義片語，除了「進展、上演」等意思外，還有「趕快、開始、登場、順利進行、(季節、夜晚)將近」等意思。此片語在口語上，也作慫恿的口吻使用，如：「好啦！請！」或是無奈的口吻，意近中文的「拜託！」

MP3
056

A: How are you **coming on** your new project?
你的新企劃進展如何？

B: So far so good.
目前還好。

A: I am wondering if I can help.
我在想我是否能幫得上忙。

B: It's very nice of you to offer.
你願意提供協助真是太好了。

相關用語 → **in progress** 進展　進階補充 → **come along** 進展

057 My dream has finally **come true**!

我終於實現了夢想！

come true是指「某種預測、夢想、希望等被證實或成為事實」的意思。片語中的come在此等於become，是「變成」的意思；true是形容詞，做主詞補語，切記不可因come為動詞，將true以truly代替。

057

A: Congratulations. You've won the contest.
恭喜你贏得競賽了。

B: Yes! What is the prize?
太好了！獎品是什麼？

A: Ten thousand dollars and a free ticket to Paris.
一萬元獎金和巴黎免費機票。

B: My dream has finally **come true**!
我的夢想終於成真了！

相關用語 **fulfill 實現**　　進階補充 **come to pass 實現**

058 If you **committed a crime**, would you turn yourself in? 若你犯了罪，會自首嗎？

commit a crime為「犯罪」之意。commit是指「犯(罪、錯)」的意思，後可接crime(罪)、error(錯)、suicide(自殺)等。此片語為慣用片語，因此commit不能用其他動詞代替。commit的名詞為commitment。

058

A: If you **committed a crime**, would you **turn** yourself **in**?
如果你犯了罪，你會自首嗎？

B: It depends.
看情況。

A: What do you mean?
你是什麼意思？

B: I would certainly do it if I thought I might get caught.
若我覺得我會被抓，那當然會自首。

相關用語 **commit to 交給**　　進階補充 **turn in 自首**

059 You forgot to **count in** the utility cost.

你忘了計入水電費。

count in為「算入、納入考量」之意。用法：S + count + 受詞 + in～。count和calculate都有「計算」的意思，其差別為：count是指「依順序逐一地計算」之意；calculate則是指「使用精密的數學程序從事複雜計算」的意思。

059

A: I have some suggestions on your business plan.
關於你的事業企劃書，我有一些建議。

B: I am so glad I can have your opinion. What is it?
我很高興能聽你的意見。是什麼呢？

A: You forgot to count in the utility cost, which shouldn't be over 10%.
你忘了計入水電費了，水電費不該超過百分之十。

B: Oh, I see. Thank you so much.
喔，我知道了。真的很感謝你。

相關用語 **count up** 共計　　進階補充 **utility cost** 水電費

060 The Board decided to **cut down** on the incentive program. 董事會決定刪減獎勵計劃。

cut down為「削減、砍斷」之意。用法：S + cut down + on + 受詞。cut、chop和hack都有「砍、切」的意思，其差別為：cut是指最通用的「劈、砍」；chop是指「用刀斧等利刃砍、劈」的意思，可算是cut中的一種特殊形式；hack則是指「粗暴亂砍」的意思。

060

A: Have you heard the news?
你聽說了嗎？

B: What news?
什麼事？

A: The Board decided to cut down on the incentive program.
董事會決定刪減獎勵計劃。

B: That's too bad!
真是太糟了！

相關用語 **cut back** 削減　　進階補充 **trim off** 削減

061

You always cut in while I am trying to finish what I'm saying. 你總在我試著說完話前插嘴。

cut in為不及物動詞；作「插嘴」的意思解時，是指「打斷別人正在進行的談話」；作「超車」的意思解時，則是指「在車輛行駛過程中，搶在前頭，攔住別人的去路」。由cut所組成的片語有：cut across「遮斷」；cut back「削減」；cut off「切斷」；cut out「刪去、關掉、安排」；cut up「切碎」。

A: I don't like the way you talk to me.
我不喜歡你跟我說話的方式。

B: What's wrong?
怎麼了？

A: You always **cut in** while I am trying to finish what I'm saying.
你總在我試著說完話前插嘴。

B: My apologies.
對不起。

相關用語 → interrupt 打斷　　進階補充 → break into 打斷

062

We believe he died from a stroke.

我們認為他死於中風。

die from為「因…而死」之意。die是泛指「死亡」最普通的字，可用於生命的結束，也可用在比喻的意思上。die from是指「由於外傷或意外原因而造成死亡」的意思。另外要注意的是，die of也可表示死因，但通常用於內在因素所導致的死亡，如疾病或饑餓。

A: I am sorry. We did our best.
很抱歉，我們盡力了。

B: Oh, no!
噢，不！

A: We believe he **died from** a stroke.
我們認為他死於中風。

B: A stroke? How could this be?
中風？怎麼會這樣？

相關用語 → pass away 去世　　進階補充 → cause of death 死亡原因

063

Do you know why cockroaches never **die out**?

你知道為何蟑螂從未滅絕嗎？

die out是指「某種事物因某種原因而逐漸消失，以致完全絕跡」的意思。在這裡的die不作「死亡」之意解，而是「逐漸消失、滅絕」的意思，可用於抽象事物如風俗文化，或實質存在如物種、人類等。

MP3
063

A: Do you know why cockroaches never die out?
你知道為何蟑螂從未滅絕嗎？

B: No, though I do believe they should.
不知道，但我相信它們該滅絕才是。

A: They can survive even without a head!
他們沒有頭也能存活！

B: Yuck! That's disgusting.
噁！真噁心。

相關用語 → extinct 滅絕的 進階補充 → die of 因…而死

064

Maybe you can **discuss** the project **with** Mr. Wang.

也許你可以和王先生討論計劃。

discuss with為「討論、商議」之意。discuss是強調從不同的角度來考慮一個問題，往往指交換意見，以便解決問題、制定方針等，通常是在友好的氣氛中進行。而如debate、argue，就有辯論和爭論、氣氛較為激烈的味道。用法：S + discuss + 事 + with + 人。

MP3
064

A: I really don't know what to do.
我真的不知道該怎麼辦。

B: What's bothering you?
你在煩惱什麼？

A: It's a collaboration project with Dr. Cooper.
和庫博醫生的合作計劃。

B: Maybe you can discuss it with Mr. Wang. He knows Dr. Cooper very well.
也許你可以和王先生討論。他跟庫博醫生很熟。

相關用語 → discussion 討論 進階補充 → know...well 對…很熟

065 Can you **divide** the cake **into** ten pieces?

你可以把蛋糕分成十份嗎？

divide into為「把…分成…」之意。用法：S + divide + sth. + into sth。into之後通常接「劃分後的形式」，如幾個小組、幾個小隊、幾個團體、幾塊或幾堆等等。若是採用S + divide + sth. + from，則是相反句型，from後須接「劃分前的形式」。

A: Can you divide the cake into ten pieces?
你可以把蛋糕分成十塊嗎？

B: Ten? But there are only eight people here.
十塊？但這裡只有八個人。

A: We have to leave some for Mom and Dad.
我們得留一些給爸媽。

B: Right.
對耶。

相關用語 · separate into 分成…   進階補充 · leave for 留給

066 Honey, can you **do me a favor**?

親愛的，能幫我個忙嗎？

do sb. a favor是指「幫某人一個忙」；而win sb. a favor則是「贏得某人歡心」，記憶時要特別注意。其他相關片語：in favor of「贊成」；out of favor with sb.「不得…歡心」；come out in favor of sb./sth.「公開表示支持」；curry favor with sb.「試圖贏得歡心」；Fortune favors the brave.「幸運青睞勇敢的人」。

A: Honey, can you do me a favor?
親愛的，能幫我個忙嗎？

B: Sure. What is it?
當然可以。什麼事？

A: Can you take Tina to school today?
你今天可以帶蒂娜去上學嗎？

B: I'd love to.
我很樂意。

相關用語 · help 幫助   進階補充 · ask for a favor 請求幫助

067

I'd never dreamed of being promoted.

我從未想過會升職。

dream of/about為「夢想、夢見」之意。用法：S + dream of/about + N/Ving。dream可當動詞和名詞，除了後接of和about來表示夢到什麼之外，也可以用that加上子句來進行陳述。相關片語有：pipe dream「無稽之談」；wet dream「春夢」。

MP3
067

A: Congratulations on your big promotion!
恭喜你升職了！

B: Thank you. I'd never dreamed of being promoted.
謝謝你。我從未想過會升職。

A: Why didn't you? You are such an excellent engineer. You deserve it!
為何沒有？你是個優秀的工程師，這是你應得的！

B: Thank you so much.
真的很謝謝你。

相關用語 • wish for 希望　進階補充 • congratulations on 恭喜

068

Why are you dressing up?

你為何盛裝打扮？

dress up當「裝扮、盛裝」的意思解時，是指為演戲等所做的刻意打扮。dress在這裡是不及物動詞，所以不能直接在dress跟up之間加上受詞，必須接在up之後。相關用語：dress code「服裝規定」；dress sb. down「責罵(口語用法)」。

MP3
068

A: Why are you dressing up?
你為何盛裝打扮？

B: I am going to Michelle's birthday party.
我要去參加蜜雪兒的生日派對。

A: Isn't that a beach party?
那不是場海灘派對嗎？

B: I think it's a good way to impress her.
我覺得這是個讓她印象深刻的好方法。

相關用語 • dressed-up 精心打扮的　進階補充 • impress 使銘記

069

My landlord is totally driving me into a corner.

我的房東完全把我逼入困境。

drive...into a corner為「將…逼入困境」之意。drive在這裡不是「駕駛」，而是「逼迫」的意思。相關片語：drive away at「努力做」；drive in「灌輸(觀念)」；drive out「驅趕」；drive a hard bargain「努力討價還價」；drive sb. over the edge「將某人逼近崩潰」。

MP3
069

A: My landlord is totally driving me into a corner.
我的房東完全把我逼入困境。

B: What did he do?
他做了什麼？

A: I asked if I could pay the rent late this time, but he said no.
我問他這次可否遲繳房租，他說不行。

B: Don't worry. I'll lend you some money. How much do you need?
別擔心，我可以借你一點錢。你需要多少？

相關用語 ► corner 困境　　進階補充 ► pay the rent 支付租金

070

Sorry about just dropping in.

抱歉，突然來訪。

drop in為「突然來訪」之意。drop在這裡是「訪問」的意思；若要標出明確的地點，則要用介系詞at，即drop in at + 地方；若要指拜訪某人時，介系詞則用on，即drop in on sb.。

MP3
070

A: Sorry about just dropping in.
突然來訪真抱歉。

B: Not at all. It's nice to see you. Would you like tea or coffee?
一點也不，很高興看見你。想喝茶還是咖啡？

A: Tea, please.
請給我茶。

B: OK.
好的。

相關用語 ► pay a visit to 拜訪　　進階補充 ► not at all 一點也不

071

The dam will **dry up** if it doesn't rain in a week.

若一週內未降雨,水庫將乾涸。

dry up表「枯竭、乾涸」。當「枯竭」解時,指的是在思想上沒有新的見解或創意。dry up的up是副詞,放在dry之後,有「使完全乾掉」的意思。此片語也可作不及物動詞用,表「曬乾」,其後接受詞。

A: The news report said the dam will **dry up** if it doesn't rain in a week.
新聞上說若一週內不下雨,水庫就要乾涸了。

B: Oh, that's awful!
噢,太糟糕了!

A: Indeed. I hate **water rationing**.
的確是。我討厭限水。

B: Me, too.
我也是。

相關用語 **dry out** 變乾　進階補充 **water rationing** 限水

072

It's time for Jason to **earn his own living**.

該是傑森自力更生的時候了。

earn one's living為「謀生」之意。living可當形容詞和名詞,當形容詞時作「活著的、有生氣的、實況轉播的」意思解,當名詞時則表示「生存、生計、生活方式」等。動詞為live,為「居住、存活」之意。

A: I think it's time for Jason to **earn his own living**.
我想該是傑森自力更生的時候了。

B: Isn't it too soon for him?
對他來說會不會太快了?

A: I don't think so. I started supporting my family at the age of 18.
我不這麼覺得。我十八歲就開始賺錢養家了。

B: I know. But can't we wait until he **graduates from college**?
我了解。但我們不能等到他大學畢業嗎?

相關用語 **make a living** 謀生　進階補充 **graduate from** 從…畢業

073

The pressure on everyone has **eased off** a lot.

每個人的壓力已減輕不少。

ease這個單字有「減輕、緩和」的意思，指免於困難、工作、痛苦、煩惱等各種壓迫的一種「安逸輕鬆的狀態」。ease off在這裡的意思是指「痛苦、局勢或神經緊張等狀態的減輕或緩和」。

A: Now that my company has hired more staff, the pressure on everyone has **eased off** a lot.
既然公司已多雇人力，每個人的壓力減輕了不少。

B: Does that mean you won't have to work overtime any longer?
所以是你不再需要加班的意思嗎？

A: Right. I should work no more than eight hours a day from now on.
是啊。從現在起，我一天不再工作超過八小時。

B: I envy you.
真令人羨慕。

相關用語 ▸ now that 既然   進階補充 ▸ no more than 不超過

074

Let's **eat out** tonight!

今晚出去吃飯吧！

eat in/out作「在家/在外吃飯」的意思解時，為不及物動詞，所以受詞不可以接在in/out的前面。eat in和eat out另外也可作「腐蝕、吃光」的意思解，此時為及物動詞。受詞若為代名詞，要接在in/out之前；如果受詞為名詞，則無此限制。

A: Let's eat out tonight!
今晚出去吃飯吧！

B: What's the event?
有什麼大事嗎？

A: Don't you remember? It's our anniversary today!
你忘了嗎？今天是我們的週年紀念日！

B: Oh, I got so busy that it slipped my mind.
噢，我忙到忘了。

相關用語 ▸ dine out 出外用餐   進階補充 ▸ slip one's mind 遺忘

075 **Even if** I promise I won't make the same mistake again? 即便是我保證不會重蹈覆轍？

even if等於even though，表「即使」，為有加強語氣意味的副詞片語。在正式的文章寫作上，even though是較正確且正式的用法，不可單用though，因為單用though是口語或非正式(也比較不被接受)的用法，必須加上even或改用although這個字才行。

A: Kelly told me **no matter** what you do, she won't forgive you.
凱莉跟我說不管你做什麼，她都不會原諒你的。

B: Really? **Even if** I promise I won't make the same mistake again?
真的嗎？即便是我保證不會重蹈覆轍？

A: She won't forgive you. You'd better forget about her.
她不會原諒你的。你最好忘了她。

B: Well, maybe she's not really the one for me.
嗯，或許她並不適合我。

相關用語 ► **even though** 即使　　進階補充 ► **no matter** 無論⋯

076 **Every time** I ride in your car, you always listen to this song. 每次搭你的車，你總是聽這首歌。

every time為「無論何時、每次」之意，在這裡當時間副詞用。相關片語：every so often「不時、偶爾」；every inch「完全」；every now and then「時常、有時」；every other day「每隔一天」。

A: What's the name of this song? It's very nice.
這首歌叫什麼名字？很好聽。

B: It's Canon, my favorite song.
這是我最喜歡的歌，卡農。

A: **Every time** I ride in your car, you always **listen to** this song.
每次搭你的車，你都在聽這首歌。

B: This song helps me escape from the chaos of the city.
這首歌可以帶我逃離城市喧囂。

相關用語 ► **whenever** 每當　　進階補充 ► **listen to** 聆聽

077 Excuse me. Where is the post office?

不好意思，請問郵局在哪裡？

Excuse me用於麻煩別人，或沒聽清楚對方說話時的道歉語。excuse是禮貌性的謙詞，指「所犯的錯誤不至於傷害到他人的人身安全，或造成他人利益之損害」，說話者不見得有錯；sorry是指「說話者的行為動作影響他人的人身安全、利益、感情等」的意思；apologize是指「說話者的行為動作深深影響他人的人身安全、利益、感情」，需正式、慎重地道歉。

A: Excuse me. Where is the post office?
不好意思，請問郵局在哪裡？

B: You go straight down the road for two blocks, and it will be on your right.
你往前直走兩個路口後，就在你右手邊。

A: Thank you.
謝謝你。

B: You're welcome.
不客氣。

相關用語 ─ pardon me 抱歉   進階補充 ─ I'm sorry 抱歉

078 I have to talk to him face to face.

我得當面和他談。

face to face為「面對面」之意。face可當動詞與名詞，當動詞時意為「面對」，當名詞時為「臉」。「面對」的相關片語有face with「面臨(困難)、面對(事實)」；face the music「面對困境」。

A: Can I see your manager, Mr. Cooper?
我可以見你們的經理，庫伯先生嗎？

B: I'm sorry; he's not in the office now. I'll have him call you back.
很抱歉，他目前不在辦公室。我會請他回電給您。

A: No. I have to talk to him face to face.
不用，我得和他當面談。

B: Then, I am afraid you might need to wait for a while.
那恐怕您得等一會兒了。

相關用語 ─ in person 親自   進階補充 ─ for a while 一段時間

079

It was so touching, especially when the music faded out. 那非常感人，尤其是當音樂漸弱時。

fade out的意思是指「電影、廣播或電視的聲音或影像漸漸變弱」。fade是不及物動詞，所以受詞不能放在fade跟out中間。反義片語：fade in「漸明、漸現」。

MP3
079

A: Did you **shed tears** at the end of the movie?
電影結束時，你有落淚嗎？

B: I did. It was so touching, especially when the music **faded out.**
我有。電影真的很感人，尤其是當音樂漸弱的時候。

A: I know. As the music faded out, the man drew his last breath.
我懂。音樂漸弱，那男人的也嚥下最後一口氣。

B: I just couldn't help but burst into tears.
我無法克制地哭得一塌糊塗。

相關用語 **little by little** 逐漸地　　進階補充 **shed tears** 流淚

080

Sorry I fell asleep during the movie.
抱歉，電影中我睡著了。

fall asleep為「睡著」之意。fall在這裡表「變為、成為某種狀態」的意思，如：fall sick「生病」。fall的動詞三態是：fall、fell、fallen。fall的相關片語有：fall back「退卻、落後」；fall down「失敗」；fall for「迷戀、上當」；fall in with「偶遇、贊同」。

MP3
080

A: Sorry I **fell asleep** during the movie.
抱歉，我看電影時睡著了。

B: That's alright. The movie was boring, and you were really tired.
沒關係。電影很無聊，而你也很累了。

A: I still am. Maybe we should **call it a day.**
我還是蠻累的。今天就到此為止吧。

B: Sure. See you tomorrow at the office!
好的。明天辦公室見！

相關用語 **sleepy** 想睡的　　進階補充 **call it a day** 結束一天

081

I was on sick leave last week and fell behind on my work. 我上週請病假，因此工作進度落後。

fall behind為「落後」之意。此片語若在後面接on，則指在某方面落後而言，為不及物動詞。behind和back都有「在後方」的意思，因此本片語的behind也可用back代替。相關片語：fall back on「跌在…之上、走投無路時求助於…」。

081

A: Are you going to work overtime again?
你又要加班了嗎？

B: I have to. I was on sick leave last week and **fell behind on my work.**
我必須加班。上週我請了病假，現在工作進度落後。

A: If you need help, just tell me.
如果你需要幫忙，就跟我說一聲。

B: I will. Thank you so much.
我會的。真的很謝謝你。

相關用語 **leave behind** 遺忘　　進階補充 **keep up with** 趕上

082

I fell down the stairs yesterday by accident.

我昨天不小心跌下樓梯。

fall down為「跌倒、病倒」之意。用法：S + fall down。由於fall down多用來直接修飾整個句子，所以後面可以不接受詞。相似片語：fall down on是「失敗」的意思，為口語用法。另一相近片語take down也是病倒的意思，但通常使用被動式。

082

A: What's wrong with your knee?
你的膝蓋怎麼了？

B: I **fell down** the stairs yesterday **by accident**.
我昨天不小心跌下樓梯。

A: You must be in so much pain.
你一定非常痛。

B: I am. I should have been more cautious.
是啊。我應該要更小心的。

相關用語 **trip** 跌倒　　進階補充 **by accident** 意外地

083

I **fell in love with** Emma.

我與愛瑪墜入愛河。

fall in love with是指「與某人墜入愛河」的意思，with接的是戀愛的對象。若不想提及對象，則可省略with。反義片語：fall out of love with「不再愛…」。另一相似片語have an affair with，同樣有指稱戀愛事件的意思，但經常帶有負面意義(如外遇)。

A: You look glorious today. Did anything good happen to you?
你氣色真好。發生了什麼好事嗎？

B: I fell in love with Emma, and she said she would go out with me.
我與愛瑪墜入愛河，她說她願意跟我約會。

A: Congratulations!
恭喜你！

B: Thank you. I am so happy.
謝謝你。我真開心。

相關用語 • **be in love** 戀愛中　進階補充 • **go out with** 與…約會

084

Can you explain why the production **fell off**?

你可否解釋產量為何減少？

fall of為「減少、掉落」之意。用法：S + fall off。作「減少」的意思解時，是指數量、程度及尺寸的減少；作「掉下」的意思解時，指物體從高處落下。fall off 為不及物動詞片語，一般而言不接受詞。

A: Can you explain why the production fell off?
你可否解釋為何產量減少了嗎？

B: We have to shut down the production line for a week due to machinery failure.
由於機台故障，我們必須停工一週。

A: When can you restart production?
何時能重新動工？

B: This Friday.
本週五。

相關用語 • **decrease** 減少　進階補充 • **shut down** 停工

085

Tokyo is so **far away** from here.

東京離這裡好遠。

far away為「遙遠地」之意，是副詞片語。若將far away連在一起，寫成faraway，則為「遠方的、恍惚的」之意，是形容詞，在使用上要特別注意。若在far away後加上from，則可接任何地點，表示對某處而言、從某處算起相當遙遠。

085

A: It's hard to say goodbye.
很難跟你說再見。

B: It's hard for me, too. But I have to pursue my dream.
我也是，但我必須追求夢想。

A: Tokyo is so **far away** from here.
東京離這裡好遠。

B: I know. But we can talk online everyday.
我知道。但我們每天都可上線聊天。

相關用語 **distantly** 遙遠地　　進階補充 **close to** 接近

086

The wording of the contract is **far from** satisfactory.

契約文字一點也不令人滿意。

far from為「一點也不」之意，是副詞片語，用來修飾後面的名詞或形容詞。由於from是介系詞，若後面要接動詞，就必須要改成動名詞。相似片語：never for a moment為「決不」的意思。

086

A: Are we going to sign the contract?
我們要簽約嗎？

B: I don't think so. The wording is **far from** satisfactory.
我認為不要。契約文字一點也不令人滿意。

A: So what should we do now?
所以我們該怎麼辦？

B: Make a call and schedule a renegotiation.
打電話安排重新協商。

相關用語 **not at all** 一點也不　　進階補充 **far from it** 絕非如此

087

I feel bad about not being able to make you happy.

無法讓你開心，我感到很抱歉。

feel bad為「心情不好、感到抱歉」之意，多用在口語上。反義片語：feel good「心情好」。相關片語：feel in bones「憑著直覺」、feel free to「隨意」、feel out「釐清」、feel with「同情」。

A: Are you alright?
你還好嗎？

B: Not really.
不好。

A: What's wrong?
怎麼了？

B: I feel bad about not being able to make you happy.
無法讓你開心，我感到很抱歉。

相關用語 ⟶ unhappy 不開心的　　進階補充 ⟶ feel sorry 感到抱歉

088

I feel like going to the movies.

我想去看電影。

feel like為「覺得、想要」之意。feel可當動詞和名詞，當名詞時為「觸感、氣氛」之意。一般在like之後所接的受詞為Ving或不定詞(to V)，也可接名詞，表示相似的對象。此片語當作「想要」的意思解時，其後一樣要接Ving、名詞或是子句。

A: What are you going to do this weekend?
你這週末要做什麼？

B: I feel like going to the movies. How about you?
我想去看電影。你呢？

A: I don't have any particular plans.
我沒有計劃。

B: Then, do you want to go with me?
那你要和我一起去嗎？

相關用語 ⟶ want 想要　　進階補充 ⟶ would like 想要

089

I think it's better for Cindy to find out the truth herself. 我想，讓辛蒂自己發現事實會比較好。

find out為「發現、揭露」之意，是指已找到或發覺；而look for「尋找」則為正要開始尋找。本片語若要接名詞，則名詞可置於find跟out之間。find的動詞三態為不規則變化：find、found、found。

MP3
089

A: Do you think we should tell her the truth?
你認為我們該告訴她實情嗎？

B: No. I think it's better for her to find out herself.
不。我想讓她自己發現會比較好。

A: It sounds so cruel.
聽起來真是殘忍。

B: We have no other option.
我們別無選擇。

相關用語 → discover 發現　　進階補充 → uncover 揭露

090

I wish I hadn't fooled around so much during my college years. 真希望我大學時期能夠少混一點。

fool around為「鬼混、虛度光陰」之意，是不及物動詞片語。around有「到處」的意思，若後面要加人，必須用with連接。此片語是美式用法，英式用法是fool about。這句片語較偏重「虛度時間的閒晃」，若是在路上漫無目的地遊走，則可用hang around。

MP3
090

A: I wish I hadn't fooled around so much during my college years.
真希望我大學時期能夠少混一點。

B: Why do you say that?
你為何這樣說？

A: If I had studied harder, I might have a decent job now.
如果我有認真唸書，現在一定有份好工作。

B: Maybe you were not that interested in your major.
或許你是對你的主修沒那麼有興趣。

相關用語 → mess around 閒混　　進階補充 → interested in 有志

091

I prefer outdoor activities; for example, rock-climbing. 我喜歡戶外活動，例如攀岩。

example的意思是「例子、榜樣」，是名詞，可衍生出許多意義相近的片語，如：give an example「舉個例子」；set an example「樹立榜樣」等。另外，書寫上常見的舉例方式包括e.g.、ex.、such as等，均可加以背誦活用。

MP.3
091

A: What kind of sports do you like?
你喜歡什麼運動？

B: I prefer outdoor activities; **for example**, rock-climbing.
我喜歡戶外活動，如攀岩。

A: Cool! I have always wanted to go rock-climbing.
酷！我一直想去攀岩。

B: Then why not come with me this weekend?
那這週末何不和我一起去？

相關用語 **for instance 例如** 進階補充 **take...for example 例如**

092

Is it for fun or for work?

是消遣，還是為了工作？

for fun是指「為了得到樂趣而去做某動作或事情」，非並認真地去執行，也可以寫成for in fun。fun是「娛樂、樂趣」的意思，形容詞為funny。相關片語：fun and games「嬉鬧」。

MP.3
092

A: I heard that you are learning Japanese. Is it **for fun** or for work?
聽說你在學日文。是消遣還是為了工作？

B: It's just **for pleasure**.
只是消遣。

A: Is Japanese difficult?
日文難嗎？

B: It was easy at first, but it became complicated and hard to understand as I progressed.
一開始很簡單，但進階後變得複雜又難懂。

相關用語 **for pleasure 為了消遣** 進階補充 **have fun 玩得開心**

093

I'll remember you **for good**.

我將永遠記得你。

for good = for good and all，為「永久、永遠」之意，後者所表達的語氣較強。相似片語：for good or evil「不論好壞」；for one's good = for the good of「為了…利益」；be good for「保持有效、會產生」。

093

A: The graduation ceremony is almost here.
畢業典禮快到了。

B: That's right. It's time for us to say goodbye to each other.
沒錯。該是我們向彼此道別的時候了。

A: I'll remember you **for good**.
我會永遠記得你。

B: Me, too.
我也是。

相關用語 **for ever** 永遠　　進階補充 **for ever and a day** 永遠

094

Amy and I never **get along** with each other.

愛咪和我向來處不好。

get along為「存活、相處」之意。當「存活」的意思解時，along可用by取代。若要用來表示「相處」，則必須加上with，再加上人，以表示跟某人相處。另外，get along with同時還有「在…方面進展」、「(雖有困難)仍繼續應付」的意思。

094

A: Amy and I never **get along with** each other.
愛咪和我向來處不好。

B: Why is that? She seems nice.
為何？她看起來人還不錯。

A: She stole my boyfriend.
她搶了我男友。

B: Now that makes sense.
現在我懂了。

相關用語 **survive** 倖存　　進階補充 **get along with** 和睦相處

095

Oh, my God! A crocodile **got away** from the zoo!

天啊！一隻鱷魚從動物園逃脫了！

get away為「逃脫、送走」之意。當作「逃走」之意解時，為不及物動詞片語；而在當作「送走」之意解時，是及物動詞片語。受詞若是代名詞，放在away之前；若是名詞，則放在away之前或之後皆可。

MP3
095

A: Oh, my God! A crocodile got away from the zoo!
天啊！一隻鱷魚從動物園逃脫了！

B: Really? When did it happen?
真的嗎？何時發生的？

A: Last night. We'd better watch out when walking on the street.
昨晚。我們走在街上時最好小心點。

B: Yes, we should.
我們真的應該如此。

相關用語 ▸ **run away** 逃跑　　進階補充 ▸ **watch out** 小心

096

When will you **get back** tonight?

你今晚何時回來？

get back在此是指「回來、收回」，back是副詞。若句義是指「從…回來」，則後面接from + 地方；若指「回到…」，則用to。此片語作「取回、收回」的意思解時，是及物動詞。受詞若是代名詞，要置於back之前；若為名詞，則置於back之後或之前皆可。

MP3
096

A: When will you get back tonight?
你今晚何時回來？

B: By seven as usual.
跟往常一樣，七點前。

A: Can you be home earlier? It's Amanda's birthday today.
你可以早點到家嗎？今天是亞曼達的生日。

B: Sure. No problem.
當然沒問題。

相關用語 ▸ **get back to** 回到…　　進階補充 ▸ **come back** 回來

097

He is getting a lot better now.

他現在好很多了。

get + 比較級形容詞,表示「漸漸進入某種狀態」的意思,better是更好,worse則是更糟。用來形容身體狀況時,worse可用weaker取代,表示越來越虛弱之意。get worse這個片語也可用動詞worsen取代。

A: Have you heard about Jack and the car accident?
你聽說傑克出車禍的事了嗎?

B: A car accident? Is he alright?
車禍?他還好嗎?

A: He is **getting** a lot **better** now.
他現在好很多了。

B: Can I go visit him?
我可以去探望他嗎?

相關用語 → recover 恢復健康   進階補充 → worsen 惡化

098

Excuse me, I think I got lost somehow.

不好意思,我想我似乎迷路了。

get lost為「迷路、迷失」之意,是不及物動詞片語,所以受詞不可加在get跟lost之間。lost是形容詞,意為「迷失的、迷途的」,動詞為lose。若用lose表示「迷路」時,可用lose one's way或lose oneself的句型。lose oneself + in/on/at + 地點;也可以用lose oneself + in + 事物,表「沉迷於…」。

A: Excuse me, I think I **got lost** somehow. Where is the SOGO Department Store?
不好意思,我想我似乎迷路了。SOGO百貨在哪裡?

B: Don't worry, you're almost there. It's just two blocks away.
別擔心,你快到了。就在兩條街外。

A: Thank you very much.
非常感謝你。

B: You're welcome.
不客氣。

相關用語 → get astray 迷路   進階補充 → be lost 迷路

099

It's almost time for school. Go and **get** your sister **up**.

上學時間快到了。去叫姐姐起床。

get up是指「從坐臥的狀態站起來的動作」，通常作「起身、坐起、起立」的意思解。「起床」另可用get out of bed來表示，字義更為鮮明。相似片語：get oneself up「穿著特別種類的衣服」。

MP3
099

A: Where is your sister?
姐姐在哪裡？

B: She is still **in bed**.
她還在睡。

A: It's almost time for school. Go and **get** her **up**.
差不多該上學了，快去叫她起床。

B: I don't want to. She always kicks me.
我不想去。她總是踢我。

相關用語 **wake up 起床**　　進階補充 **in bed 臥床**

100

Can we **go ahead** with our party plans?

我們可以繼續進行派對的規劃嗎？

go ahead為「先走、繼續」之意。用法：go ahead + with + 受詞 = continue「繼續」。此片語常用於祈使句，表示「開始吧！」或「請用！」。ahead為副詞，有「在前、向前」的意思，相關片語：ahead of「在⋯之前」；ahead of time「提早」；ahead of schedule「比(計畫中)還早」。

MP3
100

A: Can we **go ahead** with our party plans?
我們可以繼續進行派對的規劃嗎？

B: It depends upon whether Jessica, the birthday girl, will be **in town** or not.
要看壽星潔西卡是否在鎮上。

A: What do you mean?
你是什麼意思？

B: She told me she might need to go somewhere on business on her birthday.
她跟我說，她生日可能會出差。

相關用語 **go full steam ahead 全力以赴**　　進階補充 **go on 繼續**

101 I have to **go away** for a week.

我必須離開一星期。

go away為「離開、停止」之意。go是指「離開現在自己所在之處」的意思，away為副詞，有「遠離」之意。片語後接from可表示離開何事何物、從何處離開。相似片語：go away with，是「帶走、拐走」的意思。

A: I have to **go away** for a week.
我必須離開一星期。

B: For what?
為什麼？

A: My boss is sending me to Singapore for the coming exhibition.
我老闆派我去新加坡參加接下來的展覽。

B: Got it. Be careful during the trip.
了解。旅途中要小心點。

相關用語 ○ **leave** 離開   進階補充 ○ **depart from** 從…離開

102 As time **goes by**, the kids grow more and more into adults. 隨時光流逝，孩子們逐漸長大成人。

go by為「時間流逝、依據」之意。當「時間流逝」的意思解時，等同於pass by，在這裡的by是副詞；若當「依據」的意思解時，此處的by為介系詞。相關片語：go by the board「遭到丟棄或忽視」。

A: As time **goes by**, the kids **grow** more and more **into** adults.
隨時光流逝，孩子們逐漸長大成人了。

B: Yes, they do, and I am so proud of them.
沒錯，他們是長大了。我非常以他們為榮。

A: I can still remember them crawling on the floor.
我還記得他們在地上爬行的樣子。

B: They were so adorable then.
他們那時真可愛。

相關用語 ○ **pass** 流逝   進階補充 ○ **grow into** 成長為…

103 I think we'd better stop and see how things **go on**.

我想我們最好停下來看事情如何進展。

go on 為「繼續、發展」之意。用法：S + go on + Ving。此片語若當「發展」的意思解時，通常是指不好的情況。此片語多在後面加Ving當受詞；然而若受詞是名詞時，則需要以with連接。在口語中，本片語也適合用來釐清現場情況：What's going on？「發生了什麼事？」

MP3
103

A: I think we'd better stop and see how things **go on**.
　　我想我們最好停下來看事情如何發展。

B: Are you sure?
　　你確定嗎？

A: I believe this is the only and best way to get things done.
　　我相信這是唯一且最佳的處理方式。

B: OK. But I hope we won't lose the contract **in the end**.
　　好吧，但希望我們最終不會搞丟合約。

相關用語 → proceed to 繼續下去　進階補充 → in the end 最終

104 I am **going out** with Daniel tonight.

今晚我要和丹尼爾約會。

go out為多義片語，有「參加派對、公諸於世、廣播、退潮、約會、外出、熄滅」等意思。要表達為了什麼事出門，則可在go out後加上for，例如go out for dinner「外出吃晚餐」。

MP3
104

A: Do you want to go to the movies tonight?
　　你今晚想去看電影嗎？

B: No, I think I will **take a rain check**.
　　不，我想改天好了。

A: What are you going to do tonight?
　　你今晚要做什麼？

B: I am **going out** with Daniel. He is taking me to go ice skating.
　　我要和丹尼爾約會，他要帶我去溜冰。

相關用語 → date 和…約會　進階補充 → take a rain check 改期

105 Time to **go to bed**.

該就寢了。

go to bed是所有具「就寢」之意的詞語中，最普遍的用詞。值得一提的是，在英文中要表示跟誰一同就寢，應說成「go to bed with + 人」，不可說成「sleep with + 人」，因為「sleep with + 人」在英文裡的意思是表示「跟誰發生性關係」，請釐清當中的區別，以避免造成誤會。

MP.3
105

A: Time to go to bed.
該就寢了。

B: Come on. Can I wait until the show ends?
拜託可以讓我等到節目結束嗎？

A: I don't think so, Sweetie. I promised your mom that I would put you to bed by 10.
親愛的，我想不行。我答應你媽媽會準時讓你上床睡覺。

B: But she will never know!
但是她不會知道的！

相關用語 → **turn in** 就寢   進階補充 → **put to bed** 安排就寢

106 The vines are **growing over** our window.

藤蔓爬滿了我們的窗。

grow over 為「長滿」之意。此片語通常使用被動式，用法：S + be V + grown over + 受詞。grown是grow的過去分詞型。相關片語：grow out of sth.「從…發展而成」；grow by leaps and bounds「急速生長」；grow away from sb.「與某人變得疏離」。

MP.3
106

A: The vines are growing over our window. Can you do something about it?
藤蔓爬滿了我們的窗。你可以處理一下嗎？

B: What do you want me to do? Cut them off?
你想要我怎麼做？砍掉它們嗎？

A: That would be great!
那就太好了！

B: But I kind of like the shade it gives.
但我還蠻喜歡它的樹蔭。

相關用語 → **overgrow** 長滿於…   進階補充 → **thrive** 繁茂生長

107

You had better get yourself a cup of coffee.

你最好找杯咖啡喝。

had better為「最好…」之意。此片語中的had不能改成have或has，因為這是慣用法，任何時態、人稱都必須使用had。若此片語後面接不定詞(to + V)，則to可以省略。另外，had better是一個不可分離的片語，而且後面必須接原形動詞，所以否定型為had better not + V。

A: You had better get yourself a cup of coffee.
你最好找杯咖啡喝。

B: What do you mean?
你是什麼意思？

A: It seems like we are going to have to work overtime.
看來我們得加班了。

B: Oh, not again!
喔，別又來了！

相關用語 ► suggest 建議　　進階補充 ► recommend 勸告

108

You should hand in your reports by next Monday.

你們應於下週一前繳交報告。

hand in為「繳交、呈遞」之意，是及物動詞片語。當代名詞為受詞時，應置於in之前；若受詞為名詞則位置前後不拘。此片語多指「繳交作業、報告或其他文件」而言。in也可代換成over，意義相同。相關片語：hand in glove「合作」；hand in hand「攜手」。

A: Ma'am, when is the report on Double Ten Day due?
老師，雙十節的報告什麼時候要交？

B: You should all hand in your reports by next Monday morning.
你們都應該在下週一早上前繳交報告。

A: But today is already Friday!
但是今天已經是星期五了！

B: That means you'll have the whole weekend to get it done.
那代表你們有一整個週末可以做報告。

相關用語 ► submit to 遞交　　進階補充 ► in hand 在手頭的

109 Did you just **hang up** on Mom?

你剛把媽的電話掛斷嗎？

hang up是電話用語，指「掛斷電話、終止交談」的意思。其他實用的電話用語還有：hold on「不要掛斷」；put through「轉接」；engaged「電話中、忙線中」。

A: Did you just hang up on Mom?
你剛是掛斷媽的電話嗎？

B: I did. I really couldn't stand her nagging anymore.
是啊，我真的再也受不了她嘮叨了。

A: But it was extremely rude.
但這很沒禮貌。

B: I know. I really regret it. I will call back and apologize.
我知道，我非常懊悔。我會回電跟她道歉。

相關用語 • hang up on 掛…電話   進階補充 • call back 回電

110 I have to go now. **Have a good time**!

我該走了，祝玩得開心！

have a good time為「玩得開心」之意。此片語中的good是形容詞，可以換成fine、nice、pleasant和wonderful等，通常用作他人出遊前的祝福語，也可用have fun。反義片語：have a bad time「不愉快的時光」。

A: Isn't it nice to be here?
在這裡是不是很棒？

B: Yes, it is. What are you doing here?
是啊。你來這裡做什麼？

A: I am with my daughter. She loves the merry-go-round here.
我和我女兒一起來，她喜歡這裡的旋轉木馬。

B: That's great. Well, I have to go now. Have a good time!
真棒。嗯，我現在要走了，祝玩得開心！

相關用語 • enjoy 享受   進階補充 • have fun 玩得開心

111 I have a habit of going hiking every Saturday morning. 我有每週六早上健行的習慣。

have a habit of 為「有做…的習慣」之意。用法：S + have/has a habit of + Ving。此片語也可以寫成in the habit of，用法：S + be V + in the habit of + Ving。「習慣於做什麼」也可用S + be used to + Ving來表示。而S + used to + V則表示「過去習慣於(而現在不再)…」，別搞混囉！

MP3
111

A: What do you usually do on weekends?
你週末通常都做些什麼？

B: I have a habit of going hiking every Saturday morning.
我習慣每週六早上健行。

A: Cool! Where do you usually go?
酷！你通常都去哪裡？

B: Yangmingshan. The cherry blossoms are in full bloom now.
陽明山。現在櫻花盛開。

相關用語 → in full bloom 盛開　　進階補充 → go hiking 健行

112 Thank you. I just have a headache.

謝謝你，我只是頭痛。

一般身體上的疼痛在英文裡都用ache表示，在器官的後面加上「-ache」就表示該器官發生疼痛的症狀，例如toothache「牙痛」。pain也表示疼痛，但差別在ache是指持續的、一般疼痛；pain包括從身體某一部分突然的疼痛，到全身長時間劇烈的痛苦，也指內心的痛苦與悲傷。

MP3
112

A: You look pale. Do you want to take a rest?
你看起來很蒼白，想休息一下嗎？

B: Thank you. I just have a headache.
謝謝你。我只是頭痛。

A: Let me get you some aspirin.
讓我拿些阿斯匹靈給你。

B: Thank you. That's very nice of you.
謝謝你。你人真好。

相關用語 → stomachache 肚子痛　　進階補充 → take a rest 休息

113

You have to get home by 9.

你必須在九點前回到家。

have to 為「必須、一定」之意，後面一定要加原形動詞。同義詞有 must、should等，但值得注意的是，must/should後面不能加to，因為它們是助動詞，後面只能加動詞原形，不能加不定詞to。

A: Son, you **have to** get home by 9.
兒子，你必須在九點前回到家。

B: Please don't say that. The party starts at 8, which means I only have an hour.
拜託別這樣。派對八點開始，代表我就只有一小時的時間。

A: But you have to come home early. Your dad will be **furious with** you for going out before exams.
但你必須早點回家。你爸爸會很氣你考前跑出去。

B: OK.
好吧。

相關用語 ◦ **need to** 需要　　進階補充 ◦ **furious with** 狂怒的

114

I often have trouble in exporting files.

我經常在輸出檔案時出問題。

have trouble in為「有困難、有麻煩」之意。用法：S + have trouble in + (代)名詞／Ving。trouble可當名詞，也可當動詞。當名詞時，意思有「苦惱、不幸、痛苦、帶來煩惱的人、麻煩、不方便、紛爭、紛擾」等；當動詞時，意思是「使煩惱、麻煩、費力」。

A: Larry, would you please help me out here?
賴瑞，你可以來幫我個忙嗎？

B: Sure. What's wrong?
當然好。怎麼了？

A: I often **have trouble in** exporting files. Do you know how to do it?
我經常在匯出檔案時出問題。你知道該怎麼做嗎？

B: No problem. Let me show you.
沒問題。我做給你看。

相關用語 ◦ **troubled** 為難的　　進階補充 ◦ **in trouble** 處困難中

115

I haven't heard from Wendy since we graduated.

自從我們畢業後，就沒收到溫蒂的消息了。

hear from是指「收到或得到對方的消息、來信、電報」等，可以與自己產生聯繫的訊息。用法：S + hear from + (代)名詞。此片語後面通常接人，也可以接地方。hear的動詞三態：hear、heard、heard。

115

A: I haven't **heard from** Wendy since we graduated.
自從畢業後，我就沒有溫蒂的消息了。

B: Really? I remember you were very close back then.
真的嗎？我記得你們那時候感情很好。

A: We were, but I guess she's very busy with her graduate school work now.
曾經是的，但我想她現在忙於研究所課業。

B: Maybe you should call her first.
也許你該先打電話給她。

相關用語 **hear about** 得知　進階補充 **hear out** 聽完

116

I've never heard of such a thing!

我從未聽過這種事！

hear of是指「聽說過」的意思，即從別人那裡輾轉得知某人或某事，不必一定要用耳朵聽到，從其他管道或透過其他形式得知也可以。用法：S + hear of + (代)名詞。此片語也可當「答應、接納」的意思。相似片語：hear about「得知」。

116

A: I've never **heard of** such a thing!
我從未聽過這種事！

B: What is it? You seem to be very surprised.
什麼事？你好像很驚訝。

A: A news report said a monkey in the zoo fell in love with a tortoise.
新聞說動物園裡的一隻猴子愛上海龜。

B: No way! It must be a joke.
不可能！這一定是個笑話。

相關用語 **know about** 知道　進階補充 **familiar with** 熟悉的

117

OK. Please hold on.

好的，請稍候。

hold on有「稍候、繼續、抓牢」之意。此片語中的hold是不及物動詞，on是副詞，表示「繼續」，所以在受詞(即被抓牢的某物)前需加介系詞to，即hold on to + 受詞。hold on作「稍候」的意思解時，多屬電話用語，即請別人「稍待一下、不要掛斷」的意思。

A: May I speak to Mr. Lin?
可以請林先生聽電話嗎？

B: Who is this, please?
請問是哪位？

A: It's Mr. Chao from Bank of Taiwan.
台灣銀行，敝姓趙。

B: OK. Please hold on.
好的，請稍候。

相關用語 ◦ **hold the line** 稍等   進階補充 ◦ **hold on to** 緊握

118

Do you know how come onions always make you cry? 你知道為何洋蔥總讓你流淚嗎？

how come是一則非常常用的美式口語片語，它的意思是指Why is it that～?「為什麼是…？」用法：How come + S + V + 受詞，記住它和wh-問句的倒裝順序不同。

A: Do you know how come onions always make you cry?
你知道為何洋蔥總是讓你流淚嗎？

B: No. Why is that?
不知道。為什麼？

A: A study says broken onion cells release acid, which turns into gas that makes you tear.
一則研究指出，遭破壞的洋蔥細胞會釋放出可轉變成催淚氣體的酸性物質。

B: Wow. Interesting.
哇，真有趣。

相關用語 ◦ **on earth** 究竟   進階補充 ◦ **in the world** 到底

119 There will be **hundreds of** people there.

那裡一定會有很多人。

hundreds of為「數以百計、許多」之意。hundred前面若有數詞(one、two…)或表數目的形容詞時，複數不加s，如：one hundred、two hundred；通常在百位跟十位或個位之間要加and，例如：two hundred and five(兩百零五)，但在美式口語中，有時會省略and。

A: Where do you want to go today?
你今天想去哪裡？

B: Can we go to Sogo?
我們可以去太平洋百貨嗎？

A: It's the first day of their anniversary sale. There will be **hundreds of** people there.
今天是週年慶的第一天，那裡一定會有很多人。

B: But there are great sales as well.
但也會有大量的折扣。

相關用語 **few** 很少的　　進階補充 **millions of** 數以百萬計

120 **Hurry up**, or you are going to be late for school.

加快腳步，否則你上學會遲到。

hurry up主要用在祈使句中，用來催趕別人「快一點」的意思。由hurry所組成的片語有：in a hurry「急忙地」；in no hurry「從容不迫地」；hurry along「催促」；hurry on「趕往」；hurry over「匆忙地做…」；hurry through「匆忙趕完」。

A: Hurry up, or you are going to be late for school.
快點，否則你上學會遲到。

B: Relax. There is still plenty of time.
放輕鬆，還有很多時間。

A: Plenty? It's already five minutes after eight!
很多？已經八點五分了！

B: Oh, no! My alarm didn't **go off** again!
噢，不！我的鬧鐘又沒響了！

相關用語 **hasten** 趕緊　　進階補充 **go off** 響起

121 In a moment, Sir.

先生，馬上來。

in a moment是修飾時間的副詞片語，表示「立即、馬上、立刻」。同義詞包括：instantly、promptly、at once、in a minute、in no time、off hand、right now、on/upon the spot、on the instant、on the nail、in a flash、at/on sight。

MP3 121

A: Can you come into my office?
你可以進來我辦公室嗎？

B: In a moment, Sir.
先生，馬上來。

A: Great. Take your time.
很好。你慢慢來。

B: Thank you.
謝謝您。

> 相關用語 → right away 馬上   進階補充 → take your time 慢慢來

122 There were customers in and out all the time.

一直有顧客來來去去。

in and out是由介系詞組合而成的副詞片語，in是「進入、在內」，out是「離開、在外」，組成「不斷反覆進出」的含義。除了上述的意思外，還有「忽隱忽現地、無論內外、完全地」等意思。

MP3 122

A: Did you see anyone who looked suspicious in the store?
你有在店裡看到任何可疑的人嗎？

B: No, there were customers in and out all the time. Wait! There was a man!
沒有，店裡一直有顧客來來去去。等一下！是有個男人！

A: Tell me more about him.
跟我多說點他。

B: He had a huge beard and tried to get past the counter.
他留著大鬍子，試圖要通過櫃台。

> 相關用語 → ins and outs 詳細情形   進階補充 → get past 通過

123 **In fact**, we broke up.

其實我們分手了。

in fact為「事實上、其實」之意，fact有「事實、真相」的意思。由fact所衍生的詞彙和片語有：fact-finding「實情調查的」；fact of life「生活中的嚴酷現實」；get down to the facts「回到正題」；It's easy to be smart after the fact.「事後諸葛容易當」。

A: I haven't seen you with Andy for a while. Is he all right?
我好久沒看到安迪跟你一起出現了。他還好嗎？

B: In fact, we broke up.
其實我們分手了。

A: What? Why?
什麼？為什麼？

B: He cheated on me.
他對我不忠。

相關用語 → **actually** 事實上 進階補充 → **as a matter of fact** 事實上

124 There is a big apple tree **in front of** my house.

我家前面有棵大蘋果樹。

in front of為「在…前面」之意，表示物體與物體間空間上的前後關係，例如He sat in front of me.「他坐在我前面。」另外，in the front of的意思是「在…的前方」，表示物體內部的前後關係，例如The teacher is in the front of the classroom.「老師站在教室的前面」。

A: Just come to my place before five. This is my address.
在五點以前到我家來。這是我的地址。

B: OK.
好的。

A: And there is a big apple tree in front of my house. It should be easy.
我家前面有棵大蘋果樹，應該很好找。

B: That's great. See you then.
太好了，到時見。

相關用語 → **in back of** 在…後面 進階補充 → **in front** 於前面

125 How can I turn my back on a friend **in need**?

我怎能背棄危難中的朋友？

in need為「在危急中、在危難中」之意。need可當動詞和名詞，表示「需要」的意思。相似片語：in need of「需要…」。有句知名的成語就引用了這句片語：A friend in need is a friend indeed.「患難見真情」。need的形容詞為needy，意為「貧窮的」。

A: Ken asked me to lend him some money today.
肯今天要我借他些錢。

B: Again? Please tell me that you refused it.
又借？請告訴我你拒絕他了。

A: How can I **turn my back on** a friend **in need**?
我怎能背棄危難中的朋友？

B: Our family should be more important to you.
我們的家庭對你而言應該更重要才是。

相關用語 ○ **needless** 不需要的　　進階補充 ○ **turn back on** 轉身不理

126 **In other words**, your loan request will not be approved. 換言之，您的貸款申請將不被核准。

in other words為「換言之、換句話說」之意。與本片語組合形式相似的片語有：in a/one word「總而言之」；in so many words「一字不差地」；in these words「以下列措辭」；in words of one syllable「用非常簡單的話語解釋」。

A: I am afraid we're having a bit of trouble agreeing to your request for an increase in your credit line.
對於您欲增加信用額度的要求，我們有同意上的困難。

B: What do you mean?
你的意思是？

A: **In other words**, your loan request will not be approved at this time.
也就是說，您的貸款申請這次將不被核准。

B: That's too bad.
真糟糕。

相關用語 ○ **that is to say** 換言之　　進階補充 ○ **that is** 那就是

127

I believe everything will turn out fine **in the end**.

我相信最後不會有事的。

in the end為「最終、終於」之意。反義片語：in the beginning「最初」。
end和close都有「結束」的意思，其差別為：end是指「完結或終止」的
意思，是最普遍、意義涵蓋最廣的「完結」用字；close是指「已經開始的
事物暫時或永遠地中止」。

127

A: Today is really not my day.
　　我今天真的很倒霉。

B: What do you mean?
　　你的意思是？

**A: I overslept and then was caught by Ms. Chen, who said
　　she would report me to the principal.**
　　我睡過頭，被陳老師抓到，她說會報告校長。

**B: I'm sorry, but I believe everything will turn out fine in
　　the end.**
　　我很遺憾，但我相信最後不會有事的。

相關用語 **turn out** 結果是 ┃ 進階補充 **not one's day** 不順的一天

128

What are you going to do **in the future**?

你將來想做什麼？

in the future = for the future，為「未來、在將來」之意。由於本片語是表
時間關係的副詞片語，因此可被放在句首或句尾，用來修飾整句話的時間
關係。若在future前加上near，則表示「在不久的將來」。

128

A: What are you going to do in the future?
　　你將來想做什麼？

B: I want to be a nurse.
　　我想當護士。

A: Is that because nurses are always loving and caring?
　　是因為護士都很有愛心又關懷他人嗎？

**B: No, it's because they can ask people to do things they
　　don't want to do.**
　　不，是因為他們可以叫別人做不想做的事。

相關用語 **foreseeable** 可預見的 ┃ 進階補充 **in future** 從今以後

129

I'm back to Japan in the middle of June.

我將於六月中旬回日本。

in the middle of為「在…中旬、在…中央」之意，可修飾時間也可修飾地點，屬副詞片語，所以可置於句首或句尾。「在…之初」用at the beginning of；「在…的終了」用at the end of。相關片語：middle ground「妥協狀態」；be caught in the middle「夾在兩方之間」。

A: When is your flight back to Japan?
你回日本的班機是什麼時候？

B: In the middle of June.
六月中旬。

A: Isn't that just two weeks from now? I will miss you so much.
那不就是兩週後？我會很想你的。

B: You are welcome to come for a visit.
很歡迎你來看我。

相關用語 ─○ early in June 六月上旬   進階補充 ─○ late in June 六月下旬

130

They are going to join hands to work on the new research project. 他們將攜手進行新的研究計劃。

join hands為「聯手、握手」之意。此片語當「握手」解釋時，要加上介系詞with，表示跟某人握手。這裡的hand要加s，因為握手不會只有單獨一隻手，一定同時要有兩隻手才能產生「握」的動作。

A: Dr. Watson and Dr. Lee are going to join hands to work on the new research project.
華生博士和李博士將攜手進行新的研究計劃。

B: That will be the greatest project ever!
那將會是最棒的計劃！

A: And they are recruiting new assistants.
而且他們正在招募新助理。

B: How do I apply for it?
我該如何申請？

相關用語 ─○ join forces 協力   進階補充 ─○ team up with 與…合作

131 Jerry is always **joking around**.

傑瑞總是愛開玩笑。

joke around為「開玩笑」之意，與play a trick on和play a joke on在意義上大致相同。差別在於，joke around後面可直接加句點，而後兩者都是接被捉弄或被開玩笑的對象(必須是人)。play a trick on是指以行動來尋人開心；play a joke on則指用言語來開人玩笑。

A: I heard Jerry tried to ask you out.
我聽說傑瑞想約你出去。

B: No, he didn't. He is always **joking around**. This must be another one of his jokes.
我不這樣認為。他總是愛開玩笑，這一定又是他開的另一個玩笑。

A: I think he really likes you, though. I saw him **staring at** you for a long time the other day.
但我想他是真的喜歡你。我前幾天看他盯著你看了好久。

B: I hope he forgets about me. I could never fall for him.
我希望他放棄。我不會喜歡上他的。

相關用語 ► **make a joke** 開玩笑　　進階補充 ► **stare at** 凝視

132 I came back from Mr. Watson's company **just now**.

我剛從華生先生的公司回來。

just now為「剛才、現在」之意。在當「剛才」的意思解時，應與狀態動詞的過去式一起使用，如例句所示。當「現在」的意思解時，則可與現在式或未來式一起使用。

A: Where have you been?
你去哪裡了？

B: I came back from Mr. Watson's company **just now**. What is it?
我剛從華生先生的公司回來。怎麼了？

A: Mr. Chen wants to see you immediately.
陳先生想要立刻見你。

B: Uh, oh; that can't be good for me.
噢⋯，那對我來說不是好事。

相關用語 ► **a moment ago** 剛才　　進階補充 ► **at the moment** 此刻

133 You look **just the same**!

你們看起來一模一樣！

just the same為「相同」之意，可當形容詞片語也可當副詞片語。just這個字在當形容詞時，意思是「正直的、正當的」；當副詞時，則有「正巧、剛才、僅、完全、非常」等意思。

133

A: Is that your twin sister?
那是你的雙胞胎姐姐嗎？

B: Yes, she is.
沒錯。

A: You look **just the same**!
你們長得一模一樣！

B: Actually not. My parents always say we are quite different.
事實上沒有。我父母總說我們很不一樣。

〔相關用語〕◦ the same 相同的　　〔進階補充〕◦ the same as 與…一樣

134 Are you in the habit of **keeping a diary**?

你有寫日記的習慣嗎？

在「寫日記」這個片語裡，動詞一定要用keep，不能用write，因為「書寫」的英文雖然是write，但keep a diary是一種慣用法，加上keep本身有「保持某一種狀態」或「持續某事」的意思。寫日記是一種持續性的習慣，不可能今天寫，明天又不寫了，如果是這樣就不叫「日記」了，所以在使用上要記住這個觀念及用法。

134

A: Are you in the habit of **keeping a diary**?
你有寫日記的習慣嗎？

B: No, that's too much trouble for me. How about you?
沒有，那對我來說太麻煩了。你呢？

A: Yes, I keep one. I find it a good way to **engage in** self-reflection.
嗯，我有寫。我覺得這是個反省自己的好方法。

B: You are right. Maybe I should **give it a shot**.
你說得對。也許我該試試。

〔相關用語〕◦ engage in 從事　　〔進階補充〕◦ give sth. a shot 試試看

135 An apple a day **keeps** the doctor **away**.

一天一蘋果，醫生遠離我。

keep away是及物動詞片語，所以受詞可加在keep跟away之間，或是使用keep away from + 受詞。「與⋯保持距離」或「避免」的用法還有：prevent...from...、stop...from...、prohibit...from...。

A: Here you are.
　　拿去吧。

B: Apples again? Can I have something else?
　　又是蘋果？我可以吃點別的嗎？

A: Apples are good for your health. An apple a day **keeps the doctor away**.
　　蘋果對你的健康很有幫助。一天一蘋果，醫生遠離你。

B: But I have eaten apples straight for more than a week already!
　　但是我已經連續吃超過一星期的蘋果了！

相關用語 **distant from** 遠離　　進階補充 **removed from** 遠離的

136 Never give up. Just **keep on** trying.

別放棄，請繼續加油。

當keep on作「繼續做⋯」的意思解時，在on的後面要加Ving，以表示某種斷續性動作之重複。另外，keep on跟continue的用法略有不同，continue的後面可接Ving、名詞或不定詞；而keep on後面若要接名詞或代名詞，則須在on的後面先加上with。

A: Sweetheart, never give up. Just **keep on** trying.
　　親愛的，別放棄，請繼續加油。

B: There is no point in trying so hard. I can't win anyway.
　　再怎麼努力也沒用。反正我不會贏。

A: But you will get better and better! Maybe you can win next time.
　　但是你會越來越棒！也許下次你就會贏了。

B: Thank you, Dad.
　　爸，謝謝你。

相關用語 **hold on** 繼續　　進階補充 **carry on** 繼續

137

The case was dismissed because of lack of evidence.

該起案件因證據不足而遭撤銷。

lack of為「缺少、不足」之意。這句片語的lack當名詞用，所以後面必須加上of，再加上名詞或Ving作為受詞。若lack當動詞用，則不需要加of，直接加名詞即可；也可以當不及物動詞使用，用法為lack for sth。

A: Have you heard that Kevin has been accused of fraud?
你有聽說凱文被控詐欺嗎？

B: Yes, but that was two months ago.
有的，但那是兩個月前的事了。

A: What was the outcome?
結果如何？

B: The case was dismissed because of lack of evidence.
案子由於證據不足而撤銷了。

相關用語 ○ short of 缺乏　　進階補充 ○ accused of 被控…

138

Everyone laughs at my lunchbox.

每個人都嘲笑我的便當盒。

laugh at為「嘲笑、一笑置之」之意，後面接的受詞若為事物，則表示笑或譏笑的對象是某事物；若後面接的受詞是人，則表示嘲笑的對象是人。相關片語：laugh away「用笑掩飾、一笑置之」；laugh down「用笑聲打斷」、laugh sth/sb. out of court「一笑置之、用笑打發」。

A: You forgot your lunchbox, Sweetheart.
你忘記午餐盒了，親愛的。

B: I don't want to take it. Everyone laughs at it.
我不想帶。每個人都取笑它。

A: Why? It's cute to me.
為什麼？我覺得很可愛啊。

B: But not to a boy like me! It's a pink Hello Kitty lunchbox!
但對我一個男孩來說不可愛！這是個粉紅色的凱蒂貓午餐盒！

相關用語 ○ make fun of 取笑　　進階補充 ○ teaser 戲弄他人者

139

Lay down whatever you are doing and get into my office now! 放下你手邊的工作，馬上來我辦公室！

lay down為「放下、鋪設」之意，是及物動詞片語，所以在lay跟down之間可以加受詞。lay的動詞三態是：lay、laid、laid。相關片語：lay back「放回原處」；lay off「解雇」；lay stress on「著重」。

A: Lay down whatever you are doing and get into my office now!
放下你手邊的工作，馬上來我辦公室！

B: But it's Mr. Lin's urgent contract.
但這是林先生的緊急合約。

A: Nothing is more important than the thing I am going to tell you!
沒有事情比我即將要告訴你的事更重要！

B: OK. Here I am.
好。我馬上來。

相關用語 ── **put down** 放下　進階補充 ── **lay down the law** 發號施令

140

I tried to make her feel better yesterday by **lending an ear to** her. 昨天我聽她說話，試著讓她好過些。

lend an/one's ear to為「注意聽、諦聽」之意。lend是「借」的意思，借一隻耳朵給別人，那就表示別人希望你能注意聽他說話，用這種方式思考比較容易記住這則片語。

A: Sally is feeling really depressed right now.
莎莉現在非常沮喪。

B: I know. I tried to make her feel better yesterday by **lending an ear to** her.
我知道。昨天我聽她說話，試著讓她好過一些。

A: Did she tell you what is bothering her?
她有說她在煩惱什麼嗎？

B: It sounds like she's really unhappy in her job and marriage.
她似乎對於工作以及婚姻感到非常不滿意。

相關用語 ── **listen to** 注意聽　進階補充 ── **listen attentively** 傾聽

141

Let her be. She gets angry with everyone about everything. 別管她。她對任何事、任何人發火。

let...be為「不要管」之意。用法：let + 受格 + be。let是使役動詞，和make、have一樣有「讓、使」的意思，所以後面必須接原形動詞be。

A: What's wrong with Peggy?
佩姬怎麼了？

B: **Let her be. She gets angry with everyone about everything.**
別管她。她對任何事、任何人發火。

A: How can you say that? It's really mean.
你怎麼這樣說？這樣說真的很壞。

B: Is it? She **yelled at** me yesterday because I took her spot on the sofa.
有嗎？她昨天因為我佔了她沙發的位置而對我大吼。

相關用語 • **regardless of** 不管   進階補充 • **let alone** 聽任

142

Listen to your heart. It will tell you the best way to go. 傾聽你的心；它會告訴你怎麼做最好。

listen to為「傾聽、聽從」之意。這則片語當「聽人說話或聽音樂」的意思解時，後面一定要加to，不可以直接用listen + 人或listen + 音樂。listen和hear都有「聽」的意思，但兩者之間有很重要的差別：listen是嘗試、有意圖地去聽，hear通常是無心、無意中聽到。

A: What's wrong with you? You look upset.
你怎麼了？你看起來很沮喪。

B: I am having the biggest dilemma ever. I don't know what to do.
我正面臨史上最大的困境，不知該如何是好。

A: **Listen to** your heart. It will tell you the best way to go.
傾聽你的心；它會告訴你怎麼做最好。

B: OK. Then I will just buy these two dresses and not try to decide which one to buy.
好的。那我就兩件洋裝都買，不去決定該買哪一件。

相關用語 • **apply one's ears to** 傾聽   進階補充 • **hear of** 聽說

143

The research project is progressing little by little.

研究計畫正逐步進展。

little by little為「逐漸地、一點一點地」之意。此片語中的by在這裡有「累積」的意思。little是「少」，所以有「一點一點」的意思；若用degree或stage取代，則有「一個階段、一個進程慢慢發展」的意味。

A: How is your research going?
你的研究進展得如何？

B: Thanks to Dr. Huang's help, the research project is progressing **little by little**.
多虧黃博士的幫忙，研究計畫正逐步進展中。

A: Dr. Huang is not only knowledgeable but also very helpful.
黃博士既博學多聞又熱心助人。

B: He is the best instructor I've ever had.
他是我遇過最棒的指導老師。

相關用語 ▸ **bit by bit** 漸漸地　　進階補充 ▸ **thanks to** 幸虧、由於

144

They live and prosper on dead skin from humans and hair. 他們以人類的皮屑及毛髮為主食生存繁衍。

live on為「以…為主食；靠…過活」之意。這則片語在當「以…為主食」的意思解時，on是介系詞。當「繼續生活」時，on是副詞。

A: Do you know there might be more than millions of dust mites in our bed?
你知道我們床上可能有超過數百萬隻塵蟎嗎？

B: What? Yuk!
什麼？真噁！

A: And they **live** and prosper **on** dead skin from humans and hair.
而且他們以人類的皮屑和毛髮為主食生存繁衍。

B: I really should **stop** you **from** watching the Discovery Channel.
我真的不該再讓你看探索頻道了。

相關用語 ▸ **feed on** 以…為食物　　進階補充 ▸ **stop from** 阻止

145

I can never live up to Dad's expectations.

我不可能達成父親的期望。

live up to為「達到、實踐、按照」之意。用法：S + live up to + 受詞。live up to特指「遵守諾言或原則、達成期望或理想」。live在這裡等於maintain「維持」的意思，而不作「生活」解。up to的意思是「達到、高達」，另有「忙於某種活動」之意。

MP3
145

A: I can never live up to Dad's expectations.
我不可能達成父親的期望。

B: He might be a little too harsh, but he loves you a lot.
他或許有點太嚴格，但他很愛你。

A: If he does love me so much, how can he make me do things I don't like?
如果他真的這麼愛我，他怎麼能逼我做我不想做的事？

B: He just wants you to have the best future.
他只是想讓你擁有最好的未來。

相關用語 ╌ get up to 達到　　進階補充 ╌ up to 忙於

146

They have longed for a baby for a long time.

他們渴望獲得一個寶寶很久了。

long for為「渴望」之意。用法：S + long for + Ving/N。long在這裡不作「長的」解，而當作動詞，意為「渴望」。for也可以用after代換。若將for用to代換，則必須加原形動詞。

MP3
146

A: Peggy gave birth to a baby last night.
佩姬昨天晚上生了個寶寶。

B: Really? A boy or a girl?
真的嗎？男孩還是女孩？

A: A cute little girl.
一個可愛的小女孩。

B: They must be happy. They have longed for a baby for a long time.
他們一定很開心。他們期待這個寶寶很久了。

相關用語 ╌ yearn for 渴望　　進階補充 ╌ give birth to 生孩子

147

I will have Mandy look after the kids.

我會讓曼蒂照顧孩子們。

look after是「照料、照顧、留心」的意思，after是介系詞，後面所接的名詞是其受詞。look是「觀看」，after是「在後方」，「從後方觀看」就有「關照、照顧」的意思，此法有助於背誦。

MP3
147

A: Can you watch the kids tomorrow night?
你明晚可以照顧孩子們嗎？

B: I can't. I have an important meeting tomorrow.
不行。我明天有個重要的會議。

A: What can we do?
我們要怎麼辦？

B: Don't worry. I will have Mandy look after the kids.
別擔心。我會讓曼蒂照顧孩子們。

相關用語 · **take care of** 照顧　　進階補充 · **see after** 照顧

148

He's been looking at me ever since he entered the room. 自他進門後，就一直注視著我。

look at為「注視」之意。look是不及物動詞，所以需要加介系詞。look at跟watch都有看到的意思，但look at是表示「注視靜態目標或對動態目標做短暫的視線停留」，而watch則表示「注視動態目標」，通常是暗示已經觀察了一段時間。另一個意思相近的動詞see，強調的則是看到的「結果」，不若look強調的是觀看的「動作」。

MP3
148

A: Do you know the guy over there?
你認識那邊那個男生嗎？

B: Yes. Why are you asking?
認識啊。為何這麼問？

A: He has been looking at me ever since he entered the room.
自從他進門後，就一直看著我。

B: He must have a crush on you.
他一定是煞到你了。

相關用語 · **glare at** 怒視　　進階補充 · **ever since** 自從

149 I am **looking for** a birthday gift for my daughter.

我在找送女兒的生日禮物。

look for為「尋找、期待」之意。look for跟find都有「找」的意思，而其中的差別是：look for含有「正在尋找」的意思，而find則含有「已找到」的意思。search和seek也有尋找的意思，雖然是同義，但還是有些許差別：look for是通俗的日常用語；search for是「尋找所失之物或所需的資料」；seek for是指「謀求所需的東西」。

A: Good morning. What can I do for you?
早安。我可以為您做些什麼呢？

B: I am **looking for** a birthday gift for my daughter.
我在找送給女兒的生日禮物。

A: How about this? A cute, pink bag.
這個怎麼樣？一個可愛的粉紅色提袋。

B: She will love this.
她一定會喜歡的。

相關用語 **search for** 尋找　　進階補充 **look out for** 設法找到

150 We need to **look** further **into** this case.

我們需要深入調查這起案件。

look into為「調查、研究」之意，指「研究或調查某一件事」。「into」這個介系詞有「到…裡面」的意思，look into代表「深入觀看」，也就是「調查、研究」的具體行為。

A: We need to **look** further **into** this case.
我們需要深入調查這起案件。

B: What can I do to help?
我該如何幫忙？

A: Do you remember seeing any suspicious people last night?
你記得昨晚有看到任何可疑人物嗎？

B: Not really.
並沒有。

相關用語 **investigate** 調查　　進階補充 **inquire into** 調查

151

Ma'am, please look out for the traffic.

女士，請小心交通。

look out用於當別人陷於危險而不自知時，提醒對方當心。若要對方警戒某種危險事物，則應在該事物前加for或with。若look out連在一起，變成lookout，則是指「守衛、護衛」的意思。

MP3
151

A: Ma'am, please look out for the traffic.
女士，請小心交通。

B: I am sorry, but I need to save my puppy.
很抱歉，但我得救我的小狗。

A: You'd better put him on a leash, just in case he runs into the traffic.
你最好把狗拴起來，以免他跑到馬路上。

B: I will. Thank you.
我會的，謝謝您。

相關用語 • cautious 當心的   進階補充 • watch out 小心

152

Did you look it over before handing it in?

你在繳交前有仔細檢查嗎？

look over為「仔細檢查」之意，通常用於檢查文件、資料、作業等。受詞若是名詞就置於over之後，若是代名詞就置於over之前。要注意的是，當look over順序調換並且合為一個字overlook時，此時字義變成「忽略」，應當小心留意。

MP3
152

A: Tommy, I need to talk to you about your assignment.
湯米，我得和你談談你的作業。

B: What's wrong? Did I do something wrong?
怎麼了？我做錯什麼了嗎？

A: You made several typos. Did you look it over before handing it in?
你拼錯了幾個字。繳交前，你有仔細檢查嗎？

B: I am sorry. I will be more careful next time.
對不起。我下次會更加注意。

相關用語 • examine 檢查   進階補充 • check up 核對

153

Maybe you can look it up in the dictionary.

或許你可以查閱字典。

look up為「往上看、查閱」之意，是及物動詞，特別指「翻查字典或目錄」的意思，如翻查單字或電話號碼。look up另外也有「抬頭、仰望」的意思。相反片語：look down，表示「回頭、向下看」。

A: Do you know the word "Superbrain"?
你知道「超級腦」這個字嗎？

B: No. Sounds like a new word. Maybe you can look it up in the dictionary.
不知道。聽起來像個新字，也許你可以查一下字典。

A: I don't need to. I created it, meaning "Jason, the most intelligent person."
不需要。這是我創的字，意思是「傑森，最聰明的人」。

B: You are such a narcissist.
你真是個自戀狂。

相關用語 ○ consult 查閱 　 進階補充 ○ refer to 查閱

154

I made a small fortune recently.

我最近發了筆小財。

make a fortune為「發財、致富」之意。make在英文中是擁有眾多意思的字彙之一，它會隨著後面所接字彙的意義不同而有不一樣的解釋，但大致上仍保有「製造或使某物產生」的原意。make在這裡是指「賺」或「得」；fortune是「財富」的意思，為不可數名詞，但在這裡是特殊用法。

A: Wow, the car must have been expensive.
哇，這輛車一定很貴。

B: I made a small fortune recently.
我最近發了筆小財。

A: Really? Good for you! How did you make it?
真的嗎？恭喜你！你怎麼賺到的？

B: I was so lucky because I won the lottery!
我很幸運地中了樂透！

相關用語 ○ fortunate 幸運的 　 進階補充 ○ cost a fortune 所費不貲

155

If you ever make a mistake again, I might have no choice but to fire you. 若你再犯錯，我別無選擇只能開除你。

make a mistake為「犯錯」之意。指涉「錯誤」的單字很多，如：fault通常與受到的責備直接相關，側重於造成錯誤的主觀責任；而mistake和error通常較注重於犯錯的客觀事實。

A: Ma'am, they said you wanted to see me.
女士，他們說您要見我。

B: I do. I want you to take this job seriously and do your job well.
是的。我希望你工作認真點，把工作做好。

A: Yes, Ma'am.
是的，女士。

B: If you ever make a mistake again, I might have no choice but to fire you.
若你再犯錯，我別無選擇只能開除你。

相關用語 ⟶ **by mistake** 錯誤地　　進階補充 ⟶ **and no mistake** 無疑地

156

I made it from fresh raspberries and bananas.

那是我用新鮮的覆盆子和香蕉做成的。

make...from...為「製作」之意，主要用於成品不保留材料原本的性質、型態及形狀，即所製成的東西經過化學變化，例如由葡萄製成的酒。make...of...的用法則是所製成的成品保留原材料的性質，也就是說所製成的成品是經過物理變化而得到的，例如由木頭製成的家具。

A: This is the most delicious cupcake I have ever tasted!
這是我吃過最好吃的杯子蛋糕！

B: Thank you.
謝謝你。

A: What's your secret recipe?
你的秘方是什麼？

B: I made it from fresh raspberries and bananas.
我是用新鮮的覆盆子和香蕉製作的。

相關用語 ⟶ **fabricate** 製造　　進階補充 ⟶ **secret recipe** 秘方

157

It might be a good chance to make friends with kids in your class. 這或許是和班上同學交朋友的好機會。

make friends with為「交朋友」之意。此片語中的friends一定要用複數，用法：S + make friends with + 人。但同義片語keep company with中的company則必須用單數，因為company表「陪伴」，為不可數名詞。

MP3
157

A: Are you sure you don't want to come to the zoo with us?
你確定不和我們去動物園嗎？

B: I just started at this school today. I will be bored if nobody talks to me.
我第一天來這所學校，我會因為沒人跟我說話而感到無聊。

A: Don't worry about that. It might be a good chance to **make friends with** kids in your class.
別擔心那些。這或許是和班上同學交朋友的好機會。

B: You're right. Maybe I should go.
你說得沒錯。也許我該去。

[相關用語] **accompany** 陪同　　[進階補充] **associate with** 與…來往

158

Everyone in my class makes fun of my hair.
班上的每個人都嘲笑我的頭髮。

make fun of是指「用言語嘲笑、戲弄別人」的意思，fun為不可數名詞。此片語和play tricks on有些差異：make fun of多指「用言語向某人開玩笑」；而play tricks on是指「用動作向某人開玩笑」，也有戲弄的意思。

MP3
158

A: Mom, I don't want to go to school ever again.
媽，我再也不想去上學了。

B: What's wrong? Is someone bullying you again?
怎麼了？又有人霸凌你了嗎？

A: No, it's just that everyone in my class **makes fun of** my hair.
沒有，只是班上的每個人都嘲笑我的頭髮。

B: Just ignore them. I love your lovely ruby-like hair.
別理他們就好。我喜歡你紅寶石色的秀髮。

[相關用語] **mock at** 取笑　　[進階補充] **jeer at** 嘲笑

159

The novel was **made into** a TV series.

那本小說被拍成電視影集。

make...into...指的是將原料、物質等，經過加工而製成某物，用於被製作出的成品之前。若要表達「某物被製成某物」，則必須使用被動式，句法為：S + be V + made into + 名詞。

A: What are you reading?
你在讀什麼？

B: The best novel of the decade, *A Song of Ice and Fire.*
近十年來最棒的小說，《冰與火之歌》。

A: I've **heard of** it. It's so good that it was also **made into a TV series.**
我聽過它。這本小說很棒，還被拍成電視影集。

B: Really? I don't want to miss that one.
真的嗎？我絕對不能錯過。

相關用語 → **manufacture** 製造　　進階補充 → **hear of** 聽說過

160

Make sure that every detail is taken care of.

確認每個細節都照顧到了。

make sure為「確定」之意，通常後面會接不定詞(to + V)，或是接that + 子句(S + V)，表示「確認某事」的意思。除了上述語意外，make sure也可以當「查明、確信」的意思解。sure在此為形容詞，表「確信的、必定的」之意。

A: It is of vital importance for us to win the contract over ABC.
打敗ABC公司贏得合約，對我們而言十分重要。

B: Yes, Sir.
是的，長官。

A: So **make sure** that every detail is taken care of.
所以必須確認每個細節都照顧到了。

B: I'll **see to** it right away.
我立刻去處理。

相關用語 → **confirm** 確認　　進階補充 → **see to** 照料、修補

161

He made it up to fool Ms. Chen. It's not true.

那是他掰來騙陳老師的，並不是真的。

make up在此為「編造、虛構」之意。make up是擁有最多詞意的英文片語之一，make up作「組成」的意思解時，後面要接of，再接所要組成的東西。相關片語：make up for「賠償」；make up to「巴結、奉承」；make up one's mind「下定決心」。

MP3
161

A: Do you want to visit Jonathan and give him your condolences?
你想要去拜訪強納森並致上慰問嗎？

B: Why?
為什麼？

A: Haven't you heard about his grandmother's car accident?
你沒聽說他祖母出車禍嗎？

B: Come on. He made it up to fool Ms. Chen. It's not true.
拜託，那是他編來騙陳老師的，並不是真的。

相關用語 ○ **trump up** 編造　　　進階補充 ○ **hear about** 得知

162

People sometimes mistake me for her.

大家有時把我誤認成她。

mistake A for B為「誤認A是B」之意。用法：S + mistake + 受詞 + for + (代)名詞。mistake的動詞三態：mistake、mistook、mistaken。mistake可當動詞和名詞，當動詞時是「誤解」的意思，當名詞時則為「誤會、過失」的意思。

MP3
162

A: Are you and your sister twins?
你跟你姐姐是雙胞胎嗎？

B: No, she is two years older than I.
不，她比我大兩歲。

A: Wow, but you look so similar.
哇，但你們長得好像。

B: Yes, and people sometimes mistake me for her.
是啊，大家有時會把我誤認成她。

相關用語 ○ **take A for B** 誤認A為B　　　進階補充 ○ **mistaken** 誤解的

163 Most of the items on sale are not things I need.

大部分的特價商品我都不需要。

most of為「大多數、大部分」之意，用法如下：1. most + 複數名詞或不可數名詞，most其後不能加冠詞、所有格形容詞(有my、your、his、her、its等)。2. most of + 代名詞。3. most of + the/these/those/one's + 名詞。

MP3
163

A: Let's go shopping today!
今天一起去逛街吧！

B: Why? I don't need anything right now.
為什麼？我現在什麼都不需要。

A: It's the anniversary sale, and most items are 70% off!
現在正週年慶，大部分商品都打三折！

B: But most of the items on sale are not things I need.
但大部分打折的商品都不是我需要的。

相關用語 ► at most 至多　　進階補充 ► the most 極限

164 I am neither his brother nor a close friend.

我既非他兄弟，也非他好友。

neither...nor...為「既非…也非…」之意。此片語是相關連接詞，連接兩個文法作用相同的單字、片語或子句。neither A nor B的動詞應與B一致。其他用法相同的片語有：either A or B + V(動詞與B一致)；not only A but also B + V(動詞與B一致)。

MP3
164

A: Can you set me up with Daniel?
你可以撮合我跟丹尼爾嗎？

B: Why me? I am neither his brother nor a close friend.
為什麼是我？我既不是他的兄弟，也不是他的好友。

A: But he looks up to you a lot.
但是他很尊敬你。

B: Are you kidding me?
你在跟我開玩笑嗎？

相關用語 ► neither 兩者都不　　進階補充 ► look up to 尊敬

165 Never mind.

沒關係／別介意。

never mind為「別介意、沒關係」之意。此片語屬於口語片語，也可當「別管、不客氣」來解釋。mind當動詞時，後面接Ving或that + 子句；當名詞時，後面接不定詞(to + V)，意為「意見、想法」。

A: Excuse me. This is my seat.
　　不好意思，這是我的座位。

B: I am sorry. I didn't think it was taken.
　　抱歉，我以為沒人坐。

A: Never mind.
　　沒關係。

B: Let me take my bags away.
　　讓我把我的包包拿走。

相關用語　mind 介意　　　進階補充　don't mention it 不客氣

166 I am **no longer** in love with him.

我不再愛他了。

no longer為「不再」之意。longer是由long(形容詞，「長久的」的意思)所衍生出來的單字，著重於時間的延續。因為no longer在語意上為否定的意思，所以前面若再用否定動詞，則會變成雙重否定。

A: Roger is very sad that you refused to go out with him yesterday.
　　羅杰很難過你昨天不願意跟他出去。

B: Could you tell him not to ask me out anymore? I am **no longer** in love with him.
　　你可以請他別再約我了嗎？我不再愛他了。

A: Are you finished with him **for good**?
　　你和他已經完全結束了嗎？

B: Absolutely, especially after he cheated on me like that.
　　當然，特別是在他那樣背叛我之後。

相關用語　not anymore 不再　　　進階補充　for good 永久地

167

No matter what, we all love you and stand by you.

我們無論如何都愛你及支持你。

no matter what為「不論」之意。no matter為連接詞片語,若後面加how,其意思為「不論如何」;加who,其意思為「不論是誰」;加what,其意思為「不論怎樣」;加where,其意思為「不論何處」。no matter who = whoever;no matter when = whenever;no matter where = wherever;no matter how = however;no matter what = whatever。

MP3
167

A: Sweetheart, you need to cheer up.
親愛的,你得振作起來。

B: No. I'm such a big loser.
不。我真是個沒用的人。

A: Stop saying that. **No matter what**, we all love you and **stand by** you.
別這麼說。無論如何,我們都愛你、支持你。

B: Thank you, Dad.
謝謝你,爸。

相關用語 ◦ **matter** 重要性   進階補充 ◦ **stand by** 支持

168

I am sorry, but we have **no more** Coke.

很抱歉,但我們沒有可樂了。

no more為「不再」之意,著重修飾程序和數量,前方必須使用肯定語氣,相當於not...any more。此片語若變成no more + 形容詞 + than,則意思是「與…一樣…」;若變成no more than + 名詞,則意思是「僅僅、只不過」。

MP3
168

A: Sir, I am sorry, but we have **no more** Coke.
先生,很抱歉,但我們沒有可樂了。

B: What do you mean?
你的意思是?

A: We don't have **any more** Coke. Just juice and wine.
我們沒有可樂了,只剩果汁和酒。

B: That's ridiculous!
真是誇張!

相關用語 ◦ **any more** (不)再   進階補充 ◦ **no longer** 不再

169 The box is **not** heavy **at all**.

這個箱子一點也不重。

not at all為「一點也不」之意，可連在一起使用，也可分開使用。若分開使用，由於not是副詞，必須加在形容詞之前，at all則放在最後，如例句所示。not at all也可用來回應他人的感謝，意為「別客氣」。

A: Thank you so much for carrying the box.
非常感謝你幫我搬箱子。

B: Don't mention it. It's **not** heavy **at all**.
不客氣；它一點也不重。

A: It was for me, and I really don't know what I would have done without your help.
對我來說很重。而且沒有你的幫忙，我真不知道該怎麼辦。

B: I was more than happy to help you, Brenda.
布蘭達，我很樂意幫助你。

相關用語 ⊶ **not a bit** 一點也不　　進階補充 ⊶ **not nearly** 一點也不

170 **Not only** fathers **but also** mothers should come.

不僅是父親們，母親們也要來。

not only A but also B為「不僅A而且B」之意。此片語是對等連接詞片語，其後所接的字必須在詞性上相等。值得注意的是，若將not only...but also...置於句首，且連接兩個子句時，就必須以倒裝句的形式呈現。例：
Not only does he like dancing but also I like dancing.

A: The PTA meeting is tomorrow. Can you come?
家長會在明天。你能來嗎？

B: I can't. Your father will go on our behalf.
我不能。你爸爸會代表我們參加。

A: But the teacher said **not only** fathers **but also** mothers should come.
但老師說不僅爸爸們，媽媽們也要來。

B: I am really sorry, but I have an important meeting tomorrow.
真的很抱歉，但我明天有個重要會議。

相關用語 ⊶ **both A and B** 既A且B　　進階補充 ⊶ **more than** 不只

171

We chat every **now and then**.

我們有時會閒聊。

now and then為「有時、不時」之意。then也可代換成again，意義不變。此片語也可寫成every now and then。額外補充："Now or never."「機會難再，勿失良機」，這是一句經常在大賣場聽到或看到的行銷用語。

MP3
171

A: Are you familiar with Jason?
你跟傑森熟嗎？

B: Kind of. We chat every now and then.
算是吧。我們有時會閒聊。

A: What do you talk about?
你們都聊些什麼？

B: Nothing important. Just some office gossip.
沒什麼重要的事，就是些辦公室八卦。

相關用語 • occasionally 偶爾　　　進階補充 • familiar with 與…熟悉

172

Of course I will take Amy to the party.

我當然會帶艾咪參加派對。

of course為「當然」之意，是一則相當常用的口語片語。若要表示否定，則是of course not，意思為「當然不」。course大多用作名詞，有「方向、路線、進程、科目、一道菜」等意思。course亦可當動詞使用，表「(用獵犬)追獵、(液體)流動、(使馬)奔跑」等意思。

MP3
172

A: Are you going to Allen's cousin's birthday party?
你會去亞倫他堂哥的生日派對嗎？

B: Certainly.
當然會。

A: Will you take little Amy to the party?
你會帶小艾咪參加派對嗎？

B: Of course I will. I know you miss her very much.
我當然會。我知道你很想念她。

相關用語 • certainly 當然　　　進階補充 • of course not 當然不

173

I am sorry, but I am off duty now.

很抱歉，但我現在已下班。

off duty為「下班」之意。off是「離開、離去」的意思；duty是指「受到自身的正義感、道德心或良知驅使，而認為應盡的義務」。相關片語：relieve one of one's duties「解雇某人」；shirk one's duty「怠忽職守」。

MP3
174

A: Hi, I would like to **get a refund on** this handbag.
你好，我要退這個手提包。

B: I am sorry, but I am **off duty** now. Do you mind going to aisle 7?
很抱歉，但我已經下班了。您介意至七號走道嗎？

A: There are a lot of people lined up there. Can't you do it for me?
那裡有很多人排隊。你不能幫我處理嗎？

B: I am sorry, but I've already closed my till for the evening.
很抱歉，但我已關閉帳款了。

相關用語 ▸ **on duty** 上班　　進階補充 ▸ **get a refund on** 退貨

174

He's been out of the office on and off all morning.

他今早一直進進出出辦公室。

on and off為「斷斷續續」之意，也可以寫成off and on，是副詞片語，形容一件事情的無持續性，只有偶爾地、斷斷續續地發生而已。on是「持續」，off表示「停止」。反義片語：on and on「持續不斷」。

MP3
173

A: Mr. Lin's office. How may I help you?
林先生的辦公室。有什麼我可以幫您的？

B: This is Johnson. May I speak to Mr. Lin now?
我是強森。可以請林先生聽嗎？

A: I'm sorry but he's been out of the office **on and off** all morning, and now he's out again.
很抱歉，他今早一直進進出出辦公室，而他現在又出去了。

B: That's OK; I'll call him back later.
沒關係；我晚點再撥過來。

相關用語 ▸ **fitful** 斷續的　　進階補充 ▸ **discontinuous** 斷續的

175

My boss is sending me to Hawaii **on business**.

老闆派我出差夏威夷。

on business為「因公、以辦公為目的」之意，為表目的的副詞片語，通常放在句尾而不放句首。on在這裡是「從事」的意思。business在此為「事務」之意。相關詞彙有：business card「商用名片」；business class「商務艙」；business hours「營業時間、上班時間」；businesslike「效率高的」。

A: What are you doing?
你在做什麼？

B: Can't you see? I am packing.
看不出來嗎？我在打包。

A: I know. I am asking why are you packing?
我知道。我是問你為何要打包？

B: My boss is sending me to Hawaii **on business**. I'll be back next Tuesday.
老闆派我去夏威夷出差。我下週二回來。

相關用語 **for work** 為了工作　　進階補充 **for pleasure** 為了消遣

176

What **on earth** do you need more shoes for?

你究竟為何需要更多的鞋？

on earth為「在地球上、究竟」之意。在當「究竟」的意思解時，是用來加強疑問語氣，在口語中經常被拿來使用。作此用法時也可代換為in the world、in heaven等。

A: Shoes again? What **on earth** do you need more shoes for?
又是鞋？你究竟需要更多雙鞋做什麼？

B: A pretty woman can never have enough shoes.
一個漂亮女人不可能擁有足夠的鞋。

A: Yes, especially when she is a centipede.
是的，尤其當她是隻蜈蚣的時候。

B: Don't **make fun of** me!
別嘲笑我！

相關用語 **in hell** 究竟　　進階補充 **make fun of** 取笑

177

I don't want to make you feel **on edge**.

我不想讓你感到緊張。

on edge為「緊張地」之意。edge為名詞，有「邊緣、刀口」之意。與edge相關的片語包括：on the edge of「在…邊緣」；give an edge to「加劇、使激烈」；give the edge of one's tongue to「嚴斥」；not to put too fine an edge upon it「直截了當地說」；put a person to the edge of the sword「殺死某人」。

A: Good morning. Please take a seat.
早安，請坐。

B: Thank you, Sir.
謝謝您，先生。

A: I don't want to make you feel on edge. So just relax.
我不想讓你感到緊張，所以請放輕鬆。

B: I'll try my best not to be nervous. Thank you.
我會試著不緊張的，謝謝你。

相關用語 → nervous 緊張的　　進階補充 → on the verge of 瀕於

178

Mr. Chao's house is **on fire**.

趙先生的房子著火了。

on fire為「著火」之意；此片語也可當「(感情或情緒的)興奮、激動」的意思解。如果在前面加set，變成set...on fire，那麼就成了「縱火、使興奮」的意思。相關用語：fire in the belly「衝勁十足」；hold one's feet to the fire「施壓」。

A: What is that noise?
那是什麼聲音？

B: A fire engine. Mr. Chao's house is on fire.
消防車的聲音。趙先生的房子著火了。

A: Oh, that's too bad! How did it happen?
噢，太糟糕了！怎麼會著火？

B: Some naughty kids were playing with matches in his yard.
幾個調皮的小孩在他家院子裡玩火柴。

相關用語 → set fire to 縱火燒　　進階補充 → catch fire 失火

179

Are you going **on foot**?

你要走路去嗎？

on foot為「步行」之意，其中foot不可改成複數型feet。相似片語on one's feet，表「站著、復元、獨立」的意思。另外，我們通常用前往某處的動作 + by + 交通工具，來表示如何抵達某處，所以步行時也可以使用by foot，和on foot一樣表達「走路前往」之意。

MP3
179

A: Where are you going?
你要去哪裡？

B: Sogo Department Store.
太平洋百貨。

A: That's about 2 kilometers away. Are you going on foot?
那大約有兩公里遠。你要走路去嗎？

B: What else can I do? My car isn't running again.
我還能怎麼去？我的車又壞了。

相關用語 → **by train** 搭火車　　進階補充 → **by bus** 搭公車

180

This one is **on sale** and has some excellent features.

這款正在特價，且擁有一些優點。

on sale為「出售、銷售中」之意。在這則片語中，sale是名詞，為「銷售、交易」的意思。on sale是指物品銷售；for sale則是指任何事物的出售。由sale所衍生的詞彙有：saleroom「拍賣場」；sales clerk = salesclerk「售貨員(美式用法)」；sales tax「營業稅」。

MP3
180

A: We are looking for a 3-D TV.
我們在找3D電視。

B: I happen to have some pretty great models in stock.
我碰巧有些不錯的現貨。

A: Can I take a look at them?
我可以看一下嗎？

B: Sure. This one here is on sale and has some excellent features.
當然可以。這邊這台正在特價，且擁有一些優點。

相關用語 → **for sale** 待售　　進階補充 → **in stock** 有現貨的

181

On the basis of user reviews, AT&T provides better reception. 基於用戶評價，美國電話電報公司提供較佳收訊。

on the basis of為「基於…」之意。關於「基礎」的英文有basis、base、foundation和groundwork等，其意義與用法略有不同：basis和base多用於抽象的比喻，指「信念或議論」的基礎；foundation則是指「穩固或永久性」的基礎；groundwork和foundation同義，但多用於比喻。

A: There are so many plans. Which one should we go for?
有好多種方案，我們該選哪一種？

B: We should definitely go for AT&T.
我們當然要選美國電話電報公司。

A: Why?
為什麼？

B: **On the basis of** user reviews, AT&T provides better reception in this area.
基於用戶評價，美國電話電報公司在本區提供較佳收訊。

相關用語 ⟶ **on account of** 由於   進階補充 ⟶ **be based on** 根據

182

On the other hand, the price may not be affordable for us. 另一方面，我們可能無法負擔這個價錢。

on the other hand為「另一方面、反過來說」之意。和本片語組合相似的片語有：on the one hand「一方面」；on hand「現在、在手邊」；not much of hand at「不善於」；give a hand in「幫忙、參加」。

A: This apartment is perfect for us.
這間公寓看起來很適合我們。

B: You're right. It has the best backyard I've ever seen.
你說的對。它的後院是我看過最棒的。

A: **On the other hand**, the price may not be affordable for us.
但另一方面，我們可能無法負擔這個價錢。

B: Don't worry. We can handle it.
別擔心。我們應付得來。

相關用語 ⟶ **aspect** 方面   進階補充 ⟶ **on the contrary** 正相反

183

I'll be there **on time**.

我會準時到達。

on time為「準時」之意，指「不早不晚，正好在指定或約定的時間做某事」的意思，常用在如飛機、火車等等的時刻上。此片語可作形容詞片語或副詞片語。相似片語：in time「及時」。

MP3
183

A: Remember we're meeting Aunt Lauren.
記得我們和蘿倫阿姨有約。

B: Is it today?
是今天嗎？

A: Yes. Don't be late again.
是的。別又遲到了。

B: Sure. I'll be there **on time**.
好的。我會準時到達。

相關用語 ▸ **on schedule** 按時間表　　進階補充 ▸ **on the minute** 準時

184

I guess it's probably because he is **on vacation**.

我猜大概是因為他在度假。

on vacation為「在度假、度假中」之意。on有「正在從事、進行某事」的意思；vacation是名詞，有「假期」的意思。英文中有一個字的拼法和vacation十分相似：vocation，名詞，意思是「職業」，兩字易混淆，在使用上要特別小心。另一個片語on leave，意思是「休假中、告假中」，可與on vacation做一對比。on holiday也是「休假中」的意思，但vacation通常指較長的假期而言。

MP3
184

A: Can you give Jason a ring?
你可以打個電話給傑森嗎？

B: I already tried, but he didn't answer the phone.
我試過了，但他沒有接電話。

A: Really? I wonder why he didn't **pick up** the phone.
真的嗎？我好奇為何他不接電話。

B: I guess it's probably because he is **on vacation**.
我猜大概是因為他在度假吧。

相關用語 ▸ **furlough** 休假　　進階補充 ▸ **pick up** 接起

185

Please get your sandwich one by one.

請依序排隊領三明治。

one by one為「一個一個地」之意，也可以寫成one after one。由one所衍生出的詞彙有：one-parent family「單親家庭」；one way or another「以某種方法」；by ones and twos「零零落落地」。

185

A: Please get your sandwich one by one.
請依序排隊領三明治。

B: Ms. Lin, Larry cut in again!
林老師，賴瑞又插隊了！

A: Fine, I'll talk to him later.
好，我晚點會跟他談談。

B: But he took my sandwich, too!
但他還拿走了我的三明治！

相關用語 • **take turns 輪流**　　進階補充 • **cut in 插隊**

186

Honey, we are out of sugar.

親愛的，我們沒有糖了。

out of含有「沒有」的意思，根據後面所接的字彙不同，意思也隨之改變。out of date = out of fashion = old-fashioned「過時的、陳舊的」；out of town = away from town「出城」；out of sight = invisible「看不見」；out of one's mind = mad、insane「發狂、神經錯亂」；out of work = unemployed「失業」；out of control = unrestrained「失控」等等。

186

A: Honey, we are out of sugar. Can you grab some on your way home?
親愛的，我們的糖用完了。你可以在回家路上順便買一點嗎？

B: Again? Didn't I just get some two days ago?
又要買？我兩天前不是才買了一些？

A: Yes, you did, but your daughter consumes sugar like a little ant.
是啊，但你女兒像隻螞蟻般吃糖。

B: You need to stop her from doing that!
你得阻止她那樣做！

相關用語 • **out of print 絕版**　　進階補充 • **out of breath 喘不過氣**

187

I've warned you **over and over** not to hit your classmates. 我已再三警告你，不可毆打同學。

over and over為「再三地」之意，是副詞片語。接上again後意思一樣。相關片語：over and above「在⋯之外、超乎」；over against「在⋯對面」；over there「在那裡」。

MP3
187

A: Frank, I've warned you **over and over** not to hit your classmates.
法蘭克，我已再三警告你，不可以打同學。

B: But it's Jason who took my sandwich first!
但是，是傑森先拿走我的三明治！

A: No matter what problem you have, violence isn't a solution.
不論你們之間有什麼問題，暴力不是解決之道。

B: OK. Please don't tell my mom. I'll behave myself!
好吧。拜託別跟我媽說。我會乖的！

相關用語 ⟶ repeatedly 屢次　進階補充 ⟶ time after time 多次

188

He is heartbroken from his wife **passing away**.
妻子的離世讓他心碎。

pass away有「去世、度過」之意。當「去世」的意思解時，屬於較有禮貌、委婉的用詞。當「度過」的意思解時，多指時間上的度過，而非空間的度過，有「消磨時間」之意。

MP3
188

A: How is Jay doing?
傑還好嗎？

B: Terrible. He is heartbroken from his wife **passing away**.
糟透了。他太太的離世讓他心碎。

A: Hmm...It must be really hard for him.
嗯⋯他一定很難過。

B: All we can do is stand by him and support him whenever he needs us.
我們能做的就是陪伴他，必要時給予他支持。

相關用語 ⟶ depart 過世　進階補充 ⟶ pass on 過世

189

Did you see the girl **passing by**?

你有看到經過的那個女孩嗎？

pass by為「經過、錯過」之意。在當「經過」的意思解時，是不及物動詞，受詞不能加在pass跟by之間。pass是「經過、通過」的意思，by則有「旁邊、通過」的意思，合起來就有「經過、擦身」的意思。用於時間的流逝時，可與go by互換。

A: Did you see the girl passing by?
你有看到經過的那個女孩嗎？

B: Which one?
哪一個？

A: The blonde over there. I think that's Jenny.
那邊那個金髮女孩。我想那是珍妮。

B: Gosh! It is! When did she dye her hair?
天啊！沒錯！她什麼時候染頭髮的？

相關用語 ○ **walk by** 經過　　進階補充 ○ **pass through** 經歷

190

Each of you can take a piece of toffee and **pass** the box **on**. 每人可拿一塊太妃糖，然後把盒子往下傳。

pass on為「傳遞下去」之意，也就是「傳遞某物給某人」，其後要接to再接人。用法：S + pass on to + 人。此片語另外還有「繼續下去、去世」的意思，當「繼續下去」時與keep on同義；當「去世」時則與pass away同義。

A: Each of you can take a piece of toffee and pass the box on.
每個人可拿一塊太妃糖，然後把盒子往下傳。

B: Can I have two?
我可以拿兩塊嗎？

A: No, I am afraid you may not.
不，很遺憾你不能。

B: OK.
好吧。

相關用語 ○ **pass down** 傳下來　　進階補充 ○ **hand down** 傳下去

191

When are you going to **pay** me **back**?

你打算何時還我錢？

pay back為「報復、償還」之意。pay是指「為了酬謝某件工作或購買物品而付款」的意思，用法：S + pay back + to + 人。其動詞的三態為：pay、paid、paid。此片語可用於正面的報答，亦可用於負面的報復。

A: When are you going to **pay** me **back**?
你打算何時還我錢？

B: What are you talking about? I owe you nothing.
你在說什麼？我什麼也沒欠你。

A: That's not true. You borrowed five dollars from me last Friday!
才不是那樣。你上週五跟我借了五塊錢！

B: Oh, that totally **slipped my mind**.
喔，我完全忘了。

相關用語 → **give sth. back** 送還　進階補充 → **slip one's mind** 忘了

192

Pick out the red beans from the green beans.

把紅豆從綠豆中挑出來。

pick out為「分辨出、挑選出」之意，後面所接的受詞不能是代名詞，必須是名詞才行。pick和choose都有「挑選」的意思，其差別為：pick有「仔細挑選」之意，因此在購物時常用pick out來表示；而choose則是指「從一堆東西中，挑選一個出來」的意思。

A: What are you doing?
你在做什麼？

B: **Picking out** the red beans from the green beans.
把紅豆從綠豆中挑出來。

A: I can see that. I am asking you why.
我看得出來。我是問你為什麼。

B: I forgot to finish my homework. It's a punishment from Ms. Chen.
我忘記寫作業了。這是陳老師給我的懲罰。

相關用語 → **choose** 選擇　進階補充 → **pick at** 挑毛病

193

He always **picks up** what I teach him in a second!

他總能馬上學會我教的東西！

pick up為「拾起、搭載、學到」之意。在當「學到」的意思解時，是指「知識、利益等的獲得」；當「搭載」時，用法為pick sb. up。在非正式用法中，此片語還有「搭訕」的意思。相似片語：pick up with，指「與(偶然遇到的人)結識」；pick up on「了解到、注意到」。

A: My son must be a genius!
　我的兒子一定是個天才！

B: Why do you say that?
　你為何這麼說？

A: He always picks up what I teach him in a second!
　他總能馬上學會我教的東西！

B: Knowing how to use a spoon doesn't mean he is an Einstein.
　知道如何使用湯匙不表示他是個天才。

相關用語 **master** 精通　　進階補充 **get into** 學會

194

He is just **playing at** not caring.

他只是假裝不在意。

play at為「裝扮、玩票、作遊戲」之意。at是介系詞，如果後面加的是動詞，則應該改為Ving。play at在當「玩票」的意思解時，使用上是沒有被動式的。當「作遊戲」解時，後面可加遊戲的名稱，例如play at hide-and-seek「玩捉迷藏」。

A: What should we do about Mr. Damon?
　我們該拿戴蒙先生怎麼辦？

B: What do you mean?
　你是什麼意思？

A: He refused to accept our offer and it seems he is losing interest in the deal.
　他拒絕接受我們的條件，而且似乎對這次的交易失了興趣。

B: He is just playing at not caring. He will eventually sign.
　他只是假裝不在意。他終究會簽約的。

相關用語 **pretend** 假裝　　進階補充 **lose interest in** 失去興趣

195

I believe we can **play on** that and get a better price.

我想我們可以利用那點，以取得更好的價格。

play on為「演奏、利用」之意。當「利用」解時，後面必須接人的弱點或錯誤，如害怕、懦弱等。另外，許多樂器的演奏也用play on來表示。用法：S + play on + 樂器，不過on經常被省略，直接用play + 樂器。

MP3
195

A: Mr. Anderson called to ask if you would like to make more purchases.
安德森先生來電詢問您是否要增加訂購量。

B: I will if he can offer me a better price.
如果他可以給我更好的價格，我是會增加的。

A: I heard he is in need of cash. I believe we can play on that and get a better price.
聽說他需要現金，我想我們可以利用這點，以取得更好的價格。

B: Excellent! Let's go for it.
太好了！就這樣進行吧。

相關用語 • **make purchases 購買**　　進階補充 • **in need of 需要**

196

As you previously **pointed out**, global warming is getting worse. 誠如您先前所指出的，全球暖化漸趨嚴重。

point out為「指出」之意，後面通常加名詞或that子句(that + S + V)。相關片語：point of reference「參照標準」；point of view「觀點」。

MP3
196

A: As you previously pointed out, global warming is getting worse.
誠如您先前所指出的，全球暖化漸趨嚴重。

B: That is correct, and this research is aimed at finding an effective solution to it.
沒錯，本研究的目的在於找出有效的解決方法。

A: How are you going to start with your research?
您要從哪裡開始您的研究？

B: I will probably start with examining the oxygen content in the river.
我或許會從檢查河水含氧量開始。

相關用語 • **indicate 指出**　　進階補充 • **aim at 以…為目的**

197

I **prefer to** have pork.

我比較想要豬肉。

prefer to為「寧願、較喜歡」之意。用法：S + prefer to + 動詞。prefer
是動詞，其名詞是preference、形容詞是preferable。若用prefer A to B，
則表示較喜歡A，較不喜歡B。A和B也可置入動詞，但是時態兩者必須統
一。

A: Sir, we have beef and pork. Which one do you want?
先生，我們有牛肉和豬肉。您想要哪一種？

B: I prefer to have pork. Thank you.
我比較想要豬肉。謝謝你。

A: How about your drink? Tea or wine?
那飲料呢？茶還是酒？

B: Red wine, please.
請給我紅酒。

相關用語 ○ **had rather** 寧可　　　進階補充 ○ **would sooner** 寧願

198

We are scheduled to **pull down** the building tomorrow. 我們預計於明日拆除房屋。

pull down為「拆掉、拉下來、衰弱」之意。相似片語：pull down one's
house about one's ears「試圖自我毀滅」。其他由pull所組成的片語有：
pull in「到站」；pull into「將車開進去停放」；pull over「將車停靠路
邊」；pull through「恢復」；pull together「互助合作」。

A: We are scheduled to pull down Mrs. Watson's building tomorrow afternoon.
我們預計明天下午拆除華生太太的房子。

B: Fine. Who will be the supervisor?
好。誰會去監工？

A: Since she is an important client, I will do it myself.
由於她是重要客戶，我會親自監工。

B: Good. Please make sure everything goes right.
很好。請確認每件事順利進行。

相關用語 ○ **tear down** 拆掉　　　進階補充 ○ **take apart** 拆卸

199 Pull over now!

馬上停車！

pull over為「拔出、(把車)停下來」之意。在當「停住」的意思解時，是指「馬或車等交通工具停止動作」的意思。此片語另外還有「從電腦中蒐集資訊」的意思。相似片語：pull up your socks，「加倍努力」的意思。

A: Pull over now!
馬上停車！

B: Sir, what's wrong?
警官，怎麼了嗎？

A: You are speeding. Your license, please.
你超速了。請把駕照給我。

B: OK. Here you are.
好的。在這裡。

相關用語 ▸ **pull out** 拔出　　進階補充 ▸ **pull in** 到達

200 Time is up. Put down your pen.

時間到了，請停筆。

put down為「放下、寫下、奚落」之意。在當「奚落」的意思時是口語用法。相似片語：put down the drain「消費、浪費」，也是屬於口語用法。相關片語：put down as/for「把…視為」；put down to「把…歸因於」。

A: Time is up. Put down your pen.
時間到，請停筆。

B: Can I have five more minutes?
可以再給我五分鐘嗎？

A: I am afraid not. Sorry.
恐怕無法，抱歉。

B: Come on! I just have to finish the last question.
拜託！我只是要把最後一題寫完。

相關用語 ▸ **lay down** 放下　　進階補充 ▸ **put up** 建造

201

Put on your jacket.

穿上你的外套。

put on為「穿上、加開、誇大」之意。當「穿上」的意思解時，其相反片語是take off「脫下」；當「加開」的意思解時，專指火車班次的增加。相關片語：put on airs「擺架子」；put on flesh/weight「發胖」；put on one side「放在一邊」。

MP3
201

A: Put on your jacket.
穿上你的外套。

B: I don't want to.
我不想穿。

A: But it's cold outside.
但是外面很冷。

B: I just don't want to put on that stupid pink jacket.
我就是不想穿上那件愚蠢的粉紅色外套。

相關用語 ○ **dress up 打扮**　　進階補充 ○ **put off 延遲**

202

I am always willing to put out a helping hand for my friends. 我總是願意對朋友伸出援手。

put out為「伸出、熄滅、擊敗」之意。put-out是名詞，在棒球用語中是指「刺殺出局」的意思。相關片語：put out to grass「解雇」；put out feelers「試探、探勘」；put out to tender「招標」。

MP3
202

A: Jason called last night.
傑森昨晚打電話來。

B: What did he say?
他說了什麼？

A: He asked us for a loan. Do you want to give him one?
他向我們借錢。你想借嗎？

B: Sure, I am always willing to put out a helping hand for my friends.
當然，我一向願意對朋友伸出援手。

相關用語 ○ **stretch out 伸出**　　進階補充 ○ **reach out 伸出**

203 Class, please **quiet down**.

同學們,請安靜。

quiet down為「靜下來」之意。quiet是指「沒有興奮、騷擾、搖動等情緒因素,因而平靜」。quiet跟quite(相當地、完全地,副詞)拼法類似,在書寫上要多加留意。quiet可當形容詞、動詞和名詞,此處當動詞用。

MP3
203

A: Class, please quiet down. I have something important to tell you.
同學們,請安靜下來。我有重要的事宣佈。

B: What is that?
是什麼?

A: We are going to have a field trip next week.
我們下週要校外教學。

B: Great!
太棒了!

相關用語 **lower** 減弱(音量)　進階補充 **keep quiet** 保持安靜

204 Please **read over** the content before you sign the agreement. 在簽署同意書前,請先詳讀內容。

read over為「仔細閱讀、重讀」之意;而glance、run、go這些動詞與介系詞over連用時,則有「從頭到尾很快地、大略地查看某物」的意思。相關片語:read for/up「攻讀(學位)」;read out「宣讀、開除」;read the handwriting on the wall「預知未來」。

MP3
204

A: This is the application form for the new credit card.
這是新信用卡的申請表。

B: Should I sign now?
我該現在簽名嗎?

A: No, please read over the content before you sign the agreement.
不,在簽名同意之前,請先詳讀內容。

B: I see.
我知道了。

相關用語 **run through** 瀏覽　進階補充 **glance over** 簡略閱讀

205

Can you **replace** my hard drive **with** a new one?

你可以幫我換顆新硬碟嗎？

replace with為「以…代替」之意。replace是指「取代已離開的人、已不見的物或已破損的東西」，也可以指「代替某人的職位」。with後是加「用來取代的人或物」；with也可用by代替。

A: Can you come over tonight?
你今晚可以過來嗎？

B: Sure. What is it?
當然可以。怎麼了？

A: Can you **replace** my hard drive **with** a new one?
你可以幫我更換新硬碟嗎？

B: No problem.
沒問題。

相關用語 • substitute for 替代　　進階補充 • replace by 以…代替

206

It might **result from** Ken's inappropriate behavior.

那可能導因於肯的不當行為。

result from為「產生；起因於」之意，沒有被動句型，而且只能用簡單式。用法：S + result from + N。反義片語：result in「導致」。要注意的是，表現事物的因果時，應該用「果」result from「因」；或是「因」result in「果」。

A: Ms. Chen called and canceled the joint-project.
陳小姐打電話來取消和我們的合作計劃。

B: Oh, no! Did she say why?
噢，不！她有說為什麼嗎？

A: I believe it might **result from** Ken's inappropriate behavior the other day.
我想那可能導因於肯前幾天的不當行為。

B: Just make Ken apologize to her immediately!
馬上讓肯向她道歉！

相關用語 • result in 導致　　進階補充 • as a result 結果

207

Mr. Watson wants you in his office right away.

華生先生要你立刻進他辦公室。

right away為「馬上、立刻」之意。right在當形容詞時,意思是「正確的、真實的、良好的、正面的、右邊的」;在當副詞時,意思是「公正地、向右方、剛好、馬上、徹底地、非常地」;在當動詞時,意思是「糾正、豎立、拯救」。

MP3
207

A: Mr. Watson wants you in his office right away.
華生先生要你立刻進他辦公室。

B: Did he say why?
他有說為什麼嗎?

A: No, but he seems to be really angry.
沒有,但他看起來非常生氣。

B: Oh, no. I should have asked for a sick leave today.
噢,不。我今天應該要請病假的。

相關用語 → **at once** 馬上   進階補充 → **in a mere moment** 馬上

208

We ran across each other at a Christmas party.

我們在一場耶誕派對上偶然遇見彼此。

run across為「偶然遇到;穿過」之意,是不及物動詞片語,所以受詞不能放在run和across之間。across這個介系詞有「穿越、相交」的意思。相關片語:run amuck「胡作非為」;run down「弄壞」。

MP3
208

A: How do you know Ken?
你怎麼認識肯的?

B: We ran across each other at a Christmas party.
我們是在一場耶誕派對上偶然遇到的。

A: You two make a cute couple.
你們兩個是很搭的一對。

B: Thank you so much.
非常謝謝你。

相關用語 → **bump into** 遇見   進階補充 → **run into** 遇見

209

It must be the police running after a bank robber.

一定是警察正在追趕銀行搶匪。

run after為「追趕、追蹤、追求」之意。run的動詞三態：run、ran、run。after這個介系詞是「在後方」的意思，所以run after表「在後追趕」，可當實際上的追逐，也可當情感上的追求。run和go都有向前移動的意思，所以go after與本片語同義。

A: What's that noise?
那是什麼聲音？

B: It must be the police running after a bank robber.
一定是警察在追趕銀行搶匪。

A: What robber?
什麼搶匪？

B: Don't you ever watch the news? The bank two blocks away was just robbed.
你沒看新聞嗎？兩條街外的銀行剛被搶了。

相關用語 come after 緊跟　　進階補充 chase after 追趕

210

He ran away from home, which has made his mom very worried. 他逃家了，讓他的母親非常擔心。

run away為「逃跑、離家」之意。後面接from，表示從某個地方離開。此片語是指「出於任性或反抗而離家出走或遠走他方」的意思，可能是不告而別，也可能是私奔，依文意而定。但兩者有一個共通點，那就是「沒有通知就離開」。

A: Have you heard from Jack lately?
你最近有傑克的消息嗎？

B: No. What's up?
沒有。怎麼了？

A: He ran away from home, which has made his mom very worried.
他逃家了，這讓他的母親非常擔心。

B: That's too bad.
太糟糕了。

相關用語 escape 逃離　　進階補充 run away with 失去控制

211

It's such a surprise to run into you here!

在這裡遇到你真令人意外！

run into為「撞到、偶遇」之意。此外，還有「衝入、達到、和…相接」等意思。介系詞into也可用against代替，但run against沒有「撞到」、只有「偶遇」的意思。反之，如果用over代替的話，則有「撞到」甚至「輾過」的意思。

A: It's such a surprise to run into you here!
在這裡遇到你真令人意外！

B: It is! What are you doing here?
沒錯！你在這裡做什麼？

A: I've come to run some errands for my mom. How about you?
我來幫我媽媽跑腿。那你呢？

B: I've come to get some cabbage for my mom, too.
我也來幫我媽買甘藍菜。

相關用語 ► come across 偶遇　　進階補充 ► run errands 跑腿

212

Honey, we are running out of flour.

親愛的，麵粉快用完了。

run out為「用完、耗盡」之意。此外，還有「跑出去、流出、比賽到底、出局」等等其他意思。若在其後加上介系詞of，可以接用完的物品，或是跑出來的地方。相似片語：run/walk out on「拋棄」；run out of steam「精疲力盡」。

A: Honey, we are running out of flour. Can you get some for me now?
親愛的，麵粉快用完了。你現在可以幫我去買一些嗎？

B: Can you wait ten more minutes?
你可以再等十分鐘嗎？

A: What are you doing?
你在做什麼？

B: I am watching the NBA finals.
我正在看美國職籃季後賽。

相關用語 ► deplete of 耗盡　　進階補充 ► use up 用完

213

we are all sold out of cheeseburgers.

我們的吉士漢堡全賣完了。

sell out為「售完」之意。sell的動詞三態為：sell、sold、sold。由sell所衍生的用詞：sell-by date「保存期限」；sell oneself「自薦、賣身」；sell short「低估」。

A: One cheeseburger to go, please.
請給我一個吉士漢堡外帶。

B: I am sorry, but we are all sold out of cheeseburgers.
對不起，但是吉士漢堡賣完了。

A: Then, I will have a Big Mac.
那我要一個大麥克。

B: OK. Do you need a drink?
好的。您需要飲料嗎？

相關用語 • **out of stock** 無現貨的　　進階補充 • **sell off** 廉價出售

214

We should set off now if we want to catch the train.

若我們想趕上火車，現在就該出發。

set off為「出發、分開、使爆炸」之意。set動詞三態皆為set。set有「設定、裝置、校正、規定」等非常多種意思。相關片語：set down「記下、讓乘客下車」；set in「建造、開始」；set back「使受挫、使落後」；set upon「攻擊」。

A: If we want to catch the 7:00 train, we should set off now.
如果我們想搭七點的火車，我們應該現在出發。

B: That means we only have ten minutes left to get to the station.
也就是說，我們要在十分鐘內抵達火車站。

A: Can we make it in ten minutes?
我們十分鐘內到得了嗎？

B: I don't think so. Can we take the 8:00 train?
我不這樣覺得。我們可以搭八點的車嗎？

相關用語 • **start off** 出發　　進階補充 • **hit the road** 上路

215

I'm **setting up** a new shop in the downtown.

我將在市中心開立新店。

set up為「設立、設定、開店」之意。除了上述的意思之外，還有「提高、提供、增加權力、發生、高喊、康復、鍛鍊、計畫」等等其他意思，非正式的口語意思則有「招待飲料、付飲料費、激勵、欺騙他人妥協」等。

A: I am going to **set up** a new shop in the downtown.
我要在市區開店了。

B: Really? What kind of shop is it?
真的嗎？是什麼樣的店？

A: It's a pet grooming shop.
是間寵物美容店。

B: Great! Can I get a discount?
太棒了！我可以有折扣嗎？

相關用語 • establish 建立　　進階補充 • put up 建造

216

I met Adele in the airport, and she even **shook hands with** me! 我在機場遇到愛黛兒，她甚至和我握手！

shake hands with為「與某人握手」之意，with後面要加人。也可以寫成：shake sb. by the hand。shake hands是見面時的禮節，由於握手時，需要上下搖動彼此的手，所以才會用shake「搖動」這個字。另外要注意的是，這裡的hands要加複數，因為握手一定要兩隻手。

A: You know what? The greatest thing ever happened today!
你知道嗎？今天發生了我生命中最棒的事！

B: What was it?
是什麼？

A: I met Adele in the airport, and she even **shook hands with** me!
我在機場遇到愛黛兒，她甚至和我握手！

B: You are so lucky!
你真幸運！

相關用語 • handshake 握手　　進階補充 • clasp hands with 握手

217 Any great news to **share with** me?

有好消息與我分享嗎？

share with為「分享、分擔」之意，後面接人。share當動詞時，是指「以共同方式分擔工作、利害、甘苦」的意思。share也可當名詞，有「部分、分攤、股份、市場佔有率」等意思。

A: You seem to be very excited. Any great news to share with me?
你好像很興奮，有好消息要跟我分享嗎？

B: Yes. Do you remember the scholarship I told you about?
沒錯。你記得我跟你提過的獎學金嗎？

A: The one that offers full-funding?
全額的那個嗎？

B: Yes, that one - I got it!
沒錯，就是那個。我拿到了！

相關用語 → **divide with** 分享　　進階補充 → **whack up** 分享

218 **So far** so good.

目前為止一切順利。

so far為「到目前為止」之意，為副詞片語，通常放在句首或句尾來修飾全句，由於「到目前為止」表示「從過去到現在的一段期間」，所以有so far通常與完成式連用。由so所組成的片語有：so that「如此…以致於」；and so on = and so forth「諸如此類」；ever so「非常(口語用法)」；so long「再見(口語用法)」。

A: How are your wedding preparations going?
你的婚禮籌備得如何了？

B: So far so good.
到目前為止一切順利。

A: Good to hear that. If you need any help, just let me know.
真是個好消息。如果需要幫忙，儘管告訴我。

B: Thank you so much.
真的很謝謝你。

相關用語 → **up to now** 到目前為止　　進階補充 → **by far** 顯然

219

We will all **stand by** you.

我們都會幫助你。

stand by為「站在一邊、幫助、待命」之意，有support的意味。若stand by合在一起寫，變成standby，則是名詞和形容詞，名詞的意思是「可信賴的人(物)、待命信號、替身」；形容詞的意思是「備用的、等退票的」。若將stand和by順序調換合成一字，再加上er，成為bystander，則為「旁觀者」之意。

MP3
219

A: Congratulations about being elected as the chairperson of the Graduation Committee.
恭喜你被選為畢聯會的主席。

B: Thank you, but I am not sure if I can do a good job.
謝謝你，但是我不確定能不能做好。

A: Don't worry. You've got us! We will all **stand by** you.
別擔心。你有我們啊！我們會幫助你的。

B: You are definitely my best friends.
你們真是我最好的朋友。

> 相關用語 • **stand for** 支持　　進階補充 • **back up** 支援

220

I can show you how to do it **step by step**.

我可以一步步教你如何操作。

step by step為「逐漸地、一步一步地」之意，是一則副詞片語，通常放在句尾來修飾全句。此片語也可以寫成step-by-step，不過詞性就變成形容詞「按部就班的」。

MP3
220

A: I really don't understand.
我真的不懂。

B: Don't worry. I can show you how to do it **step by step**.
別擔心，我可以一步步教你如何操作。

A: That's so nice of you. Computers always give me a headache.
你人真好。電腦是我的罩門。

B: It's my pleasure.
這是我的榮幸。

> 相關用語 • **stage by stage** 逐步地　　進階補充 • **step up** 增加

221

I would like to talk over my dissertation proposal with you. 我想和您討論我的論文計劃。

talk over為「商討、討論」之意。用法：S + talk over + 事情。由talk所衍生的詞彙有：talkative「愛說話的」；talker「說話的人」；talkie「有聲電影」；talking machine「留聲機」。相關片語：talk about「談論」；talk around「說服」；talk back「反駁」；talk out「說出」。

MP3
221

A: Sir, do you have a minute?
先生，您有空嗎？

B: Yes. What is it?
有。什麼事？

A: I would like to **talk over** my dissertation proposal with you.
我想和您討論我的論文計劃。

B: Sure. Come in and take a seat.
當然好。進來坐下吧。

相關用語 ∘ confer with 商談   進階補充 ∘ talk about 談論

222

Class, let's take a break for ten minutes.
同學們，我們休息十分鐘。

take a break為「休息一下」之意。break當名詞時有「暫停、休息」的意思，也可當動詞，有「毀壞、掙脫、違反、超過」等意思，為多義單字。與break有關的片語有：break a leg「祝成功」；break down「故障」；break into「闖入」；break jail「越獄」。

MP3
222

A: Class, let's **take a break** for ten minutes.
同學們，我們休息十分鐘。

B: Can I go to the playground?
我可以去操場嗎？

A: No, you have to finish your in-class worksheet first.
不行，你得先完成課堂練習題。

B: OK.
好吧。

相關用語 ∘ take a rest 休息   進階補充 ∘ take one's ease 休息

223

Do you mind me **taking a look at** the file?

你介意我看看檔案嗎?

take a look at為「看一看」之意。用法:S + take a look at + 東西,受詞放在at的後面。take可以用have或give來代替,在look之前可加上形容詞。look在此處當名詞用。take a...的句法非常常見,例如:take a bath「洗澡」;take a fancy to「愛上」;take a rap「受到打擊」等等。

A: I would like to know about your mortgage rates.
我想要瞭解房貸利率。

B: Sorry, it's my first day at work. Do you mind me taking a look at the file?
不好意思,我今天第一天上班。你介意我看一下檔案嗎?

A: Not at all.
不介意。

B: Thank you for your understanding.
謝謝您的體諒。

相關用語 **look at** 看　　進階補充 **glance over** 簡略閱讀

224

If it's OK with you, I would like to **take a nap**.

若你不介意,我想小睡片刻。

take a nap為「打盹、小睡」之意。與睡眠相關的用詞很多,但意義不盡相同,使用時必須加以區分。nap是指白天時小睡片刻、稍作休息;doze多用於口語中,指輕微的小睡或打瞌睡的狀態;sleep是指一般晚上的睡眠、長時間的休息;slumber是指安詳、長時間的熟睡,多用於文體中。

A: It will be a long journey. What are you going to do while we are on the train?
這會是個長途旅行。我們坐火車的時候,你要做什麼?

B: Read a book, maybe. What about you?
也許看書吧。那你呢?

A: If it's OK with you, I would like to take a nap.
如果你不介意,我想睡一下。

B: Of course. Go ahead.
當然不介意。睡吧。

相關用語 **doze off** 打瞌睡　　進階補充 **nod off** 打盹

225

I can't be sure until I take apart the heater.

拆開暖器後我才能確定。

take apart為「拆卸、拆開」之意。apart是副詞，意為「分開、拆散」。take若是和名詞連接使用，結合後的take是在強調動作，意思上沒有特定的翻譯，其意義是根據後面名詞的意思而來。例如take care「保重、小心」；take a shower「淋浴」。

A: What is the problem exactly?
問題到底出在哪？

B: I can't be sure until I take apart the heater.
在我把暖器拆開後才能確定。

A: How long will it take?
那要花多久時間？

B: About two hours, and you'll be charged fifty dollars for the work.
大約兩小時，要跟您收修理費五十元美金。

相關用語 • dismantle 拆卸   進階補充 • tear down 拆下

226

Frank took away the train that she was playing with.

法蘭克拿走了她正在玩的火車。

take away為「拿走」之意，受詞可以放在take away之後或take跟away之間。take away和put away的差別在於，take away是單純的「拿走」，put away則有「收走」的意思。

A: Why is Jamie crying?
為什麼潔米在哭？

B: Her brother, Frank, took away the train she was playing with.
她哥哥法蘭克把她正在玩的火車拿走了。

A: Why didn't you stop Frank?
那你為什麼不阻止法蘭克？

B: She is the one who started the problem. The train is actually Frank's.
她才是始作俑者，那其實是法蘭克的火車。

相關用語 • take back 拿回   進階補充 • take away from 從…拿走

227

Thank you for taking care of Puffy for me.

謝謝你幫我照顧帕妃。

take care of為「照顧」之意。care前可加形容詞,表示照顧的情況或程度。這個片語還有表示「當心、注意、小心」的意思。take care of後面的受詞如果接人或有生命的生物,表示主詞所指稱的對象,保護照顧後面所述及的人或生物避免受到傷害;如果受詞接問題、任務或情況時,則表示主詞所指稱的對象會設法處理它的意思。

MP3
227

A: Thank you for taking care of Puffy for me.
謝謝你幫我照顧帕妃。

B: You're welcome. We had a great time together.
不客氣。我們相處得很愉快。

A: I am glad that she didn't make a lot of trouble.
我很高興她沒給你造成太多麻煩。

B: Not at all. I do like her a lot.
一點也不。我真的很喜歡她。

相關用語 ► **look after** 照顧　　　進階補充 ► **see after** 照顧

228

Don't be too nervous. Take it easy.

別太緊張,放輕鬆。

take it easy為「別著急、放輕鬆」之意,是口語中常用的片語,多用於安慰或鼓勵的情境。由easy所衍生的詞彙有:easygoing「隨和的」;easy listening「輕鬆的音樂」;easy money「不義之財」;easy chair「安樂椅」。

MP3
228

A: Remember to stop at the stop sign.
記得在停止號誌前停下來。

B: OK.
好。

A: Don't be too nervous. Take it easy.
別太緊張。放輕鬆。

B: OK. I'll try to chill out while I'm driving.
好。我會盡力在開車時保持冷靜。

相關用語 ► **lighten up** 放輕鬆　　　進階補充 ► **chill out** 冷靜

229

We are about to take off in fifteen minutes.

我們將於十五分鐘內起飛。

take off為「起飛、休假」之意。在當作「起飛」解釋時，為不及物動詞片語。除了上述的意思之外，take off還有「脫下、帶走、模仿、減除、飲盡」等等意思。若將take off兩字連在一起，成為takeoff，則變成名詞，意為「起飛、出發點」。

A: We are about to take off in fifteen minutes.
我們將於十五分鐘內起飛。

B: OK. I'll make sure everything is set in the cabin.
好。我會確認機艙內一切就緒。

A: Thank you. Can you get me a cup of coffee, too?
謝謝你。可以也給我一杯咖啡嗎？

B: Absolutely. It's my pleasure.
當然。我很樂意。

相關用語 land 降落　　　進階補充 about to 即將

230

I can take on responsibilities and make my own decisions. 我可以承擔責任、自己做決定。

take on為「穿上、承擔、雇用」之意，受詞若是代名詞，就要放在on之前；若是接名詞，則放在on之前之後都可以。相關片語：take on oneself「承擔」；take oneself off「走開、離開」。

A: Put on your coat before you leave.
離開前先穿上外套。

B: Mom, I am already thirty-two years old. I can take on responsibilities and make my own decisions.
媽，我已經三十二歲了。我可以承擔責任、自己做決定。

A: Since you will always be my baby, I can't stop caring about you.
因為你永遠都是我的孩子，我沒辦法停止關心你。

B: OK.
好吧。

相關用語 shoulder 承擔　　　進階補充 take upon oneself 承擔

231

ABC.com is going to take over our company.

愛必喜網路將接管我們公司。

take over為「接管」之意，是及物動詞片語，受詞若是代名詞，就放在
over之前，若為名詞，則放在over之後。若將take over寫在一起，成為
takeover，則變成名詞，意為「接管」。

**A: Rumor has it that ABC.com is going to take over our
company.**
謠傳說愛必喜網路將接管我們公司。

**B: It can't be true! Our company has been making a profit
since last year.**
不可能！我們公司從去年以來就一直有賺錢。

A: But Mr. Liao wants to sell the company and retire.
但是廖先生想要賣掉公司退休。

B: It looks like we are going to have a new boss then.
那麼看來我們要有新老闆了。

相關用語 ► step in 介入   進階補充 ► take charge 掌管

232

It took place at the community swimming pool.

那在社區游泳池舉行。

take place為「舉行、發生」之意，只用在主動句，不用於被動句；無論作
「發生」或「舉行」的意思解，後面都不可直接加受詞，而其主詞須以事
物為主。若想用被動式來表示活動被舉行，可改用hold這個字，用法：S +
be V + held + 地點或時間副詞。

A: This is a nice photo!
這張照片真好看！

B: Thank you. It's little Jason's birthday party.
謝謝你。這是小傑森的生日派對。

A: Where did it take place?
這是在哪裡舉行的？

B: It took place at the community swimming pool.
在社區游泳池舉行。

相關用語 ► come about 發生   進階補充 ► come off 舉行

233 | Can't you **take turns** playing with it?

你們不能輪流玩嗎？

take turns為「輪流」之意。英式用法是take it in turns。turn可當名詞也可當動詞，意思非常多，在此片語表示「依次輪流時的一次機會」，所以欲表達「輪到我了」時，可用it's my turn。

MP3
233

A: Honey, can you stop fighting over the toys? It's very annoying.
親愛的，你們可以不要再搶玩具了嗎？真的很惱人。

B: But Jason took away my train again!
但是傑森又搶了我的火車！

A: I know you both love the train very much. Can't you **take turns** playing with it?
我知道你們都很喜歡那台火車。你們不能輪流玩嗎？

B: I can! It's Jason who **refuses to** share!
我可以！是傑森不想分我玩！

相關用語 **by turns** 輪流   進階補充 **refuse to** 不願…

234 | I could **tell from** the way he blinked.

我可從他眨眼的方式判定。

tell from為「分辨、區分」之意。from是介系詞，所以後面接的受詞必須是名詞。用法：S + tell + A + from + B，表示分辨A與B兩樣東西。tell from除了上述的意思之外，還有「判別、判斷」之意，此時用法中的A可以省略，直接用tell from sth.來表示「判別某事物」。

MP3
234

A: How do you know that Allen was lying?
你怎麼會知道艾倫在說謊？

B: I could **tell from** the way he blinked.
我可以從他眨眼的方式看出來。

A: Wow! Amazing!
哇！真神奇！

B: I have known him ever since we were five. I know him too well.
我從五歲起就認識他了。我太瞭解他了。

相關用語 **make out** 分辨   進階補充 **distinguish from** 辨別

235

What did you **think of** the movie?

你對這部電影有什麼看法？

think of為「認為、考慮」之意，是不及物動詞片語，受詞放在of之後。當「想到」的意思解時，也可用hit upon和occur to，但這兩者和think of的用法不同：想法 + hit upon/occur to + 人；人 + think of + 想法。

A: What did you think of the movie?
你覺得這部電影怎麼樣？

B: It's definitely the best to come out in the past six months.
絕對是近六個月來最棒的一部。

A: I couldn't agree more. Robert Downey Jr. totally pulled it off again!
我很同意。小勞勃道尼再一次完美表現！

B: Absolutely! Iron man is the best!
沒錯！鋼鐵人最棒了！

相關用語 → **come out** 出版　　進階補充 → **pull off** 成功

236

You have to **think** it **over**.

你得仔細考慮。

think over為「仔細考慮」之意，後面接的受詞若是名詞，要置於over後面；若是代名詞，則放在over的前面。over可用out代替。與think相關的片語有：think little of「不重視」；think nothing of「視為理所當然」。

A: Which car do you think I should buy?
你覺得我應該買哪一款車？

B: Buying a car is a huge decision to make. You have to think it over.
買車是很重大的決定。你得仔細考慮。

A: I did, but I really don't have a clue. Can you give me some advice?
我有啊，但是我真的毫無頭緒。你可以給我點建議嗎？

B: Sure. Let's go ahead and take a look.
當然。我們一起去瞧瞧吧。

相關用語 → **ponder over** 深思　　進階補充 → **meditate on** 深思熟慮

237 Would you please **turn away** for a while?

你可以轉過身去一會兒嗎？

turn away為「轉過去、解雇、輕視」之意，是不及物動詞片語，所以受詞不能加在turn與away的中間，要放在away的後面才行。相似片語：turn away from「對…感到厭煩」。

A: Would you please **turn away** for a while?
你可以轉過身去一會兒嗎？

B: Sure. Do you want me to leave so that you can have the room to yourself?
當然可以。你要我離開把房間讓給你嗎？

A: That would be great. Thank you.
那就太好了。謝謝你。

B: You're welcome.
不客氣。

相關用語 **turn down** 拒絕　　進階補充 **turn back** 阻止

238 Would you please **turn off** the stereo?

可以請你關掉音響嗎？

turn off為「關掉、停止」之意。若受詞為代名詞，要置於off之前；若為名詞，則置於off的前後皆可。值得注意的是，turn off和close都有「關掉」的意思，但turn off多用在關掉電器類用品上，如電視、電燈等等，而close是指「關掉其他非電器物品」的意思，如窗戶、門等。兩者的區別要分辨清楚，避免錯誤使用。

A: Would you please **turn off** the stereo? It's too noisy.
可以請你關掉音響嗎？太吵了。

B: Come on! It's Mayday! Don't you like them?
拜託！這是五月天！你不喜歡他們嗎？

A: I do, but I really need to prepare for my exam tomorrow.
我喜歡，但我真的得為明天的考試做準備。

B: Oh, I see. Sorry about that.
喔，我懂了。真抱歉。

相關用語 **turn up** 調大(聲音)　　進階補充 **turn on** 打開

239 Everything is **under control**.

一切都在控制之中。

under control為「處於控制之下」之意。under是「在…下面」的意思。反義片語：out of control「失去控制」。under和control之間也可以加入所有格，表示在何人的控制之下。由control衍生的辭彙有：control center「控制中心」；control tower「(機場)控制塔」。

A: I heard there is a strike at the factory now.
聽說工廠目前正在罷工。

B: Yes, that is true. Some workers are protesting the new working hours.
是的，沒錯。有些工人靜坐抗議新的工作時數。

A: What's the situation now?
現在的情況怎麼樣？

B: We are negotiating with the union representative and everything is **under control**.
我們正和工會代表協商，一切都在控制之中。

相關用語 · in control of 控制   進階補充 · control freak 控制狂

240 The copy machine is **under repair** now.

影印機目前維修中。

under repair為「修理中」之意。under的意思是「在…之下」，後面加上名詞，表示「在什麼狀態之中」，此片語通常放在句尾，屬副詞片語。類似句法的片語有很多，例如：under arrest「被捕的」；under suspicion「有嫌疑的」，under review「檢查中」。

A: Where is the **copy machine**?
影印機在哪裡？

B: It's **under repair** now.
目前正維修中。

A: It's too bad. I have some important documents to copy.
太糟糕了。我有些重要文件要影印。

B: You can use the one in my office.
你可以用我辦公室裡的那台。

相關用語 · maintain 維修   進階補充 · copy machine 影印機

241 **Whether your proposal will be adopted or not is still up in the air.** 你的提案能否被採納仍懸而未決。

up in the air為「懸而未決」或「在空中」之意。air當「空氣、空中」時不可數，當「氣氛、狀態、樣貌」時則可數。

A: **Whether your proposal will be adopted or not is still up in the air.**
你的提案能否被採納仍懸而未決。

B: **How come? I thought the decision was going to be reached yesterday.**
為什麼？我以為昨天就已作出決定了。

A: **It should have been, but Mr. Watson still couldn't make up his mind.**
是應該要沒錯，但華生先生還無法下定決心。

B: **That is still good news for me, right?**
這對我來說仍是個好消息，對吧？

相關用語 **reach** 達成　　進階補充 **make up one's mind** 下定決心

---

242 **Up to now, everything has been going well with the data collection.** 目前為止，資料蒐集進行得很順利。

up to now為「到目前為止」之意，是一則副詞片語，可放在句首，也可放在句尾。由於此片語通常表示「從過去到目前為止的這段時間」，發生了什麼事、或在什麼狀態，所以動詞通常必須使用完成式。

A: **How is your research project going now?**
你的研究計劃進行得如何？

B: **Up to now, everything has been going well with the data collection.**
目前為止，資料蒐集進行得很順利。

A: **Then, what is your next step?**
那你的下一步是什麼？

B: **I am going to do interviews with the subjects.**
我將要訪問受試者。

相關用語 **until now** 直到現在　　進階補充 **so far** 目前為止

243

It's **up to you**.

你自己決定。

up to you為「自己決定」之意。在英文的文法中，介系詞有時候也有動詞的用法，例如：Down oars!「把槳放下！」，較常被用在口語上。但要記得若用在完整的句子當中，由於up是介系詞，所以前面必須加上be V，如例句所示。

MP3
243

A: Do you think I should attend Maria's party?
你覺得我該去瑪麗亞的派對嗎？

B: It's **up to you**.
你自己決定吧。

A: Come on. Can you give me some advice?
拜託。你可以給我點建議嗎？

B: If I were you, I would definitely not go.
如果我是你，我絕對不會去。

相關用語 **decision** 決定　　進階補充 **settle on** 選定

244

I have been **waiting for** you for nearly two hours.

我已經等了你快兩個小時。

wait for為「等待」之意。用法：S + wait for + 人。除了wait之外，await也是「等待、等候」的意思，但兩者的用法有所不同。1. await是及物動詞，wait則一般以不及物的形式出現，與for、to等介系詞連用。2. await通常接抽象名詞，如decision、announcement等；而wait for通常接明確的人或物。3. await需接Ving，wait則必須接不定詞＋原形動詞。

MP3
244

A: You are late again!
你又遲到了！

B: Sorry. The traffic is horrific.
對不起。交通一團亂。

A: I have been **waiting for** you for nearly two hours.
我已經等了你快兩個小時。

B: Let me buy you a fancy meal to **make it up to** you.
讓我請你吃頓好料的做為補償。

相關用語 **wait on** 伺候　　進階補充 **make it up to** 對…做補償

245

I woke up at three this morning.

我今天早上三點起床。

wake up 在當作及物動詞時，是「喚醒」的意思；若當不及物動詞，則是「醒來」的意思。關於醒來有四個容易混淆的字：wake、waken、awake、awaken，它們都有「醒來」和「喚醒」的意思，但awake和awaken更側重於精神面和抽象面的「醒」，例如意識到性別歧視、喚醒責任感等等。wake則是其中最普遍與常用的字。

MP3
245

A: You keep yawning all the time. Are you all right?
你整個早上都在打哈欠，還好嗎？

B: I woke up at three this morning. I am very sleepy right now.
我今天早上三點就起床了，現在很睏。

A: Three? Why?
三點？為什麼？

B: There was an important game I had to watch.
有個我得看的重要比賽。

相關用語 • **get up 起床**   進階補充 • **stay up 熬夜**

246

Watch out! The floor is wet.

小心！地板是濕的。

watch out為「小心」之意，用來當作警告、提醒的片語，所以通常都置於句首。後方加上介系詞for，可連接需小心的事物。從watch衍生的字彙和片語包括：watch fire「營火」；watch night「除夕」；watch for「等待」；watch over「監視、留意」。

MP3
246

A: Watch out! The floor is wet.
小心！地板是濕的。

B: Thank you. I almost fell.
謝謝你。我差點跌倒。

A: Be careful.
小心點。

B: I will. Thank you.
我會的。謝謝你。

相關用語 • **look out 小心**   進階補充 • **be aware of 警覺**

247

Let me **write down** your phone number.

讓我寫下您的電話號碼。

write down為「寫下來」之意。此外，還有「以文字攻擊、在文字上聲稱或認定、降低帳簿上的價格、輕描淡寫」等意思。若在後面加上介系詞as，則表示「描寫成…」的意思。write的動詞三態為不規則變化：write、wrote、written。

A: May I speak to Mr. Chang?
我可以和張先生通話嗎？

B: He is not in the office now. Do you want to leave a message?
他現在不在辦公室。你想要留言嗎？

A: Can you ask him to call me back as soon as he's back?
可以請他一回辦公室就回電給我嗎？

B: Sure. Let me **write down** your phone number.
當然好。讓我把您的電話號碼寫下來。

相關用語 put down 寫下　　進階補充 take down 記下

248

She wants us to **yield to** all her demands.

她要我們接受她的所有要求。

yield to為「屈服、接受」之意。yield是指「受到壓力或壓迫而不支讓步」的意思。to是介系詞，所以後面要接名詞或是Ving。yield本身也是多義動詞，另有「生產、讓出、放棄、投降」等意思，也可當名詞表示「產量、利潤」等。

A: How was your meeting with Ms. Chang?
你和張小姐的會議怎麼樣了？

B: She wants us to **yield to** all her demands.
她要我們接受她的所有要求。

A: What are they?
要求是什麼？

B: She wants us to give her another 20% discount.
她要我們再給她兩成的折扣。

相關用語 knuckle under 屈服　　進階補充 succumb to 屈服於

中級片語 Part 2

中級片語，係針對欲增加使用中階英語的能力、以及有心提升日常生活英語溝通力者所設計。學完本章的中級片語，英語溝通力可達十二年級程度，即有能力使用高於基礎的中階英文聽、說、讀、寫，也能較順暢地使用日用英語與他人溝通。

How to Master Dixon Idioms and English Phrases with One Single Sentence

Basic Level

Intermediate Level

High-Intermediate Level

{Part 2}

中級片語
Intermediate Level

Dixon Idioms and English phrases

249

I am going to the movies with Allen as well as Lauren. 我要跟亞倫和蘿倫去看電影。

A as well as B為「A和B」之意。與as well as連用的動詞要與主詞A一致，而不是與主詞B一致。用法：S1 + as well as + S2 + V(與S1一致) + O。英語中有所謂「就近原則」，即動詞的單複數型是依最接近它的主詞而定，例如either...or...、neither...nor...等等。但凡有原則必有例外，並非所有片語皆適用，如本片語以及rather than和but等皆不適用。

A: What are you going to do later?
你等會兒要做什麼？

B: I am going to the movies with Allen **as well as** Lauren.
我要跟亞倫和蘿倫去看電影。

A: Can I join you?
我可以一起去嗎？

B: Of course; let's **hit the road**!
當然可以，我們出發吧！

相關用語 → **together with** 和　　進階補充 → **hit the road** 上路

250

You can't abandon yourself to TV games all the time. 你不能總是沈迷於電動。

abandon oneself to為「沉溺於」之意。abandon是動詞，原意是「因不得已而放棄、捨棄人或物」；oneself為反身代名詞，需與該句主詞一致。to為介系詞而非不定詞，因此後接名詞或動名詞(Ving)，不接原形動詞。

A: You can't **abandon yourself to** TV games **all the time**.
你不能總是沈迷於電動。

B: Come on. It's just the way I try to **get relaxed**.
拜託，這只是我試著放鬆的方式。

A: Relaxed? You've been spending 15 hours playing the stupid game.
放鬆？你已經花了十五個小時玩這個蠢遊戲了。

B: Really? I thought it was only 3 hours.
真的嗎？我以為只花了三小時。

相關用語 → **all the time** 一直　　進階補充 → **get relaxed** 放鬆

251

Every resident should abide by the residential agreement. 每位居民都應遵守住戶規約。

abide by為「遵守、忠於」之意。abide和obey都是「遵守」的意思，但abide後面要加by，obey則不用，在使用上要特別注意。本片語還有另外一個意思為「承擔後果」，意近take the responsibility of...「擔負…的責任」。

A: Did you mow your lawn last week?
你上週有修剪草坪嗎？

B: No, I was away on business. Is there anything wrong?
沒有，我出差去了。有什麼問題嗎？

A: Every resident should abide by the residential agreement and mow their lawn.
每位居民都應遵守住戶規約修剪草坪。

B: I'm sorry. I'll get it done today.
抱歉。我今天會處理好。

相關用語 • obey 遵守　　進階補充 • on business 為了公事

252

According to the state law, no one should drive without a license. 根據州法，不得無照駕駛。

according to為「根據、按照」之意。according to中的to是介系詞，所以後面不接動詞，而是接名詞或代名詞。according來自於accord這個動詞，其意為「一致、符合」；其名詞為accordance；形容詞為accordant；副詞為accordingly。

A: According to the state law, no one should drive without a license.
根據州法，不得無照駕駛。

B: I am truly sorry. I left my driver's license at home.
真的很抱歉。我把駕照忘在家裡了。

A: Show me your ID. I'll look it up on my computer.
給我你的身分證。我用電腦查查看。

B: Here you are.
在這裡。

相關用語 • based on 根據　　進階補充 • look up 查詢

253

I need you to acquaint her with the company rules.

我需要你協助她熟悉公司規定。

acquaint with為「了解、熟悉」之意，有兩種用法。用法1：acquaint + 人 + with + 事，意指使某人熟悉某事。用法2為將acquaint轉為形容詞 acquainted「熟悉的」：S + be acquainted with + 人 / 事，意指主詞對 於…很熟悉。

A: Do you see the tall girl over there?
你有看到那邊那位高高的女生嗎？

B: Yes.
有。

A: That's Karen. I need you to **acquaint** her **with** the company rules.
那是凱倫。我要你跟她說明公司規定。

B: No problem.
沒問題。

相關用語 → **enlighten** 教導 　　進階補充 → **no problem** 沒問題

254

He's become addicted to video games.

他開始變得沉迷於電動。

addict to為「沉溺於某種嗜好」之意。用法：S + be addicted to + (代)名 詞 / Ving。to是介系詞，不是不定詞，所以後面不可以加原形動詞，要接 Ving或名詞。本片語通常指「沉溺於不良習慣或嗜好」。

A: I haven't seen Jack for a long time. What's he been doing?
好久沒看到傑克了。他在忙什麼啊？

B: I haven't seen him for a week, either.
我也一星期沒看到他了。

A: How come? Aren't you living together?
怎麼會？你們不是住一起嗎？

B: He's become **addicted to** video games, and he hasn't left his room for a whole week.
他開始沉迷於電動，已經整整一個星期沒離開他的房間了。

相關用語 → **indulge in** 沉迷於 　　進階補充 → **how come** 何以

255

Have you **adjusted to** your new environment?

你已適應新環境了嗎？

adjust to為「使自己適應於…」之意。片語中的to是介系詞，所以後面不接動詞，而接Ving或名詞。用法：S + adjust to + (代)名詞，或S + adjust oneself to + (代)名詞。adjust除了「適應」，還有「調整、校正」的意思，例如校準鐘錶時間等。

A: Time flies. You have been here for two months.
時光飛逝。你已來這裡兩個月了。

B: That's right.
沒錯。

A: Have you **adjusted to** your new environment?
你已經適應新環境了嗎？

B: Yes, **thanks to** your help. Everything is quite good now.
是的，多虧你的幫忙，現在一切都好。

相關用語 ○ **adapt to** 適應 　　進階補充 ○ **thanks to** 幸虧、由於

256

She is **aiming at** winning the championship.

她以奪得冠軍為目標。

aim at為「瞄準、以…為目的」之意。用法：S + aim at + 事物。aim除了上述的意思之外，還可當名詞，意為「企圖、目標」。aim當「企圖」的意思解時，表示「含有某種特殊目的，因而全力以赴」。另一個意思相近的單字intention，是指「在心中思慮的計畫」。

A: Where is Katie?
凱蒂在哪裡？

B: She is out for training.
她出門訓練了。

A: She is **working hard** for the marathon next month.
她為了下個月的馬拉松賽而努力。

B: She is **aiming at** winning the championship, and she is doing all she can.
她以奪得冠軍為目標，而她也竭盡全力。

相關用語 ○ **aim for** 致力於 　　進階補充 ○ **work hard** 努力

257

Is Miami appealing to you?

你覺得邁阿密吸引人嗎？

appeal to為「吸引、訴諸」之意。這裡的to是介系詞，所以後面加名詞或代名詞。appeal是指「表示就某事提出熱切而急迫的懇求」，在法律用詞上為「上訴」之意。appeal這個字可以當動詞，也可以當名詞，當名詞時有「請求、上訴、吸引力」等含義。

MP3
257

A: Your birthday is just **around the corner**. Do you want anything?
你的生日就快到了。你想要什麼嗎？

B: How about going on a vacation together?
一起去度假好不好？

A: Sure. Is Miami **appealing to** you?
當然好。你覺得邁阿密吸引人嗎？

B: A trip to Miami? Sounds like a great idea.
邁阿密之旅？聽來是個好主意。

相關用語 · attract 吸引　　進階補充 · around the corner 即將來臨

258

Which job are you going to apply for?

你打算申請什麼工作？

apply for為「申請」之意。用法：S + apply for + 名詞。申請工作為apply for a job；申請研究所為apply for graduate schools；申請獎學金則為apply for scholarships。apply是動詞，其形容詞是applied「應用的」、applicable「合適的、應用的」；名詞是application「申請、運用」。另一個衍生字applicant是名詞，為「申請者」的意思。

MP3
258

A: Which job are you going to **apply for**?
你打算申請什麼工作？

B: I am still **thinking about** it. How about you?
我還在考慮。那你呢？

A: I'm thinking about applying for that job as an engineer.
我想申請那份工程師的工作。

B: Wow! That looks like a really good job. Good luck!
哇！那看起來是個很棒的工作。祝你好運！

相關用語 · apply to 適用於　　進階補充 · think about 考慮

259

The disagreement **arose from** a conflict of interests.

爭論由利益衝突所引起。

arise from為「由…引起」之意。用法：S1 + arise from + S2。arise的動詞三態是：arise、arose、arisen。另外，arise也可以當「起身」的意思，但以get up最為常用。arise在當「起因」的意思時，均指「某事發生，因而引起別人注意」。

MP3
259

A: Can you explain why there was a big disagreement in the meeting?
你可否解釋，為何會議中產生嚴重的爭論？

B: The disagreement **arose from** a conflict of interests.
爭論是由利益衝突所引起。

A: What do you think we can do to **come to** a settlement?
你認為我們目前可以怎麼做以達成協議？

B: We should **meet** the client **halfway**.
我們應遷就客戶。

相關用語 ◦ come to 達成　　進階補充 ◦ meet...halfway 遷就…

260

The back yard is in a mess **as a result of** the typhoon last week. 後院因上週的颱風而亂成一團。

as a result of為「由於」之意。此處result當名詞用，為「結果」的意思。result也可當動詞用，如result from是「發生、產生」的意思；result in是「導致…的結果」之意，兩者皆為常見片語。

MP3
260

A: The back yard is in a mess **as a result of** the typhoon last week.
後院因上週的颱風而亂成一團。

B: Are you going to clean it all by yourself?
你想要自己打掃嗎？

A: I think I will. It will **save** us a lot of **money**.
我想我會吧。這樣可省下不少錢。

B: But it will take a lot of time.
但你得花很多時間。

相關用語 ◦ owing to 由於　　進階補充 ◦ save money 省錢

261

You should do as follows: apply ointment and take medicine. 你應按如下處置：塗藥以及服藥。

as follows為「如下」之意，為一慣用語。as有「如同、依照」之意，而follow是指「某人或某物跟在某人或某物之後或繼之而來，但兩者之間沒有必然的因果關係」，有「跟隨、追逐、沿著…行進」的意思。這裡的follow後面一定要加s，不可省略。

A: How do I take care of my injury?
我該如何養傷？

B: You should do as follows: apply ointment and take medicine.
你應做如下處置：塗藥跟服藥。

A: How do I apply the ointment?
我該如何塗藥？

B: Put a thin layer of the ointment on the wound twice a day.
一天兩次，在患部塗抹薄薄一層藥膏。

相關用語 ── as below 如下　　進階補充 ── take medicine 服藥

262

Karen dropped by and asked after you.

凱倫前來拜訪，並問起你。

ask after為「問候、探問」之意，用來詢問人的狀況，因此after之後接人。ask指「向別人請求、請教」之意，是相當常用的字。inquire after也是用來詢問人的近況，但也指「問人以取得某些消息或資料」。

A: Karen dropped by and asked after you this afternoon.
凱倫今天下午有來，她問候你。

B: Really? I haven't seen her for a long time. How is she?
真的嗎？我好久沒見到她了。她還好嗎？

A: She just came back from her honeymoon in Hawaii. This is a souvenir she bought for us.
她剛從夏威夷度蜜月回來。這是她買給我們的紀念品。

B: It was very nice of her to get us a souvenir.
她人真好，還給我們紀念品。

相關用語 ── greet 問候　　進階補充 ── for a long time 很長一段時間

263

What's the matter? You look at a loss.

怎麼了嗎？你看起來很困惑。

at a loss為「虧本地、困惑不解」之意。loss是名詞，意為「損失、虧損」。用法：S + V/be V + at a loss + (to + V)。loss相關片語：loss adjuster「保險公司的險損估價人」；loss leader「虧本出售的商品」。

263

A: What's the matter? You look at a loss.
怎麼了嗎？你看起來很困惑。

B: I can't figure out this math problem.
我解不出這題數學。

A: Let me have a look. Maybe I can help.
讓我看一下，也許我能幫忙。

B: You're so kind. Thank you so much.
你人真好，很感謝你。

相關用語 → **confused 困惑的**　　進階補充 → **figure out 算出**

264

We can provide you with property information to see at first hand. 我們會提供第一手房產資訊給您參考。

at first hand為「直接地、第一手地」之意，是副詞片語，通常放在句尾修飾全句。反義片語：at second hand「二手地、間接地」。first和hand可以併為一個字firsthand，既可用作形容詞也可作為副詞，意思皆為「第一手的／地」；second-hand則為「二手的／地；間接的／地」。

264

A: We can provide you with property information to see at first hand.
我們會提供您第一手的房產資訊。

B: I would also like to know the details about service charges.
我也想知道關於服務費的細節。

A: We will charge you 100 dollars per month for the broker service.
我們每個月收取一百美金的仲介服務費。

B: OK.
好的。

相關用語 → **directly 直接地**　　進階補充 → **provide with 供給**

265

I know you are not really bad **at heart**.

我知道你本質上並不壞。

at heart為「本質上、內心裡」之意，是副詞片語，通常放在句尾修飾全句。相似片語：after one's own heart「完全符合己意」；at the bottom of one's heart「在某人的內心深處」；all heart「非常慷慨仁慈」；pour one's heart out「傾吐心事」。

A: David, I know you are not really bad at heart. Why did you hit John?
大衛，我知道你本質上並不壞。為什麼你要打約翰？

B: He's been very mean to my little sister. He deserved it.
他一直對我妹妹很壞。他活該。

A: But you can always turn to me for help. Violence cannot solve problems.
但是你可以來找我幫忙啊。暴力不能解決問題。

B: OK.
好。

相關用語 → **naturally 天生地**　　進階補充 → **turn to 求助於**

266

I can't believe that the man is still **at large**.

我不敢相信那名男子仍逍遙法外。

at large為「逍遙法外」之意。此外，還有「詳細地、就全體而言」的意思。相關片語：in (the) large「大規模地、自誇地」；large as life「親自地」；live large「生活奢華」。

A: I can't believe that the man is still at large.
我不敢相信那名男子仍逍遙法外。

B: Who are you talking about?
你在說誰啊？

A: I'm talking about Jacky Liao, who illegally escaped taxes.
我在說廖傑克，那個非法逃漏稅的人。

B: Don't worry. Justice will win in the end.
別擔心。正義終將得勝。

相關用語 → **on the run 在逃**　　進階補充 → **escape taxes 逃漏稅**

267

I need you to tell me at length about what happened.

我需要你詳細交代事件始末。

at length為「最後、詳細地」之意，是一則副詞片語，可放在句首、句中或句尾來修飾全句。length是名詞，其動詞是lengthen，是指「在時間上、空間上予以延長」的意思，形容詞為lengthy「冗長的」，副詞lengthily「冗長地」。此片語比同義片語at last更正式。

A: I need you to tell me at length about what happened.
我需要你詳細交代事件始末。

B: I found Mr. Robins dumping garbage into my backyard last night.
我發現羅賓斯先生昨晚把垃圾倒在我家後院。

A: That was why you went to his house at eleven at night?
所以你在晚上十一點時去他家？

B: Right, and then he punched me in my face.
沒錯，然後他就往我臉上揍。

相關用語 → **in detail** 詳細地　　進階補充 → **eventually** 最後

268

How many years have the two Koreas been at peace? 兩韓已維持多少年的和平？

at peace為「處於和平」之意，由at這個介系詞，和名詞peace所組成。peace意為「和平、寧靜」，多數情況為不可數名詞。peace的形容詞是peaceful，副詞是peacefully。

A: Did you watch the news about the Korean nuclear crisis?
你看到韓國核子危機的新聞了嗎？

B: Yes. Pyongyang and Seoul are currently in a tense situation.
有。平壤和首爾目前處於緊張情勢。

A: How many years have the two Koreas been at peace?
兩韓雙方已維持了多少年的和平？

B: Several decades, I think.
我想是數十年。

相關用語 → **at war** 交戰　　進階補充 → **nuclear crisis** 核子危機

269

I am sorry, but Kenny isn't available at present.

很抱歉，但肯尼目前沒空。

at present為「目前」之意。present為多義且多詞性之單字；當動詞時，有「贈送、呈遞、提出、表達、上演、出現、表示、指向、瞄準」等意思；當形容詞時，為「在場的、出席的、現在的、當今的、目前的」之意；當名詞時，則是「贈品、禮物、現在、目前」的意思。在本片語at present中，present為名詞用法。

MP3
269

A: May I speak to Kenny, please?
我可以跟肯尼通話嗎？

B: I am sorry, but Kenny isn't available at present.
很抱歉，但肯尼目前沒空。

A: Can you ask him to call me back? It's Jessica.
你可以請他回撥給我嗎？我是潔西卡。

B: No problem.
沒問題。

相關用語 ○ **for the time being** 眼下　　進階補充 ○ **call back** 回電

270

Your arrogance might put you at the risk of failing.

你的傲慢可能陷你於失敗的風險中。

at the risk of為「冒…的危險」之意。risk為名詞，意為「危險、風險」，亦可當動詞表示「冒險」。其他相關片語：take risks或take a risk「冒險」；on one's own risk「自負風險、自擔責任」。risk的形容詞是risky，副詞為riskily。

MP3
271

A: Go upstairs and prepare for the math exam next week.
上樓準備下週的數學科考試。

B: Don't worry. Math is easy for me. I only need two days to study.
別擔心。數學對我來說很容易，我只需要兩天的時間準備。

A: Your arrogance might put you at the risk of failing.
你的傲慢可能陷你於失敗的風險中。

B: OK, OK. I'll go upstairs and study now.
好好好。我現在就上樓念書。

相關用語 ○ **run the hazard** 冒險　　進階補充 ○ **go upstairs** 上樓

271

Jessica is at the table. I'll get her on the phone.

潔西卡正在用餐。我讓她來聽電話。

at the table為「在吃飯」之意。相關片語：sit down at table「入席」。由table所衍生出來的相關詞彙有：tablecloth「桌布」；table cover「桌罩」；table knife「餐刀」；table salt「食鹽」。

MP3
270

A: May I speak to Jessica? It's Kevin.
我可以跟潔西卡通話嗎？我是凱文。

B: She is at the table. I'll get her on the phone.
她正在用餐。我讓她來聽電話。

A: No, that's fine. Just ask her to call me back.
不用了，沒關係。就請她回電吧。

B: OK. Bye.
好的，再見。

相關用語 **at table** 用餐時　　進階補充 **that's fine** 沒關係

272

I also go to the movies at times.

我偶爾也會去看電影。

at times為「偶爾」之意，是副詞片語，無論放在句首或句尾皆可。相關片語有：against time「趕時間」；all the time「老是、始終」(美式用法)；at all times「時常、老是」；at a time「一次、同時」；at one time「曾經、一度」；at other times「平常」；at the same time「同時」。

MP3
272

A: What do you do on the weekend?
你週末都做些什麼？

B: I play basketball, and I also go to the movies at times.
我打籃球，偶爾也會去看電影。

A: That's great. Do you want to see *The Dark Knight Rises* with me this Saturday?
太棒了。這週六你想和我一起去看《黑暗騎士：黎明昇起》嗎？

B: Definitely not!
免談！

相關用語 **on occasion** 偶爾　　進階補充 **periodically** 偶爾

273

You have been pacing back and forth for an hour.

你已來回踱步一小時了。

back and forth是一則副詞片語，指「從一個地方到另一個地方不斷往返」。用法：S + V + back and forth + 時間或地方副詞。back和forth皆為副詞，前者指「向後」，後者為「向前」，因此形成「來回地」之意。

A: You have been pacing back and forth for an hour. What's wrong?
你已經來回踱步一小時了。怎麼了嗎？

B: I went for a job interview last week. They said they would call if I got the job.
我上週面試了一份工作，他們說如果我錄取了，會打電話給我。

A: Oh, I see. Don't worry. I believe they'll call.
喔，我懂了。別擔心，我相信他們會打來的。

B: I hope so, too.
我也這麼希望。

相關用語 → **to and fro** 來回地　　進階補充 → **job interview** 就業面試

274

You should be ashamed of yourself for hitting your sister. 你該為了打妹妹而感到羞愧。

be ashamed of為「羞愧的、難為情的」之意。ashamed表示「為自己或他人做錯的事、不正當的事或愚蠢的事感到羞愧」的意思，只能用來形容人，shameful則用來形容事。

A: You should be ashamed of yourself for hitting your sister.
你該為了打你的妹妹而感到羞愧。

B: But she used my laptop without my permission!
但是她沒經過我的允許，就用了我的筆記型電腦！

A: She is a child. Can't you be a nice brother and be more tolerant?
她還小。你不能當個好大哥，多容忍她一點嗎？

B: Fine.
好吧。

相關用語 → **abashed** 羞慚地　　進階補充 → **disgraceful** 可恥的

275 You **are aware of** the problem before it gets too big.

你在問題惡化前就意識到了。

be aware of為「意識到」之意，後接事物，表示意識到某事物存在。用法：S + be V + aware of + (代)名詞。aware表示「藉觀察或感覺，而對某事物有所察覺或意識」之意。

MP3
275

A: It's a good thing that you **are aware of** the problem before it gets too big.
你能在問題惡化前先意識到，真是太好了。

B: I am just trying to do my job well.
我只是盡力做好我的工作。

A: I am glad that I have you on my team.
我很高興你在我的小組裡。

B: Thank you. I am flattered.
謝謝你。過獎了。

相關用語 **notice** 注意到   進階補充 **beware of** 小心、謹防

276 He **is bound up with** his girlfriend and has no time for us. 他跟女友黏在一起，沒空理我們。

be bound up with為「與…有密切關係」之意。bound是形容詞，指「被縛住的、受束縛」的意思。同義字與片語：have something to do with、do with、concern、relate to、have relations with、be in connection with。

MP3
276

A: Where is Andrew? I thought he was coming for dinner, too.
安德魯在哪裡？我以為他也要來吃晚餐。

B: He **is bound up with** his girlfriend and has no time for us.
他跟女友黏在一起，沒空理我們。

A: That's too bad. I didn't know he **valued** love **over** friendship.
太糟了。我不知道他重色輕友。

B: Me, neither.
我也不知道。

相關用語 **in relation to** 關於   進階補充 **value over** 重視…超過

277

I am not sure if I am capable of filling the position.

我不確定能否勝任這份工作。

be capable of為「可勝任的」之意。able、capable和competent都指「有能力的」，其中able是指「具有必要能力」；capable是指「具有做普通工作的能力」；competent表示「可以勝任某種工作的足夠能力」。

A: I'd like to appoint you to be the new team leader.
我想指派你為新任小組長。

B: Thank you, Sir. I am not sure if I **am capable of** filling the position.
長官，謝謝您。我不確定能否勝任這份工作。

A: Your performance gives me great **confidence** in you. Don't worry.
你的表現讓我對你很有信心。別擔心。

B: Thank you. I'll try my best.
謝謝您。我會全力以赴。

相關用語 **be able to** 能　　進階補充 **confidence in** 有信心

278

Did you see David? He's eager for your love.

你看大衛，他渴望你的愛。

be eager for為「渴望的、急切的」之意。eager和anxious皆表「渴望的」，其差別為：eager是指「因想做某事，或想得到某物，而感到非常興奮或熱心，有時也暗示不耐煩」；anxious強調「唯恐欲望受到挫折，或希望不能實現而感到不安、焦躁」。

A: Did you see David? He's **eager for** your love.
你看大衛，他很渴望你的愛。

B: What are you talking about?
你在說什麼？

A: Can't you see? He's been trying to **flirt with** you all night.
你看不出來嗎？他一整晚都想和你調情。

B: I am really flattered.
我真是受寵若驚。

相關用語 **zealous for** 熱望的　　進階補充 **flirt with** 與…調情

279

Amanda is going to **be engaged to** Frank!

亞曼達將和法蘭克訂婚！

be engaged to為「訂婚」之意。engaged是形容詞，為「已訂婚」的意思，另外也有「(電話)佔線中、忙於、從事」的意思。相關片語：engage oneself to「與…訂婚、答應」。

MP3
279

A: Have you heard the news? Amanda is going to **be engaged to** Frank!
你聽到消息了嗎？亞曼達要和法蘭克訂婚了！

B: What surprising news!
真是驚人的消息！

A: Not to me. Frank has **had a crush on** Amanda ever since they first met.
對我來說不是。自從他們第一次見面，法蘭克就對亞曼達一見鍾情了。

B: Oh, it's so romantic.
喔，真是太浪漫了。

相關用語 ▸ engage in 忙於　　進階補充 ▸ have a crush on 迷戀

280

I think he **is equal to** running the office.

我認為他有能力管理辦公室。

be equal to為「等於、勝任」之意。片語中的to是介系詞，所以後面加名詞。用法：S + be V + equal to + (代)名詞。因為equal的意思是「平等、等於」，所以一般而言沒有比較級的變化，不過作為「更近乎平等、比較公平」的意思解時，還是可以用比較級的形式表示。equal當名詞時，是指「同輩、對手」之意。

MP3
280

A: What do you think of Kenny?
你覺得肯尼怎麼樣？

B: I think he **is equal to** running the office, but...
我認為他有能力管理辦公室，但…

A: But what?
但是怎樣？

B: I think he needs to sharpen his communication skills.
我認為他仍需磨練溝通技巧。

相關用語 ▸ qualified 勝任的　　進階補充 ▸ competent 有能力的

281

We are looking for someone familiar with computer data processing. 我們正在尋找熟悉電腦資料處理的人。

be familiar with為「熟悉、通曉」之意。with換成to時，表示「對某人來說很熟悉」，句法為S + be V + familiar to + 人。familiar和intimate都有「熟悉」的意思，其差別為：familiar是指「由於長期的交往而變得密切、隨便、不拘形式、宛如家庭成員一般」之意；intimate是指「由於了解對方的思想、情感等而產生親密的關係」。

MP3
281

A: We are looking for someone familiar with computer data processing.
我們正在找熟悉電腦資料處理的人。

B: I have two data-processing licenses.
我擁有兩張資料處理證照。

A: What are they related to?
是關於哪方面的？

B: Word and Excel.
Word和Excel。

相關用語 unfamiliar 不熟悉的　　進階補充 acquainted with 了解

282

You will be free from service charges each time you make a transfer. 您每次轉帳都可享免繳手續費。

be free from為「免於」之意。from也可代換為of，但free of較著重於免除的狀態；free from則著重於加害物或拘束物。相關片語：free and easy「無拘無束的」；free ride「占便宜」；free lunch「不勞而獲的事物」。

MP3
282

A: Do you want to sign up for our new bank service?
您想要註冊加入我們銀行的新服務嗎？

B: What is it?
那是什麼？

A: You will be free from service charges each time you make a transfer.
您每次轉帳都可享免繳手續費。

B: How can I apply for it?
我要怎麼申請？

相關用語 sign up 註冊　　進階補充 apply for 申請

283

Everything will **be free of charge** for you today!

您今天的消費金額全免！

be free of charge為「免費」之意，是形容詞片語，通常都放在句尾。這裡的charge是名詞，為「索價、索費」的意思。此片語也可以寫成free of cost。charge和cost都是費用的意思。charge可當動詞，表示「索價、指控、充電」的意思。

A: Congratulations! You are the 100th customer today!
恭喜！您是今天的第一百位客人！

B: Thank you.
謝謝你。

A: And everything will be free of charge for you today!
您今天的消費金額全免！

B: I guess it's my lucky day!
我今天真走運！

相關用語 · **on the house** 免費 　　進階補充 · **no charge** 免費

284

Come on! You are just **being jealous of** Frank.

拜託！你只是在嫉妒法蘭克。

be jealous of為「嫉妒」之意。用法：S + be V + jealous of + (代)名詞。jealous是形容詞，其副詞是jealously，名詞是jealousy。俚語have no jealous bone in one's body指「某人不會嫉妒他人」。

A: Look at Charlotte and Frank. How happy they are!
你看夏綠蒂和法蘭克。他們真幸福！

B: But I think Charlotte deserves a better guy than Frank.
但我認為夏綠蒂值得比法蘭克更好的人。

A: Come on! You are just being jealous of Frank. I know you like her, too.
拜託！你只是嫉妒法蘭克。我知道你也喜歡她。

B: Nonsense!
亂說話！

相關用語 · **envious** 忌妒的 　　進階補充 · **with jealous care** 小心地

151

285 Why **are you opposed to** Sam's promotion?

你為何反對山姆晉升？

be opposed to為「反對」之意。片語中的to是介系詞，所以後面接名詞或Ving。用法：S + be V + opposed to + (代)名詞。to也可以換成against。oppose是指「對於對方的思想、計畫等，或對於威脅和干涉到自己的事物，予以反抗或反對」的意思。

MP3
285

A: Why **are you opposed to** Sam's promotion?
你為何反對山姆晉升？

B: I believe Amanda is much more qualified.
我認為亞曼達更有資格。

A: Why do you think that?
你為何那樣認為？

B: She **works** much **harder** and has sealed several deals for us.
她比較努力工作，而且也幫我們完成了好幾筆交易。

相關用語 ● against 反對 ｜ 進階補充 ● work hard 認真工作

286 The scent **is peculiar to** that hospital area.

這股香味是那間醫院附近特有的。

be peculiar to為「特有的」之意。同義片語：be characteristic of、be proper to。用法：S + be V + peculiar to + (代)名詞，代表S(主格)是(代)名詞所特有的特質或物件，切記不可顛倒順序。peculiar是形容詞，其名詞是peculiarity；副詞是peculiarly。

MP3
286

A: You were at Grace Hospital, weren't you?
你去過恩典醫院，對吧？

B: Yes, I was! How do you know?
沒錯，我是去過！你怎麼知道？

A: Your clothes have the scent of pine trees, which **are peculiar to** that hospital area.
你的衣服有股松樹味，那是那間醫院附近特有的。

B: Wow! You are good.
哇！你真厲害。

相關用語 ● distinctive 特殊的 ｜ 進階補充 ● particular 特有的

287

I **am used to** jogging in the morning.

我習慣晨跑。

be used to為「習慣」之意。這裡的to是介系詞，所以後面一定要加Ving。這則片語的用法：S + be V + used to + Ving。used to還有另外兩種用法：第一種是S + be V + used to + V，是指「過去習慣於，但現在不會再發生」的意思，要小心區別兩者不同；第二種是S + be V + used to + V，但這種用法的主詞則是物，指「物品被用來做某種用途」的意思。

MP3
287

A: Are you **in the habit of** exercising?
你有運動的習慣嗎？

B: Yes, I am. I **am used to** jogging in the morning.
是的，我有。我習慣在早上慢跑。

A: Me, too! Maybe we can go jogging together some time.
我也是！或許我們改天可以一起跑。

B: How about this Sunday morning?
這週日早上如何？

相關用語 ◦ **get used to** 習慣　　進階補充 ◦ **in the habit of** 習慣

288

I was the one to **bear the brunt of** it.

我是首當其衝的人。

bear the brunt of為「首當其衝」之意。brunt是名詞，意思是「衝擊、撞擊」，與impact、strike同義。用法：S + bear the brunt of + (代)名詞。動詞除了bear，也可以用take代換，意思不變。

MP3
288

A: Are you all right? You look terrible.
還好吧？你看起來很糟。

B: Mr. Watson was in a bad mood. I was the one to **bear the brunt of** it.
華生先生心情不好。我是首當其衝的人。

A: Oh, poor you. Do you know why Mr. Watson was so **grumpy**?
喔，你真可憐。你知道為什麼華生先生如此暴躁嗎？

B: I **have no idea**.
我不知道。

相關用語 ◦ **grumpy** 性行乖戾的　　進階補充 ◦ **have no idea** 不理解

289

Behave yourself, or I'll have to ask your parents to come. 檢點些，否則我得請你父母親來一趟。

behave oneself為「檢點、循規蹈矩」之意。同義片語：on one's best behavior。behave是指「舉止行為合乎禮貌或規矩」的意思，英文裡還有另一個字conduct，也是指「表現、為人」的意思，但其更強調「注重在某特定場合的行為舉動，以符合社會的道德標準」。

A: John, behave yourself, or I'll have to ask your parents to come to school.
約翰，檢點些，不然我得請你父母來學校一趟。

B: Please don't. I'll behave.
拜託不要。我會守規矩的。

A: Really? So you promise there won't be any monkey business?
真的嗎？所以你發誓不會再胡鬧了？

B: No, not any more.
不會再有了。

相關用語 ► behavior 行為　　　進階補充 ► monkey business 胡鬧

290

He is **beside himself with** anger and cannot speak right now. 他很生氣，現在無法說話。

beside oneself with為「處於某種激動情緒」之意。這裡的beside要小心不要寫成besides，因為besides是副詞，是「此外」的意思；beside則是介系詞，是「在旁邊、無關」的意思。

A: What's wrong with Jack?
傑克怎麼了？

B: He is beside himself with anger and cannot speak right now.
他很生氣，現在沒辦法說話。

A: What happened?
發生什麼事了？

B: Pete went out with his girlfriend last night.
彼特昨晚和他女友出去了。

相關用語 ► beside the point 離題　　　進階補充 ► right now 現在

291

He is in a very bad mood and will **blow up** over every little thing. 他心情很差，任何小事都能惹他發飆。

blow up的正式用法，用在「爆炸」的情形上；而非正式的用法，則為「痛斥某人」的意思。相關片語：blow out「取消、中止」。blow的動詞三態是blow、blew、blown。

A: Take my advice. Don't **knock on** Mr. Jackson's door.
聽我的，別敲傑克森先生的門。

B: Why is that?
為什麼？

A: He is in a very bad mood and will **blow up** over every little thing.
他心情很差，任何小事都能惹他發飆。

B: That's too bad. Thank you for telling me.
太糟糕了。謝謝你跟我說。

相關用語 → **blow away** 震驚　　進階補充 → **knock on** 敲打

292

The new president can **bring about** good changes.
新任總裁能帶來好的改變。

bring about為「引起」之意。bring一般指「將某人或某物攜帶到說話者所在的某地」，但在這裡是指「導致、引起」。用法：S + bring about + 受詞。因為bring是及物動詞，所以受詞可以放在bring跟about之間。

A: Have you heard the news? Mr. Kennedy is **stepping down** as president.
你聽到消息了嗎？甘迺迪先生要卸下總裁職位。

B: Really? Who will be the next president?
真的嗎？誰會是下一任總裁？

A: I don't know yet. I just hope the new one can **bring about** some good changes.
還不知道。我只希望新任總裁能帶來好的改變。

B: Me, too.
我也是。

相關用語 → **give rise to** 引起　　進階補充 → **step down** 辭職

293

Maggie and I ran into Karen by chance yesterday!

瑪姬和我昨天巧遇凱倫！

by chance為「偶然地、意外地」之意。opportunity和chance都是指「機會」，但兩者略有差異：opportunity是指「可以行動，以達到其目的或希望的機會」，而chance則主要是指「偶然」出現的好機會；另有一個alternative是指「另外的選擇、替代方案」之意。

MP3
293

A: Maggie and I ran into Karen by chance yesterday!
瑪姬和我昨天巧遇凱倫！

B: Really? How is she?
真的嗎？她好嗎？

A: She's going to get married next month.
她即將在下個月結婚。

B: Wow! What great news!
哇！真是個好消息！

相關用語 • **by accident 偶然地**　　進階補充 • **get married 結婚**

294

Mr. Kennedy is trying to cut our salary by degrees.

甘迺迪先生正試著逐步刪減我們的薪資。

by degrees為「逐漸地」之意。degree在此作為名詞，有「程度、等級」的意思。其他關於degree的片語有：degree of frost「冰點以下」；in a/some degree「有點兒」；in its degree「隨自己的身分」；not in the slightest degree「一點也不」。

MP3
294

A: Mr. Kennedy is trying to cut our salary by degrees.
甘迺迪先生正試著逐步刪減我們的薪資。

B: How do you know?
你怎麼知道？

A: He canceled the overtime pay last month, and now the bonus has been cut short.
上個月，他取消了加班補貼，現在又縮減紅利。

B: You're right. We have to do something.
你說的沒錯。我們必須做點什麼。

相關用語 • **little by little 逐漸地**　　進階補充 • **cut short 縮短**

295

They tried to bring in more revenue by means of adding taxes. 他們試圖藉加稅來增加歲入。

by means of為「用…方法或手段」之意，後接名詞。若接Ving，則可去掉means of，用by + Ving即可。用法：S + V + by means of + N。其他跟means有關的片語有：by any means「無論用什麼方法」；by no means「絕不」；by some means or other「想盡辦法」。

MP3
295

A: The government is trying to bring in more revenue by means of adding taxes.
政府正試著藉由加稅來增加歲入。

B: It looks like they're putting a bigger burden on our shoulders.
看來我們肩頭上的負擔又更重了。

A: We have to budget our life.
我們必須節儉度日。

B: You are right.
你說的沒錯。

相關用語 ▸ **bring in** 產生　　進階補充 ▸ **budget one's life** 節儉度日

296

Do you know why Mrs. Watson called off the meeting? 你知道為何華生太太取消會議嗎？

call off表「取消、宣告終止」，指「取消或打消一種既定的計畫或默契」之意。用法：S + call off + 受詞。若受詞為代名詞，可放在off前面；若為名詞則放在off之後。此片語還有另一個意思：把人或動物「喊走」。

MP3
296

A: Do you know why Mrs. Watson called off the meeting?
你知道為何華生太太取消會議嗎？

B: Her son was sick and she had to take him to see the doctor.
她兒子生病了，她得帶他去看醫生。

A: That's too bad.
真糟糕。

B: For her son, but not for us.
對她兒子是，對我們可不是。

相關用語 ▸ **cancel** 取消　　進階補充 ▸ **call on** 號召

297

The teacher just called the roll.

老師剛點過名。

call the roll為「點名」之意，roll在這裡是指「名單、名冊」。muster也有點名單的意思，故可以用來取代roll。點名時經常用到的辭彙包括：present「出席的」；absent「缺席的」；on leave「請假」等。

A: You are late again! The teacher just called the roll.
你又遲到了！老師剛點過名。

B: That's too bad. What should I do now?
真糟糕。我現在應該怎麼辦？

A: Just apologize to Mrs. Chen. She is in her office now.
去跟陳老師道歉。她現在在她的辦公室。

B: OK. Wish me good luck.
好。祝我好運吧。

相關用語 ∘ roll calls 點名　　進階補充 ∘ wish sb. luck 祝…好運

298

I would like you to carry on with the project.

我希望你繼續進行該計畫。

carry on為「繼續」之意。用法：S + carry on + N/Ving。若將carry on合在一起，寫成carryon，那就變成形容詞，為「可隨身攜帶」的意思；或是名詞「可隨身攜帶的物品」。carry是常見用語，表示「以運送工具將人或物一起運送至他處」的意思。

A: Good job! I would like you to carry on with the project.
做得好！我希望你能繼續進行這個計畫。

B: Thank you, Sir. I will do everything I can.
長官，謝謝您。我會努力去做。

A: Do you need any help from Kevin? I can have him help.
你需要凱文幫忙嗎？我可以讓他幫你。

B: No, I think I will be fine.
不用了，我覺得我可以的。

相關用語 ∘ continue 繼續　　進階補充 ∘ go on 繼續

299

I still can't believe that you will actually carry out the plan. 我真不敢相信你真的完成計劃了。

carry out為「完成、實行」之意。用法：S + carry out + 事件。常與此片語相連的詞語包括promise、dream、plan等。carry當動詞時，有「搬運、支撐、傳達、攜帶、刊登、帶有」等非常多的字義，因此必須依上下文脈絡來確認字義。

MP3
299

A: I still can't believe that you will actually **carry out** the plan.
我真不敢相信你真的完成計劃了。

B: I won't be able to without Allen's help.
沒有亞倫的幫助，我沒辦法做到。

A: Allen is very enthusiastic.
亞倫很熱心。

B: Indeed he is.
的確是。

相關用語 ∘ **put through** 完成　進階補充 ∘ **follow through** 堅持完成

300

I will need your passport to check in.
我需要您的護照以登記入住。

check in為「登記」之意，也可以寫成check into。由check所衍生的詞彙有：checkbook「支票簿(美式用法，英式用法為chequebook)」；checklist「投票名冊、核對清單」；checkup「健康檢查」。

MP3
300

A: Good morning. How can I help you?
早安。我能幫您什麼呢？

B: I would like a **double room**.
我想要一間雙人房。

A: It's 200 dollars. I will need your passport to **check in**.
兩百元。我需要您的護照以登記入住。

B: Here you are.
拿去。

相關用語 ∘ **check out** 結帳離開　進階補充 ∘ **double room** 雙人房

301 | Did you **clock in** on behalf of Jerry this morning?

你今天早上是否替傑瑞打卡？

clock in為「打卡上班」之意。clock當動詞時是「記錄時間」的意思。由clock衍生出的詞彙，包括：clocker「計時員」；clockwise「順時針方向的」；counter-clockwise「逆時針方向的」。

A: Can I talk to you for a second?
我可以和你談一會嗎？

B: Yes. What is it, Mr. Watson?
好的。華生先生，什麼事？

A: Did you clock in on behalf of Jerry this morning?
你今天早上是不是替傑瑞打卡？

B: I am sorry. It won't happen again.
對不起。不會再發生了。

相關用語 ｜ clock out 打卡下班　　進階補充 ｜ on behalf of 代表

302 | How does lightning **come about**?

閃電是如何發生的？

come about為「發生」之意，也可以當「船或風改變方向」的意思，about代換成up意義不變。由come所衍生的片語非常多，包括：come through「經歷」；come down「傳下來」；come in for「遭到、得到」；come of「起因於」等。

A: Ma'am, I still don't understand.
女士，我還是不懂。

B: Fine. What is your question?
好。你的問題是什麼？

A: How does lightening come about?
閃電是如何發生的？

B: You can refer to page 53 in your textbook.
你可以參考課本的第五十三頁。

相關用語 ｜ take place 發生　　進階補充 ｜ refer to 參考

303

I came across Josh Brolin yesterday afternoon!

我昨天下午遇見喬許‧布洛林！

come across為「不期而遇」之意，是不及物動詞片語，受詞要放在across
的後面。用法：S + come across + 受詞。相關片語：a rap across the
knuckles「嚴懲」；a shot across the bow「停止的警告」。

**A: You know what? I came across Josh Brolin yesterday
afternoon!**
你知道嗎？我昨天下午遇到喬許‧布洛林了！

B: Are you serious?
你是認真的嗎？

A: Absolutely! I also took a picture with him.
當然是！我還跟他合照。

B: How lucky you are!
你真幸運！

相關用語 • bump into 無意中遇到　　進階補充 • run into 偶然遇見

304

I believe it will come off very well.

我相信會非常成功的。

come off為多義片語，有「脫離、舉行、成功」等意思，必須依上下文來
判斷意義。若在come off後加上as，表示呈現某種特定的型態或樣貌。相
似片語：Come off it.「別裝蒜了！別胡扯！」，是屬於口語的用法，並且
用於祈使句。

A: When is your painting exhibition?
你的畫展在什麼時候？

B: It's next Tuesday.
下週二。

A: I believe it will come off very well.
我相信會非常成功的。

B: Thank you.
謝謝你。

相關用語 • make one's mark 成功　　進階補充 • take place 舉行

305

Allen's new book is coming out today!

亞倫的新書今天出版！

come out為「出現、出版、傳出」之意。此片語除上述的意思外，還有「初次登台、結果是、洩露祕密、開花」等等其他意思。相似片語：come out at「出現襲擊」；come out for「表示支持」；come out top「名列前茅」。

A: Where are you going?
你要去哪裡？

B: The bookstore. Allen's new book is **coming out** today!
書局。亞倫的新書今天出版！

A: Really? Let me join you. I want to take a look at his great work, too.
真的嗎？我跟你一起去。我也想看看他的大作。

B: Sure. Let's go.
好啊。我們走吧。

相關用語 **put out** 出版　　進階補充 **publish** 出版、發行

306

Do you know who came up with the solution?

你知道是誰想出解決辦法的嗎？

come up with為「想出、趕上」之意。用法：S + come up with + 受詞。相似片語：come up「上升、萌芽、開始流行、出現」；come up against「面對、對付」；come upon「偶遇、突襲、向人要求」；come up to「到達、達到或符合」。

A: Do you know who **came up with** the solution?
你知道是誰想出解決辦法的嗎？

B: I think it was Jerry.
我想應該是傑瑞。

A: Jerry? He really did such a great job.
傑瑞？他做得真好。

B: Indeed; it is very impressive.
的確；真的很令人印象深刻。

相關用語 **figure out** 想出　　進階補充 **strike out** 想出

307

Why are you always **complaining about** Allen?

你為何總是埋怨亞倫？

complain about為「抱怨、埋怨」之意。用法：S + complain about + 事情。介系詞about也可代換為of。complain是動詞，其名詞是complaint，兩者只差一個字母t，所以在書寫時要特別小心。

MP3
307

A: Allen is very annoying!
亞倫很煩人！

B: Why are you always complaining about Allen?
你為何總是抱怨亞倫？

A: He is such a bully that he took my lunchbox again today.
他真是惡霸，今天又搶了我的午餐。

B: Why don't you report him to the teacher?
你為什麼不跟老師報告？

相關用語 → **whine about** 發牢騷　　進階補充 → **grumble about** 抱怨

308

Whoever **concerned with** the case comes to my office. 所有與本案有關者都到我辦公室來。

concern with為「影響、關連」之意。用法：S + concern with + (代)名詞。比較一下都具有「關心」之意的care和concern兩個字：care是指「憂慮、疑懼、操心、責任等足以成為心理上負擔的事物」；concern是指「對心愛的事物表示心中的不安、關懷、關切」之意。

MP3
308

A: Have whoever is concerned with the case come to my office now.
現在，把所有跟本案有關的人都叫進我的辦公室。

B: Allen is, but he is absent today.
有亞倫，但他今天不在。

A: Get him on the phone!
打電話給他！

B: Right away.
馬上辦。

相關用語 → **involve in** 牽涉　　進階補充 → **right away** 馬上

309

Jeff is never content with an A.

傑夫不會滿意只拿到A。

content with為「使滿意」之意。content可以當動詞，也可以當名詞和形容詞。當動詞時指「滿足」的意思；當名詞時是指「內容、旨意、面積、容積」的意思；當形容詞時為「滿足的、滿意的」，其後介系詞用with。

A: What's wrong with Jeff? He looks down in the mouth.
傑夫怎麼了？他看起來情緒低落。

B: He isn't satisfied with his score on the math test.
他不滿意數學考試的成績。

A: But I thought he got an A!
但我以為他拿了A！

B: He is never content with an A. He wants the very best: an A+.
他不會滿意只拿A的。他想要最棒的A+。

相關用語 ● **discontent** 不滿意的　　進階補充 ● **satisfy with** 使滿意

310

My team members all contributed to the success.

我的小組成員對於成功皆有貢獻。

contribute to為「捐助、促成」之意。這裡的to是介系詞，所以後面要接名詞或Ving。用法：S + contribute to + (代)名詞。相關字彙有：endow、donate、subscribe。contribute是動詞，其名詞是contribution；形容詞contributive「貢獻的」、contributory「捐助的」。

A: Congratulations on your successful project.
恭喜你，計畫很成功。

B: Thank you; my team members all contributed to the success.
謝謝，我的小組成員對於成功皆有貢獻。

A: It is very nice of you to say so.
你這麼說真是貼心。

B: Without their support, the project could never have been completed.
沒有他們的支援，絕對無法完成計畫。

相關用語 ● **push through** 促成　　進階補充 ● **contributor** 貢獻者

311

Cool down; things will work out.

冷靜下來；事情會解決的。

cool down為「冷卻、冷靜下來」之意。cool在這裡是動詞，「冷卻」的意思，表示「不激動或狂熱，即使遭遇困苦也能保持冷靜」。cool down當「冷卻」的意思解時，down也可以用off來代替。有句美國諺語是：Keep your breath to cool your porridge.「不要多管閒事。」(原字面意思是：「省下你的氣來吹涼麥片粥吧！」)，就是用cool來當動詞。

MP3
311

A: Cool down, Frank! Things will work out.
冷靜下來，法蘭克！事情會解決的。

B: Are you sure? Will Ella give a nod to my proposal?
你確定嗎？艾拉會同意我的提案嗎？

A: I believe so. She likes you so much.
我相信是這樣。她非常喜歡你。

B: Thank you so much.
真的很謝謝你。

相關用語 ◦ work out 解決　　進階補充 ◦ give a nod to 同意

312

Who can best **cope with** the strike?

誰能把罷工處理得最好？

cope with為「處理」之意。用法：S + cope with + (代)名詞。cope with同時也有「競爭、對付」的意思。cope還有另一種意思為「斗篷、遮蓋物」，當名詞用；或是「加蓋、覆蓋」，當動詞用。

MP3
312

A: Who can best cope with the strike?
誰能把這次的罷工處理得最好？

B: I believe we can trust Allen to do the best job.
我相信亞倫最適合。

A: Why is that?
為什麼？

B: He has a great relationship with John, the union leader.
他和工會領袖約翰關係很好。

相關用語 ◦ handle 處理　　進階補充 ◦ deal with 處理

313

Don't worry. You can always **count on** me.

別擔心。你永遠能倚靠我。

count on是指依賴他人的幫助，為不及物動詞片語，受詞放在on之後。count為一多義字，有「計算、認為、總計」等意思，可當動詞和名詞。相關用詞：countdown「倒數」；countless「無數的」。

A: Don't worry. You can always **count on** me.
別擔心。你永遠能倚靠我。

B: Thank you. You are the best sister ever!
謝謝你。你是我最棒的姐姐！

A: It's what big sisters are **supposed to** do - help their little brothers.
這是姐姐該做的：幫助弟弟。

B: Then, can you lend me 50 more dollars?
那你可以再借我五十美金嗎？

相關用語 **rely on 依賴**　　進階補充 **supposed to 應該**

314

Didn't you **cover up** for your brother when he broke the vase? 你沒有在哥哥打破花瓶時，替他掩飾嗎？

cover up為「掩飾」之意。相關片語：cover up for + 人「替某人掩飾」。用法：S + cover up + 受詞。由cover衍生的詞彙：coveralls「連身的長袖工作服」；cover charge「(餐館、夜總會等特定場所，除飲食之外加收的)服務費、娛樂費」；cover girl「封面女郎」；coverlet「床罩」；cover story「封面故事」。

A: David, **come over** here now.
大衛，過來這裡。

B: Why are you **in such a hurry**, Mom?
媽，為什麼這麼急？

A: Didn't you **cover up** for your brother when he broke the vase?
你有沒有在你哥哥打破花瓶時替他掩飾？

B: I am sorry, but he threatened to hit me.
對不起，但他威脅要打我。

相關用語 **come over 過來**　　進階補充 **in a hurry 匆忙地**

315

Do you think we should cross out Allen from the list? 你認為我們應該把亞倫從名單上刪除嗎？

cross out為「刪去」之意。片語中的out也可以用off代替。由cross所衍生的詞彙：crossbreed「雜種」；cross-channel「穿越英吉利海峽的」；cross-eye「斜視、斜眼」；cross-question「反問、盤問」；crossroad「交叉路」；crossword「縱橫填字謎」。

MP3
315

A: Do you think we should cross out Allen from the list?
你認為我們應該把亞倫從名單上刪除嗎？

B: Hmm…I don't think so.
嗯…我不這樣認為。

A: Why not?
為什麼不？

B: He is a very hardworking worker, and he deserves to be rewarded.
他是個很認真的員工，值得被獎賞。

相關用語 ‧ **score out** 劃掉 　　進階補充 ‧ **rule out** 排除

316

Why can't you let me deal with it on my own?

為什麼你不能讓我自己處理呢？

deal with為「處理、應付」之意。用法：S + deal with + 受詞。deal當動詞時，是指「分配、發(牌)、加以(打擊)、應付、交易」的意思；當名詞時，是「成交、妥協、待遇、政策、大量、發牌」的意思。

MP3
316

A: Why can't you let go and let me deal with it on my own?
為什麼你不能放手，讓我自己處理呢？

B: Honey, are you sure?
親愛的，你確定嗎？

A: Of course I am. I am already fifteen. It's time to let go.
當然。我已經十五歲了，是你該放手的時候了。

B: But you are not old enough to drive alone.
但是你的年紀還不到能自己開車。

相關用語 ‧ **manage to** 設法做到 　　進階補充 ‧ **let go** 放手

317

I derived this poem from my mother's writing.

我從母親的文章中獲得這篇詩的靈感。

derive from為「起源於、獲得」之意，受詞可加在derive和from之間。derive是指「出自某一根源而再發展」，其形容詞是derivative，名詞是derivation。另外，derive在化學用語中是指「誘導、衍生」的意思。

A: It's such a lovely poem, Tommy.
湯米，這是首很棒的詩。

B: Thank you. I derived this from my mother's writing.
謝謝您。我是從母親的文章中獲得靈感的。

A: That's so sweet.
真甜蜜。

B: I hope she will like it as much as you do.
我希望她也會像您一樣喜歡。

相關用語 → originate 源於   進階補充 → inspired by 從…獲得靈感

318

He has devoted himself to the company.

他已為公司盡心盡力。

devote oneself to為「致力於」之意。用法：S + devote + 人 + to + 事情。此處to為介系詞，後方必須加名詞或Ving。devote和dedicate都有「專心致力於…」的意思，其差別是devote是暗示「熱忱地奉獻時間、精力於單一目的」的意思；dedicate是指「莊重而神聖地奉獻」，用法更為正式，通常用於神聖的宗教儀式上。devote的形容詞是devoted；devotee是名詞，為「皈依者、獻身者」之意；devotion是名詞。

A: Did you know Mr. Watson is going to receive an award?
你知道華生先生將要領獎嗎？

B: An award? I thought he is going to retire soon.
領獎？我以為他快退休了。

A: He has devoted himself to the company. Don't you think he deserves it?
他已為公司努力付出，你不覺得他值得獲獎嗎？

B: I couldn't agree more.
我很同意。

相關用語 → dedicate to 奉獻   進階補充 → devote to 致力於

319 Is he **digging in** his piles of books again?

他又埋首於書堆中嗎？

dig in為「苦讀、埋起來」之意，是口語用法。一個句子中如果有 "someone is digging in..."時，是指「某人很認真地進行某事」。相似片語：dig oneself in「挖壕溝以藏身」。dig的動詞三態：dig、dug、dug。

A: Where is Allen?
亞倫在哪裡？

B: Where else would he be?
他還會在哪裡？

A: Is he digging in his piles of books again? He really should take a break.
他又在書堆裡苦讀嗎？他實在應該好好休息。

B: Not before he gets admitted to NTU.
在他考上台大以前是不會的。

相關用語 **dig into 致力於** 進階補充 **take a break 休息**

320 I **dug up** a box in the garden.

我在花園裡挖到一個盒子。

dig up為「開闢、發掘、發現」之意。用法：S + dig up + (代)名詞。 dig up在非正式用法上有「雇用、使用」的意思。相關片語：dig up the hatchet「開啟戰端」，hatchet是斧頭之意；若要表示休戰，可用bury the hatchet。

A: Mom, come here and take a look!
媽，過來看一下！

B: What is it, sweetheart?
什麼事，親愛的？

A: I dug up a box in the garden. Maybe it's from ancient times.
我在花園裡挖到一個盒子，也許是古時候的。

B: No it's not. It's just the pin money I have saved over the years.
不，不是的。那只是我這些年來存的私房錢。

相關用語 **dig out 發現、找出** 進階補充 **pin money 私房錢**

321

Where can I **dispose of** these used towels?

我要如何處理這些用過的毛巾？

dispose of為「解決、丟棄」之意。用法：S + dispose of + N/Ving。
dispose + 受詞 + to + V，是「想要、傾向」的意思。dispose of若加
sb.(人)或生物時，在非正式用法中有「殺害」的意思。

A: Where can I dispose of these used towels?
我要如何處理這些用過的毛巾？

B: Are those from the lab?
那些是實驗室的毛巾嗎？

A: Yes.
是的。

B: Then they must be thrown into the green tin.
那得丟進綠色桶子裡。

相關用語 **get rid of 處理掉**　　進階補充 **throw into 丟進**

322

Frank, did you **doze off** in class again?

法蘭克，你上課時又打瞌睡了嗎？

doze off為「打瞌睡」之意。doze的意思是「假寐」，尤其是指在白天打
瞌睡之意。用以表示打瞌睡的說法還包括：drop off、drowse、catnap、
nod等等。相關片語doze away「在瞌睡中度過」。

A: Frank, did you doze off in class again?
法蘭克，你是不是又在上課時打瞌睡？

B: No, I didn't.
沒有，我沒有。

A: Then can you explain to the class what a euphemism is?
那你可以向班上同學們解釋什麼是委婉語嗎？

B: I am sorry. I think I missed that part.
對不起。我沒有聽到那個部分。

相關用語 **fall asleep 睡著**　　進階補充 **stay awake 保持清醒**

323

I sat on the porch with grandma as evening drew on.

當夜幕降臨，我與奶奶一同坐在長廊上。

draw on為「臨近、穿上、利用」之意。用法：S + draw on + (代)名詞。draw的動詞三態：draw、drew、drawn。pull和draw都有「拉」的意思，其差別為：pull是指「向自己這一邊或某一個固定方向拉」，是最普遍的用語；而draw比pull的動作，有「更平滑、更均勻的感覺」。

MP3
323

A: I'm certainly going to miss this house.
我一定會很想念這間房子的。

B: Me, too.
我也是。

A: I still remember sitting on the porch with grandmother as evening drew on.
我還記得接近傍晚時，和奶奶一起坐在長廊上。

B: It is a house full of our childhood memories.
這是間充滿兒時回憶的房子。

相關用語 ● draw in 到達   進階補充 ● full of 充滿

324

Her chances improve as the other contenders drop away. 隨著其餘參賽者棄權，她的機會增加了。

drop away為「減少、離開」之意。此外，也可當「散去、一個一個走掉」的意思。此片語是不及物動詞片語，away之後不加受詞，用法為S + drop away。此片語在當「減少」的意思解時，可代換為drop off。

MP3
324

A: Who do you think will win the election for student union president?
你覺得誰會贏得學生會長選舉？

B: I think May stands a good chance.
我覺得梅希望很大。

A: Why? Are you one of her supporters?
為什麼？你是她的支持者嗎？

B: No, I just think her chances improve as the other contenders drop away.
不，我只是認為隨著其餘參賽者棄權，她的機會就增加了。

相關用語 ● decrease 減少   進階補充 ● stand a chance 有希望

325

The Thunder have **dropped** two points **behind**.

雷霆隊已落後兩分。

drop behind為「落後」之意。用法：S + drop behind + (代)名詞，表「落在…之後」的意思。behind之後可加人或物。behind也可代換為back，同樣表示「落後」的意思，但drop back還有「掉回(原處)」的意思。

A: The Thunder have **dropped** two points **behind**.
雷霆隊已經落後兩分了。

B: Don't worry. There are still three minutes left.
別擔心，還剩三分鐘。

A: What can they do in three minutes?
他們能在三分鐘內做什麼？

B: Lots of things can happen in three minutes.
三分鐘內可能發生的事很多。

相關用語 ◦ **fall behind** 落在後面   進階補充 ◦ **keep up** 趕上

326

Do you want to **drop by** her house?

你想順道拜訪她嗎？

drop by為「順道拜訪」之意。用法：S + drop by + 地方／人。其同義片語是drop in，皆有「順便、偶然造訪，讓對方感到突然或驚喜」之意。相關片語有：drop by the wayside「脫隊休息、落後他人」。

A: Rita lives in this neighborhood.
瑞塔住在這附近。

B: Really? Do you want to **drop by**?
真的嗎？你想順道去拜訪她嗎？

A: That's a good idea. Let me give her a ring first.
好主意。先讓我打個電話給她。

B: And tell her to get some cold drinks ready for us!
跟她說幫我們準備些冷飲吧！

相關用語 ◦ **come round** 順道拜訪   進階補充 ◦ **call on** 拜訪

327

I dropped off and missed most of the movie.

我睡著了，錯過大部分的電影。

drop off當「打瞌睡」的意思時，屬於非正式用法。另外，還有「讓…下車」的意思，用法為drop sb. off，自行下車則應用get off。本片語另有「減少、下降」之意。相關片語：drop off the edge of the earth「人間蒸發」。

327

A: What do you think about the movie?
你覺得電影怎麼樣？

B: I have absolutely no idea.
我完全沒有想法。

A: Why?
為何？

B: Because I dropped off and missed most of it.
因為我睡著了，錯過大部分的電影。

相關用語 ► **doze off 打瞌睡**　　進階補充 ► **stay awake 保持清醒**

328

The check is running late due to a system malfunction.

由於系統異常，支票將會延期。

due to為「由於」之意。用法：S + V + due to + 受詞。注意此處的to為介系詞，必須加名詞或Ving。在比較重視形式的正式文章中，應避免使用due to，因為這樣的用法較口語、不正式，可以because of或on account of代替之。

328

A: I am sorry that your check is running late due to a system malfunction.
很抱歉，由於系統異常，您的支票會延誤。

B: That's fine. But can anything be done to mend this situation?
沒關係。但是否會進行任何補救措施？

A: Our technician will check and fix the system by 3 p.m.
我們的技師會在三點前進行檢查及修復。

B: Alright.
很好。

相關用語 ► **because of 因為**　　進階補充 ► **owing to 由於**

329

How did the magician **escape from** the cage?

魔術師如何從籠中逃脫？

escape from為「逃脫」之意。escape可當動詞也可當名詞，用法：S + escape from + 事情／地方。escape、evade和shun都有「逃跑」的意思，其差別為：escape是指「脫離迫切的危險或束縛」；evade是指「以巧計或詭計去躲避」；shun的意思為「對於所避開的人或物，懷有強烈的嫌惡或憎惡」。

MP3
329

A: I just can't **figure out** how the magician **escaped from** the cage.
我就是想不透那個魔術師是怎麼從籠子裡逃脫的。

B: Me, neither. It's a solid iron cage.
我也不知道。那可是個堅固的鐵籠。

A: He must have played some trick!
他一定有玩些把戲！

B: Of course. That's how he makes his show work.
當然。那可是他讓表演奏效的訣竅。

相關用語 **get away** 逃脫　　進階補充 **figure out** 理解

330

Everyone should hand in a report **except for** those with an A. 除了那些拿A的人，每個人都應繳交報告。

except for為「除了」之意。except是表示「從整體之中除去一部分」，例如：Our class went on a trip except him.「我們全班除了他都去旅行。」besides則是「從外部附加進來」，和in addition to意思相同。

MP3
330

A: Everyone should **hand in** a report **except for** those with an A.
除了拿A的那些人，每個人都得繳交報告。

B: It is not fair at all.
這一點都不公平。

A: Hardworking students deserve a break now and then.
認真的學生值得偶爾放個小假。

B: I want a nice vacation, too!
我也想有個好假期！

相關用語 **apart from** 除了　　進階補充 **hand in** 繳交

331

Maybe we can exchange our used toys for some good stuff! 或許我們可以用二手玩具換些好東西！

exchange for為「交換、兌換」之意，可用exchange with + 人代替。用法：S + exchange + 受詞A + for + 受詞B，意為將受詞A交換出去，以取得受詞B。

MP3 331

A: The flea market will be open this Sunday.
跳蚤市場本週日會開放。

B: Cool!
酷！

A: Maybe we can exchange our used toys for some good stuff!
或許我們可以用二手玩具換些好東西！

B: I hope I can find something nice.
希望我可以找到好東西。

相關用語 · **in exchange for** 交換 進階補充 · **substitute for** 代替

332

I expect you to study harder.

我期望你更用功。

expect to為「要求、期望」之意，受詞放在expect跟to之間，用法：S + expect to + V。expect、anticipate和hope都有「期望」的意思，其差別為：expect是指「對於某事的發生懷著期待」；anticipate是指「對於某事以喜悅或痛苦的心情加以期待，並且考慮對策」；hope則是指「對某事的發生懷抱希望，或是確信地加以期待」的意思。

MP3 332

A: Can I go to the baseball game with Jerry?
我可以和傑瑞去看棒球賽嗎？

B: Honey, you have an exam soon. You'd better stay home and study.
親愛的，你馬上就要考試了，最好待在家裡唸書。

A: Please! I've already studied very hard.
拜託！我已經很用功了。

B: I expect you to study harder.
我期望你更用功。

相關用語 · **await** 期待 進階補充 · **live up to expectation** 達成期望

333 Why can't you **face up to** the fact?

你為何不能面對事實？

face up to為「勇敢面對、面對事實」之意，後面所接的受詞必須是有關困難、痛苦的詞語。由face所衍生的詞彙有：face off「對峙」；faceless「匿名的、無個性的」；face to face「面對面」；face-lift「拉皮」。

MP3
333

A: Why can't you face up to the fact?
你為何不能面對事實？

B: What fact?
什麼事實？

A: The fact that you are no longer with Peggy.
你和佩姬分手的事實。

B: We are just taking a break.
我們只是暫時冷靜一下。

相關用語 · face the music 面對事實   進階補充 · no longer 不再

334 What does your snake **feed on**?

你的蛇以何為食？

feed on為「以…為食」之意，受詞可以放在feed跟on之間。此片語通常是指「給動物餵食」的意思，若要指「人以什麼為主食、以什麼維生」就要用live on，兩者的差別要弄清楚。由feed所衍生的用語如：feed back「回饋」；feed the fishes「暈船」。

MP3
334

A: Can you take care of my pet snake while I'm away on business?
我出差時，可以幫忙照顧我的寵物蛇嗎？

B: Uhm, I guess so. What does your snake feed on?
嗯…應該可以吧。你的蛇吃什麼？

A: Just feed my snake with some mice I have in a cage.
餵我的蛇吃籠子裡的老鼠就可以了。

B: Forget it. Find somebody else!
算了。你另請高明吧！

相關用語 · nourish 滋養   進階補充 · feed with 以…餵食

335

I just can't figure out why Linda didn't pass the exam. 我不懂為何琳達沒有通過考試。

figure out表「理解」，指「把一件事情自始至終研究清楚」的意思，為非正式片語，受詞若是代名詞，就必須放在figure跟out之間；若是名詞，則放在out後面。用法：S + figure out + 事情。相關片語：figure sb. as sth.「認為某人是怎樣的人」；figure on sb/sth.「計算人或物」。

MP3
335

A: I just can't figure out why Linda didn't pass the final exam.
我不懂為何琳達期末考沒有通過。

B: A little bird told me that she didn't even take the test.
有人跟我說她根本連試都沒去考。

A: Is that true?
真的嗎？

B: I don't know.
我不知道。

相關用語 → perceive 理解　　進階補充 → a little bird told me 我聽說

336

Please fill in the withdrawal slip first.

請先填寫取款條。

fill in為「填寫、代替」之意。fill是動詞，其名詞是filling，指「填充物、裝填」。fill除了「填滿」的意思外，還有「任(職)、滿足、填補(空缺)」的意思。相關片語：fill the bill「符合要求」；fill a gap「填補空隙」。

MP3
336

A: What can I do for you?
有什麼我可以幫您的？

B: I would like to withdraw fifty thousand dollars from my account.
我想從我的帳戶提領五萬元。

A: Sure. Please fill in the withdrawal slip first.
好的。請先填寫這張取款條。

B: OK.
好。

相關用語 → fill out 填寫　　進階補充 → withdrawal from 提取

337 It's a pie **filled with** blueberries - your favorite!

那是你最愛的藍莓派！

fill with為動詞片語，意思是「充滿」；若物品被充滿時，則可使用被動式
be filled with，或用be full of來表示。用法：S + fill with + 受詞。

337

A: It smells so good.
　　聞起來真香。

B: I am preparing some dessert.
　　我正在準備點心。

A: Wow! What will we have for dessert?
　　哇！我們點心吃什麼？

B: It's a pie **filled with** blueberries - your favorite!
　　吃你最愛的藍莓派！

相關用語 • **stuffed with** 填滿　　　進階補充 • **stuff up** 填塞

338 Have you ever done anything to **fit in with** your classmates? 你做過任何融入班級的行為嗎？

fit in with為「與…一致；適合」之意。用法：S + fit in with + 事情。fit當形
容詞時，和proper、appropriate都有「適合」的意思，其差別為：fit表示
「適合某種條件、目的、要求等」的意思；proper是指「當然的，或有正
當理由而本應如此」的意思；appropriate是指「非常適合於某人、某種目
的、地位、場合等」的意思，其間略有不同，使用時須多加留意。

338

A: Have you ever done anything to **fit in with** your classmates?
　　你做過任何融入班級的行為嗎？

B: Yes. I pierced my ears when I was in high school, just to make myself more like my friends.
　　有的。我高中時穿耳洞，想讓自己跟朋友一樣。

A: When did you realize you were too concerned about **peer pressure**?
　　你何時理解到當時太過專注於同儕壓力？

B: When my pierced ear got infected.
　　當我耳洞發炎時。

相關用語 • **fitter** 合適者　　　進階補充 • **peer pressure** 同儕壓力

178

339

I would like everyone to focus on the new marketing strategy. 我希望每個人專注於新的行銷策略。

focus on為「集中於」之意。用法：S + focus on + 事情。其他有關focus 的片語有：bring sth into focus「集中焦點於某事物」；in/out of focus「在 焦點上/外、清晰/不清晰」。

MP3
339

A: I would like everyone to focus on the new marketing strategy.
我希望每個人專注於新的行銷策略。

B: OK. What should we do?
好。我們該做什麼？

A: Just throw out any new ideas and suggestions.
丟出任何新的想法跟建議即可。

B: How about giving away free samples?
發送免費試用品如何？

相關用語 ● concentrate 專注　進階補充 ● give away 贈送

340

No one dares refuse her for fear of losing a job.
沒人膽敢拒絕她，以免飯碗不保。

for fear of為「以免」之意。用法：S + V + 受詞 + for fear of + N/Ving。 關於「恐懼」的字彙有以下幾種：fear是表示恐懼、懼怕最普遍的用語； dread是指「由於預知有危險、或會發生不愉快的事情而感到擔心」的意 思；fright是指「突然的驚嚇」。

MP3
340

A: No one dares refuse Ms. Chen's request for fear of losing his or her job.
沒有人膽敢拒絕陳小姐的要求，以免飯碗不保。

B: Why is that? She is not your manager.
為何？她又不是你們的經理。

A: But she is dating our manager.
但她和經理約會。

B: Oh, I see.
喔，我懂了。

相關用語 ● worry about 擔心　進階補充 ● in fear of 怕、擔心

341

Generally speaking, the money is transferred into accounts in eight hours. 一般來說，錢會在八小時內入帳。

generally speaking為「一般來說」之意，是在作文中經常使用的副詞片語，通常放在一句話或一段文章的前面。此片語也可以寫成speaking generally。和generally近義的字有usually，但usually是指「習慣上經常」的意思，而generally是指「在一般情況下、廣泛而論」的意思。

341

A: OK. This is your receipt for the transaction.
好的。這是您的交易收據。

B: Thank you. When can the recipient get the money?
謝謝你。受款方何時能收到錢？

A: Generally speaking, the money is transferred into accounts in eight hours.
一般來說，錢會在八小時內入帳。

B: OK. Thank you.
好的。謝謝你。

相關用語 → in general 一般地   進階補充 → on the whole 一般而言

342

How did you **get acquainted with** Maggie?

你怎麼認識瑪姬的？

get acquainted with為「與某人結識」之意。用法：S + get + 人 + acquainted with + 人。跟acquaint有關的片語有：make a person acquainted with sth「向某人解說某事」，切記雖然make是使役動詞，但acquainted才是「認識的、瞭解的」意思，不可誤用為acquaint。

342

A: How did you get acquainted with Maggie?
你怎麼認識瑪姬的？

B: We met at Alan's party last week, and we hit it off.
我們上週在亞倫的派對上認識，而且一拍即合。

A: She is a nice girl.
她是個很好的女孩。

B: I know. I am so glad to know her.
我知道。很高興能夠認識她。

相關用語 → acquaintance 熟人   進階補充 → hit it off 相處融洽

343

There's no way you will **get away with** it!

你不可能僥倖逃脫的！

get away with為「僥倖成功」之意，後面接的受詞可以是名詞或是代名詞。相似片語：get away是「逃開、離開、送走」的意思。在口語中，get away (with you)是「胡說、滾開」的意思。

A: There's no way you will **get away with** it!
你不可能僥倖逃脫的！

B: How can you be so sure?
你何以如此確定？

A: I heard Tommy is going to report you to Mr. Kennedy.
我聽說湯米要向甘迺迪先生舉報你。

B: Oh, no!
噢，不！

相關用語 ◦ **by chance** 意外地   進階補充 ◦ **by luck** 僥倖

344

We **get in touch with** each other all the time.

我們一直保持聯繫。

get in touch with為「保持聯絡和接觸」之意。用法：S + get in touch with + 人，為「跟人聯繫」的意思。這裡的get也可以用keep來代替。touch為「接觸、聯繫」的意思，可用contact、connection代替。反義片語：get out of touch「失去聯繫」。

A: Who was it on the phone?
你剛在跟誰講電話？

B: It was Jessica.
是潔西卡。

A: Jessica who?
哪一位潔西卡？

B: My friend back in college. We **get in touch with** each other all the time.
我大學時期的朋友。我們一直保持聯絡。

相關用語 ◦ **contact** 聯絡   進階補充 ◦ **tied up with** 密切聯繫

345

Go upstairs and study, or you'll get into trouble.

上樓念書，否則你就麻煩大了。

get into trouble為「陷入困境」之意。get into是指「自己進入或到達某種狀態」的意思，trouble則為「麻煩、困境」之意，因此此句指陷入麻煩，但不一定是指「自作自受」，也可能是因為受到牽連或拖累而惹上麻煩。反義片語：get out of trouble「擺脫麻煩」。

MP3
345

A: Go upstairs and study, or you'll get into trouble.
上樓念書，否則你就麻煩大了。

B: Can I have five more minutes, please?
可以再給我五分鐘嗎？

A: No, you have been watching TV for two hours.
不行。你已經看兩小時電視了。

B: Alright.
好吧。

相關用語 ○ troublesome 麻煩的   進階補充 ○ troubled 不安的

346

He goes wherever I go. It's impossible to get rid of him. 我去哪裡他都跟，根本擺脫不了他。

get rid of為「擺脫」之意。用法：S + get rid of + 事情 / 人。rid為動詞，本身就是「擺脫、清除」的意思，因此也可直接用rid of + 事情。相似片語：rid oneself of「使自己戒除、免除」。

MP3
346

A: Who's that kid over there?
那邊那個小孩是誰？

B: That's my little brother.
那是我弟弟。

A: Why did you bring him here? It's our prom!
你為什麼帶著他？這是我們的畢業舞會耶！

B: Because he goes wherever I go. It's impossible to get rid of him.
因為我去哪裡他都跟，根本擺脫不了他。

相關用語 ○ free from 遠離   進階補充 ○ shrug off 不理

347

Any liquid over 100 ml isn't allowed to **get through**.

超過一百毫升的液體皆不准通過。

get through為「完成、通過」之意。get through與go through「經歷、討論、舉行」的寫法相似，但意思卻大不相同，在使用上要注意。相似片語：go through fire and water「赴湯蹈火」、go through the mill「經受磨鍊」、go through the motions「做樣子」。

347

A: Open your bag, please.
請打開你的袋子。

B: OK. Is there anything wrong?
好的。有什麼問題嗎？

A: Ma'am, I am sorry. Any liquid over 100 ml isn't allowed to get through.
女士，很抱歉。超過一百毫升的液體不准通過。

B: Uh, oh. What should I do now?
噢…。我現在應該怎麼辦？

相關用語 → put through 完成　　進階補充 → pass through 通過

348

Their behavior totally **gives** it **away**.

他們的行為透露一切。

give away為「頒發、洩露」之意。因為是及物動詞片語，所以受詞可以放在give跟away之間，也可以放在give away之後。相似片語：give the whole show away「揭穿戲法、露出馬腳」；let the cat out of the bag「露出馬腳」。

348

A: I believe Frank and Sandy are having an affair.
我覺得法蘭克和珊蒂有一腿。

B: Don't gossip.
別八卦。

A: Come on! It's obvious. Their behavior totally gives it away.
拜託！很明顯。他們的行為透露一切。

B: Maybe you are right.
或許你是對的。

相關用語 → spill the beans 洩露秘密　　進階補充 → let out 洩露

349

Maria gave birth to a lovely girl last night!

瑪麗亞昨晚生了個可愛的女孩！

give birth to為「生孩子、生產」之意。用法：S + give birth to + 孩子。breed也有「繁衍、生產」的意思，但通常用於動物。與「生產」相關的詞彙有：pregnancy、conception「懷孕」；diaper「尿布」(美式用法)；napkin「尿布」(英式用法)。

A: Maria gave birth to a lovely girl last night!
瑪麗亞昨晚生了個可愛的女孩！

B: Really? That's so great!
真的嗎？太棒了！

A: It is. Do you want to visit her and the baby this afternoon?
是啊。你今天下午想去探望她和寶寶嗎？

B: Maybe later. She must be exhausted and will need a lot of rest.
或許晚一點吧。她現在一定很累，需要休息。

相關用語 **childbirth** 生產　　進階補充 **in labor** 分娩

350

Have you given in your history report yet?

你繳交歷史報告了嗎？

give in為「繳交、屈服」之意。當「屈服」的意思解時，後接to以連接受詞，即：S + give in + to + 受詞。give和present都有「贈送」的意思，其差別為：give是表示「給予他人」的最廣泛用字；present則比give正式，指「用一定的形式贈予，並暗示所給予的東西具有相當價值」。

A: Have you given in your history report yet?
你繳交歷史報告了嗎？

B: Not yet. I thought the deadline is next Tuesday.
還沒。我以為是下週二要交。

A: No, it is this Tuesday; that is, yesterday.
不，是這週二，也就是昨天。

B: Oh my God! What should I do now?
我的天啊！我現在該怎麼辦？

相關用語 **hand in** 繳交　　進階補充 **yield to** 屈服

351

He is giving himself up to the geography report **until he finishes it.** 他正埋首完成地理報告。

give oneself up to為「埋頭於」之意。相似片語：give oneself up「投降、(犯人)自首」；give oneself over to「縱情於(菸酒等)」；give oneself airs「裝腔作勢」。

MP3
351

A: Where is Larry?
賴瑞在哪裡？

B: He is giving himself up to the geography report until he finishes it.
他正埋頭完成地理報告。

A: What? I thought that one was due last Friday.
什麼？我以為那份報告上週五就要交了。

B: Miss Chen asked him to redo it by tomorrow.
陳小姐要他明天前重做。

相關用語 → immersed 專注的　　進階補充 → absorbed 全神貫注的

352

Can you give out the bread for me?

你可以幫我分麵包嗎？

give out為「分配、宣稱、用盡」之意。當「宣稱」的意思解時，其後要接名詞或名詞片語，而不接代名詞，即：S + give out + N/NP(名詞片語)。由give所衍生出來的詞彙有：give-and-take「公平交易、意見交換」、giveaway「(口語用法)放棄、有獎猜謎節目、通通有獎」、given name「名字(美式用法，等於first name)」等。

MP3
352

A: Sweetheart, can you give out the bread for me?
親愛的，你可以幫我分麵包嗎？

B: But I don't know how to do it.
但是我不知該怎麼分。

A: It's easy. Just make sure everyone has some to eat.
很簡單。只要確定每個人都吃得到一些就好。

B: OK.
好的。

相關用語 → distribute 分配　　進階補充 → hand out 分給

353

Can you **give** my **regards to** your father?

可以代我向令尊問好嗎？

give regards to為「向…問候」之意。用法：S + give + 人 + regards to + 對象。give to是指「把…獻給」的意思。regard在這裡是指「問候」的意思，因為問候別人不會只有簡單的一句，一定是有一些真誠的對答句，所以regard要加s。

A: Hi, nice to see you here.
嗨，很高興在這裡看到你。

B: Hi, Uncle Chen. Long time no see.
嗨，陳叔叔。好久不見。

A: It has been. Can you **give** my **regards to** your father?
沒錯。可以代我向令尊問好嗎？

B: No problem.
沒問題。

相關用語 **send regards to** 問候   進階補充 **ask after** 問起

354

You never **give up**, do you?

你從不放棄，對吧？

give up為「放棄」之意。up是介系詞，所以後面如果要加動詞，必須轉變成Ving。同義字與片語包括：back down、abstain from、forgo、put away、get out of、surrender、renounce。

A: You never **give up**, do you?
你不會放棄的，對吧？

B: I believe a person is responsible for his or her own success.
我相信一個人的成敗應自己負責。

A: But Linda still doesn't talk to you.
但琳達還是不跟你說話。

B: That's all right. **Patience wears out stones.**
沒關係。滴水穿石。

相關用語 **give up the ghost** 死亡

進階補充 **Patience wears out stones** 滴水穿石

355

It must be hard for you to go through all this.

經歷這一切，你一定很辛苦。

go through意為「經歷、討論、舉行」。在當「經歷」的意思解時，是指「經歷一個不愉快的經驗，或一段艱難的時光」之意。go的三態是：go、went、gone。相似片語：go through with...「完成、做完某事」。

MP3
355

A: It must be hard for you to go through all this.
你經歷這一切一定很辛苦。

B: Kind of. I am trying to handle it, though.
算是吧。然而，我正試著處理。

A: What is your secret to it?
你的祕訣是什麼？

B: Just relax and try to make myself as happy as possible.
就是放輕鬆，試著盡可能讓自己開心。

相關用語 ◦→ undergo 經歷　　進階補充 ◦→ come through 經歷

356

Which school did you graduate from?

你畢業於哪所學校？

graduate from為「畢業於…」之意。用法：S + graduate from + 地方 / 學校。graduate若當名詞，在美國是指各層級的畢業生，在英國則是專指大學畢業生。由graduate所衍生的詞彙有：graduate school「研究所」；graduation exercise「畢業典禮」(美式用法)。

MP3
356

A: Which school did you graduate from?
你畢業於哪所學校？

B: National Taiwan University.
台灣大學。

A: Hmm…you have an impressive resume. Can you start work tomorrow?
嗯…你有份令人印象深刻的履歷。你可以明天來上班嗎？

B: No problem. Thank you.
沒問題。謝謝你。

相關用語 ◦→ graduated 畢業的　　進階補充 ◦→ graduation 畢業

357

We should try to grow David out of wetting his bed.

我們應試著讓大衛戒除尿床習慣。

grow out of為「戒除、產生於」之意。此外，也有「長到穿不下」的意思。當「產生於」的意思解時，是指「構想、主意、概念或計畫等由…發展而來」的意思。用法：S + grow out of + (代)名詞。

MP3
357

A: We should try to grow David out of wetting his bed.
我們應試著讓大衛戒除尿床習慣。

B: Don't push him. He might get stressed out.
別催他。他可能會壓力過大。

A: But we have to! He is ten now, and he still wets his bed!
但我們必須這麼做！他已經十歲了，還在尿床！

B: We just have to wait for him to get over it.
我們只需要等他克服就好。

相關用語 ⟶ stressed out 緊張的　　進階補充 ⟶ get over 克服

358

Nothing. We just hang about.

沒什麼。我們只是閒晃。

hang about為「閒蕩」之意。hang about和hang round是英式用法，而美式用法是hang around。此片語也可當「圍繞、迫近」的意思解。hang的動詞三態：hang、hung、hung。記得hang當動詞「絞死」的意思時，動詞三態改為hang、hanged、hanged。

MP3
358

A: Have you been with Tom a lot these days? What are you doing together?
你這陣子常和湯姆在一起嗎？你們都一起做些什麼？

B: Nothing. We just hang about.
沒什麼。我們只是閒晃。

A: Don't you have anything meaningful to do? Like doing your homework?
你們沒有有意義的事可做嗎？像是寫作業？

B: Come on! That is so boring.
拜託！那太無聊了。

相關用語 ⟶ fool around 閒蕩　　進階補充 ⟶ do homework 寫作業

188

359

The threat of the U.S. recession hangs over Asia.

美國經濟衰退的威脅漫延至亞洲。

hang over為「威脅、延續」之意。由hang所衍生出來的詞彙有：hanger「衣架」；hangtag「商品上的說明標籤」；hangup「煩惱、難題」。

A: It seems like the threat of the U.S. recession **hangs over** Asia.
看來美國經濟衰退的威脅漫延至亞洲了。

B: To make things worse, Europe is suffering from its biggest recession ever.
更糟的是，歐洲正遭受有史以來最嚴重的經濟衰退。

A: I guess the economy won't get any better **in the short term**.
我想經濟情勢短期內不會好轉。

B: Maybe not.
也許不會。

相關用語 → **hangover** 宿醉　　進階補充 → **in the short term** 短期內

360

I happen to know that man over there!

我碰巧認識那邊那個男人！

happen to為「碰巧」之意。用法：S + happen to + V。happen、chance和occur都有「發生」的意思，其差別為：happen是表示發生事情最普遍的用語，計畫內所發生的事情跟偶然發生的事情都包括在內；chance跟happen的意思大致相同，但chance特別指原因不明事情之發生；occur屬於較為文言的用字，是指特定的事情在特定的時間內發生。

A: You know what? I **happen to** know that man over there!
你知道嗎？我碰巧認識那邊那個男人！

B: Do you mean the man with the yellow tie?
你是說那位繫黃領帶的男人嗎？

A: Yes. Is there anything wrong? You look surprised.
是的。有什麼問題嗎？你看起來很驚訝。

B: Of course I am! He is the CEO.
當然驚訝！他是執行長。

相關用語 → **by chance** 偶然地　　進階補充 → **by any chance** 也許

361

I'm wondering if the T-rex had an advantage over other species. 我在想暴龍能否擊敗其它品種。

have an advantage over為「勝過」之意。advantage是指「因處於較他人有利或優勢地位所得到的利益」，其相反詞是disadvantage，表「劣勢與缺點」。此片語也可以寫成win/gain an advantage over。

A: You know a lot about dinosaurs, don't you?
你很瞭解恐龍，對吧？

B: Kind of. I am quite interested in dinosaurs. Why?
算是。我對恐龍蠻有興趣的。怎麼了？

A: I am wondering if the T-rex **had an advantage over** any other species.
我在想暴龍能否擊敗其它品種。

B: In some cases, I'm sure. However, the Velociraptor is also a fierce one.
某些情況下我確定可以。然而，迅猛龍也是很兇猛的品種。

相關用語 ● outmatch 勝過　　進階補充 ● get the grab on 勝過

362

I want to investigate whether temperature has an effect on mood. 我想調查溫度是否會影響心情。

have an effect on為「對…有影響力」之意。用法：S + have an effect on + 事物。effect、impact、influence都是「影響」的意思。Influence和effect同時也可當動詞，後方直接加名詞，表「影響某事物」。

A: What is your research topic?
你的研究題目是什麼？

B: I want to investigate whether temperature **has an effect on** mood.
我想調查溫度是否會影響心情。

A: It sounds interesting.
聽起來很有趣。

B: Thank you, Sir.
謝謝您，老師。

相關用語 ● affect 影響　　進階補充 ● go into effect 生效

363 **You really have an eye for clothes.**

你對服裝真有眼光。

have an eye for是指「對…有鑑賞力、對事物有獨特眼光」的意思。用法：S + have an eye for + 事物。如果介系詞for改成to，意為「著眼於」；如果改成on，則變成「監視」的意思。

MP3
363

A: Which tie **goes** better **with** the blue shirt?
哪條領帶比較搭那件藍襯衫？

B: Just get the one you like.
就搭你喜歡的那條。

A: Come on. You really **have an eye for** clothes. **Help** me out!
拜託，你對服裝真的很有眼光，幫幫我吧！

B: OK. The yellow one is better.
好吧。黃色比較好看。

相關用語 → **go with** 與…相配　進階補充 → **help out** 幫助…擺脫困難

364 **A little bird told me that it has to do with** John's girlfriend. 有人說，那和約翰的女友有關。

have to do with為「與…有關」之意。在完整的句子中，have後面通常會加上something、anything、nothing這三個字。something用於肯定句；anything用於疑問句和否定句；nothing用於否定句。have nothing to do with = have little to do with，意指「與…沒關係」。

MP3
364

A: Do you know anything about John's promotion?
你知道有關約翰升遷的事嗎？

B: What do you mean by that?
你是什麼意思？

A: A little bird told me that it **has to do with** John's girlfriend.
有人說那和約翰的女朋友有關。

B: Oh, you mean that. John's girlfriend is the CEO's daughter.
喔，你說那個啊。約翰的女友是執行長的女兒。

相關用語 → **in relation to** 關於　進階補充 → **related to** 與…相關

365

Your room is in a great mess. Clean it up now!

你的房間亂七八糟的，現在就去整理！

in a mess為「亂七八糟」之意，也可當「陷於困惑」的意思解。跟mess相關的片語有：make a mess of「弄糟」。mess也可作為動詞，如mess about/around「閒蕩、多管閒事」；mess up「弄亂」。

A: Go upstairs now!
現在就上樓！

B: Why? I am watching cartoons now.
為什麼？我正在看卡通。

A: Your room is **in a great mess. Clean** it up now!
你的房間亂七八糟的，現在就去整理！

B: Can't I watch TV for ten more minutes? The show is **about to** end.
我不能再多看十分鐘嗎？節目就快要結束了。

相關用語 ∘ clean up 打掃　　進階補充 ∘ about to 即將

366

In addition, we can get some balloons.

除此之外，我們可以買些氣球。

in addition為「另外、除此之外」之意，通常放在句尾修飾動詞，如果其後要加名詞，必須使用to，即in addition to。此片語意為「除此之外」，是一種附加的概念，即「從既有的事物中再加上其他」，因而與except略有不同。例如：In addition to chocolate, I ate popcorn and chips.「除了巧克力，我還吃了爆米花和薯片。」

A: What else should we get for Linda's birthday party?
琳達的生日派對我們還要準備些什麼？

B: We will need more food and drinks. **In addition**, we can get some balloons.
我們需要更多的食物和飲料。除此之外，我們可以買些氣球。

A: Balloons? What for?
氣球？為什麼？

B: We can't even call it a party if we don't have balloons.
沒有氣球怎麼能叫派對呢？

相關用語 ∘ besides 此外　　進階補充 ∘ in addition to 除…之外(還)

367

Bring your umbrella with you in case of rain.

攜帶雨傘，以免下雨淋濕了。

in case of為「萬一、如果」之意。in case of + 名詞= if，意指「如果」。其他相似片語：in any case「無論如何」；in no case「絕不」；in that case「若是那樣的話」；get off one's case「停止批評和打擾某人」。

MP3
367

A: Bring your umbrella with you in case of rain.
攜帶雨傘，以免下雨淋濕了。

B: I don't think that is necessary. There is not even a cloud in the sky.
我認為沒那個必要。天上連朵雲都沒有。

A: You never know when it's going to pour, especially during the rainy season.
你永遠不知何時會開始下大雨，尤其是雨季期間。

B: You've got a point.
你說得有道理。

相關用語 **in the case of** 至於   進階補充 **in case** 假使

368

Who is in charge of the case?

誰負責這個案子？

in charge of為「照料、管控、負責」之意。用法：S + be V + in charge of + 人／事。charge可當名詞也可當動詞，當名詞時有「費用、責任、控告」等意思；當動詞時則有「索價、進攻、譴責」等意思。

MP3
368

A: Who is in charge of the case?
誰負責這個案子？

B: It's Andy.
安迪。

A: Get him in my office now. I want to talk to him.
叫他進來我辦公室。我要跟他說話。

B: But he is on sick leave today.
但他今天請病假。

相關用語 **responsible for** 負責   進階補充 **take charge of** 負責

369

Kobe is in danger of losing the championship for the whole team. 柯比正處於讓全隊失去冠軍的危險。

in danger of為「處於…危險中」之意。danger和hazard都有「危險」的意思，差別在danger指「可能有、但不一定迫在眉梢或不可避免的危險」；hazard指「偶然發生、或人為無法避免的事物所引發的危險」。

MP3
369

A: Come on! Not again!
拜託！不會又來了吧！

B: Calm down. It's just a game. Don't take it too serious.
冷靜下來。不過是場比賽罷了。別太認真。

A: How can I calm down? Kobe is in danger of losing the championship for the whole team.
我怎麼能冷靜？柯比正處於讓全隊失去冠軍的危險。

B: I don't think that matters to him too much. He will still make a lot of money.
我不覺得這對他來說有那麼要緊。他還是賺很多錢。

相關用語 — calm down 平靜下來　　進階補充 — make money 賺錢

370

High-tech engineers are in great demand this year.
今年，對高科技工程師的需求量很大。

in demand為「需求」之意，通常放在句尾。demand和claim都表「需求」，其差別為：demand是指「堅持要得到某種必要的事物，因為要求者有這種權力」；claim是指「要求自己有權或自認為有權可以得到」。

MP3
370

A: The news said high-tech engineers are in great demand this year.
新聞說，今年對高科技工程師的需求量很大。

B: Cool! Good news for me!
酷！對我而言是好消息！

A: What does that have anything to do with you? I thought you've already got a job.
跟你有什麼關係？我以為你已經有工作了。

B: I am thinking about job-hopping.
我正考慮跳槽。

相關用語 — in need of 需要　　進階補充 — job-hop 調換工作

371

Can you explain the package in detail again?

你能再次詳細說明本方案嗎?

in detail為「詳細地」之意,是副詞片語,通常放在句尾。detail當名詞時為「細節」的意思,當動詞時則可當「派遣、詳細敘述」的意思。

A: I am confused. Can you explain the package in detail again?
我搞不太懂。你能再次詳細說明本方案嗎?

B: Sure, but it will take a while. Do you mind coming to my office?
當然好,但會花一些時間。你介意來我辦公室嗎?

A: Sure. How about five this afternoon?
今天下午五點如何?

B: Great. I'll see you then.
好的。到時見。

相關用語 ► dwell on 詳細論述　　進階補充 ► go into details 細述

372

When the tax increase is in effect, it can help the disadvantaged. 當增稅生效後,可幫助社會弱勢。

in effect為「實際上地、生效地」之意,通常放在句中跟句尾,不放在句首。effect、consequence和result都有「結果」的意思,其差別為:effect是指「由於某種行為、行動、原因等,所直接產生的結果」,跟cause是意義相反的字;consequence是指「由於某種事產生,繼之而起的後果」之意,強調時間順序;result意指「某種行為或原因的最終結果」。

A: The government is going to increase the income tax.
政府正要增收所得稅。

B: Why are you so upset about it?
為何你如此心煩?

A: That means I will have to pay more!
那代表我要繳更多稅了!

B: When the tax increase is in effect, it can help the disadvantaged.
當增稅生效後,可幫助社會弱勢。

相關用語 ► upset about 心煩的　　進階補充 ► income tax 所得稅

373

As usual, she is in good health.

她的健康狀況如往常般良好。

in good/bad health為「健康狀況佳／差」之意。用法：S + be V + in good/bad health。健康欠佳的同義片語有：out of health、in poor health、in bad shape。由health所衍生的詞彙有：health center「健康中心」；health food「健康食品」；health insurance「健康保險」。

A: Long time no see. How is your grandmother?
好久不見。你祖母還好嗎？

B: As usual, she is in good health.
如往常般，她的健康狀況良好。

A: That's great. Send her my regards.
真好。替我向她問好。

B: Sure.
當然。

相關用語 in shape 健康良好　　進階補充 out of shape 健康不佳

374

He acts in ignorance of basic machinery operation.

他表現得好像對於基礎機械操作一無所知。

in ignorance of為「一無所知」之意。用法：S + be V + in ignorance of + (代)名詞。ignorance的形容詞為ignorant。ignorant、illiterate和uneducated都有「無知」的意思，其差別為：ignorant是指「對全盤世事、或某種特定事物沒有知識」；illiterate是指「沒有讀寫能力」；uneducated是指「沒有受過學校教育的，有時候是指沒有唸過書」。

A: Sir, I am afraid that Jeffery doesn't suit my team.
先生，恐怕傑佛瑞不適合我的小組。

B: Why is that?
為什麼？

A: He acts in ignorance of basic machinery operation.
他表現得好像對於基礎機械操作一無所知。

B: Fine. I'll transfer him to the sales department.
好。我會把他調到業務部門。

相關用語 know-nothing 一無所知者　　進階補充 transfer to 轉調

375

I like all kinds of sports, rock-climbing in particular.

我喜歡各種運動，特別是攀岩。

in particular為「特別地、尤其地」之意，可放在句中，也可放在句尾。specific跟particular均是指「挑選出來，以便比其他事物更能吸引注意」之意。specific表示要當做例子來說明，才加以引用，而particular是表示「某事物比其他事物，更具有明顯不同的性質或個性」。

A: What sports do you like?
你喜歡什麼運動？

B: All kinds of sports, rock-climbing in particular.
各種運動，尤其是攀岩。

A: Cool! Can I go with you some time?
酷！我可以找時間和你一起去嗎？

B: Sure. How about this Saturday?
當然好。這星期六如何？

相關用語 → **particularly** 特別、尤其　　進階補充 → **above all** 尤其

376

Mr. Lin is taking away our bonus in spite of the sales increase. 儘管業績提升，林先生仍要取消我們的紅利。

in spite of為「不管、無論」之意。同義片語很多，如regardless of、despite，以上和in spite of一樣，必須接名詞或Ving。而though、although、even though後方則加句子。notwithstanding加名詞/Ving和句子皆可。與spite有關的片語：in spite of oneself「不知不覺的、不由自主的」。

A: Have you heard the news?
你聽說了嗎？

B: What news?
什麼事？

A: Mr. Lin is going to take away our bonus in spite of the sales increase.
儘管業績提升，林先生還是要取消我們的紅利。

B: That's ridiculous!
太誇張了！

相關用語 → **despite** 不管　　進階補充 → **take away** 拿走

377

Don't worry; everything will be fine in the long run.

別擔心;一切終究會沒問題。

in the long run意指「經過一段時間,到後來(發現某件事情如何)」,可放在句首、句中或句尾。反義片語即是in the short run「短期而言」。這裡的run不是「跑」的意思,而是「發展、動向」之意,可用term代替。

MP3
377

A: Congratulations! When is the big day?
恭喜!大喜之日是什麼時候?

B: The wedding is scheduled for April 1. But I'm worried about our finances.
婚禮訂在四月一號,但我有點擔心我們的財務狀況。

A: Don't worry; everything will be fine in the long run.
別擔心,一切終究會沒問題的。

B: I hope so.
我也希望。

相關用語 · **ultimately** 最終　　進階補充 · **big day** 大喜之日

378

Luckily, I stopped the car in time before we crashed.

幸好,我在碰撞前及時剎住車。

in time一般是用在句中與句尾,而不用於句首,是「及時」的意思;而on time是「準時、按時」的意思,兩者的差別應分清楚。其他相似片語:in time/times of「在…的時候」;in good time「適時地」;in no time、in less than no time「立即、立刻」;in one's own good time「在某人方便的時候」;in one's own time「在某人閒暇的時候」。

MP3
378

A: I almost had a car accident this afternoon.
我今天下午差點出車禍。

B: What? Are you all right? How about the kids?
什麼?你還好吧?孩子們呢?

A: Relax. Luckily, I stopped the car in time before we crashed.
放輕鬆。幸好,我在碰撞前及時剎住車了。

B: What a close call. Just be careful next time.
真驚險。下次小心一點。

相關用語 · **timely** 及時的　　進階補充 · **close call** 千鈞一髮

379

You are **in big trouble**.

你麻煩大了。

in trouble為「起衝突、處於困境」之意，後面若要接人，必須加上with才可以。表示「與人起衝突」時，用法：S + be V + in trouble + with + 人。此片語也可以暗喻「(未婚婦女)懷孕」的意思。

MP3
379

A: You are in big trouble.
　你麻煩大了。

B: What are you talking about?
　你在說什麼？

A: I believe Dad already got your report card from Ms. Chen.
　我認為老爸已經從陳老師那裡拿到你的成績單了。

B: Oh, no.
　噢，不。

相關用語 • **plight** 困境　　進階補充 • **ask for trouble** 找麻煩

380

Believe in yourself, and all your hard work won't be **in vain**. 相信自己，你的所有努力不會白費。

in vain為「無用的」之意，可當形容詞或副詞片語。放在be V之後當作形容詞；放在一般動詞後面則是用來修飾一般動詞的副詞片語。vain是指「想法、行動、努力等未獲致好結果」的意思。其副詞是vainly、名詞是vainness。

MP3
380

A: Aren't you going to the library today?
　你今天不去圖書館嗎？

B: It's useless. No matter how hard I study, I can't get into NTU.
　沒用的。無論我再怎麼用功，都進不了台大。

A: Believe in yourself, and all your hard work won't be in vain.
　相信自己，你的努力不會白費的。

B: I hope you're right.
　我希望你是對的。

相關用語 • **without avail** 徒勞地　　進階補充 • **for nothing** 徒然

381 In view of your asthma history, you'd better start swimming. 鑑於你的氣喘病史，你最好開始游泳。

in view of為「鑑於、考慮到」之意。view是指「在視野之內看得見的景象」，同時也可當「見解、觀點」的意思。view當動詞時有「認為、考慮、觀看」等意思。相關片語：bird's eye view「鳥瞰」；come into view「看得見」。

A: In view of your asthma history, you'd better start swimming.
   鑑於你的氣喘病史，你最好開始游泳。

B: Swimming? Why?
   游泳？為什麼？

A: Swimming is good for your lungs.
   游泳對你的肺很有幫助。

B: OK.
   好。

相關用語 ● considering 考慮到　　進階補充 ● seeing that 鑑於

382 Don't interfere with my child-disciplining!
別干涉我管教孩子！

interfere with為「干涉、干預」之意。用法：S + interfere with + 事情。這裡的with也可以用in代替。interfere和meddle都有「干涉、妨礙」的意思，其差別為：interfere是指「以行動或語言加以干涉、妨礙」；meddle是指「並無權力，也未受邀請而管閒事」。

A: Don't interfere with my child-disciplining!
   別干涉我管教孩子！

B: What do you mean?
   什麼意思？

A: Just don't tell David not to worry about it when I ask him to clean up his room.
   當我叫大衛整理房間的時候，不要跟他說別擔心。

B: I am sorry. It won't happen again.
   對不起。不會再發生了。

相關用語 ● meddle in 干涉　　進階補充 ● intervene in 干涉

383

All my class **jeers at** me.

全班同學都嘲笑我。

jeer at為「嘲笑、戲弄」之意。用法：S + jeer at + 人事物。jeer是指「公然使用不雅的言詞攻擊他人，或將對方當傻瓜取笑」的意思。jeer也可當名詞，表「奚落、嘲笑的語句」。

A: Mom, can I transfer to Kevin's school?
媽，我可以轉學到凱文的學校嗎？

B: Why?
為什麼？

A: All my class jeers at me. They call me "hairy weirdo."
全班同學都嘲笑我。他們叫我「怪髮男」。

B: But, honey, Kevin is in kindergarten.
但是親愛的，凱文念的是幼稚園。

相關用語 ● **make fun of** 取笑   進階補充 ● **mock at** 嘲笑

384

You should all **keep** this formula **in mind**.

你們都該記住這個公式。

keep in mind為「記住」之意，是及物動詞片語，受詞若是代名詞，要放在keep之後；若為名詞則放在mind之後。相似片語：keep in「抑制(感情)、將(學生)留下(以示懲罰)、足不出戶」；keep in with「與…保持友好」；keep from「避免」；keep off「遠離」；keep out「阻止」。

A: Class, you should all keep this formula in mind.
同學，你們都該記住這個公式。

B: Will it be tested?
這會考嗎？

A: Yes, I believe it will be very useful on the test next week.
是的，我相信這對你們下週的考試很有幫助。

B: Yeah!
耶！

相關用語 ● **remember** 記得   進階補充 ● **bear in mind** 記住

385 **Keep up** the good work!

繼續保持好表現！

keep up在當「保持」的意思解時，為及物動詞片語，受詞若是代名詞，要放在up之前，若為名詞，則置於up之前之後都可以。當「熬夜、依然、同樣」的解釋使用時，則是不及物動詞片語。

A: I've got your report card.
我拿到你的成績單了。

B: How am I doing?
我表現得怎麼樣？

A: Excellent! Keep up the good work! I am so proud of you.
很好！繼續保持好表現！我以你為榮。

B: Does that mean I can get the latest cell phone?
這代表我可以獲得最新款的手機嗎？

相關用語 ○ remain 保持　　進階補充 ○ maintain 保持

386 You should work harder to **keep up with** the others.

你應更加認真以趕上其他人。

keep up with為「趕上」之意，是不及物動詞片語，受詞要放在with之後。此片語是指「用各種速度趕上」的意思，用法：S + keep up with + (代)名詞。此處的keep也可改用catch代換，意義不變。

A: Your teacher called today.
你的老師今天打電話來。

B: Really? What did she say?
真的嗎？她說了什麼？

A: She told me that you should work harder to keep up with the others.
她跟我說，你要更加用功，以趕上其他人。

B: But math is really all Greek to me.
但我真的搞不懂數學。

相關用語 ○ catch up with 趕上　　進階補充 ○ come up with 趕上

387

My boss **laid** him **off** this morning.

我老闆今天早上把他解雇了。

lay off在當「解雇」的意思解時,是指「由於經濟不景氣或營運不善,必須將工人解雇,非工人有過失而予以解雇」的意思,近義字有fire、expel和ax;在當「遠離某人」的意思解時,是指「某人必須停止碰觸或批評他人」的意思。

MP3
387

A: Do you remember Jack?
你還記得傑克嗎?

B: Sure. He is one of the most decent men I've ever met.
當然記得。他是我見過最得體的人之一。

A: My boss laid him off this morning.
我老闆今天早上解雇了他。

B: Oh, no. That's his loss then.
噢,不。那是他的損失。

相關用語 ► **give the sack** 解雇

進階補充 ► **kick out** 解雇

388

Do you want me to **lay out** the instruments now?

您要我現在把器具展示出來嗎?

lay out為「展示、安排」之意。若將lay跟out合在一起,變成layout,就有「安排、設計、版面設計、陳列物、宅邸、大工廠、布局」等等的意思。若在lay out之間加入人,表示「擊倒某人、嚴斥某人」;若加入的是事物,表示「散布某物、解釋事件、花錢」。

MP3
388

A: Sir, do you want me to lay out the instruments now?
先生,您要我現在把器具展示出來嗎?

B: OK. Do you know how to do it?
好啊。你知道怎麼做嗎?

A: Yes. Small to big, and from left to right.
是的。從左到右,由小到大。

B: Exactly.
沒錯。

相關用語 ► **exhibit** 展示

進階補充 ► **put on display** 陳列

389

I hope you've already **learned your lesson**.

我希望你已記取教訓。

learn one's lesson為「藉經驗獲取教訓」之意。lesson是「課程」的意思，此處引申為「教訓」。lesson也可當作動詞，有「上課」和「訓斥」兩種意義。相關片語：teach sb. a lesson「讓某人學到教訓」。

A: I hope you've already **learned your lesson**.
我希望你已記取教訓。

B: Come on. You've got to help me out.
拜託，你得幫幫我。

A: No, you really have to do your homework by yourself this time.
不，你這次真的應該自己做作業。

B: I promise I will next time.
我保證我下次會自己做。

相關用語 → **lecture** 訓斥 　　進階補充 → **read sb. a lesson** 訓斥某人

390

You can **leave a message for** him on his phone.

你可以在他的電話裡留言給他。

leave a message for為「留言給某人」之意。用法：S + leave a message for + 人。需要注意的是message「訊息」跟massage「按摩、推拿」的拼法非常相似(第二個字母一個是e，一個是a)，所以在閱讀和書寫時要特別小心。

A: Where is Jason?
傑森在哪裡？

B: He's gone out to Mr. Watson's office.
他去華生先生的辦公室了。

A: Oh, no. I have to speak to him.
喔，不。我得跟他說話。

B: You can **leave a message for** him on his phone.
你可以在他的電話裡留言給他。

相關用語 → **leave a note** 留言 　　進階補充 → **text message** 簡訊

391

He **left behind** a great legacy for the company.

他留給公司富饒的資產。

leave behind為「留下」之意。這則片語的受詞可以放在leave跟behind之間。leave的動詞三態為：leave、left、left。相關片語有：leave about「亂丟」；leave aside「不納入考慮」；leave off「停止」；leave out「省去、遺漏」；leave for「動身去…」。

A: May Mr. Johnson rest in peace.
希望強森先生能安息。

B: I believe he will.
我相信他會的。

A: He **left behind** a great legacy for the company.
他留給公司富饒的資產。

B: I couldn't agree more.
我完全同意。

> 相關用語 → **hand down** 傳下去　　進階補充 → **pass down** 傳下來

392

Mike asked me to **leave him alone** in our room.

麥克要我留他一人在我們房間。

leave sb. alone為「避免打擾某人」之意，也可用leave sb. be代替。alone是「單純的指人或物孤單或孤獨」的意思。此片語可以放在句首或句尾。另外，此片語在口語中，是指「不干涉」的意思。

A: Honey, would you go upstairs and play in your room?
親愛的，你可以上樓在自己房間裡玩嗎？

B: I can't.
我不能。

A: Why not?
為什麼不？

B: Mike asked me to **leave him alone** in our room. He is preparing for a test.
麥克要我留他一人在我們房間。他要準備考試。

> 相關用語 → **do not disturb** 勿擾　　進階補充 → **intrude upon** 打擾

393

All the class looks down on her.

全班同學都瞧不起她。

look down on為「輕視」之意。用法：S + look down on + 人。down是「向下」，因此look down有「輕視、鄙夷」的意思；反之，look up則是「向上看」，有尊敬的意思，其後的介系詞需用to接。

A: I haven't seen you playing with Tina for a long time.
　我好久沒看到你和緹娜一起玩了。

B: We are no longer friends.
　我們已經不是朋友了。

A: What happened?
　發生什麼事了？

B: She cheated on the test. All the class looks down on her now.
　她考試作弊，現在全班同學都瞧不起她。

〔相關用語〕●**despise** 鄙視 〔進階補充〕●**look down upon** 鄙視

394

He's been looking forward to his birthday.

他期待著他的生日。

look forward to為「期待」之意。切記，這裡的to是介系詞，而非不定詞，所以不能直接接動詞，要接Ving，須特別注意。用法：S + look forward to + N/Ving。forward是副詞「向前」，look forward表示「前瞻、放眼未來」。

A: Who called? You look pretty upset.
　誰打電話來？你看起來很沮喪。

B: It's my boss, Josh. He asked me to go on a business trip tomorrow.
　是我的老闆，喬許。他要我明天出差。

A: Tomorrow? But it's Andy's birthday! He's been looking forward to it.
　明天？但明天是安迪的生日！他一直很期待。

B: I know. He will be really disappointed.
　是啊。他一定會非常失望。

〔相關用語〕●**expect** 期待 〔進階補充〕●**anticipate** 期望

395

They must look up to him a lot.

他們一定很尊敬他。

look up to為「尊敬」之意。用法：S + look up to + 人。相似片語：look up「往上看、(景氣)變好、查出、探訪」；look up and down「四處尋找、上下打量」。

A: They threw a retirement party for Dr. Huang.
他們替黃博士辦了場退休派對。

B: They must look up to him a lot.
他們一定很尊敬他。

A: The faculty all love and respect him a lot.
教職員工都很愛他並且敬重他。

B: I believe they do. He is both knowledgeable and helpful.
我想他們是的。他既有學識又熱心助人。

相關用語 ● respect 敬重   進階補充 ● look down on 輕視

396

I am sorry I lost my temper.

抱歉，我動怒了。

lose one's temper為「發脾氣、動怒」之意。lose動詞三態：lose、lost、lost。temper可當「情緒」，也可當「怒氣」，需由上下文來判定。temper當動詞時則有「鍛鍊、陶冶」的意思，小心勿與拼法相似的單字temple「寺廟」混淆。

A: I've never seen you being so angry.
我從來沒見過你這麼生氣。

B: I am sorry I lost my temper. I hope I didn't scare you.
對不起我發脾氣了。希望我沒有嚇到你。

A: Actually you did, kind of. I really don't like you shouting at people.
其實有一點。我真的不喜歡你對人大吼。

B: I will try to control myself next time.
我下次會試著控制我的脾氣。

相關用語 ● get angry about 生氣   進階補充 ● get mad 發脾氣

397

It's time to make a decision.

該是下決定的時候了。

make a decision為「做決定」之意。decision是名詞，意為「決定、決心、結論、判決」，動詞為decide，形容詞為decisive「決定性的、果斷的」。此片語可直接以decide取代。相關片語：decide on sb./sth「選擇」；decide against「決定不…」。

A: It's time to make a decision.
　　該是做決定的時候了。

B: What do you mean, Sir?
　　先生，您是什麼意思？

A: I have to lay off some more staff.
　　我得解雇更多員工。

B: That's too bad.
　　太糟糕了。

相關用語 **determine** 決定　　進階補充 **settle on** 選定

398

He used to make a living by recycling garbage.

他曾以回收垃圾維生。

make a living為「謀生」之意。living在這裡當名詞，為「生計」之意，另外還有「生活方式、生存」等意思。相關片語：beat the living daylights out of sb.「重重擊垮」；every living soul「每個人」；living end「最好的人」；living death「行屍走肉」；living on borrowed time「不久人世」。

A: Have you read Mr. Jackin's autobiography?
　　你讀過傑金先生的自傳嗎？

B: Not yet. I heard it's worth reading.
　　還沒。聽說值得一讀。

A: Totally. Do you know he used to make a living by recycling garbage?
　　沒錯。你知道他曾靠回收垃圾謀生嗎？

B: Then, how did he become a billionaire?
　　那他是怎麼變成億萬富翁的？

相關用語 **earn a living** 謀生　　進階補充 **get a livelihood** 謀生

399 We are **making an effort to** attract as many new customers as possible. 我們正努力吸引更多新客戶。

make an effort to為「努力」之意。這裡的to是不定詞，所以後面要接動詞原形。用法：S + make an effort to + V。同義字和片語包括：endeavor、strive、do one's best等。

A: How is the marketing project going?
行銷企劃進行得如何？

B: We are making an effort to attract as many new customers as possible.
我們正努力吸引更多新客戶。

A: Why not focus on increasing the effectiveness of the advertising?
何不專注於提升廣告效益？

B: OK. We will work more on that.
好。我們會在該部分更加努力。

相關用語 → **strive for** 努力   進階補充 → **work on** 致力於

400 He **made believe** that his teddy bear was talking to him. 他想像他的泰迪熊在和他說話。

make believe為「假裝、想像」之意。make是使役動詞，所以後面省略不定詞to，而直接加believe。此片語的用法通常是在片語後加that做連接詞，然後再加名詞子句當受詞，但有時也可省略that。make believe若寫成make-believe，就變成了形容詞，表示「假扮的」。

A: Our little John seems to be really lonely.
我們的小約翰好像非常寂寞。

B: Why do you say that?
為何這樣說？

A: I saw him talking to his teddy bear and making believe that it was talking to him.
我看到他跟他的泰迪熊說話，並且想像它在和他說話。

B: Come on. All kids do that!
拜託。小孩子都這樣的！

相關用語 → **pretend** 假裝   進階補充 → **disguise** 偽裝

401

He never makes good on any of his promises.

他未曾履行他的承諾。

make good為「履行、達成、成功」之意，指「在某件事上能夠勝任愉快，順利達到目標」。這裡的make是不及物動詞，good是形容詞，所以後面如果有受詞，就要加介系詞in或on。用法：S + make good in/on sth。

A: I heard you've broken up with Larry.
聽說你和賴瑞分手了。

B: News spreads as if it's on wings, doesn't it?
消息傳得很快，是吧？

A: What's wrong with you two?
你們兩個怎麼了？

B: I am just **tired of** him. He never **makes good** on any of his promises.
我只是厭倦他了。他未曾履行他的承諾。

相關用語 → **carry out** 完成　　進階補充 → **tired of** 厭倦

402

It's just in case we can't make out your signature.

這只是以防我們無法辨認您的簽名。

make out為「辨別出、填寫、理解」之意。此片語有很多意義，需視上下文才能確定。相似片語：make sth out of...相等於make sth of...，意思是「以…材料製作」，但是前者比後者更具有加強以「某種材料製作」的意味。

A: Sir, I am sorry, but can you also print your name **in the blank**?
很抱歉，但是可以請您在空白處以正楷填寫您的名字嗎？

B: Is there anything wrong?
有什麼問題嗎？

A: No, it's just in case we can't **make out** your signature.
沒有，只是以防我們無法辨認您的簽名。

B: OK. Here you are.
好的。麻煩你。

相關用語 → **recognize** 辨認　　進階補充 → **in the blank** 在空白處

403

We are trying to **manage without** it.

我們正試著在故障中設法應付過去。

manage with為「設法應付」之意。用法：S + manage with + (代)名詞。manage是指「具有權限者巧妙地運用人力，並用心處理細節，以達成目的或經營事業」的意思。若將with改成without，則是在「缺乏某人或物的條件下盡善盡美」之意。

A: How is everything in the factory?
工廠的狀況還好嗎？

B: The machine is malfunctioning again, but we are trying to **manage without** it.
機器又出問題了，但我們正試著在故障中設法應付過去。

A: Have you called the technician yet?
你打電話給技師了嗎？

B: Yes, I believe he will be here in an hour.
打了，我想他一小時內就會抵達。

相關用語 • handle 處理　　進階補充 • cope with 應付

404

The union wouldn't **meet halfway** on the retirement policy. 工會不願在退休政策上妥協。

meet halfway意為「妥協」，指「採取折衷辦法向對方妥協」。受詞要放在meet的後面，而不是放在halfway的後面。halfway可當形容詞也可當副詞，在這裡是當副詞，意指「中途地、一半地」。

A: I heard the negotiation between the company and the union failed.
聽說公司和工會的協商破局了。

B: Unfortunately, you are right.
不幸的是，你說對了。

A: What happened?
發生什麼事了？

B: The union wouldn't **meet halfway** on the retirement policy.
工會不願在退休政策上妥協。

相關用語 • compromise 妥協　　進階補充 • strike a balance 折衷

405

My father named me after his favorite basketball players. 父親以他最愛的籃球員替我命名。

name after為「以…命名」之意，屬英式用法，name for則屬美式用法。由name所衍生出來的詞彙有：nameless「隱姓埋名的」；namely「那就是」；nameplate「名牌」；namesake「同名之人」。

A: You have a really special name.
　你的名字很特別。

B: Yes, my father named me after his two favorite basketball players.
　嗯，父親以他最喜歡的兩位籃球員替我命名。

A: Who are they?
　是誰？

B: Jordan and Kobe.
　喬登和柯比。

相關用語 · call after 以…命名　　進階補充 · name tag 名牌

406

I know a great place near by my house.

我知道在我家附近的一個好地方。

near by為「在附近」之意，是副詞片語，若將兩個字合在一起，寫成nearby，則是形容詞。由near所衍生出來的詞彙有：nearly「幾乎、親密地」；near-sighted「近視的」；nearside「(汽車、道路)左側(英式用法)」。

A: It's time for lunch. Do you want to have something together?
　該吃午餐了。你想一起吃點東西嗎？

B: Sure, I know a great place near by my house.
　當然好，我知道我家附近有間很棒的店。

A: That's great. Can I get a lift in your car?
　太棒了。我可以搭你的便車嗎？

B: Of course you can. It would be my pleasure.
　當然可以，這是我的榮幸。

相關用語 · close to 在附近　　進階補充 · get a lift 搭便車

407

I neglected to return her call yesterday.

我昨天忘了回她電話。

neglect to為「遺漏、忽略」之意。neglect和ignore都表「忽略」，neglect
是指「對於被期待或被要求的事情不注意、怠惰或故意不執行」；ignore
是指「故意忽視，或有時對於自己不想認知的事實故意不加理睬」。

A: Mrs. Chao called and she was really angry. Do you know why?
趙太太來電，她很生氣。你知道為什麼嗎？

B: It's my fault. I neglected to return her call yesterday.
是我的錯。我昨天忘了回她電話。

A: How could you? She is the most important client to our company.
你這樣怎麼可以？她是我們公司最重要的客戶。

B: I am sorry. I will visit her in person and make my apology to her today.
很抱歉。我今天會親自登門向她道歉。

相關用語 **slip up** 疏漏　　進階補充 **in person** 親自

408

No doubt I will accept Mr. Watson's offer.

我當然會接受華生先生的工作邀約。

no doubt為「無疑地」之意，是一則副詞片語，通常放在句首。doubt和
distrust都有「不相信」的意思，其差別為：doubt是指「對某種事物的真
實狀況不能確定」的意思；distrust是指「對於某人缺乏信任」的意思。

A: Are you going to accept Mr. Watson's offer?
你打算接受華生先生的工作邀約嗎？

B: No doubt I will.
我當然會。

A: Are you sure?
你確定嗎？

B: Come on! Sixty thousand dollars a month? I would never get anything better than that.
拜託！一個月六萬耶？我找不到更好的工作機會了。

相關用語 **undoubtedly** 肯定地　　進階補充 **without doubt** 無疑地

409

No wonder you are so tanned and energetic!

難怪你膚色健美又活力十足！

no wonder為「難怪」之意，是副詞片語，通常放在句首。wonder當動詞為「想知道」，當名詞表示「奇觀、奇蹟」。西方有一句諺語「A wonder lasts but nine days.」意思是說「任何轟動的事絕不會長久」，也就是成語「曇花一現」之意。

409

A: I haven't seen you for a while. Where have you been?
我好久沒見到你了。你去哪裡了？

B: I just got back from a nice vacation in Hawaii.
我剛從夏威夷度假回來。

A: **No wonder** you are so tanned and energetic!
難怪你膚色健美又活力十足！

B: Yes, it was a fantastic holiday!
是啊，真是個美好的假期！

相關用語 → wondering 疑惑的　　進階補充 → understandable 可理解的

410

The pay is great, **not to mention** the housing allowance. 薪資優渥，更不用提住屋津貼了。

not to mention為「更不必說」之意。mention是「提及」的意思，後方直接加名詞即可。mention可當動詞也可當名詞，都有「提及」的意思。相關用語：as above mentioned = as mentioned above「如上所述」；Don't mention it.「別提了、別客氣」。

410

A: Are you going to accept Mr. Watson's offer?
你要接受華生先生的工作邀約嗎？

B: I am still thinking about it.
我還在考慮。

A: Come on. The pay is great, **not to mention** the housing allowance.
拜託。薪資優渥，更別提住屋津貼了。

B: But I would have to go to Vietnam for two years.
但我得去越南兩年。

相關用語 → let alone 遑論　　進階補充 → make mention of 提及

411

You may file a complaint if you object to this order.

若您反對這項命令，可提出申訴。

object to為「反對」之意。這裡的to是介系詞，所以後面要接名詞或Ving。object也可當名詞，為「物體、目的、受詞」的意思，用法：S + object to + 受詞。

411

A: Ma'am, this is a court order for you to clean up your yard as soon as possible.
女士，這是要您盡速清理院子的法院命令。

B: What if I don't want to? I love the way it is now!
要是我不想呢？我喜歡它現在的樣子。

A: You may file a complaint if you object to this order.
若您反對這項命令，可提出申訴。

B: I will do that!
我一定會這麼做的！

相關用語 → **refuse** 拒絕接受   進階補充 → **what if** 假使

412

Everything I said about Jason's firing was off the record. 任何我提到關於解雇傑森的話，都是不公開的。

off the record為「不公開的、非正式的」之意。record可當動詞，也可當名詞，都是「記錄」的意思。但在讀音上是不同的，動詞的重音在第二音節，名詞的重音則在第一音節，所以在口語的使用上要特別注意。相似片語：go on record「公開發表意見」(美式用法)；on record「正式記錄的」；break the record「破紀錄」。

412

A: Everything I said about Jason's firing was off the record.
任何我提到關於解雇傑森的話，都是不公開的。

B: What do you mean?
您的意思是？

A: It means you can't write about what I told you.
意思是你不能把我說的話寫出來。

B: How am I supposed to get a good story then?
那我還有什麼好報導可寫？

相關用語 → **private** 不公開的   進階補充 → **informal** 非正式的

413

You can go to the meeting **on my behalf**.

你可以代表我出席會議。

on behalf為「代表」之意。此片語的on亦可用in代替，但一般而言on較常用。用法：S + be V + on one's behalf。behalf為名詞，意為「代表、利益」，也可用S + V + on behalf of + 人或機構的句法，意義不變。

MP3
413

A: Sir, the sales representative meeting has been rescheduled to 2 this afternoon.
先生，業務代表會議已改到今天下午兩點。

B: But I have to attend my son's Sports Day!
但是我得參加兒子的運動會！

A: Oh, no. What should we do? Should I ask them to cancel it?
噢，不。我們該怎麼辦？要我請他們取消嗎？

B: No, you can go to the meeting **on my behalf**.
不用，你可以代表我出席會議。

相關用語 → **represent** 代表   進階補充 → **in the name of** 以…名義

414

Did you bump into that girl **on purpose**?

你是故意巧遇那個女孩的嗎？

on purpose為「故意地」之意。purpose為名詞，意為「目的、意圖、用途」。此片語通常置於句尾，用來修飾動詞，以便表示某種行動乃蓄意而為。相似片語：at cross-purposes「觀點分歧」，用於兩人或團體之間。

MP3
414

A: Did you bump into that girl **on purpose**?
你是故意巧遇那個女孩的嗎？

B: Gosh! How did you know that?
我的天啊！你怎麼知道？

A: I've figured out your tricks. Is that your way to pick up girls?
我已完全參透你的伎倆。你就是這樣跟女生搭訕的嗎？

B: Yes, but I only **bump into** pretty girls.
是的，但我只會巧遇漂亮女孩。

相關用語 → **by design** 故意   進階補充 → **bump into** 巧遇

415

I am a bit **out of breath** and dizzy now.

我現在有點喘不過氣和暈眩。

out of breath為「喘不過氣」之意。相似片語：catch one's breath「喘一口氣」；hold one's breath「屏息」；waste one's breath「白費唇舌」。breath是「呼吸」的名詞，動詞為breathe，因為兩者的寫法非常相近(名詞字尾沒有e)，所以在使用上要多加留意。

A: Are you all right? You look pale.
你還好嗎？臉色有點蒼白。

B: I am a bit out of breath and dizzy now.
我有點喘不過氣和暈眩。

A: Come on. Take a seat. Let me get some water for you.
來，坐下，我拿水給你。

B: Thank you. That's very nice of you.
謝謝你。你人真好。

相關用語 → **breathless** 氣喘吁吁的   進階補充 → **take a seat** 坐下

416

Daisy and her skirt is so **out of fashion**.

黛西和她的裙子真是過時。

out of fashion為「過時」之意。反義片語：in favor「受到喜愛」；in mode「正流行」；come into vogue/style「正流行」；in (the) fashion「符合潮流」；come in「流行起來」；catch on「流行」。

A: I can't believe my eyes!
我不敢相信我的眼睛！

B: Why are you so surprised?
你為何如此驚訝？

A: Look at Daisy and her skirt! It's so out of fashion!
你看黛西和她的裙子！真是過時！

B: I don't see anything wrong with it. She looks great in that skirt.
我不覺得有什麼問題。她穿那件裙子很好看。

相關用語 → **out of date** 過時的   進階補充 → **in vogue** 正在流行

417
You have been **out of a job** for nearly a month!
你已失業將近一個月了！

out of a job為「失業」之意。此處的a job也可用work取代，均表示「工作」的意思。out of在此表示「沒有、失去」的意思。由job所衍生的相關片語：an inside job「有內賊」；devil of a job「艱鉅的任務」；lie down the job「摸魚」。

A: Aren't you going to find a job?
你不打算找份工作嗎？

B: Why should I?
我為什麼要？

A: You have been out of a job for nearly a month!
你已經失業將近一個月了！

B: I told you that I am taking a long vacation now!
我跟你說過我正在放長假！

相關用語 **unemployed** 失業的　　進階補充 **pink slip** 解雇通知

418
The shipment will not be on schedule **owing to** the bad weather. 由於天候惡劣，貨運將無法準時抵達。

owing to為「由於」之意。owing的原形動詞是owe，有「欠債、感激、歸功於」等意思。此片語通常置於句首，修飾其後接的子句。需注意to為介系詞，其後必須加名詞或Ving，和thanks to、due to等片語用法相同。

A: The shipment will not be on schedule owing to the bad weather.
由於天候惡劣，貨運將無法準時抵達。

B: When will it arrive?
貨品何時會到？

A: Next Tuesday as long as the weather improves.
如果天氣好轉的話是下週二。

B: OK.
好的。

相關用語 **thanks to** 由於　　進階補充 **on schedule** 按預定時間

419

That guy tried to pass off that fake Gucci bag as a real one. 那名男子試圖用仿古馳包以假亂真。

pass off as為「冒充」之意。這則片語的受詞放在pass off和as之間。在球賽中，pass是指「傳球」的意思。相似片語：pass off 為「消失」之意：Being washed many times, the color of the stripes passed off. 洗過好幾次後，條紋的顏色消失了。

A: That guy tried to **pass off** that fake Gucci bag **as** a real one.
那個男人試圖用仿古馳包以假亂真。

B: Good thing you noticed it was a fake.
幸好你有注意到那是假貨。

A: It wasn't too hard to see that.
並不難看得出來。

B: You're much better at spotting fakes than I am.
在認出假貨上，你比我厲害。

相關用語 ► **fake** 冒充　　進階補充 ► **pretend to be** 冒充

420

You have to pay attention to the teacher in class.

上課時，你必須集中注意力在老師身上。

pay attention to為「關心、注意」之意。此片語可以加形容程度的形容詞在pay和attention to之間，如：more、great等等，來表示程度上的多寡。attention為名詞，表示「注意」，the center of attention即「矚目的焦點」。

A: You have to **pay** more **attention to** me in class.
上課時，你得多集中注意力在我身上。

B: I am sorry, Sir.
老師，對不起。

A: Why were you **staring out of** the window?
為什麼你一直盯著窗外看？

B: There was a cute little bird in the tree.
樹上有隻可愛的小鳥。

相關用語 ► **focus on** 集中於　　進階補充 ► **stare out of** 凝視

421

He persists in asking us to move by the end of the month. 他堅持要我們在月底前搬走。

persist in為「堅持、固執」之意。用法：S + persist in + (代)名詞或Ving。last和persist都有「持續、堅持」的意思，其差別為：last是指「在良好的情況下，持續一段相當長的時間」；persist是指「持續得比預期還久」的意思。

MP3
421

A: Mr. Chen made another call this morning.
陳先生今天早上又打來了。

B: The landlord? What did he say?
房東？他說了什麼？

A: He persists in asking us to move by the end of the month.
他堅持要我們在月底前搬走。

B: No way! The lease is valid until next April.
決不！租約到明年四月前都有效。

相關用語 → insist on 堅持   進階補充 → no way 決不

422

I played a little trick on her, which obviously upset her a lot. 我開了她一個小玩笑，顯然讓她很不高興。

play a trick on為「開…的玩笑」之意。trick可用joke替換，兩者皆有「玩笑」、「惡作劇」的意思。用法：S + play a trick on + 人。萬聖節用語"Trick or treat."「不給糖就搗蛋」，其中的trick就是「惡作劇」的意思。

MP3
422

A: What's wrong with Tina? She seems to be really angry with you.
緹娜怎麼了？她好像非常生你的氣。

B: My bad. I played a little trick on her, which obviously upset her a lot.
是我的錯。我開了她一個小玩笑，顯然讓她很不高興。

A: What did you do to her?
你對她做了什麼？

B: I put a fake cockroach in her swimsuit.
我把假蟑螂放進她的泳衣裡。

相關用語 → tease 戲弄   進階補充 → practical joke 惡作劇

423

I don't like you pointing your finger at me like this.

我不喜歡你像這樣用手指著我。

point at為「指向、指著」之意。用法一：S + point at + 人 / 物，是指「用手指著物或人」的意思；用法二：S + point + 物 + at + 人，是指「拿著某物指向某人」的意思。

A: I don't like you pointing your finger at me like this.
　　我不喜歡你像這樣用手指著我。

B: I am just trying to attract your attention.
　　我只是試著吸引你的注意。

A: But you shouldn't do it in this way. It's kind of rude.
　　但你不該用這種方法。這樣有點無禮。

B: My apologies. No more finger pointing.
　　對不起。不會再用手指指你了。

相關用語 **pointy** 尖的 　　 進階補充 **point out** 指出

424

I have to prepare for tomorrow's test.

我必須準備明天的考試。

prepare for為「為…做準備」之意。由prepare所衍生出來的詞彙有：名詞preparation「準備、預習或自習」；形容詞preparatory「準備的、預習的」；preparative「準備的、預備的」。

A: How about going to the movies with me tonight?
　　今晚要不要和我去看電影？

B: I'd love to, but I have to prepare for tomorrow's test.
　　我很想，但我必須準備明天的考試。

A: What test?
　　什麼考試？

B: Don't you remember? Mr. Chen said there is going to be a math test tomorrow.
　　你不記得嗎？陳老師說明天會考數學。

相關用語 **arrange** 籌備 　　 進階補充 **in preparation for** 準備

425

Sunglasses can prevent your eyes from getting hurt by the sunlight. 太陽眼鏡可預防你的眼睛遭陽光傷害。

prevent from為「阻止、制止」之意。受詞可以放在prevent跟from之間，表示欲阻止的對象；from後則接制止去做的事，或是應該遠離的人物。keep、stop、prohibit都可用來代換prevent。用法：S + prevent from + N/Ving。

A: You should put on your sunglasses.
你應該戴上你的太陽眼鏡。

B: I don't have mine with me. It's no big deal.
我的沒帶在身上。這沒什麼關係。

A: Yes, it is. Sunglasses can prevent your eyes from getting hurt by the sunlight.
有關係。太陽眼鏡可預防你的眼睛遭陽光傷害。

B: OK. I'll keep that in mind.
好的。我會記住的。

相關用語 ▸ **big deal 至關重要的事**　進階補充 ▸ **keep in mind 記住**

426

You can start by making a list of pros and cons.
你可從製作優缺點列表開始。

pros and cons為「正反兩方」之意，是一種慣用語，所以pro和con都要加s。pro可當副詞，也可當名詞，皆指「贊成」的意思。pro還有另外一種意思「職業選手」，是professional的縮寫。

A: I really don't know what to do.
我真的不知道該怎麼辦。

B: Maybe I can give you some advice. What is it?
也許我可以給你些建議。怎麼了？

A: I don't know whether I should work in Vietnam.
我不知道是否該去越南工作。

B: You can start by making a list of pros and cons, which will probably tell you the answer.
你可從製作優缺點列表開始，那或許會告訴你答案。

相關用語 ▸ **against 反對**　進階補充 ▸ **in favor of 贊成**

427

We have to protect information from unauthorized access. 我們必須保護資訊免遭未授權存取。

protect from為「保護、免受」之意。受詞可放protect跟from之間，指保護的對象，from則接應遠離的事物。

A: Do you have any suggestion regarding our online shop?
關於我們的線上商店，你有什麼建議嗎？

B: Maybe we can make it more secure, so that consumers will be more willing to use it.
或許我們可以讓它更安全，這樣消費者就會更樂意使用。

A: What do you mean?
你的意思是？

B: We should have a better system to protect information from unauthorized access.
我們要有個更好的系統，以保護資訊免遭未授權存取。

相關用語 ► secure 使安全　　進階補充 ► be willing to 願意的

428

They will provide you with a local map and a bus schedule. 他們會提供您當地地圖以及公車時刻表。

provide with為「供給、裝備」之意。provide和supply都有「供給」的意思，其差別為：provide是指「先準備或供應必須的物品」；supply則是指「為某人、機構或地區等補充不足或必要的東西」。

A: It's my first time here. Can you recommend some interesting places to go?
這是我第一次來這裡。你可以推薦我一些有趣的景點嗎？

B: You can go to the information center first. It's on the corner.
你可以先去遊客服務中心，就座落在轉角。

A: What can I find there?
我可以在那裡找到什麼？

B: They will provide you with a local map and a bus schedule.
他們會提供您當地地圖和公車時刻表。

相關用語 ► supply with 供給　　進階補充 ► equip with 裝備

429

We should **put** more **emphasis on** boosting sales.

我們應更加強調提升業績。

put emphasis on為「強調、重視」之意，等於emphasize。put可用lay或 place代換，為「加諸」之意。這裡的on可寫成upon。

A: What do you think about the new marketing plan?
你覺得新的行銷規劃怎麼樣？

B: I believe we should **put** more **emphasis on** boosting sales.
我相信我們應更加強調提升業績。

A: I understand. Do you have any good ideas?
我理解。你有什麼好主意嗎？

B: How about giving away new posters?
贈送新海報如何？

相關用語 **stress on** 著重   進階補充 **make much of** 重視

430

There are **quite a few** men interested in Jenna.

相當多男人對珍娜有興趣。

quite a few為「相當多」之意。a few雖意為「幾個、一些」，但冠上quite 「相當、頗」後，形成「非常多」之意。quite a little在意義上與本片語相 同，但用於形容不可數之物質或抽象名詞，而quite a few則用在形容可數 的普通名詞上。

A: I would like to ask Jenna out.
我想約珍娜出去。

B: There are **quite a few** men interested in her. It will be a tough competition.
相當多男人對她有興趣，這會是場硬仗。

A: So what? That doesn't mean that I won't win her heart over all those other guys.
那又如何？這並不代表我無法打敗其他男人、贏得她的心。

B: Why are you so sure? **After all**, you are not that special, either.
你怎麼能確定？畢竟你也沒有那麼特別。

相關用語 **a great many** 很多   進階補充 **after all** 畢竟

224

431

Try to **read between the lines**.

試著領會言外之意。

read between the lines為「領會言外之意」的意思。須特別注意的是，這裡的line必須加s，因為使用between表示兩者之間，代表不只一行(line)。用來表示言外之意的單字另有implication、undernote、overtone等。

MP3
431

A: I really shouldn't have taken literature as my elective.
我真的不該選文學當選修。

B: It's not that hard.
文學沒那麼難。

A: It is to me. All that symbolism and use of euphemism really kills me.
對我來說很難。象徵用語和婉轉用語快把我逼死了。

B: Just try to **read between the lines** and appreciate what the writer tries to convey.
試著領會言外之意，並欣賞作者想表達的意思。

相關用語 ➤ subaudition 弦外之音　　進階補充 ➤ insinuation 影射

432

You can always **read his mind**.

你總能知道他的想法。

read one's mind為「知道某人的想法」之意。這裡的read是「判斷、解讀」的意思。由read所衍生的詞彙有：readability「可讀性」；reader「讀者、審稿人、(大學)講師(英式用法)」。

MP3
432

A: Should I knock on Mr. Watson's door?
我該敲華生先生的門嗎？

B: I don't know. It depends on whether you have something to tell him.
我不知道。看你是否有重要的事跟他說。

A: Come on. You can always **read his mind**. Just tell me if he is **in a good mood**.
拜託。你總能知道他在想什麼，告訴我他心情如何就好。

B: I just know that I wouldn't do that if I were you.
我只知道如果我是你，我不會敲他的門。

相關用語 ➤ get at 理解　　進階補充 ➤ in a good mood 心情好

433

Jason was reduced to a marketing agent.

傑森被降職為行銷專員。

reduce to為「迫使、降級、歸納」之意。這裡的to是介系詞，所以後接名詞或Ving。用法：S + reduce to + (代)名詞。decrease和reduce都有「減少」的意思，其差別為：decrease是指「大小、數量等逐漸遞減」；reduce則除了「減少」外，另有「降低」之意。

A: Poor Jason.
可憐的傑森。

B: What happened to him?
他怎麼了？

A: He was just reduced to a marketing agent, deprived of his original manager position.
他剛被降職為行銷專員，喪失原本的經理職銜。

B: How come?
怎麼會這樣？

相關用語 ○ degrade 降級　　　進階補充 ○ deprive of 剝奪

434

New York is also referred to as The Big Apple.

紐約也被稱作「大蘋果」。

refer to為「提到、查詢、參考」之意。若使用refer to sth as...的句型，則表示「將某物稱為…」的意思。refer的名詞為reference，表示「參考、提及、推薦函」的意思。

A: Where is your next stop on your trip?
你旅程的下一站是哪裡？

B: New York.
紐約。

A: Isn't New York also referred to as The Big Apple?
紐約不也被稱作「大蘋果」嗎？

B: Correct!
沒錯！

相關用語 ○ known as 被認為是　　　進階補充 ○ look up 查詢

435

You are the person we can best rely on to win the contract for us. 你是我們贏得合約最能仰賴的人。

rely on為「依賴、信任」之意。rely和depend都有「仰賴」的意味，其差別為：rely是指「根據過去的經驗，使人相信對方必定能完成所交代之事」；depend則是指「依賴別人的支持或援助」。

A: You are the person we can best rely on to win the contract for us.
你是我們贏得合約最能仰賴的人。

B: Thank you for your trust and appreciation.
謝謝您的信任及賞識。

A: You deserve it. Your sales skills are excellent!
這是你應得的。你的業務技巧很出色！

B: Thank you. I will try my very best.
感謝您。我會盡全力表現。

相關用語 → trust 信任　　進階補充 → depend on 依靠

436

That photo always reminds me of the good old days in high school. 那張照片總讓我想起中學時的美好時光。

remind...of...為「使回想起」之意。用法：S + remind + 人 + of + 事情。remember、remind和recall都有「回想起」的意思，其差別為：remember是指「想起從前記得或經驗過的事情」；remind是指「促使某人想起某事」；recall則是指「盡力去想起某事」。

A: It's amazing that you have kept this photo for all these years!
你還留著這張照片真令人吃驚！

B: Yes, that photo always reminds me of the good old days in high school.
沒錯，那張照片總是讓我想起中學時的美好時光。

A: You are right. That's one of my best memories, too.
沒錯。那也是我最美好的回憶之一。

B: Maybe we should organize a class reunion some time.
也許我們該找時間辦場同學會。

相關用語 → remember 想起　　進階補充 → class reunion 同學會

437

When are you going to respond to Mr. Watson?

你何時要回覆華生先生？

respond to為「回應、反應」之意。answer、reply和respond都有「回應」的意思，其差別為：answer是指「以口頭、筆寫或行動回答」；reply用在較正式的文體中，表示「經過仔細思考後的答覆」；respond是指「對某人的期望或訴苦做適當的反應」。

MP3
437

A: When are you going to respond to Mr. Watson?
你何時要回覆華生先生？

B: I still need some more time to think it over.
我還需要一些時間考慮。

A: Don't hesitate anymore. Just accept the offer.
別再猶豫了，就接受工作邀約吧。

B: The pay is great, but I really don't want to work abroad.
薪水是很棒，但我真的不想出國工作。

相關用語 • respond 反應　　進階補充 • think over 考慮

438

It might be the experience of riding on horseback ten years ago. 可能是十年前騎馬的經驗。

ride on為「乘坐」之意。用法：S + ride on + (代)名詞。ride、drive、fly、sail都是用在駕駛交通工具上的動詞，其用法分別如下：ride用在騎乘較小型的交通工具上，如機車、腳踏車、馬等；drive用在駕駛較大型的交通工具上，如汽車、火車、卡車等；若所駕駛的交通工具是在天上飛行的，就用fly；sail則用在船隻的航行上。

MP3
438

A: What's your best experience ever?
你最棒的經驗是什麼？

B: It might be riding on horseback ten years ago.
可能是十年前的騎馬吧。

A: Wow. How old were you at that time?
哇。你當時幾歲？

B: I was three then, and my dad rode with me.
我那時三歲，我爸爸和我一起騎。

相關用語 • mount 騎上　　進階補充 • dismount 下車、下馬

439

Does the name "Kevin Wang" ring a bell to you?

你對於「王凱文」這個名字有印象嗎？

ring a bell為「引起共鳴、引起反應」之意，屬於口語片語，也可當「使想起」的意思。相似片語：clear as a bell「非常清晰」；sound as a bell「非常健康」；bells and whistles「附加性能」。

A: Does the name "Kevin Wang" ring a bell to you?
你對於「王凱文」這個名字有印象嗎？

B: No, not at all. Who is he?
不，一點也沒有。他是誰？

A: I met him last night at a party. He said you two went to the same kindergarten.
我昨晚在派對上遇到他，他說你們讀同一所幼稚園。

B: I can't recall that.
我想不起來。

相關用語 → **remind of** 使回想起　　進階補充 → **recall** 回想起

440

I believe it will run up in no time.

我相信它很快就會上漲。

run up為「上漲、升起」之意。此外，run up還有「跑上去、迅速成長、建得很高、合計」等詞意。若當「高達…」的意思解時，後方的介系詞需加to，其後再接特定的數量或程度。若在run up後接against，則表「碰見」之意。

A: Can you give me some investment advice?
你可以給我一些投資建議嗎？

B: No problem. I happen to know a great stock to invest in.
沒問題。我碰巧知道一支值得投資的績優股。

A: Which one?
哪一支？

B: It's PG Company. I believe it will run up in no time.
PG公司的股票。我相信它很快就會上漲。

相關用語 → **go down** 下跌　　進階補充 → **happen to** 碰巧

441

I am searching for a birthday present for my boyfriend. 我正在找送給男朋友的生日禮物。

search for為「尋找」之意，受詞可放在search和for之間，也可放在for之後。其他有關search的片語有：search out「找出、搜出」；in search of 或in the search for「尋求」。

A: Ma'am, how can I help you?
女士，需要幫忙嗎？

B: I am **searching for** a birthday present for my boyfriend.
我正在找送給男朋友的生日禮物。

A: How about a tie?
一條領帶如何？

B: It will look perfect on him.
他繫起來會很好看。

相關用語 **hunt out 找出**　　進階補充 **search me 我不知道**

442

I want to see them off.

我想去幫他們送行。

see off為「為…送行」之意，是及物動詞片語，受詞放在off之前，且受詞必須是人。walk + 人 + to + 地方「送…人去某處、協助某人行走」和此片語的意義不同，應注意區別。

A: Where are you going?
你要去哪裡？

B: To the airport.
機場。

A: The airport? Are you going on a vacation?
機場？你要去度假嗎？

B: No, Girls' Generation are leaving today. I want to **see them off**.
不是的；「少女時代」今天離台，我想去幫她們送機。

相關用語 **farewell 告別**　　進階補充 **see out 熬過**

443

I've been trying to **seek** you **out** for a long time now.
我一直試著找了你好久。

seek out為「找到」之意。seek的動詞三態為：seek、sought、sought。受詞可放在seek和out之間，也可放在out之後。與seek相關的片語有：seek to「嘗試、試圖」；be not far to seek「近在眼前」。

A: Here you are! I've been trying to **seek** you **out** for a long time now.
你在這裡！我找你找了好久。

B: I have been here for hours. Where did you go?
我在這裡好幾個小時了。你去哪裡了？

A: It's not my fault. There are so many people here.
並不是我的問題。這裡人很多。

B: You are right. It's a little bit hard to find anyone in such a crowd.
你說得沒錯。在這樣的人潮裡要找到人是蠻難的。

相關用語 ► **seek after** 探索　　進階補充 ► **seek through** 搜查

444

Your strong ability **separates** you **from** all the others. 你優秀的能力讓你與眾不同。

separate from為「區分、分隔」之意，用法：S + separate from + 人事物。separate和part都有「分開」的意思，差別為：separate指「將原來統一或結合的東西分離」；part指「分開關係密切的人或物」。

A: Sir, they said you want to talk to me.
長官，他們說您想跟我談一談。

B: Yes, take a seat, please. You've been chosen to be the next manager.
是的，請坐。你被選為下一任經理。

A: Thank you for the recognition, Sir.
謝謝長官的賞識。

B: Your strong ability **separates** you **from** all the others. You deserve it.
你優秀的能力讓你與眾不同，這是你應得的。

相關用語 ► **stand out** 脫穎而出　　進階補充 ► **sort out** 挑出

445

He keeps showing off that he's so smart and won a scholarship. 他不停炫耀他很聰明，並且贏得獎學金。

show off表「炫耀」之意，為及物動詞片語。若受詞是代名詞，要放在off之前；如為名詞，則放在off之後。show和display都有「展示」的意思，其差別為：show是指「拿東西給人看」；display則是指「攤開或陳列某物，使其能清楚地被看到」的意思。

A: I just can't stand Jason any more.
我再也受不了傑森了。

B: What's wrong between you two?
你們兩個怎麼了？

A: He keeps showing off that he's so smart and won a scholarship.
他不停炫耀他有多聰明，並且贏得獎學金。

B: I understand. That must be annoying.
我懂。那一定很煩人。

相關用語 ∘ **swank 炫耀**   進階補充 ∘ **brag about 自誇**

446

Why didn't Jason show up at the meeting today?
傑森今天為何沒有出席會議？

show up為「出現、出席」之意，後面不加受詞。由show所衍生出來的詞彙有：show bill「廣告傳單」；showboat「賣弄」；show business「演藝事業」(簡寫為showbiz)；showcase「陳列用的玻璃櫥」。

A: Why didn't Jason show up at the meeting today?
傑森今天為何沒有出席會議？

B: I really don't know.
我真的不知道。

A: Can you give him a call and see what happened?
你可以打個電話給他，看是發生了什麼事嗎？

B: Sure. I'll do it now.
當然可以，我立刻打。

相關用語 ∘ **attend 出席**   進階補充 ∘ **assist at 出席**

447

If you are against the bill, speak up now.

若你們反對這項議案,請馬上發表意見。

speak up為「公開發表意見」之意。speak的動詞三態:speak、spoke、spoken。speak跟talk雖然同義,但speak是指「對群眾進行較正式的演說或演講」之意,而talk多意謂「個人之間輕鬆而不正式的閒聊」。

447

A: If you are against the bill, speak up now.
若你們反對這項議案,請馬上發表意見。

B: Sir, I would like to share my viewpoint with you all.
先生,我想和大家分享我的看法。

A: What is it?
是什麼呢?

B: I believe the bill needs further revising in order to serve the interests of most people.
我想,為滿足多數人的利益,這項議案需做進一步的修正。

相關用語 ○→ express 表達　　進階補充 ○→ speak out 陳述意見

448

I am going to stay up late to work on my dissertation.

我要熬夜寫論文。

stay up為「熬夜」之意,常接Ving,表示「熬夜做…」。其他有關stay的片語有:stay away「離開」;stay in「留在家裡」;stay out「留在外頭」;stay the course「跑到終點、奮鬥不懈」。

448

A: Where do you keep the instant noodles?
你把泡麵放在哪裡?

B: It's in the upper drawer. Are you hungry? I can make you a meal.
在上層抽屜。你餓了嗎?我可以幫你弄點東西吃。

A: No. I am going to stay up late to work on my dissertation. I might get hungry in the middle of the night.
不用了。我要熬夜準備論文,半夜可能會餓。

B: Oh, I see.
喔,好啊。

相關用語 ○→ sit up 熬夜　　進階補充 ○→ instant noodles 泡麵

449

You will **succeed in** your new career.

你在新的職業上會成功的。

succeed in為「成功」之意。用法：S + succeed in + 事情。succeed是動詞，指「事業或生活上獲得良好結果或達到目的」，其名詞是success，形容詞是successful，副詞是successfully。

A: When will you start your new job?
你的新工作何時開始？

B: May 1st. I am a bit nervous, though.
五月一號。我還是有點緊張。

A: I have faith that you will **succeed in** your new career.
我相信你在新的職業上會成功的。

B: Thank you so much.
真的很感謝你。

相關用語 ○ **fall through** 失敗　　進階補充 ○ **come off** 成功

450

She must be **suffering from** great pain right now.

她現在一定難受無比。

suffer from為「遭受」之意。suffer通常是指「因疾病所承受的不舒服」，與with或from連用，但以與from連用最為常見。若所患的疾病是暫時性的，如感冒、頭痛、胃痛等等，則用進行式表示。相關片語：suffer through「熬過」。

A: I want to pay a visit to Mrs. Chen.
我想去拜訪陳太太。

B: What happened to her?
她怎麼了嗎？

A: Her son died in a car accident two days ago.
她的兒子兩天前死於一場車禍。

B: She must be **suffering from** great pain right now.
她現在一定難受無比。

相關用語 ○ **undergo** 經歷　　進階補充 ○ **go through** 經歷

451 · She is just **taking advantage of** you.

她只是在利用你。

take advantage of為「利用、佔便宜」之意。take advantage of + 人，指「利用某人的弱點或缺點加以欺騙、或利用他人的優勢」。若take advantage of + 事、物或機會等，則是指「藉由利用某事、物或機會去達成某種目的」。

A: Can I borrow your car tonight?
我今晚可以跟你借車嗎？

B: Sure. Where are you going?
當然可以。你要去哪裡？

A: Jane asked me to drive her to a party.
珍要我載她去一場派對。

B: You know she is just **taking advantage of** you, don't you?
你知道她只是在利用你吧？

相關用語 · **use** 利用　　進階補充 · **make use of** 利用

452 · Don't you think little Johnny **takes after** his father?

你不覺得小約翰跟他父親很像嗎？

take after為「像、相似」之意，指「一個人的相貌、行為或性格與父母或近親相似」的意思，與look like的差別在於，look like可指人也可指物，且僅指「外表」上的相像。

A: Don't you think little Johnny **takes after** his father?
你不覺得小約翰跟他父親很像嗎？

B: Totally! He is just like a clone of his dad.
很像！他就像他爹的複製人一樣。

A: Interesting! It's a perfect example of "Like father, like son."
真有趣！是「有其父必有其子」的標準案例。

B: I couldn't agree more.
完全同意。

相關用語 · **resemble** 相似　　進階補充 · **similar** 相像的

453

Have whoever is taking charge of the project come into my office. 讓負責這個計劃的人來我辦公室。

take charge of為「負責」之意，受詞放在of之後，表示受照顧或管理的人事物。相似片語：on the charge of「被控…罪名」；charge sb. up「激勵某人」；charge at「快速襲擊、向前衝」。

A: Have whoever is taking charge of the project come into my office.
讓負責這個計劃的人來我辦公室。

B: It is Jason, Sir. However, he is in a meeting right now.
是傑森，先生。但他現在正在開會。

A: Fine. Get him into my office as soon as the meeting is over.
好。會議一結束就讓他來我辦公室。

B: Yes, Sir.
是的，先生。

相關用語 **in charge of 負責**　進階補充 **preside over 負責**

454

When will the new law take effect?

新法何時生效？

take effect為「生效」之意。其他有關effect的片語有：bring...into effect = carry...into effect「實行」；give effect to「實行、實施」；in effect「實際上」；of no effect = without effect「無效」。

A: Did you know the government has made a new law against drunk driving?
你知道政府已經制定反酒駕的新法令嗎？

B: That is terrific! When will it take effect?
太棒了！何時生效？

A: It will go into effect on July 1st.
七月一日將生效。

B: Great! I'm glad those irresponsible drivers will finally be punished properly.
太棒了！那些不負責任的駕駛，總算可以受到適當的懲罰了。

相關用語 **go into effect 生效**　進階補充 **drunk driving 酒醉駕車**

455 She always **takes** my love and care **for granted**.

她總是把我的愛和關心視作理所當然。

take it for granted為「視為理所當然」之意。這裡的it是虛受詞，真受詞是that帶出來的子句(that + S + V)，表示將某件事視為理所當然。grant是動詞，表「授與、承認」。本片語用法：S + take sth. for granted或S + take it for granted that S + V。

MP3
455

A: What's wrong between you and Cindy?
你和辛蒂怎麼了？

B: We had a fight and broke up.
我們吵了一架分手了。

A: Why was that?
怎麼會這樣？

B: She always takes my love and care for granted. I can't take it any more.
她總是把我的愛和關心視作理所當然，我再也受不了了。

相關用語 → **deserve** 應得　　進階補充 → **can't take it** 無法容忍

456 Is there anything I should **take note of**?

有任何我該注意的事嗎？

take note of為「注意、留心」之意，指「留心或注意任何重要或意義重大的事物」。其用法：S + take note of + 人 / 事情。note可當動詞也可當名詞，皆有「注意」之意。相關片語：hit/strike the right note「發揮功效」；somebody of note「名人」；make a mental note「默背」。

MP3
456

A: This is your first time operating this machine, isn't it?
這是你第一次操作這台機器，對吧？

B: Yes. Is there anything I should take note of?
是的。有任何我該注意的事嗎？

A: Remember to turn it off when you're done, or it will get overheated.
用完記得關機，否則會過熱。

B: No problem.
沒問題。

相關用語 → **heed** 注意　　進階補充 → **pay attention to** 留意

457

I want you to **take responsibility for** the team.

我要你負責小組。

take responsibility for為「負責」之意。responsibility為「責任」的名詞形，responsible是形容詞，此句片語與be responsible for的意思相同。相關片語：hold sb. responsible for sth.「認為某人應負…的責任」。

457

A: I will be away for five days. I want you to **take responsibility for** the team.
我會離開五天，我要你負責小組。

B: Sir, I am not sure if I am capable.
長官，我不確定我能否勝任。

A: You are the one I trust the most. Just **keep in touch with** me.
你是我最信得過的人。和我保持聯絡即可。

B: Thank you, Sir. I will.
謝謝長官。我會的。

相關用語 **take charge** 掌管　　進階補充 **keep in touch** 保持聯絡

458

We have to **think up** a new marketing plan.

我們得想出新的行銷企劃。

think up為「想出、發明」之意，是一則美式口語片語。think是指「歸納某種想法以達到其結論，或藉思考以形成某種念頭」的意思，up改成out後意思不變。

458

A: We have to **think up** a new marketing plan.
我們得想出新的行銷企劃。

B: Why do we need a new one?
為何需要新的企劃？

A: Mr. Watson rejected the old one, and he would like to see a new one by tomorrow.
華生先生否決了舊企劃，且想要在明天前看到新企劃。

B: Oh, no. That means working overtime again.
噢，不。代表又得加班了。

相關用語 **think out** 想出　　進階補充 **strike out** 想出

459 She has **turned a deaf ear to** me for several days.

她已對我充耳不聞好幾天了。

turn a deaf ear to為「充耳不聞」之意。用法：S + turn a deaf ear to + 受詞。由turn所衍生的詞彙有：turnabout「旋轉木馬(美式用法)」；turning point「轉捩點」；turnoff「旁道、岔路(美式用法)」；turnout「產量、出席者」；turnover「翻轉、營業額」。

459

A: Can you find some time and talk to Maggie?
你可以找時間和瑪姬談談嗎？

B: Sure. Is she all right?
好啊。她還好吧？

A: She has been angry with me and has **turned a deaf ear to** me for several days.
她一直在生我的氣，已對我充耳不聞好幾天。

B: That's too bad. What did you do exactly?
真糟糕。你到底做了什麼？

相關用語 **ignore** 忽視　　進階補充 **deaf to** 不理、不聽

460 Mandy **turned** me **down** again.

曼蒂又拒絕我了。

turn down為「減少、拒絕」之意。當「拒絕」的意思解時，相似片語turn down the thumb為「表示反對」之意。當「轉小聲」(電視、收音機等)的意思解時，不等於close down(歇業)之意。

460

A: Why are you so upset?
你為何如此沮喪？

B: It's Mandy. She **turned** me **down** again.
因為曼蒂。她又拒絕我了。

A: Did you ask her out again? I thought she **made it clear** that she doesn't like you.
你又約她出去嗎？我以為她表達得很清楚，她不喜歡你。

B: I believe that's just for now. Eventually, she will know I am the one for her.
我相信那只是暫時的。她終究會知道我才是最適合她的人。

相關用語 **refuse** 拒絕　　進階補充 **make clear** 解釋清楚

461

You can try the dress on if you like.

如果您願意的話可以試穿洋裝。

try on為「試穿、試用」之意。此片語中的on是當副詞用，如果受詞是代名詞，要放在on之前。相似片語try out，為「試用、試驗」之意，指「試驗或試用一種不曾使用過的新東西」。

461

A: Did you find anything you like?
您有看到喜歡的東西嗎？

B: Yes, I would like to take a look at the pink dress.
有，我想看一下那件粉紅色洋裝。

A: You can try it on if you like.
如果您願意的話可以試穿。

B: That would be great.
那就太棒了。

相關用語 ▸ have a try 試試看　　進階補充 ▸ trial run 試車、試航

462

You can turn the can upside down.

你可以把罐子上下顛倒過來。

upside down為「亂七八糟、上下顛倒」之意，通常放在句尾，為一副詞片語。upside當名詞時，其意思為「上面、有利的一方」。若將本片語二字相連成為upside-down則為形容詞，意為「混亂的」。

462

A: Can you give a hand? I can't open the lid.
你可以幫個忙嗎？我打不開蓋子。

B: Maybe you can turn the can upside down. It would be easier.
或許你可以把罐子上下顛倒過來，會比較容易開。

A: It is! Thank you so much.
真的耶！謝謝你。

B: You're welcome.
不客氣。

相關用語 ▸ in a mess 混亂的　　進階補充 ▸ inside out 裡朝外地

463

We are about to **use up** all the money.

我們快花完所有的錢了。

use up為「用光、筋疲力盡」之意。當「筋疲力盡」的意思解時，屬於口語用法，常用被動態表示，如I'm used up。use指「為達到某目的而使用某物、某人或某工具」的意思。

MP3
463

A: We are about to use up all the money.
我們快花完所有的錢了。

B: Really? But we are just on the half way in our journey.
真的嗎？但我們的旅程只走到一半而已。

A: Don't worry. We can cash our traveler's checks.
別擔心，我們可以兌現旅行支票。

B: Great.
太棒了。

相關用語 ⊶ **run out** 被耗盡 進階補充 ⊶ **traveler's check** 旅行支票

464

We are going to **vote for** the location for the next field trip. 我們將投票決定下次校外教學的地點。

vote for為「投票」之意，用法：S + vote for + 受詞。其他關於vote的片語有：get out a vote「拉到足夠的支持票」，屬於美式用法；one man one vote「一人一票制」；vote down「投票罷免」；vote in「票選出(人)」；vote through「投票通過」；canvass for votes「拉票」。

MP3
464

A: Today we are going to vote for the location for the next field trip.
今天我們要投票決定下次校外教學的地點。

B: Oh, yeah!
噢，耶！

A: You can nominate wherever you want to go now.
現在，你們可以提名想去的地方。

B: Disneyland!
迪士尼樂園！

相關用語 ⊶ **decide on** 考慮後決定 進階補充 ⊶ **vote out** 罷免

465

I heard that you've walked out on the research project. 我聽說你退出研究計劃了。

walk out為「退出、罷工」之意。當「罷工」的意思解時，屬於口語用法。相似片語：walk out on「遺棄」；walk out with「有曖昧、拍拖」；walk over「輕易勝過」。

MP3
465

A: I heard that you've walked out on the research project. Why?
我聽說你退出研究計劃了。為什麼？

B: There was something between Mr. Chang and I.
我和張先生間有點狀況。

A: What was it?
什麼狀況？

B: Nothing special. We just can't get along well.
沒什麼特別的。我們就是處不來。

相關用語 ── back out 退出　　　進階補充 ── get along 相處

466

Can you wind up your presentation?

可以結束你的簡報了嗎？

wind up為「使緊張、做結尾」之意。wind當名詞是「風」的意思，當動詞則是「曲折、蜿蜒、纏繞、絞起」的意思，其三態為：wind、wound、wound，注意不要與wound，名詞，「傷口」搞混。

MP3
466

A: Can you wind up your presentation?
可以結束你的簡報了嗎？

B: But I still have ten slides to go.
但我還有十張投影片要說明。

A: You have been talking for over twenty minutes. That's way too long.
你已經講了超過二十分鐘，太久了。

B: I am sorry.
對不起。

相關用語 ── end up 結束　　　進階補充 ── finish up with 以…告終

467

I am sorry that your relationship with Jack didn't work out. 很遺憾你和傑克之間沒有結果。

work out為「順利進行、耗盡體力」之意。work是指「任何勞心勞力的工作」，是所有具「工作」意義的字彙中，最常見的一個。除了前述的意思外，這則片語還有「理解、計算、解決」等解釋。

467

A: I am sorry that your relationship with Jack didn't work out.
很遺憾你和傑克之間沒有結果。

B: That's OK. It's his loss.
沒關係。這是他的損失。

A: It definitely is.
一定是的。

B: I'm certain I will meet my Mr. Right soon.
我一定很快就會遇見我的白馬王子。

相關用語 → **come off** 順利進行　　進階補充 → **go well** 順利進展

468

I would rather stay home and watch TV.
我寧願待在家裡看電視。

would rather為「寧願」之意。rather為副詞，表示「寧願」，後方直接加原形動詞，表示「寧願做某事」。衍生片語：would rather A than B是「寧願做A也不願做B」。

468

A: What are you going to do today?
你今天要做什麼？

B: I would rather stay home and watch TV.
我寧願待在家裡看電視。

A: Are you sure? It's the weekend!
你確定嗎？現在是週末耶！

B: I really want to get some rest after the final exam.
我真的想在期末考後好好休息一下。

相關用語 → **prefer** 寧可　　進階補充 → **get some rest** 休息一下

中高級片語 Part 3

中高級片語，係針對欲增強英語能力至
較成熟境界、並有心擴展英語使用範圍
者所設計。學完本章的中高級片語，英
語溝通力可達大學非英語主修系所畢業
者程度，即有能力在除了日常生活的情
境外，展現較成熟的英文聽、說、讀、
寫能力。

*How to Master Dixon Idioms and English
Phrases with One Single Sentence*

{ *Part 3* }

中高級片語

High-Intermediate Level

Basic Level

Intermediate Level

High-Intermediate Level

Dixon Idioms

and

English phrases

469

Did you **accuse** Janet **of** stealing?

你有指控珍娜偷竊嗎?

accuse A of B為「控告A犯有B罪行」之意。用法:S + accuse + 人 + of + 罪行。由accuse衍生的字彙包括:accused「被告」;accuser「原告」。此字可與另一個字convict相比照,accuse指的是「提出控告」,但被告是否有犯罪事實仍須經審判才能確定;而convict的意思則為「判決有罪」,指經審判後罪刑已經確定。

A: Did you accuse Janet of stealing?
你有指控珍娜偷竊嗎?

B: Yes, I saw her sneaking out of the warehouse.
是的,我看到她偷溜出倉庫。

A: Are you sure it was her?
你確定是她嗎?

B: Yes. I saw several toner cartridges in her bag as she passed me.
是的。她走過我時,我看到她袋子裡有好幾個碳粉匣。

相關用語 **accusation 指控**　　進階補充 **toner cartridge 碳粉匣**

470

The novel already been **adapted for** the movies.

小說已被改編成電影。

adapt A for B的意思為:為了目的B而改裝、改編A物,常用於音樂、電影和建築物等的改造。需特別注意的是,adapt、adept和adopt等單字字形相近但字義相異,adept為「熟練的」,後接介系詞at;adopt的意思則為「採納、收養」,三者意義相差甚遠,千萬別搞混了。

A: Have you read the famous novel, _Twilight_?
你讀過著名小說《暮光之城》嗎?

B: Yes, I have. It's a vampire story.
我讀過。那是一部吸血鬼小說。

A: And it's already been adapted for the movies.
而且已被改編成電影。

B: I know. Robert Pattinson is too handsome to be true!
我知道。羅伯·派汀森帥得令人難以置信。

相關用語 **rewrite 改寫**　　進階補充 **too...to... 太…而不能…**

471 Have you **adapted** yourself **to** the new school?

你已經適應新學校了嗎？

adapt to當動詞片語使用時，為「適應」之意，to為介系詞，後接名詞或動名詞。adapt可當及物動詞或不及物動詞；當及物動詞時，用法為S + adapt A to B；當不及物動詞時，用法則為S + adapt to + (代)名詞。

A: Have you **adapted** yourself **to** the new school?
你已經適應新學校了嗎？

B: I guess. It's a great place to study.
我想是吧。這是個很好的學習場所。

A: I can still **show** you **around** if you want.
如果你想，我還是可以帶你四處參觀。

B: That will be nice!
那就太好了！

相關用語 → adjust to 適應　　進階補充 → show...around 帶…參觀

472 That would be **adding fuel to the fire**.

那會是火上加油。

add fuel to the fire為非正式用法。字面上看，本片語是「在火上添燃料」、「火上加油」的意思，象徵著「使情況越發不可收拾」。相似片語：add insult to injury「雪上加霜」。insult是名詞「羞辱」，injury也是名詞「傷口」，相當於中文口語中的「在傷口上撒鹽」。

A: Why didn't you tell the teacher Jack **cut class** today?
你為何不跟老師報告傑克今天翹課？

B: The teacher already hates Jack. That would be **adding fuel to the fire**. Mr. Todd would be even angrier.
老師已經不喜歡傑克了，那會是火上加油，陶德老師只會更生氣。

A: Where did Jack go?
傑克去哪裡了？

B: He visited his grandma **in hospital**.
他去探望住院的祖母。

相關用語 → cut class 翹課　　進階補充 → in hospital 住院

473

Aside from cash, is there any other payment option?
除現金外，有其他付款方式嗎？

aside from跟apart from皆為「除此之外」的意思，然而在美式英文中，aside from比apart from更常被使用。aside是副詞，意為「在旁邊、離開」，因此和aside有關的片語都有「離開、拿開」的意思，如：lay aside「儲蓄、革除」；put aside「擱置」；set aside「保留、擱置」；turn aside「閃開、避開」等。

MP3
473

A: Aside from cash, is there any other payment option?
　　除現金外，有其他付款方式嗎？

B: We also accept credit card.
　　我們也收信用卡。

A: Then I will pay with my credit card. How much is it?
　　那我用信用卡付帳。多少錢？

B: The total is five thousand, eight hundred dollars.
　　總共是五千八百元。

相關用語 except 除…之外　　進階補充 credit card 信用卡

474

Do you have any plane tickets at a discount?
請問有打折的機票嗎？

at a discount為「打折扣、滯銷的」之意。discount可當名詞也可當動詞，當動詞時，discount on是「對…打折」的意思。要注意的是，discount當名詞時，經常與百分比連用，例如10% discount，代表的是「打九折」的意思，而非打一折。由discount所衍生的詞彙有：discount house「廉價商店(美式用法)」；discount rate「貼現率(商業用字)」。

MP3
474

A: Good morning. How may I help you?
　　早安。我可以為您做些什麼？

B: Do you have any plane tickets at a discount?
　　請問有打折的機票嗎？

A: Yes. The ticket to Bali is now only 6,666 NT dollars.
　　有的。去巴里島的機票現在只要新台幣6,666元。

B: What a bargain!
　　真是划算！

相關用語 on sale 廉售中　　進階補充 what a bargain 真便宜

475

I can't see very well **at a distance**.

距離有點遠，我看不太清楚。

at a distance為「有相當距離」之意。distance是「距離」的意思，形容詞為distant，副詞則為distantly。相關片語：keep + 人 + at a distance「與某人保持一定距離、不願與某人親近」；from a distance「從遠方」；to a distance「到遠方」。

A: Do you see the girl at the counter?
你看到櫃台邊的那個女生了嗎？

B: Which girl? I can't see very well **at a distance**.
哪一個女生？距離有點遠我看不太清楚。

A: I think she's our high school classmate, Jessica.
我想她是我們的高中同學潔西卡。

B: You're right! You have great eyesight.
沒錯！你視力真好。

相關用語 → **from afar** 從遠處   進階補充 → **around the corner** 在附近

476

We need to take Class B down **at all costs**.

我們得不計代價擊敗 B 班。

at all costs為「無論如何、不惜代價」之意。cost是「成本、代價」的意思。其他有關cost的片語有：cost of living「生活費」；cost management「成本控管」；at the cost of...「喪失、犧牲…」；count the cost「事先詳細盤算費用或得失」；to one's cost「使某人負擔費用」；cost a person dearly「使某人吃大虧」。

A: We need to take Class B down **at all costs**.
我們得不計代價擊敗 B 班。

B: But Class B has won the championship two years **in a row**.
但是B班連續兩年贏得冠軍。

A: This is the year they'll get defeated!
今年他們就會被打敗了！

B: I hope so.
我希望會。

相關用語 → **at any cost** 不計代價   進階補充 → **in a row** 連續

477
What do you think about the new retirement policy **at issue**? 你對於目前討論中的退休案有什麼想法？

at issue為「爭議中、討論中」之意。issue可當動詞和名詞，也有很多種解釋，動詞意義包括「發行、流出、放出、誕生、出版」等；名詞意義則包括「爭議、問題、發行量、流出、收益」等。

MP3
477

A: What do you think about the new retirement policy **at issue**?
你對於目前討論中的退休案有什麼想法？

B: Actually, I don't know much about it.
事實上我不太了解。

A: **According to** the new policy, the retirement age is now 60.
根據新的政策，退休年齡為六十歲。

B: What? That doesn't sound right.
什麼？那聽起來不太對。

相關用語 → in dispute 在爭論中　　進階補充 → according to 根據

478
What do you do when you are **at leisure**?
你閒暇時會做什麼？

at leisure為「在閒暇中」之意，也可寫成at one's leisure或in one's free time。由leisure所衍生的詞彙有：leisurely「從容不迫的(地)」；leisure centre「休閒中心(英式用法)」；leisurewear「休閒服」。

MP3
478

A: What do you do when you are **at leisure**?
你閒暇時會做什麼？

B: I enjoy reading, and sometimes I go to the movies. How about you?
我喜歡閱讀，有時則會去看電影。你呢？

A: I love movies, too. Let's go to a movie sometime this week together.
我也喜歡電影。本週找個時間一起去看場電影吧？

B: Sure.
好啊。

相關用語 → spare time 空閒時間　　進階補充 → recreation 消遣

479

Do you know why Allen was at odds with Mr. Burger? 你知道艾倫為何跟伯格先生吵架嗎？

at odds with為「爭吵」之意。odds有很多意思，較常見的包括「機會、不和、差異」等。跟odd有關的片語有：odds and ends「零星物品」；against longer odds「以寡敵眾」；make no odds「沒有太大差別」；take the odds「得到讓步」；What's the odds?「那有什麼關係？」。

MP3
479

A: Do you know why Allen was at odds with Mr. Burger?
你知道艾倫為何跟伯格先生吵架嗎？

B: Mr. Burger asked him to redo his new project.
伯格先生要他重做一份新企劃。

A: Why?
為什麼？

B: Mr. Burger thought Allen didn't bring out his best effort.
伯格先生覺得艾倫沒有盡力做好。

相關用語 · argue with 和…爭吵　　進階補充 · bring out 拿出

480

There are towels at your disposal in the cabinet.
櫃子裡有毛巾，你可任意使用。

at one's disposal為「供任意使用」之意，at可以用in代替。disposal是名詞，為「處理、處置」的意思，動詞型態為dispose。其他相關片語有：dispose of「處理、扔掉」；put...at one's disposal「把…交給某人自由處置」；Man proposes, God disposes.「謀事在人，成事在天」。

MP3
480

A: Welcome. Please make yourself at home.
歡迎。請把這裡當自己家。

B: Thank you for having me here during my business trip.
謝謝你讓我出差時住在這裡。

A: Not at all. There are towels at your disposal in the cabinet.
不客氣。櫃子裡有毛巾，你可任意使用。

B: Thank you.
謝謝你。

相關用語 · use at will 任意使用　　進階補充 · make use of 利用

481

Anyone who fails to hand in the report will be at his or her own risk. 沒交作業的人要自行負責。

at one's own risk為「自行負責」之意。risk是「風險」的意思，形容詞為 risky。其他關於risk的片語有：risk life and limb、risk one's neck「冒著重大危險」；run the risk of doing sth「冒著…的風險」。

A: Anyone who fails to hand in the report will be at his or her own risk.
沒交作業的人要自行負責。

B: What does that mean?
那是什麼意思？

A: It means he or she might fail the class.
就是可能會被當。

B: Oh, my!
喔，我的天啊！

相關用語 → at risk 處於危險中　進階補充 → fail to 不能

482

You shouldn't just throw your clothes at random all over the place. 你不該隨處亂丟你的衣服。

at random為「隨意地、任意地」之意，是一則副詞片語，通常放在句尾。random是指「沒有深思或確定目的、計畫、選擇的行動」，一般譯為「隨機」，為在統計和電腦領域被廣為使用的術語，例如：random variable「隨機變數」；random access memory「隨機存取記憶體」(RAM)等。

A: You should pay more attention to your personal hygiene.
你應更加注意個人衛生。

B: What do you mean?
你的意思是？

A: You shouldn't just throw your clothes at random all over the place.
你不該隨處亂丟你的衣服。

B: That's not really hygiene. At least I don't smell.
這跟衛生關係不大。至少我不臭。

相關用語 → at will 任意　進階補充 → pay attention to 注意

483

You shouldn't earn more money **at the expense of** your health. 你不該為了賺更多錢而犧牲健康。

at the expense of為「以…為代價」之意。expense和cost都有「費用、成本」的意思。相似片語：at one's expense「自費、犧牲自己」；hang the expense「盡可能地花費」。

A: Are you working a **double shift** again?
你又連值兩班了嗎？

B: Yes, and it's a good thing that they offer better pay for double shifts.
是啊，他們給連值兩班較好的薪水，真是太好了。

A: But I don't want you to earn more money **at the expense of** your health.
但我不想要你為了賺更多錢而犧牲健康。

B: Don't worry. I'll be fine.
別擔心，我沒事的。

相關用語 ► **at all costs** 不惜代價　　進階補充 ► **double shift** 連值兩班

484

I am basically **at the mercy of** Mr. Stevens.

基本上，我任由史蒂文斯先生擺佈。

at the mercy of為「任由…擺佈」之意。mercy是名詞，表「仁慈」，其形容詞是merciful；副詞是mercifully。由mercy所衍生的片語如：mercy killing「安樂死、無痛致死」。由mercy所衍生的辭彙有：merciless是形容詞，意為「無情的、殘酷的」，其副詞是mercilessly。

A: Have you found a job yet?
你找到工作了嗎？

B: Not really. I am working part-time at Mr. Stevens's factory.
還沒。我在史蒂文斯先生的工廠打工。

A: Do you have **labor insurance**? Are you in a union?
你有勞工保險嗎？你有加入工會嗎？

B: No. I am basically **at the mercy of** Mr. Stevens.
沒有。基本上，我任由史蒂文斯先生擺佈。

相關用語 ► **manipulate** 操縱　　進階補充 ► **labor insurance** 勞工保險

485

He **is** certainly **a match for** me.

他的確是我的對手。

be a match for為「與…匹敵、為…的對手」之意。用法：S + be V + a match for + 人。match當名詞是「火柴、對手」的意思；當動詞是「匹敵、相配」的意思。由match所衍生的片語和辭彙有：match up「相配」；match up to「比得上」；matchmaker「媒婆」。

A: Who is your opponent for the next round?
你下一輪的對手是誰？

B: It's Jason. He **is** certainly **a match for** me.
是傑森。他的確是我的對手。

A: Yet you must be very **excited about** having him as your opponent.
然而你一定很興奮他當你的對手。

B: Absolutely!
當然！

相關用語 • **rival** 對手   進階補充 • **excited about** 對…感到興奮

486

He **is absorbed in** making models again.

他又全神貫注於製作模型了。

be absorbed in為「全神貫注、專心」之意。用法：S + be V + absorbed in + 事情。absorb是動詞，有「吸收、汲取、使全神貫注」的意思；absorbed在這裡是形容詞，為「全神貫注的」之意。由absorb所衍生的詞彙如：absorbent「有吸收力的、吸收劑」。

A: It's lunch time. Where's Frank?
午餐時間到。法蘭克在哪？

B: I think he **is absorbed in** making models again.
我想他又全神貫注於製作模型了。

A: He has been **all nuts** about model-making lately, hasn't he?
他最近很迷模型，對吧？

B: Indeed he has.
他的確是。

相關用語 • **concentrate on** 專注於   進階補充 • **all nuts** 熱衷的

254

487

It is abundant in natural resources and wildlife.

它擁有豐富的天然資源和野生生物。

be abundant in為「豐富、充裕」之意。用法：S + be V + abundant in + (代)名詞。plentiful、abundant、copious和ample皆為「豐富的」之意，其差別為：plentiful是指「多而豐富的」；abundant是指「綽綽有餘、非常豐富的」；copious是指「生產量或可使用的量多而豐富的」；ample則是指「大大地滿足某種要求的」。

A: What will you do on Independence Day?
你獨立紀念日要做什麼？

B: I am going to Yellowstone National Park.
我要去黃石公園。

A: Sounds great. **It is abundant in** natural resources and wildlife.
聽起來很棒。它擁有豐富的天然資源和野生生物。

B: I know. I am **looking forward to** this trip very much.
沒錯。我非常期待這趟旅行。

相關用語 **be full of** 充滿的   進階補充 **look forward to** 盼望

488

I am getting **accustomed to** the new environment.

我逐漸習慣新環境。

be accustomed to為「習慣於…」之意。這裡的to是介系詞，後接Ving或名詞片語。用法：S + be V + accustomed to + 名詞 / Ving。相似片語：accustom oneself to「使自己習慣於…」。

A: You're getting **accustomed to** the new environment, aren't you?
你逐漸習慣新環境了吧？

B: Yes, Ma'am. Everyone treats me pretty nicely.
是的，老師。大家都對我蠻好的。

A: And I can see you **fit in** the class quite well.
而且我觀察到，你相當融入這個班級。

B: I try my best to do so.
我盡力而為。

相關用語 **be used to** 習慣於   進階補充 **fit in** 融入

489 Why **are you so anxious to** talk to Mr. Watson?

你為何這麼想和華生先生說話？

be anxious to為「渴望」之意。用法：S + be V + anxious to + V。anxious的意思是「渴望的」，其名詞是anxiety，副詞是anxiously。若將介系詞to改成for/about時，意思則為「為某事焦慮、擔心」的意思，此時anxious的意思為「焦慮的、擔憂的」。

A: Why are you so anxious to talk to Mr. Watson?
你為何這麼想和華生先生說話？

B: I have the perfect idea for the new marketing project.
我想到市場行銷最棒的新點子。

A: Really? That's great! I'll tell him no sooner than he comes back.
真的嗎？那太棒了！他一回來我就馬上跟他說。

B: Thank you so much.
非常謝謝你。

相關用語 **yearn for** 渴望的　　進階補充 **no sooner than** 一…就…

490 Y**ou are apt to** mix the past tense with the present tense. 你容易弄混現在式和過去式。

be apt to為「有…傾向、易於」之意。用法：S + be V + apt to + V。apt是形容詞，有「易於、傾向、恰當、善於」等意思，意義不同時後方接的介系詞也不同。表達「有某種傾向」的說法相當多，例如：be inclined to、be liable to、tend to、side with等。

A: I would like to talk to you about your composition.
我想和你談談你的作文。

B: What is it, Ms. Chen?
怎麼了，陳老師？

A: I notice that you are apt to mix the past tense with the present tense.
我注意到你容易弄混現在式跟過去式。

B: I think I am totally confused.
我想我完全搞混了。

相關用語 **be inclined to** 傾向於　　進階補充 **be apt at** 善於

491

I am confident of Nadal. He is my favorite.

我對納達爾有信心。他是我的最愛。

be confident of為「確信、有把握」之意。用法：S + be V + confident of + (代)名詞；S + be V + confident that + 子句。sure和confident都有「確信」的意思，其差別為：sure是指「確實無誤」的意思，為最常見的「確信」用字；confident是指「確信某件事情」。

491

A: Who do you think will win the game?
你覺得誰會贏得這場比賽？

B: I am confident of Nadal. He is my favorite.
我對納達爾有信心。他是我的最愛。

A: How about Federer?
那費德勒呢？

B: He is also great, but he's not the best.
他也很棒，但不是最棒的。

相關用語 ► **have faith in** 信任　　進階補充 ► **convince of** 確信

492

They are destined to be with each other.

他們是命中注定的一對。

be destined to為「命中注定」之意。destine是動詞「命定」，其名詞是destiny。用法：S + be V + destined to + V。fate和destiny都表「命運」，其差別為：fate是指「支配人或物的神或超自然力量，通常暗示著其結果是無法避免或無法改變的」；destiny可和fate互換，但含有「著重於由超自然力量所預先注定的不可改變結果」的意味。

492

A: Look at Frank and May. They're such a lovely couple.
你看法蘭克和梅。他們真是可愛的一對。

B: You are right. They are destined to be with each other.
你說得沒錯。他們是命中注定的一對。

A: Looking at them makes me want to get married, too. Will you marry me?
看著他們讓我也想結婚了。你願意嫁給我嗎？

B: Are you out of your mind?
你瘋了嗎？

相關用語 ► **doom** 注定　　進階補充 ► **out of one's mind** 失去理智

493

Sociology is quite distinct from social work.

社會學與社會工作相當不同。

be distinct from為「與…區別」之意。distinct是形容詞,意為「不同的、有區別的」,名詞是distinction;副詞是distinctly「清楚地」。distinct和distinctive詞性相同但字義不同;主要區別在:前者通常需與其他物品做比較,表示「不同、有別」;後者則表示「有特色的、特殊的」。

MP3
493

A: What are you studying in college?
你大學的主修是?

B: I major in social work.
我主修社會工作。

A: Is social work similar to sociology?
社會工作與社會學類似嗎?

B: Sociology is quite distinct from social work.
社會學與社會工作相當不同。

相關用語 ○ particular 獨特的　　進階補充 ○ be similar to 與…相似

494

Come on. You are just envious of her.

拜託。你只是嫉妒她。

be envious of為「嫉妒的」之意。用法:S + be V + envious of + 事情 / 人。由envy (名詞,「羨慕」之意)所衍生的詞彙有:envier「羨慕者」;enviable「可羨慕的」;enviously「羨慕地」。要記住的是表示羨慕的字彙中,envy、covet都帶有因羨慕引發負面的心態甚至作為;而admire才是真正由衷地佩服、欽羨。

MP3
494

A: I am fed up with Lucy and her bragging about her promotion.
我受夠露西一直炫耀她的升職。

B: Come on. You are just envious of her.
拜託。你只是嫉妒她。

A: I am not! Don't you find her a bit annoying?
我才沒有!你不覺得她有點煩人嗎?

B: No at all.
一點也不會。

相關用語 ○ jealous 妒忌的　　進階補充 ○ brag about 自誇

495

I am fed up with my boss and her nagging.

我受夠我的老闆以及她的嘮叨。

be fed up with為「感到厭煩」之意，後面接不愉快、不如意的事。用法：S + be V + fed up with + 不愉快、不如意的事。fed是feed的過去式及過去分詞。相關片語：be fed up to the back teeth「對長時期的不如意或老生常談感到厭倦」；be spoon-fed「受填鴨式教育的」。

A: Why do you want to quit your job?
你為何想離職？

B: I am **fed up with** my boss and her nagging.
我受夠我老闆以及她的嘮叨。

A: Are you going to find a new job?
你要找新工作嗎？

B: No, I want to **take a break** for a few weeks.
不，我想休息幾週。

相關用語 ⟶ **be tired of** 厭煩　　進階補充 ⟶ **take a break** 休息

496

Math is Greek to me!

我對數學一竅不通！

be Greek to為「一竅不通」之意。Greek在此是指「難懂的事、莫名其妙的話」，而不是指「希臘」。西方諺語「When Greek meets Greek, then comes the tug of war.」的意思是說「兩雄相遇，即起激鬥」。用法：事情 + be Greek to + 人，與其他表示無知的片語順序不同，例如：人 + know nothing about + 事情；人 + be utterly ignorant of + 事情。

A: Math is **Greek to** me!
我對數學一竅不通！

B: Don't give up. I can help you review it.
別放棄。我可以幫你複習。

A: That's very nice of you.
你人真好。

B: No problem.
不客氣。

相關用語 ⟶ **ignorant** 無知的　　進階補充 ⟶ **illiteracy** 文盲

497

I am inclined to stay where I am right now.

我傾向於留任現職。

be inclined to為「有…傾向」之意，此片語慣用被動式。用法：S + be V + inclined to + V。incline為動詞，表「有…傾向、易於」的意思。incline 的相關字彙為：inclination「趨勢」；inclinable「傾向的」。

A: A little bird told me you've been offered a new position on Karen's team.
有人跟我說，凱倫那組給了你一個新職位。

B: That's right, but I am inclined to stay where I am right now.
沒錯，但我傾向於留任現職。

A: Why is that?
為什麼？

B: I love my team members, and they always offer me great help when I need it.
我喜歡我的組員，他們總是適時給予我許多幫助。

相關用語 ⊶ **tend to 傾向於…**　　進階補充 ⊶ **tendency 傾向**

498

When I'm with her, I always feel inferior to her.

跟她在一起時，我總是自嘆弗如。

be/feel inferior to為「劣於」之意。用法：S + be V + inferior to + 名詞＝ S + be V + worse than + 名詞。inferior to的反義片語是superior to「優於」，inferior和superior都可當名詞，前者表示「部屬、下級」，後者表示「上司、主管」。

A: Lucy is so clever.
露西好聰明。

B: And she is so beautiful.
而且她很美。

A: When I'm with her, I always feel inferior to her.
跟她在一起時，我總是自嘆弗如。

B: Me, too.
我也是。

相關用語 ⊶ **worse than 較…差**　　進階補充 ⊶ **superior to 優於**

499

I am not well disposed to him.

我對他沒有好感。

be well disposed to為「對⋯有好感」之意。dispose在此為「使傾向於、使有意於」，用作被動式即為「有意於」，well則作副詞修飾。反義片語：be ill disposed to「對⋯覺得反感」。此片語中的to可改成toward。

A: You were rude to Jack. What is your problem with him?
你對傑克很沒禮貌。你對他有什麼意見嗎？

B: I am not well disposed to him.
我對他沒有好感。

A: Why is that?
為什麼？

B: The way he talked to Ms. Chen made me sick.
他跟陳老師說話的方式讓我感到噁心。

相關用語 ⟩ **be fond of** 喜好的　　進階補充 ⟩ **favorable** 討喜的

500

Don't beat around the bush!

別拐彎抹角了！

beat around the bush為「拐彎抹角」之意。本片語源於過去獵人在樹叢間搜尋獵物時，透過敲擊周遭的樹木來引出目標；後引申為不直接針對目標，而使用迂迴的手段來旁敲側擊之意。與beat相關的片語有：beat off「擊退」；beat out「撲滅、敲打」；beat up「痛打、攪拌」。

A: Don't beat around the bush! Just tell me where Jack is!
別拐彎抹角了！直接跟我說傑克在哪裡！

B: As his best friend and roommate, I promised not to tell. I'm sorry.
身為他的摯友兼室友，我答應他不能說。很抱歉。

A: OK. Then I'll have to tell Linda about how you cheated on her last month.
好吧。那我只好跟琳達說你上個月背著她偷吃。

B: Please don't! He is out with Maggie.
拜託不要！他和瑪姬出去了。

相關用語 ⟩ **roundabout** 繞圈子的　　進階補充 ⟩ **straightforward** 坦率的

501

He is too young to bite the dust on the battlefield.

他太年輕，不該死在戰場上。

bite the dust為「斷送、失敗、陣亡」之意。bite可用eat、lick來代替，dust則可用ground來代替。dust是「灰塵、垃圾、遺骸」的意思。

MP3
501

A: Have you heard the news? Mr. Jackson's son died in Iraq.
你聽說了嗎？傑克森先生的兒子死在伊拉克。

B: Oh, no! He is too young to bite the dust on the battlefield.
噢，不！他太年輕，不該死在戰場上。

A: I couldn't agree more. War is a terrible thing, isn't it?
我很同意。戰爭很可怕，不是嗎？

B: That's right. I hope the president can put an end to the war soon.
沒錯。希望總統能儘快結束戰事。

相關用語 ► perish 死去　　進階補充 ► put an end to 結束

502

He blamed me for the failure of the marketing project. 他因行銷企劃失敗而責怪我。

blame for為「責怪」之意。blame可當名詞也可當動詞，用法：S + blame + 人 + for + 事情。其他關於blame的片語有：Blame it!「真該死！真可惡！」(美式俚語)；A bad workman blames his tools.「笨工匠總怪工具差」；lay the blame on sb./sth.「把責任歸咎於…」。

MP3
502

A: What did Mr. Wilson talk to you about this morning?
威爾森先生今天早上跟你說了什麼？

B: He blamed me for the failure of the marketing project.
他因行銷企劃失敗而責怪我。

A: Really? That's unfair! The project was doomed to failure from the start! Everyone knows that!
真的嗎？太不公平了！這個企劃一開始就注定會失敗！大家都知道的！

B: Except Mr. Wilson.
除了威爾森先生以外。

相關用語 ► blamed 該死的　　進階補充 ► be doomed to 注定

262

503

I don't like to boast of the things I do.

我不喜歡誇耀曾做過的事。

boast of為「誇耀」之意，可把of改成about，後接用來誇耀的人或事；也可改成that後接子句。用法：S + boast of/about + N/Ving。boast衍生字彙有：boastful「自誇的」；boastfully「誇耀地」；boaster「自誇者」。

MP3
503

A: Why didn't you tell me that you won the championship?
　　為何你沒跟我說你贏得冠軍？

B: I don't like to boast of the things I do.
　　我不喜歡誇耀曾做過的事。

A: You are such a humble person.
　　你真是個謙虛的人。

B: Thank you.
　　謝謝你。

（相關用語）**show off 炫耀**　　（進階補充）**flaunt 炫耀**

504

Just bow your neck to her and promise her you won't do it again. 向她低頭，承諾你以後不會再這麼做了。

bow the neck to為「向…低頭、屈服」之意。用法：S + bow the neck to + 人。bow是動詞，表「屈服、鞠躬」，和bow相關的片語有：bow out with「(演員)退場」；bow down「屈服」；make one's bow「行禮鞠躬」；take a bow「上前謝幕」。

MP3
504

A: What's wrong with you and Amy? She said she won't talk to you any more.
　　你和愛咪怎麼了？她說她不會再跟你說話了。

B: She saw me with a girl in my arms and she was outraged.
　　她看見我抱著個女生，她氣炸了。

A: So, just bow your neck to her and promise her you won't do it again.
　　那就向她低頭，承諾你以後不會再這麼做了。

B: But it was my little niece in my arms!
　　但我抱著的是我的小姪女！

（相關用語）**succumb to 屈服**　　（進階補充）**in one's arm 在…懷裡**

505

The elevator **broke down**.

電梯故障了。

break down有「故障、失敗」之意。此外，還有「毀壞、鎮壓、分析、崩潰、健康衰弱」等其他意思。以break開頭的片語如：break into「闖入」；break off「突然停止」；break one's back「努力做某事」等。

A: The elevator broke down. I'm fixing it now. Please take the stairs.
電梯故障了，我正在維修，請走樓梯。

B: That's too bad. I have to get to the 22nd Floor for a meeting.
真糟糕。我得到二十二樓開會。

A: Don't worry. I think I can get it done in fifteen minutes.
別擔心。我想我能在十五分鐘內修好。

B: Great! I'll wait here.
太棒了！我在這兒等。

相關用語 **malfunction 故障**　　進階補充 **get...done 完成某事**

506

Then I'd better not to **break my words**.

那我最好不要失信。

break one's words為「失信」之意。這裡的break是「違反、違背」的意思，也可用片語go back on「不履行、背叛」來替代。words則代表說過的「話語」，也可用promise、commitment「承諾」等替代。

A: What are you going to buy Jay for Christmas?
你聖誕節要買什麼給杰？

B: Perhaps a dictionary. He needs to work harder on his English composition skills.
也許是字典吧。他需要更努力加強英文作文技巧。

A: But you've made a promise that you would buy him a mountain bike.
但你已承諾過要買登山腳踏車給他。

B: Then I'd better not to break my words.
那我最好不要失信。

相關用語 **eat one's words 食言**　　進階補充 **work harder 更努力**

507

A fight broke out in the federal prison.

聯邦監獄爆發打群架事件。

break out為「爆發、突然發生」之意。此外，還有「逃脫、言語突然激烈起來」的意思。關於「爆發」的用語很多，如break out、burst out通常用於戰爭或災難；火山爆發則用erupt；情緒上的忽然爆發則用flare up。

MP3
507

A: Did you watch the news this morning?
你今天早上有看新聞嗎？

B: No. Was there anything new?
沒有。有什麼新消息嗎？

A: A fight broke out in the federal prison, and two prisoners died.
聯邦監獄爆發打群架事件，死了兩名囚犯。

B: Oh, that's too bad.
噢，真是糟糕。

相關用語 ○ **outburst** 迸發　　進階補充 ○ **burst into** 情緒爆發

508

I believe you can certainly break through your limitations. 我相信你一定可以突破極限。

break through為「突破、征服」之意。用法：S + break through + 受詞。此片語的意義相當多，包括「穿透、突出、刷新(紀錄)、克服」等。若將兩個字連在一起，成為breakthrough，則變成名詞的「突破、創新」，通常與make連用，如make a breakthrough。

MP3
508

A: When is your next marathon?
你下一場馬拉松賽是什麼時候？

B: It's next Saturday, and I am worried that I can't make it through the whole race.
下週六，我擔心無法跑完全程。

A: Don't worry. I believe you can certainly break through your limitations during the Taroko Gorge marathon.
別擔心。我相信你一定可以突破極限、征服太魯閣峽谷的。

B: Thank you.
謝謝你。

相關用語 ○ **look through** 識破　　進階補充 ○ **make it** 完成

509

A reform must be **brought into effect**.

改革必須實施。

bring...into effect為「實行、實施」之意。用法：S + bring + 受詞 + into effect。effect是「結果、效果」的意思。由bring開頭的片語有：bring along「攜帶」；bring around「說服」；bring down「減低、打倒」。

A: A reform must be brought into effect for the betterment of the company.
為了使公司更好，必須實施改革。

B: I don't get it. What do you mean?
我不明白。你的意思是？

A: The promotion system is a mess, and only **apple polishers** get promoted.
升遷制度很糟，只有馬屁精會升遷。

B: I couldn't agree more.
我非常贊同。

相關用語 • **get afoot 實施**　　進階補充 • **apple polisher 逢迎者**

510

I will **brush up on** some basics with my sister.

我會和姊姊一起複習基礎原理。

brush up on為「複習」之意，屬美式用法，英式用法不加on。brush當動詞時是「刷、擦」的意思，當名詞時則是「刷子、刷狀物」。由brush所衍生的片語有：brush aside「漠視」；be as daft as a brush「行為愚蠢」(英式口語用法)；tar sb. with the same brush「一丘之貉」。

A: How is your preparation for the math quiz on Friday going?
星期五的數學小考你準備得如何？

B: I will **brush up on** some basics with my sister tonight.
我今晚會和姊姊一起複習基礎原理。

A: That's awesome! Can I be part of your study group?
真棒！我可以加入你們的讀書小組嗎？

B: Sure. It's seven thirty at my place.
當然可以。七點半在我家。

相關用語 • **review 複習**　　進階補充 • **brush off 置之不理**

511

He's burning the midnight oil for the midterm.

他正為了期中考熬夜。

burn the midnight oil從字面上看來，是「挑燈夜戰」，意為「熬夜」。與oil相關的片語有：pour oil on troubled waters「使冷靜」；be no oil painting「不吸引人的」(英式非正式用法)；oil the wheels「促成」。

MP3
511

A: Jack's light is still on. Do you want me to **check on** him?
傑克房裡的燈還亮著。要我去看看他嗎？

B: No, you don't have to. He's just **burning the midnight oil** for the midterm.
不，不必。他正為期中考熬夜。

A: That's too bad. Lack of sleep will dull his senses.
這樣真不好。缺乏睡眠會讓他變得遲鈍。

B: I know. I've told him a million times.
我知道。我已經跟他說過幾百遍了。

相關用語 ∘ **stay up** 熬夜   進階補充 ∘ **check on** 檢查

512

Jessica burst into tears in class.

潔西卡上課時突然大哭。

burst into為「情緒的突然發作」之意。介系詞into後通常接表示某種情緒的動名詞或名詞，例如burst into tears「突然哭泣」；burst into laughter「突然大笑」等。此片語也可當「突然闖入」之意解。

MP3
512

A: Do you know why Jessica **burst into** tears in class?
你知道為何潔西卡上課時突然大哭嗎？

B: The teacher played a song that **reminded** her **of** her grandmother.
老師放的歌讓她想起祖母。

A: She must have loved her grandmother very much.
她一定非常愛祖母。

B: More than you can imagine. She was brought up by her grandmother.
比你想像的還愛。她是由祖母帶大的。

相關用語 ∘ **burst out** 突然…起來   進階補充 ∘ **remind of** 使回想起

513

Mr. Watson holds the post by virtue of his family connections. 華生先生憑藉家族背景獲任該職。

by virtue of為「由於、憑藉」之意。by可用in代替。virtue是「美德、德行、優點」的意思。相關片語：make a virtue of necessity「把必須做的事變得有趣」；extol the virtues of sb./sth.「讚揚某人或某事」；Virtue is its own reward.「為善即是善報」。

A: Mr. Watson holds the post by virtue of his family connections.
華生先生憑藉家族背景獲任該職。

B: What do you mean?
你的意思是？

A: His sister is the president's wife.
他姐姐是總裁夫人。

B: No wonder they seem to be really close.
難怪他們走得很近。

相關用語 ▸ hold the post 擔任…職務　　進階補充 ▸ no wonder 難怪

514

Let's call it a day.

今天到此為止吧。

call it a day為「結束一天的工作」之意，通常以祈使句呈現，如例句所示。與call相關的片語包括：call for「要求」；call one's names「用無禮的字句描述他人」；call the tune「擁有最高權力」；have first call on「擁有優先使用權」。

A: It's five already! Let's call it a day.
已經五點了！今天到此為止吧。

B: Not for me. I have to finish the report.
我不行。我得把報告做完。

A: Come on! It's Friday!
拜託！今天是星期五！

B: Sorry. You can leave first.
抱歉。你可以先走。

相關用語 ▸ finish 完成　　進階補充 ▸ call a halt 命令停止

515

I am afraid we cannot choose but to remove part of it. 我們恐怕別無選擇，只能把部分移除了。

cannot choose but為「只好、不得不」之意。用法：S + cannot choose but + to V。此句型另有兩種表示法，同樣可表達「不得不」的意思，即cannot but和cannot help but，but後面都必須先加上不定詞to再加上原形動詞。要注意的是，當choose換成用名詞型choice表達的時候，句型變成have no choice but，後接原形動詞。

MP3
515

A: Ma'am, the pipes are clogged with lumps of hair and food.
女士，水管被毛髮和食物碎塊塞住了。

B: What should we do now?
現在該如何處理？

A: I am afraid we cannot choose but to remove part of it.
我們恐怕別無選擇，只能把部分移除了。

B: That's too bad.
真是太糟了。

相關用語 ⟶ by choice 出於選擇   進階補充 ⟶ clog with 堵塞

516

I thought I caught a glimpse of you and Mandy.
我以為我瞥見了你和曼蒂。

catch a glimpse of為「瞥見」之意，這裡的catch可用have或get代替。glimpse可以當動詞和名詞，都是「瞥見」的意思，即「目光輕微拂過、不經意掃視到」之意，和glance較類似，但與look「有目的的注視」不同。

MP3
516

A: Did you go to Jason's Bar last night?
你昨晚有去傑森酒吧嗎？

B: No, I was at home watching the NBA finals.
沒有，我在家裡看美國職籃冠軍戰。

A: Really? I thought I caught a glimpse of you and Mandy.
真的嗎？我以為我瞥見了你和曼蒂。

B: Mandy was with a guy? Are you sure?
曼蒂和一個男生在一起？你確定嗎？

相關用語 ⟶ glance over 簡略閱讀   進階補充 ⟶ gaze at 凝視

517

Aren't the prices they charge for the mini-bar ridiculous? 小冰箱食物的收費不是貴得荒謬嗎？

charge for為「為…收費」之意，受詞可放在charge和for之間。用法：S + charge for + (代)名詞。for之後加上需收費的事物，例如服務、餐點或其他商品。與charge相關的片語有：get a charge out of sth「非常享受某事」；in charge of「負責某事」；be charged up「振奮、充滿活力」。

A: Aren't the prices they charge for the mini-bar ridiculous?
小冰箱食物的收費不是貴得荒謬嗎？

B: I know. It's way too expensive.
我知道，貴得離譜。

A: Absolutely! Five dollars for a can of soda?
真的！一瓶汽水要五元美金？

B: Don't tell me that you did take something from the bar!
別跟我說你有拿小冰箱的東西！

相關用語 • no charge 免收費用   進階補充 • way too 太過

518

I am glad that you've cleared the air with Mandy.
我很高興你和曼蒂誤會冰釋了。

clear the air為「化解誤會、冰釋前嫌」之意；也可以按字面解釋，表「使室內空氣新鮮」。由clear所組成的片語如：clear out「清除、趕走(口語用法)」；clear throat「清嗓子」。

A: I am glad that you've cleared the air with Mandy.
我很高興你和曼蒂誤會冰釋了。

B: Me, too.
我也是。

A: It was awful to see you two acting so cold towards each other.
看著你們對待彼此如此冷淡，真的很難受。

B: Don't worry. We are fine now.
別擔心，我們現在沒事了。

相關用語 • clear away 收拾   進階補充 • clear off 擺脫

519

My mom came down on me like a ton of bricks.

我被母親嚴厲指責了。

come down on為「申斥；支持某方」之意。用法：S + come down on + 人／事情，這裡的on可用upon代替。相似片語：come down「降下、走下(樓梯)、(聲勢、地位)衰弱、(故事、習俗等)世代相傳」；come down to earth「回到現實」。

519

A: How is it going?
還好嗎？

B: Terrible. My mom came down on me like a ton of bricks.
糟透了。我被母親嚴厲指責了。

A: Why is that?
為什麼？

B: She caught me throwing out my report card.
她抓到我把成績單扔掉。

相關用語 → **dress down** 責罵　　進階補充 → **like a ton of bricks** 嚴厲地

520

Do you want to come forward and volunteer for the new assignment? 你願意站出來加入新案子嗎？

come forward從字面上看即有「往前站」的意思，因此可引申為「自告奮勇」。come也可代換為step。與forward有關的片語有：put your best foot forward「盡善盡美」；bring sth. forward「公開揭發某事」；put forward sth.「提出建議」。

520

A: Do you want to come forward and volunteer for the new assignment?
你願意站出來加入新案子嗎？

B: I am not sure if I can handle it.
我不確定能否處理得宜。

A: Don't worry. I believe you can.
別擔心，我相信你可以。

B: Then, I'll give it a try.
那麼，我想試試看。

相關用語 → **stand up for** 支持　　進階補充 → **volunteer for** 志願

521

The meaning really came home to me after your explanation. 你的解釋讓我完全理解其含義了。

come home to為「令某人了解」之意。用法：S + come home to + 人。come home若不加to，則為「回家」之意；若在to後方加上roost，則為「得到惡報」。其他關於home的片語有：go to one's long home「安息、長眠」；nothing to write home about「乏善可陳」。

521

A: The meaning really **came home to** me after your explanation.
你的解釋讓我完全理解其含義了。

B: It's no big deal. I am glad I could help.
這沒什麼。很高興能幫上忙。

A: Can I buy you a drink to thank you?
我可以請你喝個飲料以示感謝嗎？

B: Sure. It's so nice of you.
當然。你人真好。

相關用語 ◦ realize 理解   進階補充 ◦ at home with 熟悉

522

When will the new regulations come into effect? 新規定何時生效？

come into effect為「生效」之意。effect是「效果」的意思，相關片語包括：snowball effect「滾雪球效應」，指事情的規模或重要性越來越大，或發展得越來越快；ripple effect「漣漪效應」，指一個接一個連環性地影響他者；domino effect「骨牌效應」，指一系列地造成其他事件或狀況。

522

A: When will the new regulations **come into effect**?
新規定何時生效？

B: Next Monday.
下週一。

A: In such a short time?
這麼快？

B: Yes, Mr. Watson wants to cut expenses immediately.
是的，華生先生想立刻縮減開支。

相關用語 ◦ take effect 生效   進階補充 ◦ in effect 生效

523 | Your project has **come into** Mr. Watson's **notice**.

你的企劃引起華生先生的注意了。

come into notice為「引起注意」之意。notice可當名詞和動詞，均為「注意」的意思。與notice相關的片語包括：sit up and take notice「突然注意到」；at a moment's notice「立即地」。

MP3
523

A: Congratulations! Your project has **come into** Mr. Watson's **notice**.
恭喜！你的企劃引起華生先生的注意了。

B: What do you mean?
你的意思是？

A: Mr. Watson asked me to **forward** your reports to the rest of the board.
華生先生要我把你的報告轉發給董事會其他成員。

B: That's great!
太棒了！

相關用語 ‧ **take notice of** 注意到　　進階補充 ‧ **forward to** 轉寄

524 | The term is **coming to an end**.

學期即將結束。

come to an end為「完成、結束」之意，come to a happy end則是「圓滿結束」的意思。end可當動詞和名詞，當動詞時本身即是「完畢、結束」的意思；當名詞時則是「末端、盡頭、結尾」的意思，和ending不一樣，ending通常指「故事、戲劇等的結局」。

MP3
524

A: Mom, the term is **coming to an end**.
媽，學期即將結束了。

B: Oh, indeed it is.
喔，真的是。

A: I am wondering if I can go camping with Allen in summer.
我在想，暑假是不是可以和亞倫去露營。

B: Of course. You deserve it.
當然可以。這是你應得的。

相關用語 ‧ **on end** 連續地　　進階補充 ‧ **make ends meet** 使收支平衡

525

Compared with a Toyota, a Honda is much more economical. 和豐田相比，本田較省油。

compared with為「比較」之意。compare是「比較、研究人與人或事物與事物間，相同或相異之程度，從而衡量其相對價值」的意思；近義字contrast則是指「為強調兩者之間的差異所做的比較」。

MP3
525

A: Why do you think we should get a Honda **instead of** a Toyota?
你為何覺得我們該買本田車，而不買豐田車？

B: **Compared with** a Toyota, a Honda is much more **economical.**
和豐田相比，本田較省油。

A: But you spend less on tax and maintenance with a Toyota.
但豐田車需繳的稅較少，保養上也比較便宜。

B: What a difficult choice it is.
真是個困難的抉擇。

相關用語 ── compare to 把…比作… 進階補充 ── instead of 反而

526

How do you feel about **competing with** Alice?

你對於與愛麗絲競爭有什麼感覺？

compete with為「與…競爭」之意。用法：S + compete with + 人 + (for + 事情)。由compete衍生的字彙包括：competitive「競爭的」；competition「競爭、角逐、比賽」；competitor「競爭對手」。

MP3
526

A: How do you feel about **competing with** Alice?
你對於與愛麗絲競爭有什麼感覺？

B: Kind of nervous. She has won the championship for the last two years.
有點緊張。她是前兩年的冠軍得主。

A: Don't worry. I believe you can beat her.
別擔心。我相信你可以打敗她。

B: Thank you. You are making me feel much better.
謝謝你。你讓我感覺好多了。

相關用語 ── contention 爭論 進階補充 ── contend 競爭

527

He has been confined to a wheelchair since he broke his left leg. 自從他左腿斷掉後，一直都坐輪椅。

confine to為「把…限制在」之意。用法：S + confine + 受詞 + to...。confine和limt的差別在於，前者通常指行動和能力等範圍上的限制，而後者可指數量、能力、時間和範圍上的限制，適用範圍較前者來得廣。

MP3
527

A: I heard Jeff had a car accident. Is that true?
聽說傑夫出車禍了，是真的嗎？

B: Unfortunately, yes. He is in the hospital now.
很不幸，是的。他現在在醫院裡。

A: That's too bad. How is he?
太糟了。他還好嗎？

B: Not so good. He has been confined to a wheelchair since he broke his left leg.
不太好。自從他左腿斷掉後，一直都坐輪椅。

相關用語 → **restrain** 限制　　進階補充 → **restrict to** 限制於

528

Your restaurant doesn't conform to the regulations on hygiene. 您的餐廳不符合衛生管理條例。

conform to為「符合」之意。用法：S + conform to + (代)名詞。由conform所衍生的詞彙有：conformable「一致的、適合的」；conformity「順從、符合」；conformation「結構、型態」；conformist「遵奉者」。form本身有「規範、形式」的意思，字首con-則是「共同」，組合後整個單字為「符合」之意。

MP3
528

A: I am afraid your restaurant doesn't conform to the regulations on hygiene.
您的餐廳恐怕不符合衛生管理條例。

B: What should I do?
我應該怎麼辦？

A: You have to fix all these problems within a month.
你得在一個月內改進這些缺失。

B: Yes, Ma'am.
是的，女士。

相關用語 → **tally with** 符合　　進階補充 → **answer to** 符合

275

529 We'll be **confronted with** a fine if the contract doesn't go out today. 若今日未送出合約，我們將遭罰款。

confront with為「面臨」之意，介系詞with也可換成by。confront的名詞型為confrontation，通常指涉衝突、敵對情況的面臨，如面對困境、敵人、危險等。如果要表達「面臨轉機」則可用動詞face來表示。

MP3
529

A: We'll be **confronted with** a fine if the contract doesn't go out today.
若今日未送出合約，我們將遭罰款。

B: I am sorry. I will take it to Mr. Wang's office in person.
很抱歉。我會親自送去王先生辦公室。

A: When will that be?
會是在什麼時候？

B: By 4 this afternoon.
今天下午四點前。

相關用語 • up against 面臨　　進階補充 • in the face of 面對

530 The exhibition **consists of** over 100 drawings.
本展覽包含超過一百件畫作。

consist of為「由…構成」之意。用法：A + consist of + B(A由B所構成)。compose、constitute也是「構成」的意思，其用法如下：A + compose of + B；A + constitute + B(A構成了B)，與本片語間的差別必須特別注意。

MP3
530

A: Do you want to accompany me to the Pier 2 Arts Exhibition?
你想陪我去駁二藝文展嗎？

B: It depends. What is it about?
看情況。是什麼展覽？

A: The exhibition **consists of** over 100 creative drawings by local artists.
展覽包含超過一百件當地藝術家的創意畫作。

B: It sounds like fun. Let's go.
聽起來很有趣。我們走吧。

相關用語 • comprise 由…構成　　進階補充 • consist with 符合

531

Please **convince** Helen **of** my innocence.

請讓海倫相信我是清白的。

convince of為「使確信」之意。用法：S + convince of + (代)名詞。受詞可加在convince和of之間，介系詞of之後則接「被說服相信的事物」。convice和persuade雖然字義相近，但仍有不同，convince是指「讓對方信服某種意見的真實性」，persuade則指「說服某人進行某種行動」。

MP3
531

A: I'd like to **ask you a favor**.
我想請你幫個忙。

B: Sure. What is it?
好啊。什麼忙？

A: Helen thinks I am cheating on her. Please **convince** her **of** my innocence.
海倫認為我背叛他，請讓她相信我是清白的。

B: Only if you are innocent.
那也要你真的無辜。

相關用語 ▸ **persuade** 說服　　進階補充 ▸ **ask sb. a favor** 請⋯幫忙

532

My grandfather **corresponded with** Mrs. Liu until she died. 祖父到劉太太死前都有和她通信。

correspond with為「與⋯通信、符合」之意。用法：S + correspond with + 人／東西。由correspond所衍生的詞彙有：correspondence是名詞，表「一致、聯繫」；correspondent亦是名詞，表「通訊記者、特派員」。

MP3
532

A: My grandfather **corresponded with** Mrs. Liu until she died.
祖父到劉太太死前都有與她通信。

B: How long was that?
那是多久？

A: It must have been over twenty years.
一定有超過二十年。

B: Wow, that is a long time. They must have been very good friends.
哇，那算很久。他們一定是很好的朋友。

相關用語 ▸ **correspondence** 信件　　進階補充 ▸ **correspond to** 符合

533

I don't want to see Hank cutting a poor figure like this. 我不想看到漢克出醜。

cut a poor figure為「出醜、露出可憐相」之意，也可寫成cut a sorry figure。與figure相關的片語有cut a fine figure「(男士)顯得優雅體面」；figure sth. up「增加」；figure in sth.「參一腳」。

533

A: Can we go now? I don't want to see Hank cutting a poor figure like this.
我們現在可以走了嗎？我不想看漢克出醜。

B: Come on. It will be fun!
拜託，會很有趣的！

A: I don't think trying to put 10 hotdogs altogether in one's mouth is fun.
我不認為一次塞十根熱狗進嘴裡很有趣。

B: You are such a spoilsport.
你真是個掃興鬼。

相關用語 • **make a scene 出醜**　進階補充 • **spoilsport 破壞樂趣者**

534

It dawned on me that Allen has been cheating on me. 我突然明白亞倫一直背著我偷吃。

dawn on為「突然明白」之意。dawn原意是「黎明、破曉」，為名詞；在這裡當動詞，為「明白、頓悟」的意思。用法：S + dawn on + (代)名詞。此外，這裡的on也可用upon代替。注意主詞是事情，介系詞on後接的是「突然理解事情的人」。

534

A: It dawned on me that Allen has been cheating on me.
我突然明白亞倫一直背著我偷吃。

B: Why do you say so?
你為何這麼說？

A: I found the love emails he sent to Cindy. They have been dating for a year.
我發現他寄給辛蒂的電子情書。他們已經約會一年了。

B: A year? I can't believe it!
一年？我不敢相信！

相關用語 • **tumble to 突然明白**　進階補充 • **comprehend 領會**

535

All the Board members are prohibited to deal in company shares. 所有董事會成員禁止交易公司股份。

deal in為「交易、成交」之意。用法：S + deal in + 東西。此處的介系詞in也可用with來代替。與deal相關的片語包括：big deal「了不起的事」(通常用於反語，如It's not a big deal.「沒什麼大不了。」)；get a raw deal「受到不公平的待遇」；cut a deal「進行協議或安排」。

A: All the Board members are prohibited to **deal in** company shares.
所有董事會成員禁止交易公司股份。

B: For the entire year?
一整年嗎？

A: No, only in July when we are re-electing Board members.
不，只有在七月，重選董事會成員時。

B: OK. I got it.
好。我知道了。

相關用語 → exchange 交易   進階補充 → trade in 交易

536

No one can deprive you of your freedom.

沒人能剝奪你的自由。

deprive of為「剝奪、喪失」之意。用法：S + deprive of + 事物。受詞可加在deprive和of之間，指涉「被剝奪的對象」；介系詞of後則加上「剝奪的事物」。deprive的名詞是deprival，形容詞是deprivable「可剝奪的」。

A: That's enough! Now you are grounded.
夠了！你被禁足了。

B: No! You can't **deprive** me **of** my freedom.
不！你不能剝奪我的自由。

A: I wouldn't if you had come home by ten last night.
若你昨晚十點前到家，我就不會這麼做。

B: I promise I won't do it again.
我保證下次不會再這樣了。

相關用語 → oust of 剝奪   進階補充 → divest of 剝奪

537

Do you think we can dine on the turkey from last night? 你覺得我們能吃昨晚的火雞嗎？

dine on = dine off，為「以某物供餐」之意。dine是動詞，意思是「用餐、宴請、供餐」。其他由dine所衍生的片語有：wine and dine sb.「款待某人吃大餐」；衍生的字彙則有：diner「用膳者、餐車」；diner-out「經常在外用餐者」；dinette「小餐廳、便餐(英式用法)」。dinette set「置於廚房一角的小餐桌椅」。

537

A: What are we going to have for dinner?
　　我們晚餐要吃什麼？

B: Do you think we can dine on the turkey from last night?
　　你覺得我們能吃昨晚的火雞嗎？

A: I don't think that will be enough for both of us.
　　我不覺得那夠我們兩人吃。

B: We can have a pizza also if you want.
　　如果你想，我們可以再吃個披薩。

相關用語 • **dine in** 在家吃飯　　進階補充 • **dine out** 外出用餐

538

Buying a new car will really dip into your purse.
買新車真的很花錢。

dip into one's purse為「揮霍、浪費」之意。dip into是「探究、涉獵、瀏覽」的意思。dip可當動詞和名詞，有「浸泡、下沉、汲取、洗澡(口語用法)」等多重意義。相似片語：dig/dip into one's pocket「自掏腰包」。

538

A: I am thinking about getting a new car.
　　我正考慮買輛新車。

B: Again? That will really dip into your purse.
　　又買？那真的很花錢。

A: It's a birthday gift for you.
　　是給你的生日禮物。

B: Really? Thank you, Sweetheart.
　　真的嗎？謝謝你，親愛的。

相關用語 • **waste** 浪費　　進階補充 • **squander on** 浪費

539

What Allen did to you is nothing less than **dirty work**. 亞倫對你做的事真的很卑鄙。

dirty work為「卑鄙行為」之意。此外，也有「不愉快的工作、不法行為」等意思。此片語前要加do或does當動詞：S + do/does + dirty work + (to + 人)。dirty和filthy都有「骯髒」的意思，其差別為：dirty指「被任何污染物弄髒」，而filthy則強調「髒到令人憎惡的地步」。

A: What Allen did to you is nothing less than dirty work.
亞倫對你做的事真的很卑鄙。

B: Thank you for taking my side.
謝謝你站在我這邊。

A: I am just telling the truth. He can't date your girlfriend behind your back!
我只是說實話。他不能背著你和你女友約會！

B: Both of them did a terrible thing to me.
他們兩個對我做了件很糟糕的事。

相關用語 → **mean** 卑鄙的　　進階補充 → **nothing less than** 不亞於

540

Can you **dish out** the mashed potatoes?
你可以把馬鈴薯泥分到每個人的盤子裡嗎？

dish out為「分到個人的盤子裡」之意，屬非正式用法。其他由dish所衍生的片語有：dish the dirt「散布流言蜚語」；side dish「小菜」；do the dishes「洗碗」；lay sth. in one's dish「把某事歸咎於某人」。

A: Honey, can you dish out the mashed potatoes?
親愛的，你可以把馬鈴薯泥分到每個人的盤子裡嗎？

B: Sure.
好。

A: Be sure to divide them into six equal parts for everybody.
記得為大家分成六等分。

B: No problem.
沒問題。

相關用語 → **dish up** 把…盛到盤裡　　進階補充 → **divide into** 劃分

541

It seems you can do nothing but apologize to her.

看來你只能向她道歉了。

do nothing but為「只、僅」之意。but是副詞，在此後接原形動詞。用法：S + do nothing but + V。要分清楚的是，but後面不一定接原形動詞，如片語cannot choose but「別無選擇」中，but就要接不定詞to。

A: What's wrong with you and Amy? She is so angry with you.
你跟愛咪怎麼了嗎？她很生你的氣。

B: I stood her up last Saturday.
我上週六放了她鴿子。

A: Oops. It seems you can do nothing but apologize to her.
糟糕。看起來你只能向她道歉了。

B: I did, but she wouldn't forgive me.
我有啊，但她不願意原諒我。

相關用語 · only 僅、只　　進階補充 · stand sb. up 失約於…

542

He is a rich man that used to be down and out.

他是個曾經落魄的有錢人。

down and out為「窮困潦倒、落魄」之意。down有「消沈、低落」的意思，out則有「偏離、出局」的意思。此片語可當形容詞與副詞片語，若將三個字用"-"(hyphen，連字號)連在一起，寫成down-and-out，就變成形容詞，意為「落魄的」。

A: Do you know Mr. Watson was once broke?
你知道華生先生曾經破產嗎？

B: But he is extremely rich now.
但他現在超有錢。

A: He is. It's hard to imagine that such a rich man like him used to be down and out.
沒錯。很難想像他這樣的有錢人曾經落魄過。

B: I can't imagine it, either.
我也無法想像。

相關用語 · in poverty 窮困地　　進階補充 · badly off 境況不佳的

543

I've **drawn a blank** on where to buy.

我不知該在哪購買。

draw a blank原意是指「抽空籤」，在此引申為「未找到、希望落空、終於失敗」之意。其他與blank相關的片語有：blank sth. out「忘記、清除」；blank check「空頭支票」；one's mind goes blank「失憶、腦筋一片空白」。

MP3
543

A: I heard that you were looking for a new house.
聽說你正在找新房子。

B: Yes, but I've **drawn a blank** on where to buy. Everywhere is so expensive.
是啊，但我不知該在哪置產。到處都很貴。

A: Don't worry. I might have something good for you.
別擔心。我或許有好東西可以給你看看。

B: Really? That's fantastic!
真的嗎？太棒了！

相關用語 ○ drop through 落空   進階補充 ○ blank check 空白支票

544

I don't understand what you're **driving at**.

我不懂您的意思。

drive at表「意指」，屬口語用法，且通常採進行式，置於句尾。使用此片語時，前面一定要加what，用法：S + V + what + 人 + drive at...，或是直接用what + be V + 人 + driving at。

MP3
544

A: Sir, I am sorry, but I don't understand what you're **driving at**.
長官，不好意思，但是我不懂您的意思。

B: I am saying that you can **pack up** and leave now.
我的意思是你現在可以收拾東西走人了。

A: Please don't fire me. I'll work harder.
請別解雇我，我會更努力工作的。

B: I don't think you'll be able to.
我不覺得你會。

相關用語 ○ mean by that 意指   進階補充 ○ pack up 整理行裝

545

Don't forget to **drop me a line** some time.

別忘了偶爾寫封信給我。

drop sb. a line指「寫短信給某人」的意思。line的原意是「線」，在此引申為short message，「短信、短函」之意。與drop相關的片語包括：drop a clanger「說錯話(英式口語)」；drop a hint「暗示」；drop into one's lap「不勞而獲」。

545

A: Have a great life in New York!
　祝你在紐約生活順利！

B: I will try my best to survive there.
　我會盡力在那兒生存的。

A: Don't forget to **drop me a line** some time.
　別忘了偶爾寫封信給我。

B: I will.
　我會的。

相關用語 • **letterform** 信箋　　進階補充 • **letter box** 信箱

546

When will you **embark on** your new science project?

你何時會開始新的科學計劃？

embark on為「從事」之意，這裡的on也可用upon代替。用法：S + embark on/upon + (代)名詞。embark為多義字，當及物動詞時表「使上船(或飛機)、裝載、使從事、投資」；當不及物動詞時表「上船(或飛機)、從事、著手」。此處是不及物動詞的用法。當及物動詞時，用法為人 + be embarked on + 事。

546

A: When will you **embark on** your new science project?
　你何時會開始新的科學計畫？

B: There is no project for me anymore.
　我這邊已經沒有任何計畫了。

A: Why not? I though Dr. Copper **asked for** your help.
　為何沒有了？我以為卡柏博士找你幫忙。

B: He did, but the university cut the budget for the project.
　是啊，但學校把計畫經費刪掉了。

相關用語 • **go into** 從事　　進階補充 • **ask for** 要求

547

The economy has emerged from the previous recession. 經濟情勢已從先前的萎靡中復甦。

emerge from為「出現、出身」之意。用法：S + emerge from + (代)名詞。emerge是動詞，意為「浮現、出現」，由emerge衍生的詞彙有：emergence「出現」；emergency「危急、應急」；emergency act「緊急法令」；emergency case「急救箱」。

547

A: It seems the economy has **emerged from** the previous recession.
看來經濟情勢已從先前的萎靡中復甦。

B: Is that true? How come I haven't found a decent job yet?
真的嗎？那我為何還找不到適合的工作？

A: That's because you ask for too much.
那是因為你要求太多。

B: Come on! Sixty thousand NT dollars per month isn't too much, is it?
拜託！每個月六萬塊錢不算多吧？

相關用語 ○ **turn up** 出現   進階補充 ○ **rise above** 克服

548

The bay is enclosed by the azure ocean.

海灣被蔚藍的海圍繞著。

enclose with/by為「圍繞」之意。被動式用法：S + be V + enclosed with/by + (代)名詞。受詞可加在enclose和介系詞之間，with和by之後則加上「用以圍繞的事物」。

548

A: The bay is **enclosed by** the azure ocean. It's so beautiful!
海灣被蔚藍的海懷抱著，真美！

B: Indeed it is.
的確很美。

A: And it's so romantic, too.
也很浪漫。

B: I'm glad you like it.
我很高興你喜歡。

相關用語 ○ **surround** 圍繞   進階補充 ○ **encircle** 環繞、包圍

549

He endeavored to end racial discrimination during his entire life. 他一生致力於終結種族歧視。

endeavor to為「盡力」之意。endeavor是美式寫法，英式寫法是endeavour。其他類似的例子有：favor/favour「贊成」；color/colour「顏色」；behavior/behaviour「行為」；honor/honour「榮耀」等，前為美式、後為英式。

MP3
549

A: Do you know anything about Martin Luther King Jr.?
關於馬丁‧路德‧金恩，你知道些什麼？

B: He endeavored to end racial discrimination during his entire life.
他一生致力於終結種族歧視。

A: Then have you read his "I have a dream" speech?
那你有讀過他的「我有一個夢想」的演講稿嗎？

B: Of course! It's the most impressive speech ever!
當然有！那是最令人印象深刻的演講了！

相關用語 ○ strive for 努力   進階補充 ○ take pains 盡力、費苦心

550

He endowed the church with his house.

他把房子捐給教會。

endow with為「捐贈、賦予」之意。用法：S + endow with + (代)名詞。此片語當「賦予」的意思解時，通常用來表示「與生俱來的特質」，多採被動式運用，用法：S + be V + endowed with + 受詞。endow的名詞型為endowment，意為「捐贈、天賦」。

MP3
550

A: Have you heard the news? Mr. Wang passed away last Sunday.
你聽說了嗎？王先生上週日過世了。

B: May he rest in peace.
願他安息。

A: And he endowed the church with his house.
而且他把房子捐給教會。

B: He was such a decent man.
他真是個好人。

相關用語 ○ donate to 捐贈   進階補充 ○ pass away 過世

551 Can you **equip** the trunk **with** a spare tire?

你可以把備胎裝進後車箱嗎？

equip with為「裝備」之意。用法：S + equip + 受詞 + with + (代)名詞。equip和furnish都有「裝備」的意思，但equip可用於人，furnish則是用於家具、房間等空間和建築方面的裝備。

A: Can you equip the trunk with a spare tire?
你可以把備胎裝進後車箱嗎？

B: Sure, but why do we need an extra tire?
當然可以，但我們為何需要另備輪胎？

A: Just in case we get a flat tire.
以防爆胎。

B: Got it.
了解了。

相關用語 **equipment** 裝備　　進階補充 **just in case** 以防萬一

552 He got **excused from** military service.

他被免除兵役。

excuse from為「免除(義務)」的意思，屬動詞片語。excuse當名詞時則有「理由、藉口」的意思。其他關於excuse的片語有：excuse oneself「辯解、請求免除或離開」；in excuse of「為…辯解」；make an excuse (for)「(替…)辯護」；without (good) excuse「沒有(正當的)理由」。

A: I thought your brother was in the army.
我以為你哥哥從軍去了。

B: He was about to join, but he got excused from military service.
他原本即將要去，但後來免役了。

A: Why?
為什麼？

B: They found he has flat feet.
他們發現他有扁平足。

相關用語 **exempt from** 免除　　進階補充 **about to** 即將

553

Prof. Hoffman expanded on his political opinions.

霍夫曼教授闡述他的政治見解。

expand on為「闡述」之意，這裡的on也可用upon代替。expand有「展開、使膨脹、擴充、發展、詳述」等字義，可當及物動詞，亦可當不及物動詞。在這裡是當不及物動詞，因此需在受詞前加上介系詞on或upon加以連結。

553

A: Why were you absent from class yesterday?
　你昨天為何缺課？

B: I was sick. What happed in class?
　我生病了。班上有什麼事嗎？

A: Prof. Hoffman expanded on his political opinions during the whole class.
　霍夫曼教授一整節課都在闡述他的政治意見。

B: Luckily I was sick.
　幸好我生病了。

相關用語 ○ **elaborate on 闡釋**　進階補充 ○ **expound 解釋**

554

Jason seems to have fallen into disgrace.

傑森似乎失寵了。

fall into disgrace為「失寵」之意。disgrace、dishonor、infamy和ignominy都是名詞，為「丟臉」的意思，其差別為：disgrace是「丟臉、不名譽，或是失去他人的尊敬與寵愛」；dishonor是指「失去原有的榮耀、名譽或自尊」；infamy是指「惡名昭彰」的意思；ignominy則是指「由於公開的恥辱而為眾人唾棄」之意。

554

A: Poor Jason. He seems to have fallen into disgrace.
　可憐的傑森，他似乎失寵了。

B: Why is that?
　為什麼呢？

A: He was expected to win the contract, but he didn't.
　他被指望會贏得合約，但他並沒有。

B: Oh. Poor Jason.
　噢。可憐的傑森。

相關用語 ○ **fall out of favor 失寵**　進階補充 ○ **in favor 得寵**

555

This time, I really **fell to the ground**.

這次我真的一敗塗地。

fall to the ground為「一敗塗地」之意。相關片語：to the ground是「徹底地、十分地」之意；fall to有「開始、變成」的意思。和ground相關的片語有：break new ground「開創新局」；run into the ground「失敗」；stand one's ground「堅持己見」。

MP3
555

A: Cheer up!
開心點！

B: I can't. This time, I really **fell to the ground**.
我無法。這次我真的一敗塗地。

A: It's only a small **setback** in your career. Don't give up!
這只是你職業生涯裡的小挫敗，別放棄！

B: Well, I will try to be more **optimistic**.
嗯，我會試著樂觀一些。

相關用語 **setback** 挫敗　　進階補充 **optimistic** 樂觀的

556

I don't **feel up to** the position.

我不覺得有能力勝任該職。

feel up to為「可以勝任」之意。用法：S + feel up to + 事情／工作，此片語屬於口語用法。其他有關feel的片語有：feel for sb.「感同身受」；feel sth. in one's bones「心知肚明」；get the feel of sth.「開始熟悉某事」；feel out「釐清」。

MP3
556

A: I heard that you've been promoted to the position of manager.
我聽說你被升為經理。

B: Yes, but I don't **feel up to** the position.
是的，但我不覺得自己有能力勝任。

A: Don't be ridiculous. No one can do a better job than you.
別亂說了，沒人可以做得比你好。

B: Thanks. I'll try my best.
謝謝。我會盡力而為。

相關用語 **qualified** 勝任的　　進階補充 **capable** 有能力的

557

You were trying to fish for compliments from him.

你試圖獲得他的稱讚。

fish for為「探聽、尋找」之意。fish當動詞時，是「探求、搜索」的意思。
此字衍生出一句諺語「All is fish that comes to his net.」，意為「來者
不拒」。其他由fish所組成的片語有：be like a fish out of water「格格不
入」；drunk as a fish「爛醉如泥」；have other fish to fry「另有要事」；
make fish of one and flesh of another「差別待遇」。

A: I don't like the way you talked to Prof. Kao yesterday.
我不喜歡你昨天跟高教授講話的樣子。

B: What do you mean?
你的意思是？

A: It was like you were trying to fish for compliments from him.
你看來像試著想獲得他的稱讚。

B: I didn't mean to do that.
我並非有意那麼做。

相關用語 ∘ **yearn for** 渴望　進階補充 ∘ **mean to** 打算、有意

558

Can you have someone fix me up with a new one at a good price? 你可以安排人幫我弄一台價格合理的新冷氣嗎？

fix up「安排、修理」之意，是口語用法。fix的相關片語有：fix on「確
定、集中於」；be in a fix「身處困境」；a quick fix「捷徑」；get a fix on
sth.「瞭解某事」。

A: The air conditioner is out of order.
冷氣壞了。

B: What? It's the third time this month.
什麼？這個月壞第三次了。

A: Can you have someone fix me up with a new one at a good price?
你可以安排人幫我弄一台價格合理的新冷氣嗎？

B: No problem.
沒問題。

相關用語 ∘ **arrange** 安排　進階補充 ∘ **out of order** 發生故障

559

He **flunked out** of the class.

他被退學了。

flunk out為「退學」之意。flunk指「學業不及格、被當掉」的意思，屬美式口語用法，可當及物動詞和不及物動詞，當及物動詞時指「使某人不及格」，如My teacher flunked me.「老師把我當掉」；當不及物動詞時則指「考試不及格」，介系詞用in，如She was very sad for flunking in the final exam.「她因期末考不及格而非常難過」。

A: I haven't seen Jack for a while. Is he sick?
我好一陣子沒看到傑克了。他生病了嗎？

B: No, he **flunked out** of the class.
不，他被退學了。

A: Really? **How come?**
真的嗎？為什麼？

B: He failed 7 out of 11 subjects last semester.
他上學期十一科中有七科被當。

相關用語 **drop out** 退學　進階補充 **how come** 為什麼

560

For all that I have done, I still can't win her heart.

儘管我做了這麼多，還是無法贏走她的心。

for all that為「儘管如此」之意，是副詞片語。for all that通常置於句中，that後接子句，與even though、even so的用法相同。另外兩個也表示「儘管」的詞彙和片語：despite和in spite of，前者可接名詞或接that + 子句，後者則需接名詞。

A: **For all that** I have done, I still can't win Jessica's heart.
儘管我做了這麼多，還是無法贏走潔西卡的心。

B: **At least** you've tried.
至少你試過了。

A: You are right. I will never regret it, though, because I **gave it a shot.**
你說得沒錯。我不會後悔，因為我努力過。

B: I am glad to hear that.
我很高興聽你這麼說。

相關用語 **at least** 至少　進階補充 **give a shot** 嘗試

561

Could you please lower your tone **for God's sake**?

可以請你看在上帝的份上，降低你的音量嗎？

for God's sake為「看在上帝的分上」之意。sake是名詞，意思為「理由、緣故」。美語中有許多與God(上帝)相關的片語，如：a God-given right「天賜的理由」；put the fear of God into sb.「極度驚嚇」；play God「扮演極具影響力的角色」；be in the lap of the Gods「難以預料」。

A: Could you please lower your tone for God's sake?
可以請你看在上帝的份上，降低你的音量嗎？

B: What's the matter?
怎麼了？

A: I'm trying to solve this math problem, but I can't concentrate.
我試著解這題數學，但我無法專心。

B: No problem.
沒問題。

相關用語 ○ forsake 摒棄　　進階補充 ○ math problem 數學題目

562

For the sake of the company, this deal must be sealed. 為了公司，這筆交易非談成不可。

for the sake of表「為了」之意，通常放在句首或句中。表達「為了」的片語相當多，但用法不盡相同，例如in order to、so as to必須接原形動詞；in the cause of用法則與本片語相同，後接名詞或Ving。

A: For the sake of the company, this deal must be sealed.
為了公司，這筆交易非談成不可。

B: I understand, but Mr. Cooper hasn't made up his mind.
我了解，但庫伯先生尚未下定決心。

A: What's bothering him?
他在考慮什麼？

B: I don't know. Maybe he's not satisfied with our offer.
我不知道；或許他不滿意我們的出價。

相關用語 ○ for 為了　　進階補充 ○ in behalf of 為了

563

It would be nice if you could take Kevin's place for the time being. 若你可以暫代凱文，那就太好了。

for the time being為「暫時」之意，屬時間副詞片語，經常置於句尾。與time相關的片語非常多，例如bide one's time「伺機而動」；from time to time「有時」；give a hard/tough time「使人處於艱困或尷尬的處境」；once upon a time「很久以前」；take your time「慢慢來、不急」。

A: It would be nice if you could take Kevin's place for the time being.
若你可以暫代凱文，那就太好了。

B: Of course I could. What happened to him?
當然可以。他怎麼了？

A: He had a car accident and can't come to work for two weeks.
他出了車禍，兩週無法工作。

B: Oh, that's too bad.
喔，真是太糟糕了。

相關用語 • **temporarily** 暫時地　　進階補充 • **for the moment** 暫時

564

I know he frowns upon it.

我知道他皺眉表示不悅。

frown on/upon為「皺眉、表示不滿」之意。用法：S + frown on/upon + 事情。frown和scowl的比較：frown是指「由於不贊成、困惑或思索而皺起眉頭」；scowl則是指「由於脾氣不好或不滿而皺眉」。

A: I don't think Dad is going to let you drive his car to school.
我不覺得老爸會讓你開他的車去上學。

B: Really? But he didn't say no.
真的嗎？但他沒說不准。

A: But I know he frowns upon it.
但我知道他皺眉表示不悅。

B: I thought he was just in a bad mood this morning.
我以為他只是今天早上心情不好。

相關用語 • **disagree** 不同意　　進階補充 • **frown at** 對…表示不滿

565

If you don't get a move on, we're going to miss the movie. 如果你不快點，我們將會錯過電影。

get a move on為「趕快」之意。move可當動詞也可當名詞，此處為名詞，「採取行動」的意思。與move相關的片語包括：move about「四處走動旅行」；move along「往前走、離開」；move in on「逼近、奪取」；move on/off「出發、離開」；move out「搬出」。

A: If you don't **get a move on**, we're going to miss the movie.
如果你不快點，我們將會錯過電影。

B: OK. Let me grab my purse.
好。讓我拿個皮包。

A: Do you have your **membership card** with you?
你有帶會員卡嗎？

B: Check. Let's move!
有。走吧！

相關用語 • hurry up 趕緊   進階補充 • membership card 會員卡

566

He always tries his best to get things across to us.
他總是盡力讓我們理解事情。

get across為「使⋯被理解」之意。受詞可放在get和across之間，表示兩者之間成功地溝通、傳遞訊息之意。此片語另可表示「越過、渡過」的意思。與across相關的片語包括：run across「偶然遇到」；cut across「直接切穿、遮擋」；fire a shot across one's bows「事前警告」。

A: Mr. Lemon is the best coach ever!
雷門先生是最棒的教練！

B: How do you know?
你如何得知？

A: He always tries his best to **get** things **across** to us without patronizing.
他總是盡力讓我們理解事情，且不抱傲慢態度。

B: Sound like a great and humble coach.
聽來是個優秀而謙虛的教練。

相關用語 • get at 理解   進階補充 • make sense of 理解

567

It's a class about how to get ahead in the advertising business. 是門有關如何推展廣告業務的課程。

get ahead為「進步、領先」之意。副詞ahead有「在前方、預先」的意思。與ahead相關的片語包括：be/keep/stay one step ahead「略勝一籌」；go ahead with sth.「直接去做」；ahead of schedule「進度超前」；look ahead「展望未來」。

567

A: Where are you going?
你要去哪裡？

B: School. I have a class at four.
學校。我四點有課。

A: What class?
什麼課？

B: It's a class about how to **get ahead** in the advertising business.
是門有關如何推展廣告業務的課。

相關用語 ▸ **take the lead** 領先　　進階補充 ▸ **ahead of** 在…之前

568

I'll get even with Jay for what he has done to me.

我會為了杰對我所做的事向他報復。

get even with為「報仇、報復」之意。用法：S + get even with + sb.。even有「平等、相等」的意思，所以此句的意思為「與某人扯平」，即「報復」之意。與even相關的片語有：get an even break「與他人擁有相同機會」；on an even keel「保持平靜、不做劇烈變動」。

568

A: I swear I'll **get even with** Jay for what he has done to me.
我發誓，我會為了杰對我所做的事向他報復。

B: Calm down. Just let it go.
冷靜一點。算了吧。

A: No way. He went **way over the line**.
不可能。他太過分了。

B: Fine. But you won't achieve anything by getting even.
好吧。但報復無法讓你得到任何好處。

相關用語 ▸ **revenge** 報仇　　進階補充 ▸ **way over the line** 過分

569

When can you **get** your marketing report **in**?

你何時可繳交行銷報告？

get in為「到達、收穫」之意，受詞可放在get與in之間，也可放在in之後；當「到達」時為不及物動詞，沒有受詞的問題。相關片語：get in one's hair「惹惱某人」；get in touch with oneself「探討某人的內心世界」。

569

A: When can you **get** your marketing report **in**?
你何時可繳交行銷報告？

B: By the end of this week.
本週結束前。

A: Great. I have high expectations concerning it.
很好。我對你的報告期望很高。

B: Thank you, Sir.
謝謝您，先生。

相關用語 **hand in** 繳交　進階補充 **get into** 使陷入

570

I **get** so much **out of** it.

我從中獲得良多。

get out of為「獲得、迫使說出」之意。用法：S + get out of + (代)名詞。相似片語：get out from under「脫離困境、解除危難」；get out of line「違規」。口語上常用的一句話，"Get out of here!"「滾出去！」就是由get out組成的。

570

A: Do you enjoy playing basketball?
你喜歡打籃球嗎？

B: Of course. I **get** so much **out of** it.
當然。我從中獲得良多。

A: Like what?
像是？

B: Like learning to build teamwork while strengthening my body.
像是在強化身體時、一邊學習如何團隊合作。

相關用語 **obtain** 獲得　進階補充 **gain from** 獲得

571

You have to find a way to get over her.

你必須找到淡忘她的方法。

get over在口語用法中為「克服、恢復、結束(不愉快或麻煩的事)」之意。介系詞over有「結束、跨越」的意思，因此本片語除了「克服、恢復」之外，還有「熬過、忘卻」的意思。

571

A: **You have to face the fact that you and Emily are finished.**
你必須面對你和艾蜜莉已經分手的事實。

B: **I know, but I still have feelings for her.**
我知道，但我仍對她有感覺。

A: **You have to find a way to get over her.**
你必須找到忘了她的方法。

B: **I'll try.**
我會努力。

相關用語 → overcome 克服　　進階補充 → let go 放手、放開

572

I need to get the whole picture of what happened. 我需要了解事情的全貌。

get the whole picture of為「了解整個情況」之意。這裡的picture是指「情況、局面」的意思；get在這裡是「了解、知道」的意思，而不是一般常用的「得到、拿到」之意。用法：S + get the whole picture of + 受詞。與picture相關的片語有：be out of the picture「狀況外」；keep/put sb. in the picture「帶某人進入狀況」。

572

A: **I need to get the whole picture of what happened.**
我需要了解事情的全貌。

B: **Ms. Chen asked for more discounts, and we refused.**
陳小姐要求更多折扣，但我們拒絕了。

A: **Is that why she refused to sign the contract with us?**
所以她拒絕與我們簽約？

B: **Yes. Max Computer offered her a lower price and thus won the contract.**
是的。邁克斯電腦給她更低的報價，並因此贏得合約。

相關用語 → get the picture 了解情況　　進階補充 → refuse to 拒絕

573

Roses give off a graceful scent.

玫瑰散發出高雅的香味。

give off為「散發」之意。介系詞off也可以out代換，都有「散發、分布」的意思。與give相關的片語包括：give sb. a buzz/bell「打電話給某人」；give sb. a hand「伸出援手」；give the sack「裁員」；give sth. the thumbs up/down「贊成／不贊成某事」。

A: Thank you for the flowers.
謝謝你的花。

B: Do you like them?
你喜歡嗎？

A: Of course I do. Roses are my favorite. They give off a graceful scent.
當然喜歡。玫瑰散發出高雅的香味，是我的最愛。

B: I am glad you like them.
我很高興你喜歡。

相關用語 ∘ emit 散發   進階補充 ∘ send out 放出

574

The earthquake gave rise to a great tsunami in Japan. 地震在日本引起巨大海嘯。

give rise to為「引起」之意。rise在這裡是名詞，為「源頭、發源」之意。除上述字義外，rise當名詞還有「增加、上升、高地、加薪(英式用法)」的意思。除當名詞外，rise也可當動詞，有「上升、高聳、起立、增強、發生、浮現」等意思。

A: It was such a disaster.
真是太慘了。

B: What are you talking about?
你在說什麼？

A: The earthquake gave rise to a great tsunami in Japan. A lot of people died.
地震在日本引起巨大海嘯，許多人喪生。

B: May they rest in peace.
願他們安息。

相關用語 ∘ bring about 引起   進階補充 ∘ rest in peace 安息

575

I think he will **go mad**.

我覺得他會發瘋。

go mad為「發狂、發瘋」之意,這裡的go也可以run或become代替。由mad所組成的片語有:drive/send a person mad「逼某人發狂」;go/run mad after/over sb./sth.「發狂似地追求」。發瘋還有兩種非正式的說法:go nuts和go bananas。

MP₃
575

A: Are you all right?
你還好嗎?

B: No, not at all.
不,一點都不好。

A: What's wrong?
怎麼了?

B: I'm really worried about my friend. He's under so much pressure – I think he will go mad.
我非常擔心我的朋友。他壓力太大,我覺得他會發瘋。

相關用語 ► **go crazy** 發瘋   進階補充 ► **under pressure** 在壓力下

576

Can you **go on** some **errands** for me now?

你現在可以去幫我跑腿嗎?

go on errands為「跑差事、辦差事」之意,這裡的go也可用run代替。errand的意思是「差事、差使」;本片語中的errand一定要加s,為慣用法。其他由errand所組成的片語有:go on a fool's errand「白費心機」;由errand所衍生的詞彙有:errand boy「(公司、商店的)小弟、工友」。

MP₃
576

A: What are you doing in the study?
你在書房做什麼?

B: Studying. What else could I be doing?
唸書。我還能做什麼?

A: Can you go on some errands for me now?
你現在可以去幫我跑個腿嗎?

B: Again? I just did that an hour ago!
又來?我一個小時前才跑過!

相關用語 ► **berth** 差事   進階補充 ► **fool's errand** 徒勞奔波

577 | I feel as if I **have one foot in the grave**.

我覺得我好像快要死了。

have one foot in the grave表「臨死之際」。grave是名詞，為「墓穴」的意思。由grave所衍生的片語有：silent as the grave「完全沉默」；dig one's own grave「自尋死路」。

MP3
577

A: I feel as if I **have one foot in the grave**.
我覺得我好像快要死了。

B: Sweetheart, what's wrong with you?
親愛的，你怎麼了？

A: I have had a headache for several days. It's killing me.
我已經頭痛了好幾天，快痛死我了。

B: I think we'd better take you to the doctor's for a checkup.
我想我們最好帶你去讓醫生檢查一下。

相關用語 • **living death** 生不如死　　進階補充 • **graveyard** 墓園

578 | You put your **heart and soul** into the job.

你為工作付出所有心力。

heart and soul為「熱心地、賣力地」之意，也可寫成heart and hand。由heart所衍生的詞彙和片語如：heartache「心痛」；heart attack「心臟病發作」；heartbeat「心跳」；heartbreak「心碎」；heartbreaker「令人心碎的人事物」；heartbroken「心碎的、斷腸的」；heart failure「心臟衰竭」等。

MP3
578

A: Congratulations. Here is your sales bonus.
恭喜，這是你的業績獎金。

B: Thank you.
謝謝你。

A: You're welcome. You deserve it because you put your **heart and soul** into the job.
不客氣。你為工作付出所有心力，這是你應得的。

B: I am just trying to do the best job I can.
我只是盡力做好我的工作。

相關用語 • **exert oneself** 盡力　　進階補充 • **heart to heart** 誠懇的

579

Did we **hit the mark** for the month?

我們有達成月目標嗎？

hit the mark為「達到目的」之意。此外，也可當「中肯、一語中的」的意思解。其他由hit所組成的片語有：hit a home run「成功、達成」；hit a/the wall「遇到瓶頸」；hit the books「臨時抱佛腳」；hit the jackpot「中頭彩、大舉成功」；hit the sack「睡覺」(口語用法)。

MP3
579

A: Sir, here is the monthly sales report.
　　長官，這是本月業務報表。

B: OK. Did we **hit the mark** for the month?
　　好。我們有達成月目標嗎？

A: I am afraid not. We are more than five percent **short of the target**.
　　恐怕沒有。我們距離目標還差超過五個百分點。

B: That's fine. Just keep working.
　　沒關係。請繼續努力。

相關用語 → **reach the goal** 達成目標　　進階補充 → **short of** 少於

580

We **held our breath** while a man put his head in a lion's mouth. 當男人把頭放進獅子的嘴裡時，我們屏住氣息。

hold one's breath為「屏息以待」之意。用法：S + hold one's breath + 介系詞 + (代)名詞。由breath所組成的片語有：below one's breath「低聲細語地」；catch one's breath「鬆一口氣」；get one's breath「恢復平靜」；give up one's breath「死亡」；lose one's breath「喘不過氣」。

MP3
580

A: How was the circus performance last night?
　　昨晚的馬戲團表演如何？

B: Awesome! We **held our breath** while a man put his head in a lion's mouth.
　　很棒！當男人把頭放進獅子的嘴裡時，我們屏住氣息。

A: Sounds exciting.
　　聽起來很刺激。

B: It was, and you definitely should go.
　　是很刺激，你一定要去看看。

相關用語 → **in one breath** 齊聲說　　進階補充 → **breathtaking** 驚人的

581

Gina held her ground, and Mike didn't give in, either. 吉娜堅持己見，麥克也不肯讓步。

hold one's ground為「堅守立場」之意。ground在這裡是指「立場」，hold則是「維持、撐住」的意思。其他與hold有關的片語包括：hold back「避免」；hold down「成功維持；抑制」；hold one's feet to the fire「造成壓力」；hold off「延遲」；hold one's tongue「住口」。

581

A: What's wrong with Gina and Mike?
吉娜和麥克怎麼了？

B: They **got into a fight** yesterday. I think they might break up.
他們昨天吵了一架，我覺得他們可能會分手。

A: What happened?
怎麼回事？

B: It's about their wedding. Gina **held her ground**, and Mike didn't **give in**, either.
是關於他們的婚禮。吉娜堅持己見，麥克也不肯讓步。

相關用語 ○ **get into a fight** 吵架　　進階補充 ○ **give in** 讓步

582

The drums are not in harmony with the Chinese flutes. 鼓和中國竹笛不協調。

in harmony with為「與…協調一致」之意。反義片語：out of harmony with「不調和」。harmony是名詞「和諧」，既可表示音韻上的調和，也可用來指涉人際關係上的和睦。

582

A: Would you please **turn** that **off**? It's killing me!
你可以把那個關掉嗎？快讓我煩死了！

B: What's wrong? Don't you like the music?
怎麼了？你不喜歡這個音樂嗎？

A: Not at all. The drums are not **in harmony with** the Chinese flutes.
一點也不。鼓和中國竹笛不協調。

B: It sounds great to me. I like it.
我覺得很好聽。我喜歡。

相關用語 ○ **accordance** 和諧　　進階補充 ○ **turn off** 關掉

583

Mr. Chen seems to be in low spirits today.

陳老師今天似乎心情不好。

in high/low spirits為「心情好／差」之意。in spirit表示「在精神方面」，而在spirit前加上形容詞，用來表示精神狀態的好壞。表示「情緒低落」時，low也可用poor來取代。

A: Mr. Chen seems to be **in low spirits** today.
陳老師今天似乎心情不好。

B: How can you tell?
你怎麼知道？

A: He dropped the chalk three times in twenty minutes.
二十分鐘內，他掉了三次粉筆。

B: You are right. That is weird.
沒錯。是很怪。

相關用語 → **spiritual** 精神上的　　進階補充 → **leading spirit** 領袖

584

They gave that to him in memory of his devotion.

為感念他的付出，他們送了他那個。

in memory of為「用以紀念…」之意。用法：S + V + in memory of + 人。memory、remembrance、collection和reminiscence都有「紀念」的意思，其差別為：memory指「將學習或經驗記下來或想出來的能力」，也就是「記憶力」；remembrance指「想起記憶中的事情或回憶的過程」；collection指「設法對記憶模糊或一時想不起的往事加以回想」；reminiscence則是指「靜靜地回憶或追憶」。

A: What a beautiful medal!
真是個漂亮的獎牌！

B: Thank you. My father's colleagues gave that to him **in memory of** his devotion.
謝謝你。父親的同事為感念他的付出，送了那個給他。

A: That is so sweet.
真是太貼心了。

B: Indeed it is.
的確是的。

相關用語 → **memorize** 記住　　進階補充 → **memory lane** 往事感懷

303

585

To be honest, I am in opposition to it.

老實說，我不同意。

in opposition to為「與…意見相反」之意。opposition的原意是「對抗、相反」，其動詞為oppose、形容詞為opposite、副詞為oppositely。相關片語：as opposed to sb./sth. = in comparison with sb./sth.「與某人或某事物相比」；oppose A against/to B「把A和B進行對照或比較」。

585

A: What do you think of the new marketing project?
你對新的行銷企劃有什麼想法？

B: To be honest, I am in opposition to it.
老實說，我不同意。

A: Why is that?
為什麼？

B: I find it a ridiculous and silly plan.
我覺得這是個既荒謬又愚蠢的企劃。

相關用語 → in support of 支持　　進階補充 → to be honest 老實說

586

It's very costly in terms of the time you've spent.

就你所花的時間而言是很貴的。

in terms of為「就…而論；在…方面」之意。用法：S + V + in terms of + 名詞。其他由term所組成的片語有：be on good/bad terms with sb.「和某人關係友善／不友善」；come to terms(with)「開始接受、著手處理」；in the long term「長期來說」。

586

A: This is the most expensive garage to my knowledge.
這是就我所知最貴的車庫。

B: What are you talking about? We only spent 500 dollars remodeling it.
你在說什麼？我們只花了五百美金改建。

A: That is cheap, but it's very costly in terms of the time you've spent.
是很便宜，但就你所花的時間而言是很貴的。

B: You are right. I spent more than three months on it.
沒錯。我花了超過三個月的時間。

相關用語 → speaking of 說到　　進階補充 → with respect to 有關

587

He has indulged himself in that game for that last two days. 他最近兩天沈迷於那遊戲。

indulge in為「沉迷、放縱」之意。用法：S + indulge in + (代)名詞。相似片語：indulge oneself with + (代)名詞「讓自己好好享受某事物」。

MP3
587

A: Where is John?
約翰在哪裡？

B: Where else can he be since Diablo 3 was released just two days ago?
既然兩天前暗黑三發售了，他還能在哪裡？

A: Don't tell me he is in his room!
別跟我說他在房間裡！

B: He has indulged himself in that game for that last two days.
他最近兩天都沈迷於那遊戲。

相關用語 • **addicted to** 沉迷於　　進階補充 • **indulgent** 放縱的

588

He insists on that price, and won't give in.
他堅持那個價格，且不肯讓步。

insist on為「堅持」之意。用法：S + insist on + (代)名詞。insist的用法很特別，若強調堅持某人的某種行為時，用法為：S + insist on + one's Ving，如：He insisted on her coming to the party.「他堅持要她參加派對。」此外，insist後面也可不用介系詞，改用that + 子句。

MP3
588

A: Mr. Lee wants us to reduce the price by 10%.
李先生想要我們降價一成。

B: Tell him we've already given him the lowest market price.
告訴他，我們已經給了他市場最低價。

A: But he insists on that price, and won't give in.
但他堅持那個價格，且不肯讓步。

B: OK. It seems we have no choice but to forget about this contract.
好的。看來我們別無選擇，只能放掉這個合約了。

相關用語 • **persist in** 堅持　　進階補充 • **forget about** 放棄、忘記

589

You really **keep abreast of** the sports news.

你總跟得上體育新聞。

keep abreast of為「不落人後、與…並駕齊驅」之意。動詞keep也可改用 stay代換，意義不變。abreast是副詞，為「並列、並排、並肩」的意思。 相關片語：abreast of/with「保持與…並列」，為副詞片語。

A: Who do you think will win the MVP award for this season?

你認為誰將贏得本季最有價值球員？

B: I am not sure. Maybe Kobe or Lebron.

我不確定。或許是科比或是雷霸龍。

A: You are right. You really **keep abreast of** the sports news.

沒錯。你總跟得上體育新聞。

B: Sure – I'm a big basketball fan.

當然，我是死忠的籃球迷。

> 相關用語 • **keep pace with** 並駕齊驅　　進階補充 • **keep up** 保持

590

You should really try to **keep your temper**.

你真該試著控制你的脾氣。

keep one's temper為「控制脾氣」之意。temper是「脾氣、情緒」的意 思，與temper相關的片語有：a hot temper「急性子」；get into a bad temper「發怒」；show temper「動怒」；get out of temper「動怒」；in a temper「生著氣」；recover one's temper「恢復平靜」。

A: You should really try to **keep your temper**.

你真該試著控制你的脾氣。

B: I know, but that guy was being ridiculous!

我知道，但那男的太誇張了！

A: He did nothing but ask me for direction, and you yelled at him.

他不過就是跟我問路，你就對他大吼。

B: He was trying to **hit on** you!

他正試著跟你搭訕！

> 相關用語 • **lose one's temper** 動怒　　進階補充 • **hit on** 搭訕

591

She knocked her head against the doorknob this afternoon. 她的頭今天下午撞到門把。

knock against為「撞到、碰到」之意。用法：S + knock against + (代)名詞。與knock相關的片語有：knock down「殺價、推翻」；knock it off「住口」；knock off「下跌、中止」；knock one's socks off「徹底擊潰」；knock up「使筋疲力竭」；take a knock「受到負面影響」。

591

A: What's wrong with little Jamie?
小潔米怎麼了？

B: She knocked her head against the doorknob this afternoon.
今天下午，她的頭撞到門把。

A: How did she do that?
她怎麼撞到的？

B: She dropped her pen on the floor and then hit her head as she was standing up again.
她的筆掉在地板上，當她起身時撞到了頭。

相關用語 ∘ hit against 碰撞   進階補充 ∘ ram against 撞擊

592

Johnson knocked out his opponent in the last minute. 強森在最後一分鐘擊倒對手。

knock out為「擊昏、打敗」之意。若把knock out連成一個字，成為knockout時，可當形容詞，意為「擊倒對手的、淘汰的」；也可當名詞，意為「擊倒、讓人留下深刻印象的人事物」，常用來指稱迷人的女性。

592

A: Nice punch!
好拳！

B: What are you watching? A boxing match?
你在看什麼？拳擊賽嗎？

A: Yes. Johnson knocked out his opponent in the last minute of the round and won!
沒錯。強森在最後一分鐘擊倒對手贏得比賽！

B: Wow. It sounds like it was exciting.
哇。比賽聽起來很刺激。

相關用語 ∘ knock down 擊倒   進階補充 ∘ strike down 擊倒

593

Last but not least, please get it done by 3.

最後但不容忽略的是，請在三點前完成。

last but not least為「最後但不容忽略的」之意，節選自莎士比亞名句，常用於演講或作文時的總結。一般撰寫英文論說文時，常用first of all、secondly等序列方式陳述論點；當提到最後一點時，可用finally、lastly，也可使用last but not the least。

593

A: Please type up the contract.
請把這份合約謄打出來。

B: No problem.
沒問題。

A: Last but not least, please get it done by 3 this afternoon.
最後但不容忽略的是，請在今天下午三點前完成。

B: I will try my very best.
我會盡力而為。

相關用語 ◦ **at last** 最後　　進階補充 ◦ **from first to last** 自始至終

594

I really don't want to **let** Dad **down** again.

我不想再讓父親失望。

let down是「使失望」的意思，let sb. down，則是「讓某人失望」的意思。本片語也可當「放下、掉落、減速」的意思解。與let相關的片語如：Let bygones be bygones.「過去的就讓它過去吧」。

594

A: Honey, you should go to bed now. It's really late.
親愛的，很晚了，你該睡了。

B: I want to study for a little while more.
我想再讀一會兒書。

A: Why are you studying so hard?
你為何如此認真唸書？

B: I really don't want to let Dad down again.
我不想再讓爸爸失望。

相關用語 ◦ **disappoint** 使失望　　進階補充 ◦ **frustrate** 失望的

595

Someone must have let out confidential information to them. 一定有人洩露機密給他們。

let out為「洩漏」之意，受詞可放在let和out之間。除上述的意思外，let out還有「釋放、發出、放寬、放鬆、散會、解雇、放假、結束」等意思。俚語let the cat out of the bag，也是「洩露消息」的意思。

A: Ma'am, I am afraid ABC Computers has stolen our marketing plan.
女士，我擔心愛必喜電腦已竊取我們的行銷企劃。

B: Really? How?
真的嗎？怎麼會？

A: I believe someone must have let out confidential information to them.
我想一定是有人洩露機密給他們。

B: Find out who the spy is as soon as possible!
儘快找出間諜是誰！

相關用語 give away 洩露　　進階補充 blab out 洩露

596

I'd say yes on the condition that we don't live with your parents. 只要不與你父母同住，我就願意。

on the condition that為「只要、以…為條件」之意。condition有「情況、形勢、條件」的意思，當動詞則表「為…的條件」之意。

A: What should I do so that you will accept my proposal?
我該怎麼做才能讓你接受我的求婚？

B: I would only say yes on the condition that we don't live with your parents.
只要不與你父母同住，我就接受。

A: That's impossible. My mom won't stand for me leaving her behind.
不可能的。我媽經不起我留她一人。

B: See! That's why I want to break up with you. You Mommy's boy!
瞧！這就是我要和你分手的原因，你這個媽寶！

相關用語 in condition 身體健康　　進階補充 break up 分手

597

That topic is hot **on everyone's tongue** now.
那是目前討論度最高的話題。

on everyone's tongue為「被眾人談論著」之意。tongue的原意是「舌頭」，由tongue組成的片語包括：find one's tongue「(受驚後)恢復說話能力」；give/throw tongue「狂喊」；hold one's tongue「保持緘默」。

A: Do you know that Henry is going to be the new manager?
你知道亨利是新科經理嗎？

B: Yes, it's hot **on everyone's tongue** now.
嗯，這是目前討論度最高的話題。

A: I wonder how he became so successful in such a short time.
我好奇他是如何在這麼短時間內獲得成功。

B: Not me. I know that he's dating Mr. Chen's daughter.
我不好奇。我知道他是陳先生女兒的男友。

相關用語 ● talking point 話題 進階補充 ● tongue twister 繞口令

598

The government is trying to **play down** the impact of the global recession. 政府試圖降低全球經濟衰退的影響。

play down為「輕視；減低⋯重要性」之意。受詞為代名詞時，可置於play和down之間；受詞為名詞時則可置於play down之後。

A: The stock market is **going up** again. It seems the economy is getting better.
股票指數再度上漲，看來經濟漸有起色。

B: I don't think so. The government is just trying to **play down** the impact of the global recession on us.
我不覺得。政府只是試圖降低全球經濟衰退對我們的影響。

A: What do you mean?
你的意思是？

B: The government is investing a lot in the stock market to make it look like a **bull market**.
政府大量投資股市，讓股市看似行情看漲。

相關用語 ● go up 上升 進階補充 ● bull market 牛市

599

She always puts her nose into my business.

她總是干涉我的職務。

put one's nose into為「干涉」之意。這裡的put可用poke或thrust代替。與nose相關的片語包括：get up one's nose「激怒某人」；give sb. a bloody nose「擊敗某人」；have one's nose in the air「自命清高」；keep one's nose clean「愛惜羽毛、不做違法亂紀的事」。

MP3
599

A: I don't want to work for Ms. Chen anymore.
我不想再替陳小姐工作了。

B: Why is that?
為什麼？

A: She always **puts her nose into** my business.
她總是干涉我的職務。

B: That's really very annoying.
那真的是很煩人。

相關用語 ◦ **nose out** 發現   進階補充 ◦ **nose about** 探聽

600

He used to be my best friend until he queered my pitch. 他在破壞我的計劃前，是我最要好的朋友。

queer one's pitch為「破壞某人計畫」之意，屬英式用法，也可寫成queer the pitch for sb.。queer可當形容詞、動詞和名詞，分別為「古怪的」、「使陷入窘境」和「同性戀者」之意，原先含有貶意，用以指稱不同於主流的「異類」，但自九〇年代起，成為一群反主流學者的自稱，用以表示所有「非異性戀」的性別或性取向團體，便queer成為去汙名化的辭彙，中文直譯為「酷兒」。

MP3
600

A: I thought Jack is your best friend.
我以為傑克是你最要好的朋友。

B: He used to be until he **queered my pitch**.
在他破壞我的計劃前是的。

A: What do you mean?
你的意思是？

B: He asked Mandy out **even though** he knew I liked her.
即使他知道我喜歡曼蒂，還是約她出去。

相關用語 ◦ **blow it** 將…搞糟   進階補充 ◦ **even though** 即使

Index

國家圖書館出版品預行編目資料

一句話搞定萬用狄克生片語 / 張翔、薛詩怡 著. --初版.--
新北市：知識工場出版 采舍國際有限公司發行，
2012.09 面；公分・ --（Excellent；51）
ISBN 978-986-271-243-6 (平裝)

1.英語　　2.慣用語

805.123　　　　　　　　　　　　101012481

知識工場・Excellent 51

一句話搞定萬用狄克生片語

出 版 者／全球華文聯合出版平台・知識工場
作　　者／張翔、薛詩怡　　　　　　印 行 者／知識工場
出版總監／王寶玲　　　　　　　　　英文編輯／何牧蓉
總 編 輯／歐綾纖　　　　　　　　　美術設計／May

台灣出版中心／新北市中和區中山路2段366巷10號10樓
電話／（02）2248-7896
傳真／（02）2248-7758
ISBN-13／978-986-271-243-6
出版日期／2023年最新版

全球華文國際市場總代理／采舍國際
地址／新北市中和區中山路2段366巷10號3樓
電話／（02）8245-8786
傳真／（02）8245-8718

港澳地區總經銷／和平圖書
地址／香港柴灣嘉業街12號百樂門大廈17樓
電話／（852）2804-6687
傳真／（852）2804-6409

全系列書系特約展示
新絲路網路書店
地址／新北市中和區中山路2段366巷10號10樓
電話／（02）8245-9896
網址／www.silkbook.com

Knowledge is everything！

知識工場
nowledge.

Knowledge is everything！

Knowledge is everything！